PATHOGEN

Praise for *Trigger*

"*Trigger* by first-time author Jessica L. Webb is an action-packed adventure. Webb has a great writing style, and her storytelling is outstanding."—*Romantic Reader*

"[A] brilliantly tense and thrilling story that unraveled bit by bit, drawing the reader even further in."—*Inked Rainbow Reads*

By the Author

Trigger

Pathogen

PATHOGEN

by

Jessica Webb

2016

PATHOGEN

ISBN 13: 978-1-62639-833-7

This Trade Paperback Original Is Published By
Bold Strokes Books, Inc.
P.O. Box 249
Valley Falls, NY 12185

First Edition: December 2016

Credits
Editor: Jerry L. Wheeler
Production Design: Stacia Seaman
Cover Design by Melody Pond

Acknowledgments

I would like to thank the entire Bold Strokes Books team, who made my secret, quiet dream of becoming a published author come true. So many people had a hand in bringing this book to life, and I am so incredibly grateful for your time, energy, and dedication.

Special thanks to my editor, Jerry Wheeler. We make a good team, narrowed eyes and all.

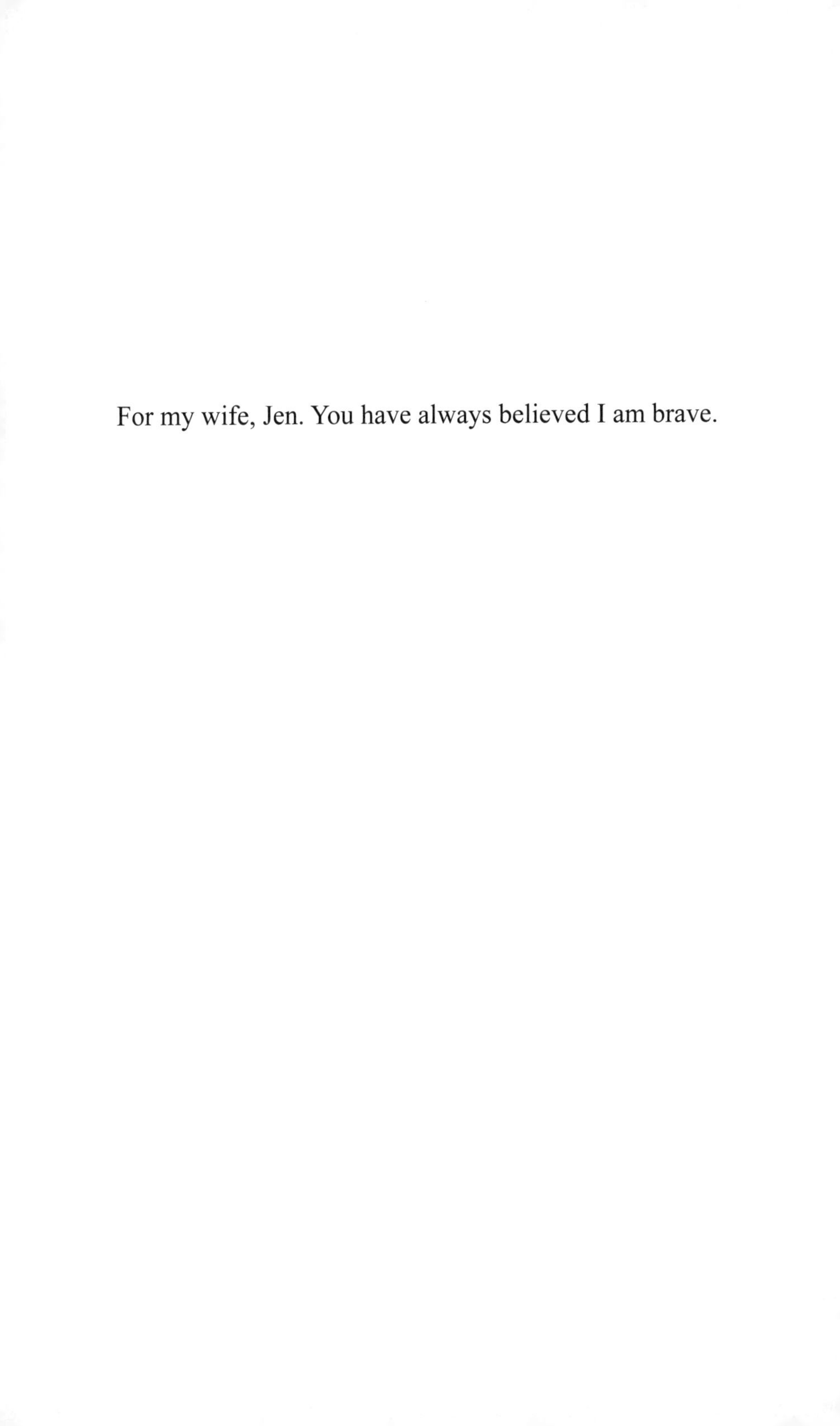

For my wife, Jen. You have always believed I am brave.

CHAPTER ONE

Kate was furious.

She stood at the nurse's station in her Vancouver East Emergency Room, hands wrapped around a takeout cup of coffee. It was lukewarm. Cold, really. But she tried to let it calm her, to let her anger dissipate into the familiar noise and movement of the morning rush. She was vaguely aware of the four med students who had been shadowing her for the past week as they whispered quietly to each other. It was the perfect opportunity to walk them through the trauma they'd just seen. Time to teach them about the crucial skills of team communication and have them identify the critical components of airway-breathing-circulation in the sixteen-year-old stabbing victim they'd just watched Kate work on for the last hour. But Kate was too angry still to do any of that, not after having to weather the insults and accusations from a trauma surgeon with a superiority complex. So she stood with her coffee, looking down at the e-Chart of the kid they'd just lost, trying to pull herself together.

"Don't you see patients of your own anymore, Morrison? Or do you just turn up at traumas to show us how it's done?" Craig dropped his e-Chart carelessly on the desk, rubbing the heels of his palms into his eyes. He was at the end of a double shift, and it showed.

"Funny," Kate said shortly. Craig was her closest friend and ally at Van East. Apparently, Kate didn't have the patience for anyone today.

Craig looked at Kate through bloodshot eyes. "Don't let him get to you. Davidson's an asshole, and you know it. He couldn't have saved that kid if he'd been standing in the ambulance bay with his scalpel in hand."

Kate grunted noncommittally, though she did feel a bit better hearing it from someone else. The med students shuffled uneasily behind them, and Kate tried to pull her day back into focus. She turned to them, their faces eager, unsure, and possibly bored.

"Each of you find a case. I want a complete history and treatment options, no input from each other or the residents. And don't get in the way of the nurses. Find me in an hour."

They scurried away, and Kate felt a pang of guilt. Usually she looked forward to medical students. They forced people to think about what they were doing and why. And they often provided comic relief for those who had been here too long. Kate wasn't sure if it was this cohort or whether she was generally feeling impatient, but somehow these med students made her feel old. Old and tired.

"Is it me or are the med students getting younger?" Craig's voice was plaintive.

This time Kate cracked a smile. "I was just thinking the same thing. It's possible, Dr. Nielson, that we are getting old."

"God, I feel it today," he groaned.

A nurse stopped Craig to follow up with a patient, and Kate took the last few moments to look out through the window. When she had left her apartment just a few hours ago, it had been a gentle, warm morning with just the subtlest hint summer was behind them and a wet, cool season was slowly making its way over the mountains.

Just then a familiar, uniformed figure came in through the revolving doors. Kate's heart gave a quick kick at the sight of Andy in her RCMP uniform, a windbreaker over the light grey shirt and soft body armour vest. Out of habit, Andy scanned the room as she walked in and Kate smiled as Andy's clear grey eyes came to rest on her. Andy stopped, one finger hooked into her belt, holding a coffee in one hand, her shoulders back, her almost six-foot frame looking every inch the RCMP sergeant she was. Andy gave a slow smile, and even across the room, to Kate it felt like a private moment, as if that look could only ever be for her.

They'd been back from Seattle four months. They'd returned from their too-brief stay in the Montana mountains, love-drenched and happy, to a frenzy of media attention. It had been overwhelming, more so given they were trying to navigate the beginning of their relationship. All Kate wanted to do was turn around and hide out with Andy in the small cabin they'd shared for three days. Things settled down, and now life had almost returned to normal. Except the part where Andy walked casually into her ER, and Kate still reacted like a schoolkid with a crush.

Andy walked up to the nurse's station, and Kate put down her cold coffee, accepting the scalding one from Andy in return.

"Hi," Kate said quietly. "You're lucky you caught me."

"Lucky, yes," Andy said. Her smile was brilliant, beautiful.

Kate sought out the details of Andy's face she knew so well now. The soft lines at the corner of her eyes when she smiled, her blond hair pulled back off her face, even her straight posture which would relax the moment Kate's hand drew a line down her spine.

"I thought you'd be home sleeping by now," Kate said, taking in the circles just visible under Andy's eyes. Kate knew Andy had worked an overnight. She should be at her apartment already, sleeping.

"Something came up," Andy told her with a small, knowing smile. It had become an all-encompassing catch phrase for both of them. It could mean anything: a trauma, a distraught family, a deadline, a new lead, one more patient, one more phone call. Often it simply meant they'd lost track of time and had gone over their shift. Until now, neither of them had someone waiting for them who could compete with their work.

"And I take it that *something* isn't resolved, since you're here in uniform," Kate said, digging.

"Finns caught me just as I was heading off shift. He's handed me an out-of-district case, apparently at the superintendent's request."

"Which means what?" Kate asked. She transferred the cup to her other hand, relieving the intense heat against her palm.

Craig interrupted before Andy could answer. "Sergeant Wyles, how's life?"

Andy tipped her hat solemnly at Craig. "Dr. Nielson. I can't complain."

"You're in the wrong place for not complaining," Craig said, half serious. He brightened quickly. "Hey, you guys should come by for dinner this weekend. Anya's been asking for weeks."

Kate answered for them both. "We're heading up to Andy's parents place next weekend for her brother's fortieth birthday."

"Is this the first time you're meeting the family?" Craig asked, looking interested.

"Yep," Kate said.

"Are you nervous?"

"I've never gone home to meet my girlfriend's family before. What if I do it wrong?" Kate answered Craig's questions but kept her eyes on Andy. She simply smiled reassuringly.

Craig picked up his e-Chart, shaking his head. "I'm pretty sure all the same rules apply, Morrison. I'll tell Anya we'll aim for end of September." With a quickly sketched farewell, Craig left to see patients.

Kate took their moment of silence to sip her hot coffee. It was absolute heaven. "So, you were telling me about an out-of-district case?" she asked Andy.

"Right. I'll be heading up north for an overnight to check out a situation in Hidden Valley. They've got someone up there, but Finns wants me to check in. I'm sure the local detachment is going to love that," Andy said with a wry smile.

"When are you back?" Kate said, trying not to let her disappointment show. Her work hours had ruined their fair share of plans, too.

"I'm supposed to be done by noon, so I should be back in the city around four tomorrow."

"Sure, and my shift *should* be done at seven," Kate muttered under her breath, making Andy laugh. "So this is suck-up coffee, then," Kate said, indicating the cup in her hand.

"Something like that." Andy lowered her voice before she spoke again. "I also thought maybe you had a hard night." Kate could see Andy scanning her eyes, gauging her reaction. Kate knew she didn't need to bother. She could never keep anything from Andy.

Kate shrugged in response.

"I thought so."

"Practicing mind reading, are you?" Kate said, trying to lighten the mood.

"No, I stopped by your place earlier. I was hoping to catch you before you left."

Kate's heart skipped at the thought, and she pictured Andy using the key she had given her to come into the apartment. She imagined the surprise of seeing Andy as she was getting ready for work, imagined kissing her in the kitchen…

Kate shook her head, the knot of curls bouncing against the back of her neck. She still struggled with how strong her feelings were for Andy. How she had to temper them in public. She'd never felt like this, not about anybody, not once.

"Why does that make you think I had a hard night?" she asked, focusing on Andy's words.

"There was a pot of tea by the sink and the bed was made. You only drink tea when you can't sleep, and you only make the bed in the morning when you wake up before the alarm," Andy said.

Kate didn't say anything as she looked out over the ER. One of her med students wrote furiously in a chart as the patient, clearly enjoying the captive audience, gave what looked like his entire life story. Kate considered going to rescue him, then changed her mind.

"Nightmares?" Andy asked softly, bringing her back.

Kate gave her a tight, humourless smile. Andy sighed, looking down at Kate's left arm. Kate controlled the urge to touch the perfectly healed but still pink scar that encircled her arm just below her elbow. She knew it would only make the grim look on Andy's face that much worse.

"I'm fine."

Which was entirely true. Most of the time, she never thought about those few terrifying hours when a deranged man had tried to remove the skin of her arms and hands. She didn't have panic attacks or flashbacks, and she didn't spend any time thinking about what had almost happened. But sometimes while she slept, Angler showed up in her dreams. He never did anything, just stood back with a smirk on his face and watched her. His inaction was somehow more frightening than anything he could say or do in her dreams.

"I'm fine," she said more firmly, until Andy tore her eyes away from the scar on Kate's arm. Kate knew that scar haunted Andy, but she couldn't figure out how to make that stop.

One of Kate's med students sidled up to the nurse's station, eyes on her chart. She started to speak to Kate, then seemed to realize she'd walked into a private conversation. The woman blushed, squeaked, and shuffled down the hallway, obviously waiting until Kate was done.

"I guess my five minutes are up," Andy said, shifting the belt around her hips. "What time are you off tomorrow?"

"Same as today, seven."

"See you at your place then?" Andy said. They spent most of their time together at Kate's small, one-bedroom Mount Pleasant apartment. Having Andy there already felt familiar.

"Yes."

They had a silent, charged moment as they looked at each other. Kate felt Andy give the smallest of sighs, a gesture she was sure Andy had not meant for her to catch. Kate stretched up suddenly and touched her lips to Andy's with the lightest, most fleeting touch.

"See you tomorrow," Kate said, listening to the rapid, erratic pounding of the blood in her veins. They had not been together long enough for a kiss, even a brief, public kiss to be anything but a promise for more the next time they were alone together.

Andy backed away, eyes dancing. "See you tomorrow."

Kate ran her bare feet over the smooth surface of her hardwood floors, finding the knots and grooves with her toes. She was sitting on the oversized beige couch in her living room wearing the scrubs she'd had to change into at the hospital after a catheterization gone awry. She was trying to focus on the report in front of her. Her supervisor, Dr. Angstrom, had caught her just before her shift ended to tell her the trauma surgeon from the day before had registered a complaint against the ER. Kate, already exhausted after another long shift of trying to see and treat her walk-in patients, direct traumas as they screamed into the ER, and keep an eye on her med students, had not handled his criticism and condescension well. She'd defended herself, Angstrom hadn't listened, Kate had pushed, and Angstrom had stuck her on a committee to prove he was managing his team. And to top it all off, he'd reminded her that the medical student profiles and resident schedules were already two days late, and he expected them by the next morning. Defeated, Kate had said nothing more.

Pushing thoughts of her supervisor away, Kate looked at her phone. It was seven thirty and still no new messages. Andy had texted her earlier, saying she'd be late. It was to be expected, really, in this long day that had no end. *Focus*, Kate demanded of herself. She wanted to be done by the time Andy arrived. Kate's stomach flipped at the thought. *Focus.*

She was rearranging the residents' schedules when she heard the key in the lock and Andy walked in, still in uniform, and dropped her bag by the front door. With her grey eyes on Kate and a slight smile on her face, Andy pulled off her windbreaker and hung it on the hook by the door. Sitting perfectly still on the couch, Kate watched as Andy pulled off her soft body armour vest, the Velcro sounding loud in the silence, and hung it with her jacket. Still, neither of them said anything, though Kate was suddenly very aware of the blood pounding through her body as Andy pulled at the belt around her waist, the sly grin still playing about her lips. Once Andy had hung her belt on the hook, she put her hands in her pockets, her dark pants with the distinctive yellow stripes down the sides hanging low on her hips.

"Hi," Andy said, leaning against the doorway. Her eyes hadn't left Kate's from the moment she'd walked in the door. Kate remembered to breathe.

"Twenty minutes," Kate said finally. "I need twenty minutes to finish this report for Angstrom."

"Sure."

Kate watched Andy unclip the holstered revolver from her belt hanging by the door. She knew Andy would put it on the bedside table in the bedroom, as she always did. What Kate didn't know was whether or not Andy had always done this, or whether it was because of what happened the morning Angler had broken into their hotel room and taken Kate away. Kate couldn't bring herself to ask.

On her way by, Andy leaned down and kissed Kate lightly on her lips.

"Sorry I'm late," she whispered, and then she kept walking back towards the bedroom.

Kate tried to focus on the schedules in front of her, but the dates, times, and names blurred together as she listened to Andy moving around her apartment. She felt the soft tread of Andy's feet on the floorboards, heard water splashing in the sink in the bathroom through the half-open door. Then, as Kate randomly began assigning names to boxes on the chart in front of her, she felt Andy climb over the back of the couch, sliding down behind her, long legs coming to rest on either side of her. Andy still had on her uniform pants, though her feet were bare and Kate could see the delicate bones, her high arches, the runner's calluses. Kate very much wanted to run her fingers over Andy's bare feet, up her calves, over her knees and thighs.

"I'm almost done," Kate said, gripping the pen tightly in her hand.

"I can be patient," Andy said and sat very still. That didn't stop Kate from feeling the heat coming from her body.

Kate had only filled in three more boxes when she felt Andy's hands on her back, fingers tracing the shape of her curved spine as she hunched over the report. Kate smiled to herself and closed her eyes as Andy reached under her shirt, fingers slightly chilled against her skin.

"Liar," Kate said, throwing down her pen.

Andy slid one hand around Kate's waist, pulling her back until they were pressed together. Kate tilted her head against Andy's shoulder, feeling Andy's lips on her neck as she ran her hands over Andy's bare arms.

"Did you overestimate your patience?" Kate asked, her eyes still closed.

"More like I underestimated how sexy you are in scrubs."

With a quick movement, Andy pulled Kate's shirt over her head, ran her hand down her back, and unclipped her bra, pushing it off her shoulders. Kate could feel the hardness of Andy's nipples through the thin cotton of her sports bra as Andy leaned back into the thick couch cushions, pulling Kate with her. Kate gripped Andy's legs, feeling the muscles underneath her fingers as Andy ran her hands over Kate's body. Kate pushed back into her hard and heard Andy respond with a groan in Kate's ear and a thrust of her hips, so she did it again and felt Andy's teeth on her shoulder. Kate tried to sit up. She wanted to face Andy, to be able to touch her. But Andy anticipated her movement and gripped her hard around the waist. Kate tried to fight back, but Andy wrapped her legs around Kate's, pinning her. Kate dug her fingers high into Andy's thighs and Andy pulled against her calves, spreading her legs farther. Kate, groaning, gave in, and she could feel Andy smile into her neck as she submitted to Andy.

Andy resumed her exploration of Kate's body, with one hand this time, the other still binding them tightly together. Kate knew her body had not been loved so completely or unself-consciously before Andy. It had been like that from the beginning, that first time in the hotel and then the three days in the cabin where Kate had learned the language of loving Andy. No thoughts then, as Andy moved her hand past the waistband of her scrubs. And as Andy's fingers finally found what they were seeking, her moan of pleasure was as loud as Kate's. No thoughts, just the sound of her own ragged breathing, the exertion of straining against Andy's hold on her, the feel of her fingers between her legs, circling and stroking again and again until Kate couldn't contain it anymore and her body arched into orgasm, the sensation lasting an exquisitely long time, ending with Andy's satisfied sigh in her ear.

Andy was quiet behind her, though Kate could feel the tension in her body. Andy released her and Kate stood up shakily, turning to see Andy properly for the first time. God, she was beautiful. With her hair slightly chaotic now around her bare shoulders, just a white sports bra showing off her athletic body, her pants low on her hips showing the waistband of her boy-cut baby blue briefs. Kate could also see the jagged, thick scar just above Andy's left hip, the result of stitches from a gunshot wound being violently ripped open twice. Before Kate could think about it, Andy reached out and pulled Kate to her, the urgency of her lips betraying her need. Kate ran her hands down Andy's chest, reaching under her bra, seeking out her sensitive nipples. Finding them hard, she touched them lightly with her fingertips, then harder, circling and pinching then backing off and coming back again until Andy was breathing hard, gripping Kate's hips, thrusting against her. Kate knew it wasn't enough. She could feel Andy's body aching for release, so she raised herself and reached between them to undo the button and zipper of Andy's pants. Andy tilted her hips. Kate knew what she wanted, so she slipped two fingers inside, feeling all of Andy's muscles tense as she leaned her head back against the couch, eyes closed.

But Kate didn't want to make it that easy. She pulled back and raised herself just above Andy, kissing her throat, up to her ear, smothering Andy's groan. She could feel Andy's hands on her hips, pulling her down, but Kate resisted for just a moment longer, then slipped her fingers inside again, lowering herself onto Andy. She did it again and again until Andy, every muscle in her body vibrating, came against her, both their bodies rocking with the power of it until finally they fell against each other, spent.

Kate lay wrapped around Andy, lips against her neck, the air trapped and hot between them. Eventually she felt Andy lightly stroking her back until she shivered at the touch. She sat up and met Andy's lazy, smiling gaze.

"How about a shower, and then I'll make something to eat?" Andy said, arms now wrapped around Kate's waist.

Kate ran her fingers through the loose ends of Andy's blond hair. "Sounds like the perfect end to a shitty day."

Andy searched Kate's face. "Want to talk about it?"

Kate loved this about Andy. She understood that sometimes you wanted someone to share in the frustrations or heartache of your day, but some days there were just no words.

Kate decided to summarize. "Lost a sixteen-year-old, got into a playground fight with a trauma surgeon, pissed off Angstrom, and almost completely ignored my med students. And I got peed on."

"A shitty day," Andy confirmed, bringing one hand up to massage the back of Kate's neck.

"Want to tell me about yours?"

Andy frowned, the furrow between her eyebrows becoming more pronounced, the corners of her mouth pulling tight. Her grey eyes told Kate she was wrestling with something.

"Sure, but while I make supper," Andy said finally. "I think if we don't get off the couch now we might not move again all night."

Kate kissed Andy lightly on the corner of her mouth. "That's not the worst idea I heard today," she murmured but stood up, pulling Andy with her.

Half an hour later, Kate was sitting on the kitchen counter in her pyjamas, her red hair loose and damp around her shoulders. Night had fallen, and the air that came in through the partially open window was early October warm, bringing with it the sounds of the street three floors below. Andy pulled food from the fridge and cupboards, arranging items neatly on the counter. Kate watched as Andy, her grey T-shirt just hiding the blue briefs that hugged her thighs, washed vegetables in the sink. Kate loved to see Andy in her kitchen, moving around like she belonged here, like they belonged here together.

"So, what was the assignment that Finns gave you?" Kate asked, legs swinging against the worn wooden cupboards.

Andy kept her eyes down, carefully slicing red peppers into long, thin strips.

"I'm not really sure what to tell you about it, actually."

"You mean what you're allowed to tell me?" Andy shared a lot of her work with Kate, although she was also used to the unapologetic evasion.

"No, that's not it. I just don't have a handle on why I was sent up there," she said, handing Kate a few slices of pepper before tipping the rest of them into the sizzling pan on the stove.

Kate chewed on the pepper, waiting. Andy chopped onions and zucchini with the same controlled deliberateness, the frown of concentration on her face having nothing to do with the task in front of her.

"Why don't you start at the beginning?" Kate suggested.

Andy looked up from her completed knife work, then covered the short distance to kiss Kate lightly before opening the fridge and pulling out the ingredients for a sauce.

"Finns gave me a last-minute, out-of-district assignment, telling me Superintendent Heath has requested I personally go up to Hidden Valley and check out a situation there." She paused and looked over at Kate. "Do you know anything about Hidden Valley?"

"Just that it's north of Whistler, and my chances of affording a house there are about as good as Angstrom proposing marriage to me during my shift tomorrow."

Andy laughed and whacked her on the leg with the back of a wooden spoon. "Yes, it's crazy rich, even by Vancouver standards. They've got a municipal helicopter landing pad so they can commute to the city, even though it's only a two-hour drive. They're on the Whistler side of the 99, a fact they're very proud of, and they're utterly exclusive, something they're far too rich to say out loud. They just show you in everything they do." Andy seemed more amused than judgemental. Kate figured this was one of the things that made Andy a great cop, the way she could get a handle on people but not judge them.

"Finns gave me nothing more than the name of the constable up there, a guy named Ferris. Nice guy, pretty laid back given that I've just invaded his territory. So I assume Ferris is going to give me the rundown of the case, persons of interest, evidence gathered. But there's nothing. No active case file, no police report, no complaint filed. Just four seemingly unconnected people who show similar presentations of a moderate flu-like illness, with symptoms lasting up to a month."

Andy paused as she added the sauce to the vegetables, the hot, sizzling smell of garlic and ginger spreading throughout the kitchen.

"How is that a case for the RCMP to investigate?" Kate said.

Andy raised her hands helplessly. "This is what I'm asking myself yesterday afternoon, sitting in the small-town police department. So I started digging."

Kate smiled. "Of course you did. And what did you find?"

"For one thing, it turns out Superintendent Heath has a personal connection to Hidden Valley. His eldest daughter, Natalie Cardiff, lives in Hidden Valley with her two kids and her husband, Michael Cardiff, who is a local councillor running for member of parliament in the fall election."

"Interesting," Kate said.

"Interesting, yes. Relevant? I'm still not sure." Andy lifted the lid off the rice, scooped a few pieces onto her spoon and blew on it gently. She took a careful bite between her perfect front teeth, then shook her head and returned the lid. "So once I start asking questions, it turns out the uproar over this flu, or whatever it is, has more to do with an article written by a small mountain-town newspaper about the effects of influenza outbreaks on elections."

Kate felt these two pieces of information war for sense in her head. "What?"

Andy gave Kate a quick smile, like she had anticipated that reaction. "Apparently the journalist, a young guy with the *Squamish Herald*, quoted a study out of Sweden linking a decrease in voter confidence and voter turnout on viral outbreaks. More importantly, he quoted this study in a newspaper article after getting into a verbal altercation with Michael Cardiff. According to Constable Ferris, the journalist warned Michael Cardiff that his election results would suffer unless he changed his platform on two-tiered health care."

Kate tried to tie politics to influenza and failed. She ignored the erroneous interchanging of virus and influenza. It wasn't the time for a medical lesson. "So remind me again what you were investigating?"

"Apparently the article was seen as, and this is a quote from the constable in Hidden Valley, 'a threat.' And the fact that several people in a fairly small population are now sick has imaginations running wild."

Andy checked the rice one more time, then switched off the stove. Kate set the table with plates, cutlery, and glasses. She opened the fridge, held up a bottle of half-flat lemon Perrier and a bottle of white wine. Andy indicated the wine, then scooped huge mounds of steaming brown rice onto their plates, topping it with the vegetables. Kate, who hadn't had a drink in over seven years, poured herself some of the Perrier, and they sat down together at the small table shoved up against the wall in her apple green kitchen.

Andy held up her glass. "To a night off together."

"To a girlfriend who likes to cook," Kate responded. They clinked glasses, sipped their drinks, and then picked up their forks.

"Does it still feel strange to say that?" Andy asked, after a moment's silence.

Kate shrugged. "A little."

Andy waited for her to elaborate, but Kate wanted to hear more about Andy's case, not to discuss her journey to accepting her new lesbian identity. Not that Andy, who had been out since she was eighteen, ever pushed. Not once, not ever. But Kate knew she worried about it. She could tell Andy wished she would give it more thought. Kate was content to be with Andy, to love her and completely share her life with this incredible woman. The label seemed shockingly unimportant.

"So, the non-case in Hidden Valley," Kate prompted, scooping another forkful of rice and vegetables.

Andy took a sip of her wine, her grey eyes appraising. Kate waited it out. Andy finally shook her head, a slight smile on her lips.

"Fine. So Ferris shows me what background he has on this journalist, which so far amounts to pretty much nothing. But I figure Finns would want more, so I ask more questions about the four patients. You know, when they got sick, any connections between patients, physicians. Any connection to the journalist, to the Cardiffs, to the election. Nothing very interesting comes up."

"Other than the fact that they've been sick for so long," Kate added. She couldn't help thinking that the description of the influenza was just a bit off.

Andy nodded her agreement, like she hadn't forgotten.

"Was Public Health involved?"

"Yes, that's who I had to hang around to meet with today. The guy had to drive up to Hidden Valley to meet with me, which he wasn't very happy about. He told me he investigated the cases and nothing showed up that caused him any concern or alarm. He stopped just short of saying the town was overbearing and completely out of line. It was hard not to agree with him."

"So now what?"

Andy pushed her empty plate away and leaned back in her chair. "Now I find some way to fill a report about whether or not this was a credible threat and if so, what action needs to be taken."

"You've got a bizarre job," Kate said, also leaning back in her chair. She lifted her feet onto Andy's lap across from her.

"I'm not the one who got peed on today," Andy reminded her, running her hands over Kate's bare feet, fingers on her ankles, palms cupping her calves.

"Do you think that's the end of it?"

Andy took a moment with Kate's question.

"No," she finally said. "No way. I have a feeling this non-case is nowhere near over."

Chapter Two

Rain fell in a constant spray of mist, challenging Andy's wiper blades. Blankets of dense clouds had covered the city for days, as if they were settling in for the next six months. Kate looked out the side window of Andy's old Corolla, watching the city give way to the endlessly long suburbs, then finally to the small towns which dotted the eastern leg of the Lougheed Highway.

It was Saturday morning, the first full weekend Kate had had off in months and the first weekend she and Andy had off together, ever. They were driving up to Andy's parents' place, an hour northeast of Chilliwack, for her brother's fortieth birthday. Andy's whole family would be there for the weekend, all three brothers and the various wives and offspring. Kate was nervous.

"So Mark is the oldest. He's a pilot, and he's married to Shayna, and they have a boy and a girl named Denver and Brindle," Kate said, though they'd already been through this more than once.

"Yes. And don't get me started on the names. Apparently, unique names are all the rage up in Whitehorse. It's a good thing they're cute," Andy said, smiling at Kate.

Kate didn't return the smile. She was too intent on getting this right.

"And Zach and his wife Deanna are expecting their first and they live in Calgary."

"Yes," Andy said patiently. When Andy looked over at Kate, she seemed amused, like she knew exactly what Kate was doing asking these questions. "And Brandon's the birthday boy, and he's probably got three girlfriends, none of whom he ever brings home."

Kate watched through the blur of rain as they passed a lump of runners in bright gear, running in near precision down the highway. She felt Andy's hand on her knee and looked up into her sweet, grey eyes.

"Why are you so nervous?" Andy asked her gently.

"Because it's important," Kate told her, knowing that was really only half the answer.

Andy seemed to know it, too. She squeezed Kate's leg with a gentle pressure and left her to her own thoughts. Yes, Kate was nervous because this was important. But it was more than that. Kate didn't know how to navigate any of this. Until Andy, her adult relationships had been brief and boring. She never had enough time or chemistry to get involved much past dates and phone calls, awkward mornings, and drawn-out excuses for breakups. But what she had with Andy was important. Unfortunately, that didn't stop Kate from feeling slightly disconnected, like she lacked the confidence needed to show everyone else how much Andy meant to her.

"Who was the last girlfriend you brought home?" Kate said.

Andy signaled, checked her blind spot, and overtook a slow-moving truck on the highway before answering. "Rachel. That was almost three years ago now."

Kate knew all about Rachel, the physiotherapist who had cheated on Andy with the captain of the UBC women's lacrosse team. They'd been together a year and half and had lived together most of that time.

"And did your family like her?" Kate was unsure which answer would make her feel worse.

Andy looked quickly at Kate. "Not particularly. Though, by the time I brought her home, neither did I really, so I can't exactly blame them." Kate still couldn't return Andy's smile. "My parents are going to love you, Kate."

"You're just saying that to make me feel better."

"Right, because I'm so well known for making people feel warm and fuzzy," Andy said sarcastically.

Kate finally laughed, the action easing some of the tension in her body. Andy looked relieved to hear Kate's laugh.

"I'm serious, Kate. I was talking to my dad the other night, and he said that he and my mom couldn't wait to meet you. Apparently my mom has known from the day she watched the press conference in Seattle on TV that you are important to me."

"Seriously?"

"My mom is very…intuitive," Andy said finally.

"And she's known you a long time."

Andy nodded. Kate knew Andy had a very interesting relationship with her mother, who had raised her from the time she was three. Kate was curious about Elaine Wyles, the woman who had raised three wild boys and taken in Andy, the child who had resulted from her husband's one affair. Andy rarely mentioned her biological mother, who had died just after her third birthday. She did have a picture of the two of them in her apartment; Andy as a chubby, smiling toddler sitting on her mother's lap, one hand holding a length of her mother's blond hair.

"All right, fine. I'll quit my whining," Kate finally said, giving her head a shake.

Andy flashed her a grin. "Good," she said, "because we're almost there."

Just a few minutes later, Andy pulled off the highway, heading north on a county side road. Houses and farms sped by at varying intervals, then long stretches of trees with glimpses of a winding, muddy river. Finally, they pulled off onto a gravel road, Andy gunning the engine to make it up the hill on loose rocks. The long tree-lined driveway opened up to a huge yard with a sprawling, side-split house in the middle. Kate could see where various additions had been added over the years with an extension out the back and a third level overlooking the forest that served as a backyard. There was a long, barn-like shed at the end of the driveway with an assortment of cars parked out front.

"Looks like everyone's here," Andy said, killing the engine. Just as she did, her cell phone rang. Andy checked the caller ID. "It's the guy up in Hidden Valley. Give me a sec."

The rain had picked up, and with the windshield wipers still, Kate could see little through the windows. She thought about Andy growing up here with her three much older brothers, thought about the chaos she imagined they were about to walk into. Her own childhood had been much quieter with just herself and her younger sister, Sarah. As an eight-year-old, Kate would have been more likely to be reading a book or doing crafts than riding her BMX bike over a homemade ramp, as she imagined Andy did at that age.

Kate tuned into Andy's half of the phone conversation.

"This morning? Have they established a cause of death?" Andy pinned the phone between her shoulder and ear, grabbing the notepad and pen she kept in the console. Kate watched Andy scrawl *respiratory distress* on the paper, and her brain kicked into gear. Andy had told her most of the patients only presented with mild to moderate flu-like symptoms. Nothing Andy said four days ago indicated anyone presented with serious, life-threatening complications from the still-unnamed illness.

Kate grabbed another pen, found a gas station receipt, scribbled on the back *pre-existing med. conditions?* and handed it to Andy. Andy took it, nodded, and spoke Kate's question into the phone while she continued to scrawl notes.

"Call again if anything else comes up over the weekend. Right, yes…And if you don't hear back by mid-morning Monday, then give me a call and I'll see what I can do from this end. Thanks, Ferris, you, too." Andy disconnected the call with one hand, gripping her notebook with her other. Kate waited, giving Andy space to think. After only a moment Andy started talking, her voice factual and even. Her sergeant's voice.

"One of the patients with flu symptoms died this morning. They're going to try to get an autopsy for early next week."

"Were there pre-existing medical conditions?" Kate asked.

"I don't have all the details, but apparently the patient was into her second year of remission from breast cancer. Ferris is going to see if he can get all the information for me." Andy looked down at her notes.

"I take it you'll be heading back up to Hidden Valley next week?" Kate asked tentatively.

Andy looked up. "Probably. Finns made it clear I was supposed to stay on this case that still isn't a fucking case." Kate wasn't sure exactly what Andy was feeling: angry, distracted, or concerned. "It's hard to feel annoyed that work is creeping into my time off when someone just lost their life," she finally said, and Kate felt a surge of compassion. She was familiar with that sensation of internal conflict. "Let's go inside. The longer we wait in the car, the cruder Brandon's jokes are going to get." Andy flashed Kate a grin, leaned in, and gave her a quick kiss full on her mouth.

They opened their doors, the rain immediately soaking into every porous surface. Grabbing bags from the backseat, they dodged the puddles in the driveway and ran up the front steps that led to a large porch. Andy shoved the door open with her shoulder and Kate got her first glimpse of Andy's childhood home. It was very open, the front entrance leading into a large living room with comfortable-looking, mismatched furniture. Kate counted four huge shelves filled with books interspersed with beautiful, intricate wood carvings and colourful child-like paintings. A carving of a salmon seemed to hold place of honour on the wall, its distinctive, static shape managing to show life and movement, a testament to the First Nations artist who brought it into creation. Up a set of six stairs, Kate could see the dining room that looked down onto the living room and the kitchen just beyond that. The décor was simple and homey and felt like the people who lived here gave little thought to what the latest trends indicated for home decorating and instead chose to revel in their own comfort.

Andy put down their bags and pulled off her boots and Kate followed suit.

"Finally!" a voice called, and Kate watched as a tall figure in baggy shorts and a T-shirt, dark brown hair long around his ears, launched himself down the six stairs in what was clearly a familiar movement. Kate caught a flash of perfectly white teeth and smiling brown eyes before the man hooked Andy around the neck in a bearish hug. Andy hugged him back, the smile on her face so incredibly happy, Kate felt all the nerves that had been collecting in her body over the last few weeks completely melt away.

"I thought we were going to have to turn the hose on you two. What were you doing sitting out in the car steaming up the windows?"

Kate watched as Andy balled her fist and punched her brother in the kidney. Kate either missed the part where Andy cushioned the blow or she had really just hit him that hard.

"I got a call from work, you ass," she told him, letting him go and stepping back. "Brandon, I'd like you to meet Kate. Kate, this is Brandon."

Kate held out her hand to the youngest of Andy's brothers. "Nice to meet you," she said, looking at him full on for the first time. "And happy birthday."

"Thanks," he said with a smile, shaking her hand. "I'm glad you could make it. We've all been dying to meet you." He said the last with a slightly suggestive tone and had to block the second kidney shot Andy aimed at him.

"Break it up, children, let the adults through."

Two more very tall, dark-haired men were taking their turns hugging Andy now, and Kate realized all three had the same complexion, as if they constantly had the look of having spent the summer out in the sun. The contrast to Andy's pale skin and blond hair was striking.

Andy was introducing her to Mark, who had a beard, and Zach, who was the most clean-cut of the three of them. They were all talking over each other, joking and throwing insults. Looking at the four siblings standing together, tall, athletic, laughing, Kate thought they looked like the poster family for a BC healthy outdoor living campaign.

"All right, let's move this party upstairs. Mom and Dad are serving lunch."

Andy held out her hand to Kate, eyes shining. "So far so good?" Andy said as they walked through the living room and up the stairs.

"I feel very short. Is there a height restriction I should know about?"

Andy laughed. "The kids are shorter than you, so you're fine."

"Sure," Kate muttered. "For a few more years."

It was loud in the dining room, which Kate could now see opened onto a huge kitchen. Adults milled about, carrying dishes to the tables and pulling food from the fridge. In the kitchen there was another round of introductions. Mark's wife Shayna was friendly and energetic, and Zach's wife Deanna was seven months pregnant and looked uncomfortable. As she looked around, Kate could just see the legs of a kid, dirty socks hanging loose, from under the kitchen island, then a blur of colour launched itself from the other side of the room, hitting Andy around her knees. When they both looked down, a small dirty face with long, light brown hair gave them an impish grin.

"You can't possibly be Brindle Truscott-Wyles," Andy said to the little girl, and the impish grin got bigger. "Because Brindle is much, much smaller."

"It's me, Auntie Andy! Grandpa says I'm huge!"

"You are huge, Brin. You're growing before our eyes." A man, tall, of course, with receding sandy blond and grey hair and a runner's build, came out of the kitchen, wiping his hands on a dishcloth.

Andy gave him a hug, which he returned happily, then stepped back to look at Andy, his light eyes clearly shining with pride.

"It's good to see you, sweetheart."

"Dad, I want you to meet Kate. Kate, this is my dad, Simon."

Simon took Kate's hand in a two-handed shake, and the look of delight on his face was unmistakable.

"Kate, it's lovely to meet you. We're really happy you could make it this weekend, and I apologize in advance for my sons, who will certainly find some way to offend you over the next two days."

Kate laughed, feeling much more at ease, even standing amongst the noise and chaos of the kitchen. She heard a door slam, and she watched a short woman with black and grey-streaked hair come in through a back door, rain splattered and with an arm full of vegetables. She had a darker complexion than her sons, a rich brown with high cheekbones and striking almond-shaped eyes, evidence of her First Nations heritage. Andy crossed the kitchen, helped her with the load, and then hugged her, the small woman reaching up to pull Andy's face down to kiss her cheek. Andy turned and held her hand out to Kate. She walked over, and, as Andy's mother's eyes met hers, Kate realized with a shock that she had been pinned by that same look before. She'd seen it the very first time she'd met Andy.

Kate had some idea she was being introduced to Andy's mom, Elaine, and they were shaking hands. Elaine hadn't yet blinked. Kate at first felt like shrinking away from the scrutiny, then she realized she knew perfectly well how to stand up to that look. She'd done it more times than she could count with Andy. As their silent exchange continued, Kate felt like everyone was watching and waiting to see how this would play out despite the chaos around them. After what felt like a long time, Elaine smiled. Any tension Kate felt dissolved instantly.

"Welcome to our home, Kate," Elaine said.

"I'm happy to be here." And she meant it.

The day was wonderfully loud and long. After lunch, they walked en masse through the forest, jeans soaked up to their knees in the wet grass, drops from the rain-heavy branches above them falling in constant drips onto their heads. They hiked up to an old zip line, Brandon daring Zach to ride it naked back down the path. Zach declined, though Kate had the feeling any of the four siblings would have taken that dare ten years ago. They were obviously mellowed, their exuberance showing in the retelling of stories, re-enactments of dares and jokes gone bad from decades ago. Simon and Elaine walked with Denver, a quiet kid who seemed undisturbed by the noise and chaos around him, though equally uninterested in adding to it. His little sister made up for his quiet, her energy and noise seemingly boundless.

After a dinner of barbecued hamburgers and late-season corn, they sat outside on damp logs and folding chairs, the delicious heat of a campfire roasting their fronts, the chill of the night air creeping under their clothes at their backs. The kids had left the campfire earlier, Brindle wailing her discontent over Mark's shoulder. Conversations melted around them, people's faces blurred by the light of the fire while at the same time defined by the edges of dark. Kate shivered, a delighted feeling at being even a small part of this family. She felt Andy's arm around her waist, pulling her in closer, and she looked up into Andy's grey eyes. Kate had never seen her this off the grid, never this far from her city-cop persona. Kate returned Andy's smile, happy.

As the night deepened, Simon and Elaine stood up from their place across the fire, coming to kiss each member of their family good night, including Kate, which for some reason made a lump form in her throat.

"Who's going to take me up on a run in the morning?" Andy's dad asked, looking around the circle expectantly. Kate noticed Zach and Brandon averting their gaze.

"I'll go with you, Dad," Andy said, kicking the leg of Brandon's chair, and Kate thought she heard Andy whisper the word *pussy* in his general direction.

"Excellent. See you at six." They all murmured their good nights as a log shifted in the fire, sending a spiral of sparks shooting up into the sky.

Mark returned from putting the kids to bed, two boxes of beer from the fridge clanking his arrival.

"Dude, you're old," Andy said to Brandon, taking a beer from her oldest brother and twisting off the cap.

"Whatever, Sergeant Blondie," Brandon said, doing the same before tossing the lid in the fire.

"Excellent comeback, Brando. I assume you've been working on that all day."

"Kate, are you going to let her talk to me like that?" Brandon said, his hurt tone sounding utterly insincere.

"I can't think of a good reason why not," Kate told him, making Zach, sitting next to Brandon, laugh.

"Because it's my birthday. In fact, you should be drinking with me because it's my birthday. Grab a beer," he said to Kate, holding up his own.

Kate laughed. "No, thanks."

"No, really. Kate, I think you and I would have a good time drinking together."

"I don't doubt that for a second, Brandon."

Kate could feel Andy press her fingers lightly into Kate's side. She looked up at Andy, smiling reassuringly. Kate then looked across the fire where Mark had pulled Shayna onto his lap. They rested comfortably against each other, two people who had obviously been together a long time, talking in low tones, sharing a beer.

Brandon wasn't backing down. "Kate, come on. I want to hear your life story. Or at least what the hell you could possibly see in my little sister. So grab a beer."

Kate probably should have thought through what she said next. She didn't.

"I can't, Brandon, because I'm pregnant."

There was dead silence. No one said a word, the only sound came from the hissing and popping of the fire.

"Don't worry," Kate said into the silence. "It's Andy's."

Mark was the first to react, spitting his mouthful of beer as he laughed. Then all of them lost it, Shayna hitting Mark on the back as he choked, Zach howling and punching Brandon, sending him half flying out of his chair. Beside her, Andy was looking down at Kate, laughing and shocked.

"Was that your first gay joke?" Andy said as her brothers continued to laugh, the sound echoing out into the night.

"Yes, I think it was."

Andy kissed her lightly, laughter still in her throat.

Brandon, his composure regained, stood with a deliberate dignity and crossed the campfire over to where Andy and Kate sat. He held out his hand to Kate.

"Well played, Kate. And welcome to the family."

Kate shook his hand, grinning.

He then put his hand heavily on Andy's shoulder. "You've got your hands full with this one, Blondie. Best of luck to you."

As the conversations drifted around her and the night air deepened into cold, Kate listened and watched Andy and her family telling what had obviously become familiar stories. Kate loved the ease of being here, of watching Andy with her brothers, people who had known her almost her entire life. Kate felt, just for a moment, a pressure of sadness on her chest, the ache of missing her own younger sister, of knowing she would never have this. Kate shied away from the feeling, settling into Andy, feeling the warmth and steadiness of her presence.

Just after midnight, Andy led Kate inside the house and up a series of stairs to the converted attic that served as storage and a guest room. Andy pushed open the windows partway, letting in some of the cool night air. Kate looked down onto the dark yard, the line of trees just visible in the light. Andy came up behind her, slipped her hands around Kate's waist, and kissed her hair.

"I love you," Andy said into Kate's ear.

Kate smiled and pictured the first time she'd ever heard those words from Andy. It was in Montana and they'd been sitting on the porch covered in a blanket after a rainstorm had swept passed. Andy had spoken the words quietly but with conviction.

"I love you, too."

They made love quietly, sweetly, swallowing the sounds of their desire, just the rustle of sheets, the slight friction of warm skin against skin. And then they slept, sated and content, wrapped around each other.

❖

Kate woke to Andy sitting on the edge of the bed in running shorts and a long-sleeved shirt, pulling on ankle socks. It was still dark outside, the night not yet ready to let go. Andy, seeing Kate awake, leaned over and kissed her eyes.

"Go back to sleep. I'll see you in a few hours."

Kate did so easily, effortlessly.

The next thing she heard was the front door slamming, a child's shriek of defiance, and an adult's admonishing voice. It was lighter now, the diffuse daylight of sun filtered through clouds lighting up the room. Kate listened to voices outside, car doors slamming, the sound of an engine and tires through puddles. The house settled back into silence. Kate got up, stretched, and, smelling the wood smoke in her hair, decided to shower.

The house was still quiet as she made her way downstairs in jeans and a sweatshirt, her hair damp and unbound. She followed the smell of coffee into the brightly lit kitchen. Elaine stood at the sink with a knife in hand, a bushel of peaches at one elbow and a huge bowl of yellowy segments at the other.

"Good morning," Elaine said, looking up to smile, then returning to her task. "Coffee's on the stove, milk and cream in the fridge, sugar on the counter."

"Thanks," Kate said, helping herself. "Where is everyone?"

"Andy and Simon are still out running, Mark and Shayna took the kids down to the river, and Zach and Dee went into town to pick up a few things."

"Someone should have woken me up," Kate murmured, a little embarrassed. She leaned back against the counter.

"We were all under quite strict orders not to, actually," Elaine said.

"Andy," Kate said. She looked up to see Elaine's eyes on her, appraising, though she didn't see anything critical about the look.

"Yes, my daughter is very protective of those she loves."

Kate was startled by the boldness of the woman's words, though she tried not to let it show. Silence settled around them, the only sound that of Elaine's repetitive movements, the paring knife tearing wetly into the soft flesh of the peaches.

"What my husband thought we were going to do with a bushel of peaches is totally beyond me," Elaine said finally. "I think he enjoyed the picture of them more than he thought about how we would use them." She shook her head, long dark hair swinging against her back.

"Can I help?" Kate asked.

"Please do. Knife in the top drawer on your left."

Kate grabbed a knife, and Elaine passed her an armful of peaches. They worked in silence, Kate segmenting the peaches, pulling off the skin, slicing the halves into quarters before adding them to the huge bowl.

"Andy says you love being a doctor and that you are very good at your job," Elaine said.

"I do love being a doctor," Kate said, unaware of the clarification she'd just made.

"But you don't love your job," Elaine stated. Kate was reminded again of how effortlessly Andy could pull information from people.

"Some days I feel like I practice bureaucracy more than I practice medicine," Kate tried to explain. "It's not exactly what I imagined as I was working my way through medical school."

"And I think my daughter was not what you imagined when you thought about finding a partner," Elaine said. Kate could hear the question in the statement.

"No, she isn't what I imagined," she said honestly. Kate's hands were sticky, the juice running down her fingers and wrists. She reached for another peach, sank the knife against the pit, and circled it around in a fluid movement.

Silence enveloped them again as they worked. Kate wasn't sure if she was ready for this conversation. But then Elaine took a turn Kate wasn't expecting.

"If you'd asked me thirty years ago if my family was complete, I would have said yes. Absolutely. I had my husband, my work, my community, and my three healthy, lively boys. I could not have imagined Andy, of course I couldn't. But now there is no way for me to picture my life without my daughter." Elaine added the segments from her hand into the bowl and paused to look up at Kate. "I wonder, Kate, if life is less about what we can imagine our lives to be and more about what we do with it once we see it."

Kate met Elaine's gaze and held it for a moment. She knew a thoughtless agreement would not be enough, so she concentrated on her task, thinking. But Andy and Simon's return saved her from having to formulate an intelligent, thoughtful response. They were both soaked, the top halves of their shirts drenched, their shoes squelching noisily on the floor. Simon gave Kate a cheerful good morning, then excused himself to shower and change. Andy's eyes sparkled, her cheeks bright red, always at the peak of energy when she returned from a run. As she crossed the kitchen and gave Kate a swift kiss on her cheek, she balanced on the balls of her feet, as if she was still running. Kate's heart thumped at the sight of her, at the feel of Andy's warm lips against her skin.

"How was your run?" Kate asked.

"Good. Long. Rainy." Andy snagged a few peaches from the bowl and threw them into her mouth. "What are you two talking about?"

"Not much," Elaine answered for them. "The meaning of life, that sort of thing." She gave Kate a sidelong smile as she said it.

"Not fair, Mom," Andy said lightly. "Kate looks like she's only had half a cup of coffee." She stole a few more peaches. "I'm going to have a shower."

They listened to Andy's tread on the stairs, and Kate noticed they had almost finished the bushel of peaches.

"Maybe she's right," Elaine murmured. "Perhaps I'm not being fair."

Kate smiled. "I don't mind. Andy has changed my life. I think I just haven't figured out all the ways she's changed it yet." It was the closest she could come to a real answer.

Andy came back into the kitchen in her shorts and sports bra, a towel around her shoulders. She was holding her cell phone, peering at it with a frown on her face Kate hadn't seen since they arrived. She hadn't missed it. "Has my phone been ringing?"

"I didn't notice it," Kate answered, reading the lines of worry around Andy's eyes.

"Finns has called me three times but hasn't left a message."

"What does that—" Kate started, but was interrupted by the phone ringing in Andy's hand.

Andy met Kate's eyes, blinked, and then turned on her phone, heading into the dining room.

Kate watched her go, noticing the way Andy's shoulders were tensed, her back rigid. She sighed and picked up the last peach. Elaine was watching her.

"I see that you are protective of those you love, also."

Kate didn't say anything, helping Elaine clean up the peach pits and skins, rinsing her hands under the tap. Andy came back into the room, her grey eyes guarded. She stopped just inside the doorway with her phone in hand.

"What is it?" Kate asked. She could feel Elaine behind her, watching them.

"Superintendent Heath's eighteen-year-old granddaughter is exhibiting the same flu symptoms as the others. Finns wants me in his office at seven tomorrow morning." She said it all in a monotone, her eyes never leaving Kate's.

"And?" Kate asked, waiting for the rest.

Andy paused, like she couldn't get the words out.

"He wants you there, too."

CHAPTER THREE

Vancouver's RCMP E-division headquarters at Thirty-seventh and Heather was old and cramped, with too many people from too many divisions in too little space. Andy said it had only gotten worse once they announced the shiny new headquarters in Surrey, as if the second the idea of more space was planted, the current space became unbearably confining. Kate had been here a few times after Seattle to give testimony and sign off on official reports. The building itself was a study in rectangles, most of them reflecting the early morning sunlight, the rest an opaque seventies aqua colour just now starting to look fashionable again.

The floor was nearly empty this early in the morning, and they stopped briefly at Andy's cubicle. Kate's heart warmed at the sight of the pictures she had centred on her corkboard. Alongside a photo of a much younger Denver holding a squirming baby Brindle, there was a photo of Andy in her blue serge uniform standing with Kate, her nephew Tyler, and her mom, Marie. It had been taken at the commendation ceremony about a month after they'd returned from Seattle. Andy followed Kate's gaze and gave her a small but real smile, then indicated with a nod of her head that they should keep going. It was the only crack in her rigid posture, her unreadable expression. Andy had been varying degrees of untouchable since getting the phone call from Finns the day before.

Staff Sergeant Finns called them in as soon as Andy knocked on his door. He was a handsome man with neatly parted grey hair and a strong jaw that held the evidence of a very recent shave. "Thank you for coming in so early this morning," he said.

Kate gave a small smile of acknowledgement. Andy sat perfectly still in the chair next to her, saying nothing. Finns seemed unperturbed by this, and Kate realized he was probably quite used to her work demeanour.

"Sergeant Wyles, last week I asked you to unofficially assess the credibility of the threat from the journalist and any link to the four cases of unidentified influenza in Hidden Valley. I read your report and agree with your assessment of low risk, given the limited amount of information at hand. With some new developments, a fifth case, and a reportable death, we're going to be increasing our presence."

Finns paused and looked back and forth between them, as if waiting for them to speak. Kate took her cue from Andy and said nothing.

"Superintendent Heath has personally requested both of you. Sergeant Wyles, you don't get a choice. This is your newest assignment, and it's your main priority." He left his eyes on Andy until she acknowledged this with a nod, though her expression didn't change. Kate could feel the tension rolling off her body.

"Dr. Morrison, Superintendent Heath is familiar with your work from Seattle and would like you to be involved in liaising with the Squamish-Whistler Health team, Public Health, and the coroner's office. Unlike Sergeant Wyles, it is your decision whether or not you want to take on another temporary consultant position with E-division."

He paused again, looked between them, and cleared his throat. It was a small gesture, but Kate read it as a nervous one. "Now, the RCMP does not usually allow those who are involved to work together, but under the circumstances, the superintendent is willing to overlook—"

The sentence was not complete, the words barely out of Finns's mouth, when Andy interrupted. "Willing to overlook or unwilling to acknowledge, which is it?"

"I understand you have concerns, Sergeant Wyles, but we are dancing a strange line here."

"No, actually, we're not," Andy said in a voice that left no room for disagreement. "If it is documented that Dr. Morrison and I are in a relationship, then it will also be documented that the superintendent has signed off on breaching protocol. I'm not letting this come back to bite me in the ass."

"Sergeant Wyles—" Finns began, a warning in his tone.

Andy ignored it. "Staff Sergeant Finns, I am willing to take an assignment which will possibly take me away from home for who knows how long, and I'm willing to drag Dr. Morrison into the field if that's what she decides to do. But I am not willing to walk into a highly politicized situation without any kind of protection because the superintendent is a homophobic prick unwilling to officially recognize my sexual orientation."

Kate had never heard Andy talk about this in public, but the truth of her words did nothing to diminish the harshness. Kate swallowed the awkwardness of the moment, unsure what to do or think or say. Instead, Kate watched Finns's reaction. She couldn't detect any hint of shock or anger at Andy's words, insubordinate as they were. Finns looked at Andy impassively for a long time, then he switched his gaze to Kate. She was surprised to see a smile in his eyes.

"My wife keeps asking me when I'm going to slow down, start taking it easy, and cruise into retirement. And I keep telling her that while Sgt. Andy Wyles is still in my division, that's just not possible."

Kate gave a small smile. Finns obviously respected Andy a great deal.

Sergeant Finns turned his eyes back to Andy. "I'll have you covered, Wyles."

The simple words were apparently enough for Andy. She nodded once but still didn't relax her posture. "What happens next?"

"I want you up there tomorrow. The autopsy is scheduled for Wednesday morning."

"And the new developments you referred to? Has the credible threat risk been reassessed?" Andy said.

"You'll find out everything you need to know tomorrow, Sergeant Wyles. As you can imagine, this assignment has the potential to be very high profile."

"You mean because Superintendent Heath's son-in-law is running for MP in the fall election." Andy made it a question and a statement.

Finns gave her that same long, impassive look. Kate wondered if they often had conversations that simply involved staring contests. Finns was almost as good at it as Andy.

"I expect your professional discretion, Sergeant Wyles."

"And you'll get it. I'd just like to know what I'm walking into."

"You know as much as I do. The rest is up for you to investigate," he said pointedly. Andy acknowledged the order with a small, definitive nod.

"Do you have any questions, Dr. Morrison?" Finns asked, turning to Kate.

"Only a hundred," Kate mumbled and felt a small amount of tension ease out of the room as Finns gave her a smile. "When do you want an answer from me?"

"By the end of today, if possible. I know it's overstepping, but Superintendent Heath has already been in contact with the director of Vancouver East about the possibility of you taking a brief leave from your job. Apparently, they golf together," he said with a straight face.

"Okay. I should know in a couple of hours," Kate said, avoiding checking with Andy to see what her reaction would be.

"Well then, I think that's all we need to cover this morning. Dr. Morrison, thank you." He stood and shook her hand.

Andy guided Kate resolutely out of Finns's office and across the office floor, not quite touching but also not allowing her to slow down. She grabbed her jacket and hat from her desk on the way. Maybe it was the expression on Andy's face, but no one stopped to talk to them, other than acknowledge a quick good morning. It wasn't until they were halfway down the stairs to the lobby that Kate recognized a friendly face.

"Katie!" Jack gave an exuberant wave as he pushed back the two laptop bags he had slung over his shoulder, further rumpling his button-up shirt.

Kate took the last few steps quickly, managing to give Jack a hug despite his heavy load. She missed Jack, although she probably saw him more than anybody outside of work, her family, and Andy.

"What are you doing here? Are you dropping off Andy at work or something? Are you guys living together now? Did you get my last text? The one about the gaming cheats for Tyler?" Jack's questions tripped over each other, his brown eyes shining excitedly.

Kate laughed. "Yes, I got your text, and yes, I passed it on to Tyler, who thinks you're a god. No, we're not living together, and Andy is actually about to take me to work." Kate didn't mention the meeting, leaving it up to Andy to share the details.

Jack looked at his partner quizzically. "What's happening, Wylie? Anything I should know about?"

"Finns wants Kate on an out-of-district case. Superintendent's request," Andy said shortly.

Jack's eyes widened. "The one up north?"

Andy nodded. Jack looked back to Kate.

"Are you going to take it?"

Kate shrugged, again avoiding Andy's expression. She wanted to have the discussion with Andy privately, when Andy couldn't use her professional wall to hide behind.

Jack, obviously sensing tension between them, said good-bye and took off up the stairs.

"Buy me a coffee?" Kate said, attempting to keep her tone light. It was just after eight, still plenty of time before her shift started at Van East.

"Sure. Let's walk."

Kate shoved her hands into the pockets of her light jacket, wondering how cold it would be up in the mountains of Hidden Valley. She stopped herself, mentally backed up a few paces, and tried to start from the beginning. Kate liked the idea of working for the RCMP again. She'd enjoyed working through the case in Seattle with Andy and Jack and the rest of the multi-division team. It had stretched her in a way working in the ER had never done. Taking a break from Angstrom and his useless protocols and committees wasn't so unappealing, either. But Kate felt like this decision was somehow bigger than any of these small pieces. Last time, the situation had escalated so quickly she never really got a choice. But Staff Sergeant Finns had just presented her with a clear and very personal decision. This time when she left her place in the ER, it would be to consciously pursue something else entirely. Even on a temporary basis, it felt like a statement Kate was making about her life. *And what exactly am I saying?*

Kate could feel Andy's eyes on her and she met the look, allowing the uncertainty she felt to show.

"I'm just trying to figure out how I'm going to make the decision," Kate said, hoping to start the dialogue. Andy said nothing and kept walking towards the busy Cambie Street intersection. Kate tried again. "I take it you would rather I had given Finns an unequivocal 'no'?"

"Not necessarily," Andy said in a neutral tone, indicating with her head that they should turn left.

Kate felt the first stirring of annoyance. She quashed it almost immediately. Maybe Andy needed to know where she stood first, before giving her opinion.

"I like the idea of working on another case," Kate said. "Particularly one that doesn't involve me as a target," she added, smiling slightly.

Andy didn't say anything, not even returning the smile. Kate wondered if Andy would ever be able to talk about Seattle without looking so murderous. Maybe Andy was thinking about everything that had happened last time Kate had been a consultant with the RCMP. But she couldn't be sure because Andy still wasn't talking.

They arrived at Starbucks, the expected line snaking back towards the door. While they waited, Kate people-watched, noting the expensive outdoor jackets in shades of jade and cranberry and amber, not a single one showing signs of wear. Women talked to each other in too loud tones, wearing their babies or their yoga mats on their backs. She watched how they reacted to Andy in her uniform, to the glowering look on her face. Kate remembered being intimidated by that expression, not understanding what was behind it. She knew better now. Kate knew she had to get Andy talking.

Coffee finally in hand, they walked back out into the warm October air. Andy took them on a different route back to headquarters, and Kate deliberately slowed her pace. She only wanted to have this conversation once.

"May I have the privilege of knowing your opinion, Sergeant Wyles?"

"It's your decision," Andy said shortly.

"Thanks. I'd already figured that part out, actually," Kate said, acid leaking into her tone.

Andy looked at Kate, but her eyes gave away very little. "I'm trying very hard not to influence you."

"Why? I just want to know what you think about all this," Kate said, not understanding. Wasn't this what people did in a relationship, talked things out, asked for the other person's thoughts and opinions?

"Because it's your life, Kate. I don't want you to feel like you have to do anything or be anything you're not."

Kate took a moment with Andy's words. "Are we still talking about me taking on a case with your division?" Kate asked.

"Yes," Andy said slowly.

"Really? Because I feel like somehow we're back to talking about my sexuality."

Andy flicked her eyes to Kate, then back to the sidewalk in front of them.

"I just think—" Andy started, and then stopped as a group of kids came screaming up the sidewalk. The kids darted around them, laughing, before taking off down the street. Andy waited until they were off in the distance before continuing. "I just think a lot has happened to you in the last few months, and you haven't had very much time to process any of it. Things are finally settling down and now you're being asked to once again leave everything that's familiar."

Kate lifted the tab on the lid of her coffee, allowing some of the steam to escape into the still air. She didn't know what to say, didn't know if she should be aiming for familiar in her life. But Andy seemed to know. Andy always seemed to know.

"So it's not just one thing you're worrying about," Kate said.

Andy watched Kate carefully now. "I'm not doubting your abilities, Kate. I have every confidence in you. In fact, I know exactly why Heath and Finns want you on this case."

"Why?"

"Because you're smart, you're fast, you see things other people don't. You can walk into any situation with any group of people and get them to listen to you and trust you. It helps that you were good with the media. You came across as professional and approachable but not attention-seeking," Andy said succinctly.

"So I'm good at it, and I like it. Isn't that an answer?"

"It's one answer."

Kate decided she needed to be direct.

"Do you hate the idea of working with me again? Would you prefer I wasn't involved in your work?" Kate knew it wasn't fair to try to pin the decision on Andy like this, but she needed to know.

"No, Kate, I don't hate the idea," Andy said softly. "Not at all."

They didn't say anything more as they approached the parking lot, walked to Andy's car, and got in. Andy didn't start the car, though. She sat and looked out the windshield at the now full lot. Kate took her first sip of coffee, waiting.

"It might not be easy. On us, I mean," Andy said finally.

"We've done it before," Kate reminded her.

"That wasn't what I would call easy," Andy said, her voice sharp. Kate knew she was thinking about Angler, about the scar on Kate's arm.

"Nothing happened, Andy," Kate said firmly, wishing they could get past this. "*I* know what happened with Angler was an isolated incident. My arm healed faster than your gunshot wound, and I didn't have any lasting side effects from the lorazepam overdose. Nothing happened. Nothing is going to happen."

Andy was quiet, playing with the lid of her coffee, an uncharacteristically nervous gesture.

"I don't know," she finally murmured. "I've always secretly suspected your IQ dropped a few points after the overdose," Andy said and smiled.

Kate looked at Andy, stunned, before punching her on the shoulder.

"Hey now, no assaulting the police officer." Andy laughed. Kate felt relief spread through her body at the sound.

They were quiet for a minute as the tension that had built from yesterday eased away.

"So should I tell Finns you've made a decision?" Andy asked.

Kate met Andy's eyes, her beautiful grey eyes which looked at her in a way no one ever had before.

"You can tell him I'll take him up on his offer. I'll go up to Hidden Valley."

"Okay," was all Andy said, and she checked her watch. "Then I should get you to your last shift."

CHAPTER FOUR

Kate was underwhelmed by her first impression of Hidden Valley. After driving through Whistler, with its over-the-top, Disneyfied version of a chalet town, Hidden Valley seemed at first very plain. As Andy continued driving, though, Kate started to see the differences. Whistler was bright and carefully coloured, dramatically displaying its imitation of nature in the rocks and stones and wood of the architecture. But Hidden Valley actually accomplished what Whistler only boasted. Huge houses were tucked into crevices of the mountain and the slopes of the valley. Even Kate, who knew absolutely nothing about architecture, could see the line of form and function blur around the edges, or meet exactly in the middle as they were supposed to. Kate had never aspired to this kind of grandeur, but she could appreciate the style with which Hidden Valley had been built.

Andy drove the Yukon past grand, countrified houses into the heart of a very small, quaint town. One main intersection branched off into smaller, tree-lined streets. The buildings continued the trend of understated brick and stone, with enough plain siding to make it look like a miniature Christmas town without the snow. Andy pulled off the main street and parked outside a grey brick building, much smaller and more utilitarian than those surrounding it. Kate could see the RCMP logo displayed in the front window. Andy killed the engine and looked over at Kate before zipping up her storm jacket, settling her hat on her head, and climbing out of the car.

The inside of the building was small and simply decorated. The posters on the wall promoted community awareness and bicycle and road safety as opposed to the anti-drug and poverty awareness posters of downtown Vancouver. These posters gave off friendly encouragement and lacked the feel of caution and desperation of those in the city.

Andy walked confidently up to the reception area, free of glass or any other protective covering. Kate felt like she was walking into a dentist's office, not the only law enforcement in a fifty-kilometre radius.

"Good morning," Andy said politely to the woman behind the desk. The secretary looked to be in her late fifties, her short grey hair feathered and sprayed into one perfect, unmoving wave.

"Welcome back, Sergeant Wyles. Constable Ferris is out on a call but should return within half an hour. Could I get the two of you some coffee while you wait?"

"Yes, thanks. It's Judy, right?" Andy asked.

"That's right." Judy seemed touched Andy had remembered, fingering the gold chain around her neck in an unconscious motion.

"Judy, this is Dr. Kate Morrison."

"Hello, we've been expecting you."

Kate wasn't sure, but she suspected she heard a note of frost in the woman's voice. Or at the very least, reserve.

"It's nice to meet you," Kate said, giving her most pleasant smile. Judy seemed slightly taken aback, though Kate couldn't figure out why.

Judy took their coffee orders and immediately disappeared around back. Kate gave Andy a questioning look.

"You'll notice a very entrenched social hierarchy out here," Andy said wryly, under her breath.

"You mean blue collar, white collar?" Kate asked.

Andy nodded.

"Great," Kate muttered, but didn't say anything else as Judy returned with two mugs, cream and sugar for Kate, black for Andy.

"There's a Starbucks and a few independent coffee shops in town," Judy said, settling herself behind her desk once more. "But Constable Ferris seems to like the way I make it, so we've always got a pot going in the back."

Kate sighed as she took her first sip. "This is absolutely perfect, thanks."

Judy smiled tentatively back.

The front door of the office opened just then as Constable Ferris returned from his call. He was older than Kate had expected, and his stomach bulged slightly with the paunch of the middle-aged. When he took off his hat, Kate saw his receding hairline. As he happily introduced himself to Kate, his handshake firm and his eyes kind, Kate could see what Andy meant by someone who seemed hard to ruffle.

"Come back into my office, you two. I see you've already got a cup of the Judy blend," he said, indicating their cups.

Once they were seated in the simple, small office at the back of the building, Ferris jumped in immediately, surprising Kate with his directness.

"Sergeant Wyles, I'd like to apologize for not getting back to you in the past few days. As I'm sure you have already figured out, I was instructed not to say anything until you were here. Now that you're sitting here in an official capacity, I think we should get all the information out on the table."

"Excellent. Maybe we can start from the beginning to get Dr. Morrison up to speed."

"September first, a journalist from the *Squamish Herald* by the name of Paul Sealy comes up to Hidden Valley, wanting to interview Michael Cardiff about the upcoming election. Michael Cardiff says he doesn't have time and, according to sources, words are exchanged."

"Threats?" Kate said, deliberately using the word.

"Depends who you ask," he said. "Witnesses say Mr. Sealy accused Michael Cardiff of refusing to represent half the constituents in Hidden Valley, namely those whose annual income is less than a hundred thousand dollars."

"Okay," Kate said, frowning. "Doesn't sound like a threat."

"Apparently Mr. Sealy then moved on to specifics." Constable Ferris emphasized the last word. "He asked Mr. Cardiff about the possibility that his stance on a two-tiered medical system could be seen as contrary to the Charter of Rights and Freedoms."

"Which sounds like a political statement phrased as a question to me," Andy said.

"There's more," Constable Ferris continued. "According to witnesses, Mr. Sealy's parting words were that Michael Cardiff would regret supporting a bill that could potentially see his voters too sick to even come out to vote him into office."

"And then people got sick," Andy said, seeking confirmation from the constable.

"Three days later, the *Squamish Herald* published an article about the effects of influenza on voter turnout. Only brief mention was made of Cardiff and his electoral campaign," Constable Ferris said. "And *then* people started getting sick."

"And Cardiff thinks those two things are connected?" Andy asked, her tone perfectly even, but her grey eyes betraying her disbelief. Kate understood. Seasonal influenza didn't really care all that much about politics.

"Michael Cardiff has said nothing. When interviewed, he gave a description of the incident, said he expected the situation to be monitored and has said nothing since."

"Until his daughter got sick," Kate said.

"That's right. Which, let's be honest, is why we're all here today."

"My staff sergeant mentioned new developments," Andy probed.

"Yes, that," Constable Ferris said, logging in to his computer. "When you were last here, we had looked at Paul Sealy's background and found his affiliation with the Green Party and his presence at some low key rallies and protests. But no real red flags." He stopped and turned his monitor so Kate and Andy could see. "Until my new constable found this."

Kate looked at the screen capture that Ferris had blown up. It was a Tweet from @PaulTheSealy which said, "Can refusing medical services to those in need be considered an act of bioterrorism? Watch the fall elections to find out #BCpoli."

"Posted September first," Andy said.

"Right, same day as his altercation with Cardiff. It was pulled down a day later, at his employer's request. But it's the Internet, nothing is ever really gone."

"Have you spoken to Mr. Sealy about this?" Andy said.

"I'm meeting him at the *Squamish Herald* office the day after tomorrow. You're welcome to come along."

Andy nodded, still looking at the screen as if she could glean more motivation from the words. Kate wondered if this short social media blast had changed Andy's mind about the credibility of a threat. With a gap in the conversation, though, Kate decided to ask her medical questions.

"While we're here, could I get a breakdown of the timeline for the patients?" Kate asked.

"I know someone who can answer that question far better than I can," Constable Ferris said. "Grab your coat, Dr. Morrison. I'll take you on a tour of the town, and then we can head over to the hospital. The chief of staff, Dr. Brenda Doyle, is expecting you."

Kate sat in the back of the Yukon and Andy drove while Constable Ferris navigated them outside the town limits. The houses here were simpler, smaller, and interspersed with attached houses and a few low apartment buildings.

"This is the outskirts of town. Most of the farmhands, seasonal workers, and people who support the service industry live here, including two of the flu patients."

"Any connections between the patients that jump out at you?" Andy said.

"It's Hidden Valley, Sergeant Wyles. Everyone's connected. Even people who don't particularly wish to be."

Kate could see Andy thinking through the implication of his answer. But it wasn't enough information for Kate.

"What about significant connections, contagion-related connections," Kate pressed. "People who live together, work together, go to school together, that kind of thing."

"I've started looking, but no pattern has emerged yet. To tell you the truth, since I'm no expert in influenza or contagion, I'm not really sure how to track that kind of information."

"And Public Health wasn't interested in investigating?" Kate asked him, knowing the answer but wanting to see how he handled the answer.

"Nope. And at this point I really don't blame them. Up here on the left is the James ranch. It's an Ozarc original," he added in a slightly mocking tone.

"What's an Ozarc?" Kate said.

"Ah, you clearly haven't checked out the Hidden Valley Wiki site," he said, in the same mocking tone.

"I'm afraid I didn't get a chance," Kate said dryly.

"Nicholas Ozarc is considered the founder of the town, or at least its current incarnation. He was your typical handsome, rich, genius ski bum in the late sixties whose father cut him off at twenty-one and told him to make his own way. According to Hidden Valley legend, he spent the next five years building up the Whistler marijuana industry and made himself a little money. He then got cleaned up, decided environmental green was the way of the future and invested in environmentally sound building supplies.

"Since he dabbled in architecture"—Kate could almost hear Ferris rolling his eyes—"he had a vision of creating a town entirely of his own design that he and his rich pals could play in. What you see is half his vision, the rest kind of snowballed." He then pointed out the window. "Take a left up here, we'll drive by the entrance to his place."

"He still lives here?" Andy asked.

"If you want to call it living. He's an utter recluse. No one has seen him in town in over a decade. His fourth wife left a few years ago and his only son, Chris, is home, taking a year off from university."

"I take it that Ozarc properties are expensive," Kate said to the constable.

"Minimum of ten million," Ferris confirmed. "And that was a small acreage during the worst of the economic crisis a few years ago." He pointed out the window, and Kate saw a long, low stone wall that stretched along one side of the road and off into the distance.

"Here's the Ozarc original. Very few people have ever seen the house." Other than the elaborate stone wall, and the gated entrance, there was very little to see. "Keep driving, and a few properties down is the Cardiff residence, another Ozarc."

They toured around Hidden Valley for another twenty minutes, Ferris giving them bits of trivia relating back to the patients and their families. They wound in a circuitous route until they were at the hospital in the northwest end of town, tucked under the shadow of the mountain range. The hospital itself was bigger than Kate had expected. Its three-story building took up half the block and seemed extreme for the relatively small population size. She wasn't surprised as much by its grandeur. The richly rough stone blocks and large, glassed-in entrance took the edge away from the institutional feel of most hospitals. By this time, Kate expected nothing less of Hidden Valley.

"Valley General Hospital," Ferris announced unnecessarily. "Fifteen acute care beds, fully staffed emergency room, x-ray, and laboratory. It also houses clinics for orthopaedics, dermatology, and physical rehabilitation."

"All the clean living services, then," Kate said, almost to herself.

"What do you mean?" said Ferris, intrigued.

"No sexual health clinic, no mental health division, no dialysis, no diabetes management, no women in crisis," Kate ticked off the top of her head.

"I never really thought of it that way," Ferris said as Andy pulled into the big lot.

As they walked across the parking lot into the main entrance of the hospital, Kate couldn't shake the feeling something was just a little bit off. It had an open main reception area which Ferris bypassed, leading them directly down the brightly lit hallways to the small emergency room. As they passed the double doors into the Valley General ER, Kate figured out what was missing: noise, chaos, energy. Kate felt like she could be walking onto any ward, not the busiest section of any hospital, city or rural.

A woman with a fashionable auburn bob and a pressed lab coat over a skirt and blouse was walking towards them. Kate guessed she was in her late forties and, from the stern look on her face, took her job incredibly seriously.

Constable Ferris introduced both Kate and Andy to Dr. Brenda Doyle, chief of staff at Valley General Hospital. Kate tried not to be intimidated by the firmness of her handshake.

"Dr. Morrison, Sergeant Wyles," Dr. Doyle began, "I think it's only fair to be honest with you. Constable Ferris and I have a disagreement as to how we should proceed from here. Since there is no active criminal case, we are bound to protect our patient's confidentiality. I can share what I have reported to Public Health in terms of general influenza information, but any other decision would have to be approved by the hospital's board of directors."

Kate very quickly tried to read between the lines of what she was hearing. Dr. Doyle wasn't wrong, and she didn't even seem particularly combative about it. Mostly she seemed cautious. All at once, Kate could clearly hear Staff Sergeant Finns's voice in her head, *I expect your professional discretion*.

"How are things progressing with Public Health?" Kate asked. "Any headway?"

Kate's question seemed to briefly throw Dr. Doyle, as if she had expected opposition to her statement instead of Kate's simple assumption that they were on the same side. She paused and openly studied Kate before answering.

"They have been notified of the recent death, but are waiting for the results of the autopsy before deciding how to proceed."

"And are they sending someone down to witness the autopsy?"

Another cautious pause, as if Dr. Doyle was trying to find the trap in Kate's question. "No, I don't believe so. But I understand that you will be there to witness?"

"That's right."

Dr. Doyle was studying her again, her expression somewhere between suspicious and appraising. Kate took the scrutiny, thinking the doctor's caution bordered on paranoia. Dr. Doyle then looked between Ferris and Andy before centring her gaze back on Kate. Kate knew it was dismissive and rude to leave the two officers out of the conversation, but she resisted the urge to check Andy's reaction.

"Perhaps I have my facts wrong," Dr. Doyle said finally. "You do work for the RCMP, don't you, Dr. Morrison?"

"Temporary consultant," Kate said. "My day job is ER physician down at Vancouver East Hospital."

This simple, truthful statement seemed to ease at least some of Dr. Doyle's reservations. Before she had a chance to speak, they were interrupted by a tall man wearing a dark grey business suit that perfectly fit his broad shoulders. He was immaculately and expensively dressed. He wore the haggard expression of someone under stress who hadn't seen a lot of sleep recently.

"Dr. Doyle, I've been looking for you." The man addressed Dr. Doyle, but he took in each member of the group with intense precision.

"Mr. Cardiff," Dr. Doyle said, "may I introduce you to Dr. Morrison and Sergeant Wyles."

He shook their hands, Kate's entirely swallowed by the man's grasp. "My father-in-law speaks very highly of you both."

Kate wasn't sure if this was meant to flatter them or warn them.

"Mr. Cardiff, I was just explaining to Dr. Morrison and Sergeant Wyles the limits of what information I can—"

He cut her off immediately with a quick shake of his head. "That's why I was trying to find you. I want them read in immediately."

Dr. Doyle look startled but quickly composed herself. "Michael—" she started, but was cut off again.

"Brenda." He looked this time only at Dr. Doyle. "The directors just finished meeting via Skype." He held up his smartphone as if it was evidence. "We had the required number of votes, Jeff was there from legal, and they're putting together the decision now. Current circumstances demand appropriate, fast action."

Dr. Doyle gave him an appraising look. While they were squaring off, Kate chanced a look at Andy. Her eyes were impassive, but she gave the smallest gesture with her hand. *Wait, watch, let it play out.*

"What's the decision?" Dr. Doyle said, sounding resigned. Kate could only imagine the number of competing pressures this woman dealt with. "What is the board asking for?"

"We're asking for this team"—he indicated Kate, Andy, and Ferris without looking at them—"to be granted full access to the patient and hospital records. We need Dr. Morrison to be granted temporary authorization to practice medicine at this hospital." He paused and very subtly leaned in towards Dr. Doyle. Kate found the gesture both aggressive and compelling. "I'm asking you to help me *contain* this."

Kate automatically looked to Andy, then quickly looked away again when she saw that Andy had also caught the emphasis in that statement.

Dr. Doyle was holding Michael Cardiff's gaze, but Kate could see her fidgeting with the pen in her pocket. "I'll take a look at the decision when it comes in, Michael."

"This afternoon. Please," he added, almost as an afterthought. "While we wait for an official answer, I'd like Dr. Morrison brought up to speed on Serena's condition."

Kate felt a moment of unease. She couldn't help feeling like she was being manoeuvred. She was just about to voice her concerns when Andy took a step forwards and inserted herself into the conversation.

"Just to be clear, Mr. Cardiff, Dr. Morrison has been assigned here to liaise with the various agencies involved in the suspected influenza case for *all* the patients involved. She is not here to act as Serena's personal physician."

Kate thought she caught a flash of anger on Cardiff's face, either at calling him out so publicly or simply for Andy being able to see so quickly to the heart of his motivation.

"Thank you for the reminder, Sergeant Wyles, but it is unnecessary. My concern extends to all the patients affected by this illness as well as their families." His voice was smooth, and his perfect politician's smile was both easy and insincere.

Andy simply looked at him, in no way acknowledging the political drivel. If he had any thought Kate and Andy would bend to his wishes simply because they were brought here by his father-in-law, Andy was quickly attempting to adjust his thinking.

The awkward introduction concluded, Dr. Doyle escorted Kate to a private patient room. Eighteen-year-old Serena Cardiff was asleep in the bed, an IV drip secured with tape to the back of her left hand. Kate quietly flipped through the young woman's hospital chart. Nothing really jumped out, no red flags, nothing out of the ordinary. Kate looked at the patient. She seemed small for eighteen, or maybe she only seemed that way in comparison to her father. Her hair was long and dark, though it lacked the shine of someone who had seen a shower in the last two days. Kate sighed, unsure what she had to offer in this case, then walked out into the hallway.

Andy and Constable Ferris were talking to a thin woman with dark hair that hung with blunt precision just past her jaw. She was wearing a grey sweater and the fabric looked soft and expensive. The woman held the sweater closed with one arm held tightly across her body, her other hand clutching a Starbucks coffee. Michael Cardiff was talking on his cell phone, just down the hall. Kate didn't need the introduction to know who this was. Natalie Cardiff's handshake was light, her fingers cold despite the coffee.

"How is my daughter?" she asked Kate.

"Sleeping, which is probably the best thing for her right now."

"She's been sleeping a lot. It's hard to wake her, and when she *does* wake up, she seems disoriented for a long period of time."

Kate let the anecdotal facts shift into the medical information from the chart. "I take it that's not typical? My thirteen-year-old nephew is impossible to wake up," Kate said with a friendly smile.

Natalie returned the gesture, though it seemed like effort. "No, Serena and my other daughter Julia are often up at dawn to go down to see their horses before school."

"What about eating habits and exercise?"

"Nothing's changed."

"How are things at school and with her friends?" Kate stopped herself from asking if she had a boyfriend, realizing how many times she had made this assumption in the past.

"Fine, everything's fine." Natalie looked down the hallway towards her husband, then gripped her coffee and took a sip. "What does this have to do with Serena being sick?"

"I'm just trying to get a picture of what's going on. The medical charts can only tell me so much. I need to put it in some kind of context, to know if what Serena is experiencing is normal or a cause for concern. That kind of information could be helpful."

Kate watched as a look of relief briefly lit up Natalie's face, as if Kate had just given her permission to be involved and not merely an impotent bystander. She still held herself rigid, her one arm wrapped almost protectively around her body. Kate tried to smile reassuringly, knowing her reassurance could only extend so far, standing in the hallway of a hospital ward.

She turned to Andy and Ferris. "I'd like to see Dr. Doyle again, if possible."

"I'll take you to her," Cardiff said, stalking over to the group, his phone clenched in his oversized hand. "She's following up with the board's decision, and she wants to see you. This way."

Kate couldn't help but notice Andy bristle at the aggressiveness with which he addressed Kate. Cardiff either didn't notice, or he didn't care. He was already walking down the hallway, thumbing through his phone. Kate gave Andy a lighthearted shrug and a small smile, wishing she could reassure her with a touch but recognizing this wasn't the time or the place.

"Michael, I've got a few questions for you while Dr. Morrison is in with Dr. Doyle," Constable Ferris said when they stopped in front of a partially open door.

"I want to be in that meeting."

"That won't be necessary, Mr. Cardiff," Andy said in her professionally neutral tone. "We can apprise you of any information that directly affects your daughter or her care." Kate knew she was making her own strategic move, reminding him that his influence had boundaries.

Michael glared at Andy but didn't say anything. Ferris pointed down the hallway towards a series of doors.

"Dr. Doyle is the third on the right," he said, and Andy nodded and continued walking down the hallway with Kate.

"Slick," Kate muttered under her breath. Andy rewarded her with a tight smile.

Dr. Doyle called them in immediately when Andy knocked on the door. Kate wondered who'd she meet when they walked through the door, the cautious hospital administrator or the team player.

"Dr. Morrison, here are copies of the charts for all the patients. The white folder is a copy of the information we've shared with Public Health." Dr. Doyle handed her a stack of brown office folders.

"That was fast," Andy said.

"Things tend to happen quickly around here."

Kate held the files in her lap, clearing her head of the politics. "Before I get into these, I'd like to hear your timeline of events."

"A general overview is all I've got time for." Dr. Doyle sounded annoyed.

Kate mentally added it to her growing list of descriptions for the woman. "A general overview would be perfect."

Dr. Doyle tapped a few keys on her keyboard and peered at her screen. She scowled and picked up her glasses and put them on before she started to read.

"September 7, the first case of suspected influenza identified in sixteen-year-old Tessa James. She was treated by family doctor. September 9, second case of suspected influenza reported in forty-two-year-old Mary Johnston, a cleaning lady from in town. She was also treated by her family doctor, different practice. September 10, third and fourth cases of suspected influenza reported in twenty-five-year-old Chase Noonan, stable hand, and in sixty-four-year-old Roberta Sedlak, retired teacher. Chase Noonan was seen at the walk-in clinic and Mrs. Sedlak was seen by her family doctor and sent home. Mrs. Sedlak was hospitalized on September 29 for respiratory distress and died in critical care on October 1. And as you know, Serena Cardiff, age eighteen, is our fifth case of suspected influenza, reported September 30 by her family doctor. All cases were reported as suspected influenza, none confirmed."

"List of symptoms?" Kate intentionally mimicked Dr. Doyle's curt tone.

"Fever, headache, bodily aches and pains, extreme and long-lasting fatigue, muscle weakness, burning sensation in the chest, sore throat, and wet cough."

"So your basic flu bug then," Kate couldn't help but add, more for Andy's benefit than anything.

Dr. Doyle said nothing, seeming resigned to wait for Kate's next question. Kate felt the pressure of time, of Dr. Doyle's stare, of Michael Cardiff's, and the RCMP's expectations. But she had so little to go on. She stole a moment, pushed at the pressures until they were in the background and listened again to Dr. Doyle's words in her head.

"So why is Tessa James the first patient?"

"What do you mean?"

"I assume Hidden Valley was hit the same as other communities during the flu season." She waited for Dr. Doyle to indicate her agreement. "So what sets Tessa James apart from what you would consider the last influenza case of the flu season?"

"I see what you're asking. It wasn't until the third case of influenza that specifically seemed to target weakness and exhaustion that we started looking back."

"And that led you to Tessa James?" Kate confirmed.

"Yes."

"How far back did you look?"

"To the beginning of the flu season, so last November."

That made sense to Kate. It was what she would have done. She trusted Dr. Doyle, but she still itched to sort through the information herself. Kate glanced quickly at Andy, telling her she was done.

"Dr. Doyle, Constable Ferris tells me there are two coroners who serve Valley General, is that right?" Andy asked.

"Yes, though we don't often have cause for the coroner's office to be involved."

"Any idea which coroner they are sending out tomorrow morning?" Andy asked.

Dr. Doyle seemed to make a show of looking through her notes. "No, although that's not unusual."

Andy said nothing, letting the silence stretch. Kate watched Dr. Doyle fidget.

"Do you have any other questions, Dr. Morrison?"

Kate squared the corners of the case files. She pushed aside the questions of threats and pressures and power struggles. She thought about Natalie Cardiff just a few hallways away, about Serena Cardiff lying in the hospital bed, about the autopsy she was going to witness tomorrow morning.

"How hard would it be to get me every chart for every suspected influenza case in the last year?"

❖

Kate rubbed at her eyes with the heel of her hands, then took a sip from the water bottle that Andy had brought a few hours ago after refusing to bring Kate another coffee. She wasn't exactly sure how long she'd been sitting in this small meeting room with the blinds drawn to keep out distraction. Dr. Doyle had set her up on the computer at first, but after two hours of scrolling through data files, Kate had requested the archived hard copies, needing to physically move the papers around and sort through the information in her own barely logical structure. Even after hours with the files, Kate felt like she knew very little. Questions about the September cluster and the length of the illness still knocked around her head. Kate forced herself to not try to form conclusions, simply absorb the information and look for connections.

Needing to separate herself from the medical files for a moment, Kate pulled up the article from the *Squamish Herald* that had been the catalyst for her and Andy's presence on this case. She hadn't pulled anything new or relevant from the article when Andy walked in.

"Pack up, we're heading out."

She gave Andy a tired smile. "You like ordering me around, don't you?"

Andy grinned and started helping Kate pack up the files, careful to keep some semblance of order to Kate's chaos. They hadn't had a chance to talk all day. As they walked silently, side by side, through the quiet hospital corridors and out into the cool, clear night, Kate forced her mind away from the medical charts and tried to remember all the things she wanted to ask Andy.

"You were great today," Andy said, once they were in the car.

"Was I?" Kate asked, rubbing again at her gritty, dry eyes.

"Yes, you managed to knock down more barriers than I could have in one day."

"That's because you wear a gun. And you don't smile very often."

Andy laughed. "You're right. I'm definitely not setting up to be the good guy here."

"That's on purpose, isn't it?" Kate said. "You stepped in with Michael Cardiff so I wouldn't have to."

"You need to have a positive relationship with the hospital and the patients and the families, I don't. Even if I did, I would never be able to ask the kinds of questions you can. They will always be looking for my motive, always on the defensive."

Kate thought about Andy's response, seeing the scene in the ER with Dr. Doyle and Cardiff in a different light. "What do you think about Cardiff?" Kate asked.

Andy pulled onto the highway, the Yukon's engine roaring as they merged onto the quiet, darkened road. "Right now I think he's a politician who is worried about his daughter," Andy said carefully.

"Instead of a worried father who happens to be a politician," Kate clarified.

"Exactly. Is that what you see?"

Kate took a moment before answering. "That's my first instinct. But I think when people are under stress, they tend to fall back on what they know, what's safe. If pushing people around and using his considerable charm and power to take control of a situation is what Cardiff is used to, it's not exactly surprising he's trying that now."

They were both quiet, thoughtful, Kate watching the lines disappear underneath the car in the headlights without really paying attention.

"You think Cardiff is charming, do you?" Andy asked. Kate detected the slightest smile in her tone.

"Very funny. You have to admit he's persuasive."

"He's a bully."

"That, too. Did you ever find out who's going to be performing the autopsy tomorrow?"

"No. Ferris couldn't find the information either. People keep telling me that it's not that unusual, but it seems odd to me."

Kate shrugged. It didn't really matter to her who was performing the autopsy. She just knew she had to be there. Hopefully, it was someone who didn't mind a lot of questions. Kate considered the questions she had, already beginning to prioritize them as Andy pulled off the highway onto a side road, winding around in the forested darkness until they came upon the large white sign with blue letters, proudly proclaiming the Sea to Sky Inn. Outside of prime tourist season, either summer or ski, the place was pretty quiet.

The room was plain and clean, the king-size bed with its blue and green striped cover dominating the space. A desk with a high-backed chair was in one corner, with a tiny kitchenette across from the bathroom. Andy put down their bags and immediately pulled out her laptop, setting it on the desk and powering it up. Kate put her bag down on the bed as she looked around.

"This seems vaguely familiar, doesn't it?" Kate said.

Andy looked up from logging into the hotel's Wi-Fi. "What does?"

"You and me in a roadside motel. You typing up reports for Finns late into the night while I sleep."

Andy smiled, tucking her now loose hair behind her ears. "I imagine it will be a little different this time."

"You think?" Kate asked, pulling out her pyjamas from the top of her bag. Andy was quiet and Kate was about to check on her when she felt Andy's hand on her back. Kate turned around. She hadn't even heard Andy cross the room.

"For starters, I couldn't do this last time we were together in a roadside motel." Andy ran her hand down Kate's face, from her temple down her jaw until one finger grazed over her bottom lip. Kate shivered at the touch. "Or this." Andy pushed Kate's hair away from her neck and kissed her there, lips travelling up to Kate's ear, then back down towards her shoulder.

"But you thought about it, didn't you?" Kate asked. Her eyes were closed, the familiar, delicious pulse that Andy excited in her coursing through her body.

Andy pulled back, and Kate opened her eyes.

"It took every ounce of willpower I had *not* to think about it," Andy said with a smile.

Kate sighed and reached up to tangle her fingers into Andy's hair. "I know the feeling."

Andy laughed, and then she leaned down to kiss her, very gently at first, slowly. It built like a slow wave, the pressure of her lips, the depth and urgency behind it, the way their hands moved across each other's bodies in rhythm to the kiss. Soon there were no thoughts of reports or autopsies or patients. Soon there were no thoughts at all.

CHAPTER FIVE

Kate woke the next morning to early dawn light in the motel room. She was only briefly disoriented by her surroundings, taking a moment to shift facts and reality and place them in the motel outside of Hidden Valley. She looked up to see Andy was already awake, lying on her back with her arms crossed under her head, apparently staring at nothing. Kate ran her hand across Andy's stomach, fingertips travelling over the ridges of her scar. She pulled herself in closer and watched the slow smile she loved so much spread across Andy's face.

"No run this morning?" Kate asked, her voice still gravelly with sleep.

"Maybe tomorrow."

"You didn't run last time. When we were in Seattle, I mean."

Andy traced a light pattern on Kate's arm. "Turns out I couldn't force myself away from you unless it was absolutely necessary."

They lay in bed, listening to the sound of each other breathing and the logging trucks on the highway in the distance.

"What are you thinking about?" Andy said, breaking the silence.

"The autopsy. It's been a while since I've seen one."

"Are you worried?"

"No, not at all. It's just been a long time since I dealt with a coroner and even longer since I've observed an autopsy."

"Well, it'll be my first."

Kate looked up, studying Andy's face. "Are *you* worried?" Kate had a hard time imagining anything that could throw Andy.

"Maybe. A little," Andy confessed. "What's it like?"

Kate thought back to her med school years. "Cold," she said finally. "Surprisingly bloodless, which makes the whole thing very unreal."

"Cold and bloodless," Andy repeated, like she was mentally preparing herself.

Kate watched the room become brighter by imperceptible degrees, the light seeping in and around the curtained window.

"Is it strange that I like that I can lie in bed with you even though our conversation is about dead people?" Kate said.

Andy laughed lightly. "Definitely. But I know exactly what you mean." Andy looked over Kate's shoulder to the clock on the bedside table. "We should get moving. Showing up together and late could be a bad start."

They showered and dressed quickly, Andy stopping to pick up the piece of paper that had been slipped under the door during the night on their way out.

"Message at the front desk," Andy read. "I'll ask them about where we can get breakfast this morning."

The day was cool and cloudy. A damp wind lifted Kate's hair off her neck and wormed its way under her layer of clothes. Kate had a flash of regret at leaving their warm bed behind, a quick image of spending the day in bed with Andy lighting up her thoughts. She shivered with the cold, waiting for the Yukon's heater to kick in while Andy picked up their message at the front desk. Andy pulled open the door, balancing two large white Styrofoam cups.

"Judy," Andy explained, passing Kate her cup. It felt wonderfully warm, and Kate wished she could wrap her body around it. "There's a diner one exit down the highway. We'll head there."

The diner was more of a truck stop. The actual building was dwarfed by the dozen or so eighteen-wheelers that surrounded it. They received a brief moment of silence when the two of them walked in, Andy in uniform with her bulky storm jacket and hat pulled low, but then the buzz of conversation picked up again. Their breakfast came fast and hot, Kate burning her tongue on her perfectly cooked over-easy eggs. Andy took a few bites of her bagel, then pushed the rest of it around her plate.

"It will be better with something in your stomach," Kate finally said. "Trust me."

They were in and out of the diner so fast that Judy's coffees were still warm in the truck. They drove in silence to the hospital, fat drops of rain beginning to hit the windshield just as they pulled off the exit for Hidden Valley. As they drove through town, the only sound Kate could hear was the Yukon's wipers streaking loudly across the glass.

"I'm having a serious case of déjà vu," Kate said, earning a small laugh from Andy. "All that's missing is Jack's chatter from the backseat."

"He wasn't very happy about being left behind." Andy sipped her coffee as she navigated the slick roads.

"He texted me yesterday. Said he was working on a project?"

"Yeah, but I made Finns promise we could have access to Jack for anything we need."

They pulled around the back of the hospital, following Constable Ferris's directions. Only two other cars were in the lot. One was a nondescript minivan, and the other was a bright orange Volkswagen bug, which seemed garish in their dark, wet surroundings. Kate could just see the vanity plate attached to the orange car: DM MD.

"Jesus fucking Christ," Andy said suddenly.

Kate turned quickly to look at Andy, who was staring out at the cars with a look of loathing. "What's wrong?"

"You've got to be fucking kidding." Andy seemed to be talking to herself as she parked the Yukon as far from the other cars as possible and pulled out her phone.

"Andy?" Kate felt the alarm rising in her chest.

Andy dialed. "I need to call Finns."

Kate waited, fidgeting, wanting to know what had Andy so rattled. Andy muttered another curse, then stabbed at the numbers on her phone again.

"Lydia, it's Andy. I need to speak to Finns and he's not answering his…With Heath? I need to talk to him. Either one, then, thanks." There was a pause, Andy still glaring out the windshield. Kate jumped when Andy spoke again, her voice loud and harsh. "Do you want to explain to me what Mona Kellar is doing here?" A pause. "Then who did? Pulling strings, then…no, I wasn't aware of that. You see no conflict of interest?" Another angry pause. "Given our history? I don't think it's possible." Kate watched Andy drop her shoulders and run her free hand over her eyes. "Yes. No, I'll make it work. Yes, I'll report by the end of the day. But you'll be getting my off-the-record report later." Andy hung up the phone, eyes grim, staring down at nothing. Kate waited, the unease in her stomach increasing the longer Andy went without speaking.

Minutes ticked by, the rain a constant, heavy backdrop. Andy finally looked up. “Cardiff decided that the local coroner would not be sufficient, so he called in the only forensic pathologist in all of western Canada. Dr. Mona Kellar.” Andy spat out the name. She pointed out the windshield at the orange VW bug. “That’s her car, I recognize the license plate. DM MD stands for dead man’s doctor.”

“Nice,” Kate said. “But a forensic pathologist seems like overkill for suspected influenza.”

“Apparently her family is connected to Hidden Valley, to Nicholas Ozarc himself.”

Kate waited, but Andy fumed silently, her body rigid with tension. “You mentioned a history,” Kate said softly.

Andy looked up at Kate, her grey eyes bleak. “I don’t have time to get into it now, but Mona Kellar hates me. Absolutely loathes me.” Kate was dying to know why, but held her silence. She watched as Andy convulsively gripped the steering wheel. “And I have no doubt that she’s going to take it out on you.”

“Me? I’ve never even met her.”

“Doesn’t matter. Look, this woman is a sociopath. She’s aggressive and underhanded and intelligent. She has no respect for personal boundaries and takes pleasure in hurting the people around her.”

Kate continued to stare at Andy, barely able to keep up with the torrent of hate that poured out. She’d never heard Andy talk like this about anyone. Mixed in with the anger was an edge of desperation and fear, but Andy didn’t seem to be worried about herself.

“What should I do?” Kate asked. She was trying to keep a semblance of calm for Andy’s sake.

Andy spoke with her hands still clenched to the wheel. “Keep all conversation about the autopsy. Try not to reveal anything about your private life. Chances are she’s already dug up as much as she can on you.”

“Then she knows we’re together.”

“Undoubtedly.” Andy ran her hand over her eyes again, took a breath, and then she unexpectedly slammed her fist against the steering wheel. “What the hell have I gotten you into?”

Kate waited until Andy's breathing had calmed before she spoke again. "I don't think I have the energy to deal with this Dr. Kellar as well as your stress *and* your guilt. So let's assume I can handle two out of three. Drop the guilt." She reached over and ran her hand lightly over Andy's knee, feeling the tension in her body.

Andy picked up Kate's hand. She ran her fingers around Kate's wrist, prying her hand open gently with her thumb before entwining their fingers together.

"I can't protect you in there. Coming to your defense will make things a hundred times worse. But if you want me to, if you *need* me to, I will."

Kate squeezed Andy's hand. "I know. Let's get this over with."

Kate and Andy signed in at the reception area. Andy showed her badge to the bored-looking man behind the desk, and Kate held up her temporary RCMP ID Judy had given her. This area was almost never seen by the public eye, so it lacked the comforting elegance that the rest of the hospital boasted. The morgue and autopsy areas were overlit, the unnatural whiteness leaching everyone and everything of colour. As if all bodies passing through this area must take on the cold semblance of the corpses it serviced.

They were led by an assistant in green scrubs to a change area where they were given surgical gowns and thin paper booties to slip over their shoes. They hung up their jackets and pulled the green surgical gowns over their clothes, the tight-fitting cuffs stretching around their wrists. The forensic technician, who introduced herself as Olivia, came a moment later to collect them and lead them down the hall.

The autopsy room had the same white look, even more so given that the light reflected off the countless stainless steel surfaces. It was much smaller than the ones Kate had seen in Vancouver, the walls covered by racks and rows of implements, bottles, trays, and tools. Kate looked around, refamiliarizing herself with the processes and implements for examining the dead. As she checked out the oversized sinks, the tile floors sloping down to a drain, the deep-set tables with troughed edges, she thought about how much of an autopsy was about the preservation and analysis of bodily fluid. It was so different than Kate's trauma rooms, where blood, urine, and vomit regularly leaked out, only to be impatiently wiped away.

Kate checked on Andy, who stood just inside the doorway, arms stiff at her sides. She wanted to say something, smile, anything, but the door swung open and Olivia returned. She held the door open for a woman in her early fifties, slightly taller than Kate with wiry bottle-orange hair that frizzed around her face. As she clomped into the room, Kate could see her face was slightly puffy with the shadow of a double chin and mean brown eyes that somehow seemed to clash with her alarmingly orange hair. She wore an oversized black T-shirt tucked into high-waist jeans and heavy lace-up work boots. Kate wasn't sure exactly what she had been expecting, but this woman was not it.

The woman clomped over to Kate and held out her hand. "Dr. Morrison, I'm Dr. Kellar. I hear I get you as assistant today."

"More of an observer." Kate shook the woman's hand and attempted a smile, trying to give her the benefit of the doubt.

"Assistant," Dr. Kellar insisted, not raising her voice but taking a very small step in towards Kate.

Kate resisted the instinct to lean away, and instead she looked over at Olivia, who was prepping the table.

"Sure," Kate said. "Assistant."

Dr. Kellar gave what supposedly passed as a smile, though it somehow made her eyes more mean than friendly. "Excellent, glove up. Olivia, get the body."

Dr. Kellar walked over to the table, pulled a surgical gown over her clothes, and added a heavy white plastic apron that tied around her back. She still had not acknowledged Andy, who was standing perfectly still near the door. Olivia returned wheeling a metal gurney with a body wrapped in white plastic. She expertly positioned it by the table and Kate, pulling on her gloves, walked over to help transfer the body to the table. The body was stiff and heavy, cold and unyielding, under Kate's hands. The name *Roberta Sedlak* flashed across Kate's mind as she remembered the name of the dead woman.

Kate stood back as Dr. Kellar prepped. She adjusted lights, lined up trays, and repositioned tools attached to tracks in the ceiling overhead. She then gestured for Olivia to unwrap the body, keeping her gloved hands against her chest like a surgeon. It seemed a curious pose to Kate, as this position was usually held to keep a surgeon's hands sterile. Here, though, it was to prevent contamination of evidence.

Once the body was exposed, Dr. Kellar reached up to a plastic-wrapped instrument attached to a black wire. It was a microphone, Kate realized, and Dr. Kellar paused before switching it on.

"Tell me Dr. Morrison, how do you feel about assisting in an autopsy while your lover watches?"

Kate knew she should have been prepared for this. Hadn't Andy given her enough warning out in the car? Kate looked into the light eyes of the forensic pathologist staring at her over the surgical mask. They were bright, they were calculating, they were interested.

"I'm ready whenever you are, Dr. Kellar," Kate said, her voice steady. She could see Andy out of the corner of her eye, but she refused to look over. Olivia looked between the two doctors, unsure, and then focused her eyes on the tray of instruments in front of her, head down. *Smart woman*, thought Kate.

"But I'm curious. Given the nature of your occupations, I wonder if you ever lie in bed together and discuss the gruesome details of your day."

That was so close to her earlier conversation with Andy that she suddenly felt very exposed, as if this twisted woman had been witness to their private moment. Kate took a breath.

"I'm ready whenever you are, Dr. Kellar," Kate said again. Then she dropped her gaze to the table between them. No one moved. The moment stretched, and Kate forced herself to keep breathing slowly, steadily. The sound of the microphone clicking on echoed loudly in the silence.

"Wednesday, October 6, 9:03 a.m., at Valley General morgue. Present are Dr. Mona Kellar, Dr. Katherine Morrison, Nurse Olivia Peterson, and Sergeant Andrea Wyles." Kate heard no change in Dr. Kellar's tone as she repeated their names for the official record. Kate thought for a moment maybe the worst was over, maybe she could focus on the autopsy about to take place. She then thought about what Andy would have to say about that, remembered the look on her face in the car. Kate decided to not let her guard down once through the whole procedure. It was going to be a very long few hours.

Dr. Kellar continued with her official, verbal report.

"Post-mortem exam of Roberta Sharon Sedlak, female, aged sixty-four. We'll start with the external physical exam."

For a woman who seemed dumpy and unkempt, she was meticulous in her process. Kate watched as Dr. Kellar took photos, weighed the body, and gave a description of the woman's skin, hair, eyes, and features. She began the physical exam at the crown of the woman's head, working her way down, taking note of features and appearances, cataloguing this woman's inconsistencies and imperfections in great detail. She gave a detailed description of the scar on the underside of the woman's left breast, a result of a four-year-old lumpectomy. Dr. Kellar worked her way quickly down the body, talking only to herself, ignoring her audience. When she attempted to roll the body to examine the back, Kate reached over to assist, getting no acknowledgement. Once the external exam was complete, Dr. Kellar stood at the head of the table and picked up her scalpel.

"What symptoms did the patient present with upon being admitted to the hospital?" Dr. Kellar said suddenly, addressing no one in particular. Kate looked quickly at Olivia, who merely widened her eyes slightly.

"Influenza symptoms and respiratory distress," Kate said.

"What influenza symptoms? Be more specific," Dr. Kellar barked.

"Fever over forty degrees lasting more than four days, complaints of burning in the chest, coughing, muscle aches and pains, and extreme fatigue. Difficulty breathing, including pain when breathing, began at home approximately five hours before being admitted to hospital."

"ER treatment?"

Kate gave a silent thanks for her memory, for her ability to access information quickly.

"Nasal cannula of forty percent oxygen upon being admitted, chest x-ray confirmed fluid in the lungs, diuretics administered PO initially and then by IV along with steroids as symptoms progressed. Respiratory distress became acute and patient succumbed two days after being admitted. Cause of death ruled as rapid onset pulmonary edema without an identifiable cause."

"What was this woman's occupation?"

"Teacher, retired."

"Who brought her into the ER?"

Kate quickly scanned the file in her head and came up blank. "I don't know, but I'm sure I could find out if you think it's relevant."

Dr. Kellar ignored the offer, seeming happier now that she'd found a question Kate couldn't answer. She still held the scalpel poised over the body, staring at Kate. "And I always assumed she didn't like people smarter than her."

Kate felt a rush of tight anger, hating the way Mona Kellar spoke so familiarly about Andy, still pretending she wasn't even there. But Kate kept her silence.

"Beginning internal examination at 9:57 a.m.," Dr. Kellar said. She immediately sank her scalpel into the patient's chest, drawing a swift, dark line from shoulder to shoulder, down her chest and stomach with a slight deviance to the left around the navel, stopping at the top of the pubic bone. She then very carefully used her scalpel to peel back the skin, muscle, and soft tissue connecting flesh to bone.

As Kate watched the forensic pathologist working, she wondered at the woman's choice of incision. Most coroners preferred the Y cut, giving them better access to the thoracic cavity. The T cut, as Dr. Kellar had just so expertly demonstrated, was used when the coroner was being particularly sensitive to the family. It was much easier to cover once the autopsy was complete. She didn't have time to speculate on the motives behind the decision because Dr. Kellar was handing her a wicked set of gardening shears.

"Dr. Morrison, the chest plate."

It was not a suggestion. It was a challenge.

Kate took the shears, opening and closing them in her hand, getting the feel of them. Next she placed her left hand at the bottom of the exposed rib cage. Then she hesitated, hating the thought of asking for help but knowing it would be disastrous to get it wrong.

"Lateral incision on both sides of the chest, approximately six inches from the centre sternal line?" she asked, keeping her eyes on the rib cage.

"That's right." Dr. Kellar's voice had changed. It was lower, creepier. "Cut away, Dr. Morrison."

Kate cut. Her movements were careful but strong, feeling the give of tissue and bone through the instrument into her fingers, her wrist, her arms. She was sweating slightly by the time she'd finished one side. Without asking, she moved to the other side of the table. Dr. Kellar did not give Kate any extra space. Kate tried to ignore the crawling of her skin at having to work so closely to this woman. She focused on the task in front of her, trying not to sigh with relief as she finished, taking her original position across the table.

She was thankful Dr. Kellar had taken over again, starting the delicate task of removing any soft tissue that had adhered to the underside of the chest plate before removing it all in one piece. Kate looked into the dead woman's chest cavity. It had been years since she'd seen the heart and lungs so clearly displayed in their predictable, orderly manner. She could see immediately in front of her what she had seen in the x-rays, swollen tissue from fluid build-up and inflammation of the pleural space. A very neat presentation of pulmonary edema.

Dr. Kellar, however, was frowning down into the chest cavity, her hands still against the table. She bent over the body, seeming to whisper to herself. Kate caught Olivia's eye. The nurse shrugged imperceptibly. Finally, Dr. Kellar picked up a large gauge needle and a vial, pulling fluid from various spots on the lung, using a sterile swab to pick up the leaking pleural fluid, and dropping that into an encased capsule before handing them all silently to Olivia, who carefully jotted down the appropriate information.

Kate had a hundred questions, but kept silent. This was not a teaching case, and she knew at the very least she would get the autopsy report. Instead she watched the proceedings, letting no detail go by unnoticed, absorbing every move that Dr. Kellar made and committing it to memory so she could take them out later and sort through relevant information. The only sound was that of the faint, wet tearing of flesh and of Dr. Kellar's almost constant stream of barely audible self-talk. She spent the most time in the chest cavity, working on the lungs before moving to the heart. After about three hours, as Dr. Kellar was removing and weighing the other vital organs, Kate stretched her back, feeling the strain of standing in one position for so long. She knew immediately it was a mistake.

"Get out if you can't handle the physical strain of simply standing up, Dr. Morrison," Dr. Kellar said, her voice harsh in the silence.

Kate bit the inside of her cheek, fighting the acid retorts that came quickly to her lips. She didn't say a word. Dr. Kellar turned to Olivia.

"Get me some water. From the fridge," she ordered, and Olivia left the room quickly.

Kate's stomach plummeted uncomfortably as Dr. Kellar reached up to turn off the microphone. She could swear she felt Andy tense also, even across the room.

"Tell me how you met," Dr. Kellar said, in the same demanding tone she'd just used with the nurse.

"No." Kate attempted to infuse as much neutrality as possible into the refusal.

Dr. Kellar smiled. "You haven't looked at her once in the last four hours. Why is that?"

Kate said nothing, wishing Olivia would hurry back. The audience didn't seem to stop Dr. Kellar from trying to make Kate uncomfortable, but at least she provided some type of outside witness.

"Did you have sex with her this morning? I know you're sharing a room. So it would be RCMP-sanctioned sex, wouldn't it? Though according to my sources, it wouldn't be the first time."

Kate could feel the flush of anger and embarrassment rise in her cheeks and tried to force it back down. She had nowhere to look—not at Dr. Kellar dominating her view and not at Andy, standing by the door. Thankfully, at that moment, Olivia walked back in with three frosted bottles of water. She offered one to Andy, who refused with a shake of her head, then another to Kate, and the third to Dr. Kellar, who did not take her eyes off Kate's face as she opened it and drank half of the contents in one loud gulp. Kate, taking small sips from the water bottle, could see Andy out of the corner of her eye, back ramrod straight, shoulders squared. In her mind's eye, Kate could also see the tightness of her jaw, the hard lines around her eyes. As Dr. Kellar threw her water bottle into the garbage and picked up her scalpel again, Kate forced her attention away from Andy. There was nothing she could do.

Another two hours, and Kate's eyes were getting dry. The back of her legs ached from standing for so long, and hunger rolled in her stomach. Dr. Kellar gave her closing observations into the microphone and asked the nurse to close up. Dr. Kellar stretched her back and shoulders, rotated her head, flexed her wrists. Kate resisted the urge to copy her, somehow knowing it would only invite more derision. She waited to be dismissed, feeling a sudden surge of empathy for her med students back at Van East.

"What's your conclusion, Dr. Morrison?"

The question caught Kate off guard. Dr. Kellar hadn't asked her opinion once in the almost six hours they'd been here. It was another test, another challenge.

"I saw pulmonary edema from an infection, primary or secondary, I don't know. I'd want Public Health to run the tests, though."

"Assholes," Dr. Kellar said. "We'll meet to discuss my findings tomorrow." She pulled off her gloves, snapping them in the silence, and then removed her apron and gown, tinged brown now with bodily fluid. She then carried them across the room and Kate watched as she approached the door and deposited them into the bypass waste bin. Then she crossed to Andy, turned to make sure Kate was watching them, and whispered something in her ear. Andy kept her eyes ahead, not acknowledging her presence. Dr. Mona Kellar then left the room.

As the door swung silently closed behind her, Kate let out the first real breath she'd felt since the autopsy started. As she began to remove her own gloves and gown, she studied Andy's face. Her eyes were guarded, her jaw tense. Kate sighed and turned to the technician.

"Do you need my help to finish up?" she asked.

Olivia smiled and looked up from where she was putting in careful stitches. "No, but thanks for asking. That was an interesting autopsy," she said, her eyebrows raised.

Kate gave her a knowing smile but said nothing.

Moments later they were out in the fresh air, leaving the autopsy room and the bodies and the fluid and the awfulness of the last few hours behind them. Kate shuddered, wishing that she could shower, find some way to rid herself of what had just happened. Kate walked as close as possible to Andy, feeling reassurance just from the brush of Andy's sleeve against hers. They stopped at the hospital coffee shop, ordering overpriced sandwiches and large coffees before carrying them to the small meeting room Kate had taken over as her temporary office.

Once they were inside, doors closed and blinds drawn, Kate sat down with a loud sigh. It felt amazing to be off her feet. As she unwrapped her sandwich and bit into it, she watched Andy remove the lid of her coffee, her sandwich untouched on the table.

"Not hungry?" Kate said. It was the first thing she'd said to her since getting out of the car this morning, and it seemed inadequate.

"Yes and no."

In all the chaos of the morning, the phone call to Finns, and the last-minute warnings about Mona Kellar, Kate had forgotten that Andy had just witnessed her first autopsy. And she'd been nervous.

"You okay?"

"Shouldn't I be asking you that?" Andy said. Kate could hear the self-recrimination in her tone.

"Me? I'm fine. Still hungry though. So, if you're not going to eat your sandwich, pass it over."

Andy shook her head, relaxing her shoulders a fraction. She tossed Kate the sandwich. Kate unwrapped it and took a huge bite.

Andy laughed. "You're unbelievable."

"Years of practice," Kate said through her mouthful. "You'll be hungry in a few hours, trust me."

They were silent. Kate made short work of the sandwich while Andy took tentative sips of her coffee.

"You'll tell me later, right?" Kate asked, her voice lowered.

Andy nodded, her eyes darkening. "Yes, everything."

With her belly full, and her legs and back no longer screaming their complaints, Kate let her mind free flow with the information from the last two days. She put aside the issues of politics and inflammatory media reports. She put aside, for now, whatever history Andy had with Dr. Kellar. Kate thought about the autopsy, the questions about infection and influenza. She looked at the charts, stacked neatly in the corner.

"Do you have to be anywhere this afternoon?" Kate asked Andy, relieved to see a small amount of colour returning to Andy's pale face.

"No. Why?"

"Can you help me sort through charts, then?"

"Is this because you need my help or you think I need to keep occupied?"

"Both," Kate said. She stood up and brought the pile of charts over to the table, depositing them in front of Andy before dropping into the chair beside her.

"Okay, what am I looking for?"

"Any mention of fatigue or muscle ache unrelated to injury goes in this pile. Everything else goes over here."

The next hour was quiet, a relaxed quiet, a stress-free quiet. They sorted through paperwork, through charts, scanning pages of symptoms and complaints, searching for commonalities. As she picked up one of the last charts, she noticed something. She looked at the piles in front of them, each chart neatly labeled with the patient's name.

"I need you to do something for me," Kate said suddenly.

"What?"

"I need a circle of people. If this is truly influenza, then those closest to the patients are at the highest risk of getting sick. That includes siblings, parents, partners, and coworkers. I want to know if any of them got sick, even an unreported illness." Kate watched Andy pull out her notepad and scrawl some notes. "I don't need it now, not even today. Maybe tomorrow, with Ferris?"

"Sure, I can do that. Anything else?"

"We're going to need to put pressure on Public Health. Failing that, do you think the hospital or Cardiff could get some kind of independent lab to take results?"

Andy rolled her eyes. "I'm sure he'd be delighted at the opportunity to throw his weight around."

"Let's wait and see what Kellar says tomorrow."

The name brought instant tension back into the room, and Kate shook her head, annoyed at herself. "Sorry."

"Don't be. I'll feel better once you know what's going on."

Kate looked at the stacks in front of them. "Three more charts, then we're out of here."

The day outside had gone from cool to warm and was heading back down to cold again when Kate and Andy pulled into a deserted rest stop at the side of the highway. They'd stopped at a posh little grocery store in town and picked up some food, including breakfast for the next morning. They made their way back through the trees until they found a damp wooden picnic table where they set down their food. Andy opened her take-out container of squash and cheese ravioli, and as the smell hit her, Kate kicked herself for saying she wasn't hungry. She was. Again. Andy popped two in her mouth and chewed slowly. Apparently her appetite was back.

"Good?" Kate asked.

Andy only nodded as she scooped up two more. Kate looked around, the trees swaying above them, the sky darkening into twilight. They probably only had another forty-five minutes until sunset. Kate wondered if it was enough time to hear Andy's story. She tried not to stare at Andy's dinner.

"I shouldn't tease you." Andy pulled a second fork out of the bag and pushed the oversized container into the centre of the table. "I have no idea how you can eat so much and not gain weight."

Kate stuffed two of the raviolis into her mouth. God, they were good. "High stress job and a sexy girlfriend. You should try it."

"I do. Daily," Andy said.

They ate in silence, listening to the wind, happy to be alone together.

"Should I start?" Andy finally asked, putting down her fork.

"Yes."

"I had just graduated Depot and had been a rookie with E-Division about three months when I first came across Mona Kellar. She was consulting on a high profile double homicide. The investigation was long and involved, so she was around headquarters a lot. I wasn't on the case because I was too new, but my mentor, Lincoln, was connected to it. I was shadowing him most of the time." Andy stopped and took a sip of water and Kate watched her eyes darken. "After Dr. Kellar and I were first introduced, she started talking to me all the time, seeking me out at work, waiting for me in the parking lot after my shift. I was twenty-four, she was in her forties. Time hasn't improved her all that much."

"Did she know you were gay?"

"Yeah, I guess. It wasn't something I ever hid."

"Is *she* gay?"

"She's a predator," Andy said. "She'll jump on anything that moves."

Kate got a mental image of this, and she shuddered reflexively.

"Exactly," Andy said. "Her attention got worse, people started talking, and I just tried to avoid her as much as possible. One night I'd stayed late trying to finish something for Lincoln, and she was waiting for me at my car. She came onto me strong and tried to kiss me. When I stopped her, she got angry. Really angry. Told me if I didn't sleep with her, she would lodge a sexual harassment complaint against me, saying I had made inappropriate advances. Mona Kellar made it perfectly clear that if I didn't have sex with her, my career would be over before it had started."

Kate looked at Andy with wide eyes, her skin crawling, her heart hammering with sympathy and a startling, intense hatred.

"What did you do?"

"Nothing at first. Kept it to myself. I respected Lincoln, but I barely knew him and was too embarrassed to take it to him. And she was so much worse after, constantly trying to touch me, saying suggestive things in front of other people. I couldn't go anywhere on my own. I even had to wait until someone else went to the bathroom and follow them in so she couldn't corner me. It was awful. And I couldn't fight back the way I wanted to, mainly with my fists, because she held so much power."

Andy looked down at the table, at her hands wrapped around the plastic water bottle. Kate waited and let her order her thoughts.

"This went on for a couple of weeks, and her advances and threats kept escalating. Eventually one of the staff sergeants, a woman named Rosalie Kurtz, pulled me into her office even though she wasn't my supervisor. Kurtz had been watching what was going on and already suspected what was happening. She made me tell her everything, which I did." Andy paused and smiled bleakly. "So we set up my very first sting operation."

"How did you do that?"

"It was simple. Kurtz parked her car in the lot near mine, I stayed late at the office and let Mona Kellar follow me out of the building to my car. She very helpfully replayed the same scene, threats and all. Kurtz then got out of the car and told her if she ever threatened me again or came anywhere near or merely hinted that there had been anything between us, she would lodge a formal complaint with the RCMP and Kellar's own career would suffer."

Andy suddenly pushed aside the water bottle and reached across the table for Kate's hands. She wove their fingers together, both of them slightly slick with oil from the pasta.

"And that was the end of it?"

"Pretty much. She left me alone, ignored me like she did today. I was still angry, though, and I wanted to launch my own sexual harassment case. It pissed me off that she could still walk around and everyone treated her like a god. Kurtz said she'd back me up if I wanted to go forward with it, but convinced me I wouldn't be doing myself any favours. I've had to work with Kellar once since then, about four years ago. She was a nightmare. We lasted a whole three days until Finns pulled me off the case and assigned someone new. I hated he might think I was incompetent so I told him, off the record, about what had happened." She paused, shrugged, looked Kate in the eye. "And that's it."

Kate looked back at her and held her hands. "Today must have been hard."

Andy gave her a bleak smile. "It took everything I had to not turn around and drive you back to Vancouver when I saw her car in the parking lot."

"I survived."

"Of course you did."

The wind picked up in a sudden gust, lifting Kate's hair off her neck and swirling it around her face. She brushed it back, realized evening was passing them by, and it was heading rapidly into night.

"We should get going," Andy said.

"Wait. Tell me what Kellar said to you before she left the autopsy room."

Andy didn't say anything for a moment then reached across the table and tucked a loose curl behind Kate's ear.

"She told me to have fun talking about her all night." Andy suddenly smiled the first real smile Kate had seen since leaving the motel this morning. "Which is an excellent reason to stop talking about her right now."

Kate returned the smile and ran her fingers over the backs of Andy's hands and wrists, making her shiver.

"I think we should go back to the motel, run a bath, and see if we can come up with a few more reasons to stop talking about her."

Andy smiled again. "Deal."

CHAPTER SIX

Kate woke with a start, heart thumping a wild, uneven staccato in her chest. She rolled over to an empty bed and a silent room, vaguely remembering Andy kissing her forehead on the way out the door for her run. Kate lay back against her pillow, letting her breathing return to normal, the adrenaline of a forced awakening diffusing through her body. She tried to remember what she'd seen in her nightmare. Angler, of course, just as silent, just as malevolent, the same knowing smirk on his round face. But this time, he was leaning against an invisible wall and tossing a scalpel in the air. In her dream, Kate watched it flip end over end, flinching every time he caught it by the handle.

Kate pulled back the covers, shivering slightly against the chill damp air of a morning in the mountains. Her bare feet hurt against the cold tile in the bathroom, but she still stopped to look at herself in the mirror. Her left cheek still held the faint red lines of her pillow, her eyes were puffy, pre-coffee slits, and her hair hung in thick, twisted ringlets. Kate splashed water on her face in an attempt to rid herself of the Angler dream, then went back out and crawled into bed to wait for Andy.

She didn't know if it was the nightmare or Andy's absence, but Kate felt unsure and somehow misplaced lying in the motel room on her own. Like she couldn't quite connect her life, herself, to these surroundings. She thought about what Dr. Doyle had said on the first day, how she'd seemed relieved when Kate told her that she had a day job, a *real* job, as a doctor back in Vancouver. But Kate had barely thought about Van East in the last few days. She could feel it slipping away, moving farther out of reach on the other side of a widening void. But she didn't know what was supposed to fill that new space.

Kate heard the key slide into the lock and Andy pushed open the door with her shoulder, two Styrofoam coffees balanced in one hand. Andy's cheeks were flushed a light pink, her hair pulled back under a tight black skullcap that covered her ears. Her bright green running jacket was still covered in raindrops. As Andy handed Kate the coffee, lightly kissing her with cold lips, Kate's unease slipped away, unnoticed.

"I didn't think you'd be awake yet," Andy said, sitting down at the desk and untying her laces.

Kate made a split-second decision not to tell Andy about the nightmare. Andy seemed lighter somehow this morning, the weight of yesterday gone. Why ruin it?

"You know how I like to wake up early on days I don't have to," Kate murmured, making Andy laugh. Kate took her first sip of coffee, leaning up against the headboard of the bed. She watched Andy pull off her running gear, adding items to the wet pile, then she grabbed her favourite grey UBC Women's Basketball sweatshirt and pulled it on. Andy scooped up the pile, headed into the bathroom to hang everything to dry. Kate listened to the sound of the water splashing in the sink. She was content sitting under the covers with her coffee, listening to Andy move around their shared space, letting Andy's energy be enough for both of them.

"Breakfast?" Andy asked as she came out of the bathroom.

"Sure."

Andy went to their kitchenette, pulled items out of the fridge, dumped the mini coffeepot off its tray, loaded it up, and brought everything over to Kate.

"Breakfast in bed, even better."

Andy grinned as she scooped organic raspberry yogurt and gluten-free granola from the grocery store downtown into one of the water glasses, shoved a plastic spoon into it, and passed it to Kate. They ate in silence, Andy refilling her own glass twice while Kate was on her first.

"You're pretty much perfect, you know that, right?" Kate said as Andy stretched across the foot of the bed.

"Fuck off," Andy said to her affectionately, throwing a balled-up napkin at Kate that landed by her knee.

"I'm serious." Kate laughed. "You're the best girlfriend I've ever had." Andy laughed with her, eyes sparkling. "Move in with me," Kate said suddenly, impulsively. "When we get back to Vancouver, move in with me."

Andy was silent, the smile fading on her lips until it looked like she was forcing it to still be there. Kate's heart thumped in her chest, the rejection of Andy's silence rising like a cloud between them. Kate dropped her gaze and started cleaning up the dishes.

"Kate." Andy's voice was low.

Kate didn't look up. She untangled herself from the covers, carried the tray over to the kitchenette, and started rinsing the dishes in the tiny sink. When she was finished and had nothing else to occupy her hands, Kate stood very still, trying to force back the tears that threatened.

Kate heard the creak of the bed as Andy stood up and crossed the room. Andy stood by her side, ran her hand down Kate's arm, letting her fingers rest against the inside of Kate's wrist. Andy waited, as Kate knew she would. Andy would never force Kate to look at her. Kate stared down at nothing, feeling Andy's fingers against the pulse in her wrist. She finally looked up into Andy's searching, grey eyes.

"I love you, Kate. I love you more than I've ever loved anybody, you know that," Andy said.

The cabin, the rain in the trees, Andy's voice. Always this memory, this flash picture of that perfect moment.

"But you don't want to live with me," Kate said, hating how weak her voice sounded. How pathetic.

"You're wrong," Andy said softly. "I do want to live with you. How many times have I showed up after my shift at two o'clock in the morning, even after I told you I was going to sleep at my place? Because I hate going to bed without you."

Kate turned to face Andy, the admission covering a small part of the rejection. "Then why?"

Andy took Kate's other hand, holding them tightly in her own. "I already worry enough that I'm pushing too hard, that I'm not giving you enough space."

Kate instantly thought back to their conversation outside E-division headquarters. Her suspicions made her next words harder than she intended. "Space for what, Andy?"

Kate knew Andy was navigating carefully, but she didn't have it in her right now to make it any easier.

"To figure things out."

"Meaning what?" Kate asked, exasperated.

Andy was silent, which only confirmed what Kate already suspected. "I get it," Kate said. She pulled her hands out of Andy's and began arranging dishes that didn't need to be arranged. "I need to be a card-carrying lesbian before you'll move in with me, is that it?"

Andy didn't answer. Even though Kate couldn't see her face, she could feel the waves of hurt coming off her. For reasons Kate didn't have time to think about, Andy's hurt only made her angrier.

"Is there a length of time that has to pass or a test I need to take? Do you need me to march in next year's Pride Parade?" Kate stared down into the sink, gripping the edge of the counter.

"That's the opposite of what I'm trying to say," Andy finally said. Kate could see Andy's shoulders slump in her peripheral vision. "Fucking hell, how did I get this so wrong?" she asked herself quietly.

As suddenly as Kate's anger had risen inside her, it dissipated. She slipped her arms around Andy's waist and Andy wrapped her in an embrace that told her she wasn't ever going to let her go. Kate allowed herself to feel comforted, leaning into her, smelling the mixture of coffee and rain and Andy.

"Not so perfect now, am I?" Andy murmured into Kate's hair.

Kate pulled back to look into Andy's eyes.

"I'm sorry, Kate," Andy said, before Kate had a chance to speak. "I'm trying so hard not to push you, and all I'm doing is backing you into a corner. I just know that this takes time."

"Falling in love with you hardly took any time at all," Kate said, giving her a small smile.

Andy returned it, running one hand over Kate's cheek, under her eyes, a light touch on her jaw and neck. "But the rest of it, Kate. I know that it takes time to figure out what it means, to shift it around in your head until it makes sense to you. It takes time to say the words and to apply them to yourself. To hear people at work talk about it, to explain to the phone company that I'm not your husband, to decide what words to take offense to, to figure out how you feel about this community that everyone will just assume you are a part of."

Andy took a breath, her thumb resting against Kate's cheek, her fingers brushing back Kate's hair. "So yes, I want to live with you, because any morning I wake up without you hurts. And yes, I worry, because I think moving in together will just force the issue, and I never want you to feel any pressure."

Kate rested her head against Andy's hand, turning her face slightly to kiss her palm. She felt relieved, the question of rejection having entirely left her.

"Am I making any sense?" Andy asked, the worry still showing in her eyes.

"Yes," Kate told her, running her hand down Andy's back, trying to reassure her with her voice and her touch. "You love me. And you're still trying to protect me," she added, with a smile.

Andy leaned down to kiss her once, so very softly, on her lips. "I do. And I am."

The tension eased out of Kate's body. For now, this was enough.

Kate walked into Serena Cardiff's room, expecting to only see the patient asleep, as Dr. Doyle had described her just a few minutes ago. Instead she found a man in his early twenties, his light brown hair a little long and a lot messy, holding Serena Cardiff's hand. Serena herself was sitting up, though she was very pale and Kate could see the nasal cannula of oxygen tucked behind her ears. Kate thought about the autopsy yesterday, the fluid on the lungs, the pinkness of infection. She quickly channelled those thoughts elsewhere, forcing herself to look at the symptoms and the patient in front of her.

"Hi, Serena. I'm Dr. Morrison. I met your mother and father the other day."

"Hi," Serena said. Kate could hear the weakness of the young woman's body as she forced herself to expel enough air to make sound.

The young man stood, gave Kate a warm smile, and held out his hand. "I'm Nathan Tomms, Serena's boyfriend."

Kate shook his hand and returned the smile.

"My sister, Julia," Serena said, pointing to the chair behind Kate. The teenage girl curled up in the chair with her long legs hugged tightly to her chest had been so quiet Kate hadn't noticed her.

"It's nice to meet you, Julia," Kate said, taking in the pale skin, the large brown eyes, and her long brown hair hanging like a curtain. She looked like nothing more than a scared, long-limbed colt. Kate looked back and forth between the two sisters.

"I take it you're not supposed to be here," Kate said to Julia, with a smile. She guessed Julia was around thirteen. Julia shook her head.

"I'm not either, for that matter," Nathan said, squeezing Serena's hand.

"Lucky for you both I'm merely a doctor and not hospital security, so if Serena doesn't mind you being here while I check on her, that's fine by me."

This earned a smile from Serena. Kate saw the effort required.

Kate walked over to the foot of the bed and read the chart. Serena had started experiencing difficulty breathing in the middle of the night, hence the oxygen. She saw a note about a chest x-ray being ordered but no results.

"Did they send you down for a chest x-ray, Serena?"

"No, not yet."

Kate scanned the rest of the chart, but nothing else jumped out at her. She wanted to see those chest x-ray results, to know for sure if there was fluid on Serena's lungs, and how much.

"Mind if I take a listen?" she asked, holding up her stethoscope.

Serena shook her head, leaned forwards in the bed. Kate moved aside the cotton gown, noting its softness compared to the ones they had at Van East. She moved the head of the stethoscope around Serena's back, listening to the gurgle and crack of the fluid as it shifted around her lungs. It sounded to Kate like pneumonia could be settling in, but she still wanted to see the test results.

"Serena, I know it's going to be uncomfortable, but I need you to take a deep, slow breath in and let it out again slowly."

Serena breathed in slowly through her mouth and had just started to release it when a coughing spasm hit. Her thin body convulsed with the effort her lungs made to release whatever had triggered the cough. Kate put her hand on the girl's shoulder as Serena doubled over in bed, hands covering her mouth. Finally it passed, Serena taking in wheezy gulps of air as she leaned back against her pillow, eyes closed.

"Dr. Morrison…" Kate looked up at Nathan's pale face. He pointed to the streak of foamy, pink blood on Serena's palm.

"It's okay, Nathan. Why don't you get her a tissue from the table," Kate said calmly. Nathan reached for the box at the head of the bed and tenderly wiped at her hand. Serena still hadn't opened her eyes.

"Serena, are you all right?"

Serena nodded once.

"Good. You rest, I'm going to go check on that chest x-ray."

Kate started walking out of the room but then caught a glimpse of Julia. She was curled into an even tighter ball on the blue plastic chair, her eyes wide and transfixed on her sister.

"Julia, would you mind showing me where to go? I still don't know my way around this hospital very well."

Julia silently unfolded herself from the chair and followed Kate into the hallway.

"All right, where would I find the nurse's station?"

Julia pointed down the hall to the left.

"Your sister has been sick for a while, hasn't she?" Kate said as they walked together.

"Yeah, but I knew it was really bad when she wouldn't even ride Calliope." Julia's voice was feather-light and shy.

"I take it that's a horse, not a motorcycle."

A small smile from the tall, pale girl.

"Good. I don't see a lot of horse injuries, but I've seen more motorcycle injuries than I can count." Kate smiled at her as they approached the nurse's station.

A young-looking nurse with bright red hair and freckles was tapping at the keyboard and looked up at their approach.

"Hi, I'm Dr. Kate Morrison. I'm consulting with the RCMP. I was just looking for Serena Cardiff's nurse." She tried out her warmest smile on the nurse, hoping it would have the same effect it seemed to have had on Judy a few days ago.

"Right now that would be me, I'm Lucy. What can I do for you, Dr. Morrison?"

"I saw on her chart that a chest x-ray was ordered, but I don't see the films or results anywhere."

Lucy seemed to pale under her freckles. "The x-ray went down last night, and they're just getting it back online now. That's why there's a delay. I'm sorry, Dr. Morrison."

"Unless you're the one who took a hammer to the machine, there's no need to apologize," Kate said. "Any idea what the backlog is?"

Lucy smiled tentatively. "About an hour, they're running emergent cases first. I can check and see if we can get Ms. Cardiff in sooner, though."

"An hour should be fine, but could you do me a favour?"

Given the stunned look on her face, Kate had to wonder if a doctor had ever uttered those words to the nurse before.

"Of course." Lucy recovered quickly.

"Could you call my cell if the x-ray is going to be much longer than an hour?" she said as she wrote down her number and passed it to the nurse.

"Yes, I can do that."

"Great, and if you could check in on Serena when you get a minute, she just had a bronchial spasm with mild hemoptysis, so I'd like someone to keep an eye on her."

"Sure."

"Thanks, Lucy."

Julia walked Kate back to the room.

"Can I ask a question?" Julia asked quietly.

"Julia, I can pretty much guarantee that the answer to that question will always be yes," Kate said.

"I know 'hemo' means blood, but what does the rest of the word mean?"

Kate smiled to herself. Clearly a bright kid. One who paid attention.

"Ptysis is the rest of the word. It means spitting. So when I told the nurse Serena had a bronchial spasm with mild hemoptysis I was really just saying she had a big cough with a little blood."

As they approached Serena's room, Julia slowed her pace. "Dr. Morrison, how sick is my sister?"

Kate stopped in the hallways and waited until Julia looked up to meet her eyes. "She's definitely sick, and she's not recovering as quickly as I'd expect from the flu. But right now she's doing okay." Kate paused. "Is that enough of an answer?"

Julia nodded and ducked her head before she said thanks and headed into the room.

Kate followed her in, finding Serena asleep with Nathan holding her hand.

"She okay?" Kate asked Nathan, picking up the chart and jotting down the expectorated blood as well as the x-ray order.

"Yeah," he responded. He checked his watch and then rubbed tiredly at his eyes.

"You okay?"

"Fine. I've got to get to work soon, but her mom should be back from her massage appointment any minute."

Kate kept her expression neutral but felt surprise and judgement at hearing Natalie Cardiff had gone to a massage appointment while her daughter was in the hospital. She tuned back in to Nathan as he sighed.

"I should head out before she gets here," he said. He looked over at Julia, who had curled herself back in the chair. "Hey, Junior, would you sit with Serena until your mom gets here? She seems to like it when someone holds her hand."

Julia climbed quickly out of the chair, blushing. Nathan leaned over and kissed Serena's forehead.

Kate checked her watch also, realizing she had somewhere she needed to be, too. "I've got a meeting now, Julia, but I'll see you later."

Julia nodded, but didn't take her eyes from her sister.

Kate followed Nathan out into the hallway, falling in step beside him.

"Serena's getting worse, isn't she?" Nathan said. It wasn't hard to hear the strain in his voice.

"She's not showing improvement, and she should be," Kate said. "But she's holding her own right now and she seems strong."

They reached the end of the hallways and were just about to take the main set of stairs down to the next level when Nathan stopped. Kate followed his gaze to the floor below and saw Michael Cardiff opening the door for his wife. Nathan sighed and took a few steps back down the hall.

"I should take the back stairs," he said, sounding resigned. "I'll see you later, Dr. Morrison."

Kate descended the stairs, wondering about the apparent strain in the relationship between Nathan Tomms and his girlfriend's family. She was curious about his evasion, though it didn't really set off any red flags for her. He'd been quietly open about his presence not being approved of by the family, like it was common knowledge. She was still thinking about this when she arrived at the small meeting room.

Andy and Constable Ferris were seated at the far side, surrounded by paper, and Dr. Doyle and Dr. Kellar at the other side, saying very little. Kate found what she hoped was a neutral spot in the middle.

"We're just waiting on Public Health, Dr. Morrison. They're just getting back from Vancouver with some results. We should be getting started in a moment," Dr. Doyle said formally.

Kate sat down and poured herself a coffee from the carafe in the middle of the table, busying her hands with adding milk and sugar. Taking her first sip, she looked at Andy over the rim of her cup. Andy was sitting stiffly in her seat, far from relaxed, but when she looked up to meet Kate's eyes, she managed a small smile. Kate took another sip of coffee and she could feel Mona Kellar's eyes drilling into her from the other side of the room. She ignored it, checked her watch, and let her mind wander to Serena's x-rays.

Finally a tall, thin, grey-haired man wearing khakis and a rumpled shirt walked in, nodded his hello to the assembled group, and sat down. Dr. Doyle introduced Dr. Clifford Salinger, twenty-year veteran with BC Public Health, then moved quickly to get the meeting started.

"Dr. Kellar, if you could present your findings."

Dr. Kellar reached over for a remote control, flicked on a projector Kate hadn't even seen mounted in the ceiling, and a screen came down in the corner of the room.

"Autopsy results support cause of death as acute onset pulmonary edema." The projector transitioned to a picture of the exposed chest cavity and Kate saw again the fluid, the infection. She reflexively pulled out her cell phone and checked for an update from the nurse, Lucy, before turning back to the pictures. "Point of infection was found here." She clicked again, and the slide now showed a close-up of the upper left quadrant of the lung. "This is where the victim had a small tumour that had just begun to infiltrate the lining of the lung. I've taken a sample to confirm, but I would guess lung mets, recurring cancer. Either way, once the lung tissue was infected, it spread aggressively throughout both lungs. The general course of antibiotics and PIO diuretics and even the steroids could not possibly have stayed ahead of that rapidly progressing infection. I also concluded that other than hourly chest x-rays to monitor fluid levels, there was no way for the medical team to know how quickly the lungs were going to fill with fluid."

Kate felt the stirrings of a quiet, generalized alarm. She checked her phone again. Nothing.

"Some place you need to be, Dr. Morrison?" Dr. Kellar's voice was biting.

"Just waiting on results for a patient," Kate said sweetly. "Please continue."

She watched as the muscles on one side of Mona Kellar's face twitched convulsively, clearly hating that Kate gave her permission to continue her own presentation.

"What my results could not verify is the nature of the infection," Dr. Kellar continued. "Given the victim's symptoms previous to being admitted to the hospital, I would suspect a viral infection, but would not conclude any such statements until lab reports were back. Which is why I drove the samples myself to Dr. Salinger's office. Dr. Salinger, I'd like to hear what you've got."

Kate couldn't help but wonder about Kellar's motives for driving the samples to Public Health. Were they scientific or self-interested or controlling or blaming? It could be any of those, and Kate knew she was far too biased to choose the most likely and most flattering option that Dr. Kellar realized the community-wide implications of such an aggressive virus. Kate shifted uncomfortably in her seat. She wanted to talk to Andy.

Dr. Salinger passed Dr. Doyle a memory stick, and the BC Public Health logo popped up on the screen.

"Dr. Kellar brought us blood, lung fluid, and tissue samples yesterday afternoon. Although her methods were unorthodox, it was a good thing that she did because it gave us time to take it to the provincial CDC labs in the city." Dr. Salinger clicked the remote and another image came up. Kate could see a single, sphere-shaped viral cell magnified significantly.

"Here's what we found. An as yet unspecified, non-influenza viral infection."

The room was silent. Kate realized this was a significant and worrying conclusion. Dr. Salinger clicked again, and the image magnified yet again to focus on the external layer of the virus.

"Here's where things get more concerning. In studying the pathophysiology of the virus, we noticed the hemagglutinin cleavage factor, though in structure extremely similar to a common H1 strain found in the vicinity two years ago, does not react to human protease."

"You tested every one, did you Dr. Salinger?" Dr. Kellar asked, not even turning to address the man.

"Of course not," Dr. Salinger said mildly, still addressing the screen. "We tested it against the common ones in the throat and lungs. When it didn't react, we concluded it was non-influenza. We still don't know exactly how it cleaves."

"Or when," Kate muttered to herself, staring intently at the screen.

"Sorry?" Dr. Salinger said.

Kate felt every eye on her. She hadn't realized she'd spoken loudly enough to be heard. "I'm just thinking about the nature of the virus and the infection. When the virus enters the body, where it travels, and how long until it cleaves, or is switched on."

Dr. Salinger gave her a tired smile. "All things I spent most of the night lying awake thinking about, Dr. Morrison. Are you a specialist in the field?"

Kate gave a small laugh. "No, not at all. I'm an ER physician, so right now I'm doing some fast recall from my lab rotation a few years back."

"Excuse me, would it be possible to get a layman's explanation of what's going on? You guys lost me back at hemaglues," Constable Ferris said.

"Dr. Morrison, why don't you explain it to the man?" Dr. Kellar challenged from the far end of the room. "I imagine you speak cop better than the rest of us."

Kate turned to Ferris and Andy, ignoring the barbed jab.

"All influenzas are viruses, but not all viruses are influenzas," Kate started. "That part I think you probably already get. This viral infection seems to mimic a common flu bug that Dr. Salinger has seen before in this area." Dr. Salinger confirmed with a brief nod of his head. "Each virus has unique properties. The most significant are the way in which it invades and takes over the host body, in this case, humans. Each virus has a unique trigger, something it reacts to or binds to in the human body that activates it. A protease. The activation allows the virus to set up shop, replicate itself, and wreak havoc in the human body. Although this one looks like a common influenza, it doesn't seem to bind like an influenza."

"Is it infectious like influenza?" Andy asked.

Kate could hear Dr. Kellar's voice, low but meant to carry across the room. "It speaks."

Kate ignored her entirely, as did Andy.

"No, it doesn't seem to be."

"So we don't know how Roberta Sedlak was infected?" Ferris asked.

Dr. Salinger answered. "No. And it will be impossible to guess unless we can identify this specific strain."

"Dr. Salinger, what are your next steps?" Dr. Doyle asked.

"Take samples from all the other patients presenting with similar symptoms and send them and Ms. Sedlak's results to the NML in Winnipeg."

"Directly to Winnipeg? Don't we need to run this by BC's Centre for Disease Control?" Dr. Doyle asked.

Dr. Salinger shrugged. "We're taking some liberties, but I don't think we should let this get caught up in process. So I'll need help bypassing the usual channels," he said pointedly.

Dr. Doyle considered him for a moment and then acquiesced with a quick nod.

"Lost me again," Constable Ferris interrupted. "NML?"

"National Microbiology Laboratory," Dr. Salinger explained. "Canada's version of the Centers for Disease Control in Atlanta."

Ferris wrote it down in his notes.

"Constable Ferris, Sergeant Wyles, is there anything you wanted to add from the...investigative end of things?" Dr. Doyle asked with a clear note of distaste in her tone.

With a quick nod of approval from Ferris, Andy answered. "We've got nothing helpful to add right now."

Kate took apart the meaning of every word in Andy's brief answer. She had questions, but they would have to wait.

"Same time tomorrow, everyone?" Murmured agreements met Dr. Doyle's question.

Kate stayed in her chair as Dr. Doyle and Dr. Salinger left the room. She was hoping Dr. Kellar would join them so she could have a minute with Andy and Ferris before heading back up to check on Serena. No luck. Dr. Kellar sat unmoving in her chair, staring down the table. Kate sighed and drained the last of her coffee before standing up, dropping her phone in her pocket, and heading out the door. She had almost made it into the hallway when that distinct, slimy purr of a voice caught up with her.

"No good-bye kiss?"

CHAPTER SEVEN

Kate stared at the x-rays on the monitor. She'd been staring for twenty minutes. Nothing had changed in that time, but she continued to look as if it could help her predict the next few hours. The silver ring on her finger was almost hot from the friction of being constantly twisted against her skin. Kate leaned back in the chair, her eyes not leaving the monitor. She was sitting at the nurse's station, almost completely oblivious to the world around her. Serena's results showed fluid on her lungs, and her high white cell count only indicated she was fighting off *something*. They wouldn't know until tomorrow if it was the same infection as Roberta Sedlak. This thought made Kate twist the ring around her finger harder. She wanted to be able to do something now, not wait until tomorrow.

"Hey."

Kate swiveled in her chair to see Andy leaning against the desk.

"Hey, yourself. You were quiet in the meeting this morning."

"Not much to say."

"Nothing from your meeting with the journalist this morning?"

Andy looked around briefly, then turned back to Kate. "Not much. We met with Sealy and his boss from the paper. Other than the 'unfortunately phrased tweet'—his boss's words, not mine—we still don't have anything. No link to any virus, no threat to the community."

"And no real reason to be here."

Andy shook her head. "We're going to follow up on a few more leads this afternoon, but I'm going to set up a call with Finns and Heath tomorrow. So, yeah, it looks like we'll wrap this thing up."

Kate stole a look at the monitor again, at the films from her patient. *Her* patient. She struggled briefly with the responsibility, the possession. Then she looked back to Andy.

"Serena will be in good hands," Andy said quietly, knowingly.

"I know she will."

They were interrupted by Lucy arriving back at the nursing station. Andy straightened. "I'll let you get back to it. Want a coffee?" she said to Kate.

"Sure, please."

"Lucy? Can I get you anything?"

Lucy blushed faintly but simply shook her head.

With a quick smile, Andy headed back down the hallway. Kate forced herself not to watch. She went directly back to Serena's chest film. In an instant, she heard Dr. Kellar describing how the doctors couldn't have known about the fluid build-up unless they'd had hourly films. Kate looked around her slowly, the fancy equipment, the shiny electronics. She looked up at Lucy, who was inputting orders into a chart.

"Lucy, I'm going to have Serena go down for two more films, spaced one to two hours apart. Could you call down to x-ray and see if that's possible?"

"Sure, Dr. Morrison, I can do that."

Kate twisted her sister's ring around her finger, captivated again by the images on the monitor. She almost didn't hear Lucy addressing her.

"She's all kinds of intimidating."

Kate swiveled in her chair to look at the red-haired nurse. "Who? Sergeant Wyles?"

"Don't you think she's intimidating?"

Kate smiled and half turned back to the monitor. "Not once you get to know her," she murmured.

Lucy didn't pursue it and Kate let it drop. Moments later, the phone rang. "It's Dr. Doyle," Lucy said, "she wants you in the ER immediately."

Kate ran down the stairs into the ER. A nurse directed her towards a curtained area where a young male doctor with sandy-blond hair was fitting a mask over a man's face. The patient seemed to be in his early twenties, his hair and eyes dark, his skin extremely pale, especially considering the energy he was expending simply to draw a breath. He was wearing cargo pants that were dirty at the knees, a serious-looking pair of hiking boots, and a thermal shirt. Kate looked around the curtain to see two others in similar gear, sitting in plastic chairs, looking tired and stressed.

Dr. Doyle quickly introduced Kate to Dr. Eric MacKay, then began reeling off information about the patient.

"Keith Grange, age nineteen, complained of flu symptoms for the last few weeks but decided to go camping with his friends anyway. He reported trouble breathing this morning which progressed rapidly. His friends barely got him down from the campsite."

Kate flipped through the chart as she listened to Dr. Doyle. She watched the patient's chest heave with strain.

"Films?"

"Portable is on its way."

Kate took the stethoscope from around her neck and held it up halfway, waiting for approval from the ER doctor before asking the patient to lean forwards. She didn't have to search. The moment she pressed her stethoscope against his back, Kate could easily hear the ominous sounds of fluid infiltrates. She glanced up at Dr. MacKay, who nodded knowingly.

"Keith, can you talk?"

Keith shook his head, but even this slight movement caused him to bark out a long, expressed cough. She picked up his hand and held it in her own.

"Okay, I'm going to ask you some questions. If the answer is yes, squeeze my hand. If it's no, don't do anything, okay?"

Keith nodded slowly.

"Have you been sick for more than a week?"

Squeeze.

"Have you been sick for more than three weeks?"

Squeeze. This put him in the same cluster as the others. Kate filed this away.

"Have you ever had asthma?"

Nothing.

Kate held the man's hand, felt it trembling in her own. Her mind buzzed with the autopsy report, the picture of Serena's films, the sound of the crackles in this man's lungs, the image of Roberta Sedlak's open, infected lung tissue.

"Have you ever had issues with breathing or with your lungs before?"

Keith squeezed then pulled his hand away, took hold of the bottom of his shirt. The movement triggered a spasm and Keith started to cough. It was a long, rolling, painful cough with Keith doubled over in the bed, his dark hair now plastered to his face with sweat. When the cough finally abated, a fine, pink spray covered the white sheet of the hospital bed. Kate adjusted the mask on Keith's face, forcing herself to push away the image of Serena, bent over and coughing just one floor above them. *Not this bad. Not this bad* yet. As Kate formulated her thoughts, she saw Andy and Ferris arrive in the ER.

"I want him on a CPAP machine with high-flow oxygen along with a cardiac monitor. I want to see how his heart is handling all this. Diuretics, preferably bumetanide, by I.V. and broad-spectrum antibiotics, just in case. Let's get some blood work, full panel, and include an extra marked for Public Health." If the ER doctor had any issues taking orders from an outsider, he didn't show it. "Did I miss anything?" Kate directed the question at both doctors.

"No. I'll go check on x-ray," Dr. Doyle answered for them both.

Kate turned to Andy and Ferris. "Constable Ferris, is this guy a local?"

"I don't recognize him."

"Could you talk to his friends? Find out how long his symptoms have lasted, where he's from, where he's been, and any medical history you can get on him."

Ferris's expression was serious as he backed out of the curtained area.

"Anything I can do?" Andy asked, staying out of the way. Kate looked at her without really seeing her, then turned back to Keith, who was leaning back with his eyes closed, his breath fogging the mask every time he exhaled.

"Just give me a minute," Kate said, more to herself than Andy. She pulled up Keith's grey thermal shirt, wondering at his movement a few minutes before. What had he been trying to tell her? She inspected his rib cage and his chest and was just about to pull his shirt back down, defeated, when she saw it. The small divot was very faint, just catching the overhead light and creating a shadow where the skin should have been smooth.

"Lung biopsy." It was a long shot. Kate didn't know very many reasons someone so young would have had a lung biopsy. But when she'd asked about trouble with his lungs, she was sure Keith had been trying to show her something.

Kate suddenly turned to Andy. "I need to speak to Serena's parents. And we need those results from Public Health. Now."

While she waited for Natalie and Michael Cardiff, Kate leaned against the desk and compared the chest films from Roberta Sedlak, Serena Cardiff, and Keith Grange. She knew it was a bad idea. She would likely be pulled off this case tomorrow, the care of Serena and Keith in the capable hands of Valley General Hospital. Still, she scanned each one until she'd memorized every pocket of fluid and air and every dense wash of tissue and bone. Cardiff's gruff voice pulled her from her near hypnotic trance.

"Dr. Morrison, you wanted to see us."

She looked up to see Serena's parents standing uncomfortably in the doorway of the ER. Kate forced herself to smile, to give an indication of reassurance after hastily calling them down from their daughter's room.

"How's Serena doing?" she asked.

"Sleeping right now," Natalie said, her free hand clenched tightly by her side.

"Maybe you should tell us how our daughter is doing. I understand you've ordered continuous chest x-rays?" Cardiff said in the same gruff voice, bordering on rude.

Kate closed the windows that showed the other two patient's films, then opened Serena's last two chest x-rays. She swiveled the monitor so the parents could see.

"I ordered two more repeats to her original x-ray, it's true. I may have overreacted." She pointed to the first set of films. "Here's the fluid that's trapped in her lungs, most likely from an influenza-related pneumonia." She pointed to the next set. "Two hours later, and we see no change. If x-ray is clear in another two hours, I'll send her down again just to be sure."

Kate saw Natalie's shoulders sag, her whole body folding in on itself, as if she had lost the fight to keep it together. Her husband didn't seem to notice. His posture and stony expression remained unchanged.

"You called us down here just to show us the results?" he asked.

"That and I wanted to ask you about any history of respiratory issues or anything related to the chest or lungs that Serena may have experienced."

Natalie had just opened her mouth to speak when her husband cut her off.

"I don't understand, Dr. Morrison. You've had access to Serena's complete medical file for three days now. Shouldn't you be able to get that information from there without calling us down here?"

Kate took a breath and looked him straight in the eye before answering.

"I have your daughter's medical chart memorized, including her birth weight of six pounds, eight ounces and hospitalization at the age of nine for appendicitis. I can repeat it verbatim if you like, but that would be a waste of everyone's time." Kate held the man's gaze, counted slowly to three to give him a chance to respond before she continued. "The chart shows only injuries and illness for which Serena sought medical attention. I want parent information, the kind of things only you know about your daughter. Specifically about her breathing or her lungs. Anything."

Natalie looked up at her husband, pleading, thinking. Kate could see that she held something clenched in her fist.

"The fall she took in the spring, Michael."

"That was her ribs, and she was fine."

"Tell me about it," Kate said immediately.

"It was back in March," Natalie said. "Serena's horse refused a jump, and she went over the horse's head and landed on the poles. She got right back on. She told her instructor she was fine. It wasn't until about two weeks later that I happened to see a bit of yellow bruised skin. Serena refused to see a doctor about it."

Kate made a mental picture of the event, the bruised skin, the pressure on the ribs folding against the delicate tissue of the lungs.

"Left side or right side?" Kate asked, pulling up Serena's x-rays.

"Right side," both parents answered.

Kate moved the image around on the screen, searching silently for a long time.

"There." Kate pointed at the films. "A very small, healed crack. Your daughter is tough. That must have hurt to ride with." Her voice was even but her thoughts spiked with anxiety. *Was the lung bruised by that cracked rib? If the tissue was compromised...*

"What does this mean?" Cardiff said, peering at the image as if he didn't quite believe what Kate was telling him.

As Kate figured out what she was going to say, she saw Andy come back into the ER, indicating she needed to talk to Kate.

"It could be a complication to her recovery," Kate said finally, knowing it wasn't enough.

"Does this have anything to do with the autopsy results? We are expecting to hear something."

"Not all the information is in from the autopsy, and I imagine the hospital and Public Health will make the decision as to if and when to release that information to the public. Serena's blood samples are being analyzed and we are closely monitoring her condition."

She waited for another verbal attack, felt it building as his chest seemed to swell. Then his cell phone rang, and he glared at Kate before pulling it out and storming back through the double doors of the ER. Natalie gave Kate an apologetic smile and followed her husband.

Kate rubbed the heels of her palms into her eyes. It had already been a really, really long day. As Andy joined her at the desk, Kate wanted nothing more than to lean in against her and have Andy massage the back of her neck with one hand. Not possible, she knew, so she settled for simply looking at her, for gaining some semblance of strength and energy from her grey eyes.

"Apparently, Dr. Salinger has samples from everyone except Chase Noonan, but Ferris has gone down to the farm where he works to see if he can bring him in."

"Good. Hopefully, we can get all of them in this afternoon. Do you know what happened with the samples heading to the NML?"

"I can answer that, Dr. Morrison," Dr. Doyle said as she put down a stack of files on the desk beside Andy. Kate noticed she was still impeccably dressed and made up, as if she'd just stepped out her front door in the morning. In comparison, Kate felt rumpled and sweaty, and she unconsciously reached up to tuck a frizzy curl behind her ear.

"Roberta Sedlak's sample went out about an hour after our meeting this morning. Dr. Salinger is taking it himself to Vancouver and having it shipped from there. I phoned the NML to let them know what we're sending. I talked to a Dr. Levesque, who said the soonest we can have a result is three days."

Three days, thought Kate. Where would she be in three days? Back in Vancouver? Back in her own ER?

As if reading her mind, Dr. Doyle spoke directly to Andy.

"It looks as if we didn't need your assistance after all, Sergeant Wyles."

Andy didn't say anything. After a brief, awkward silence, Dr. Doyle picked up her files and walked away. Andy rolled her eyes, which was so uncharacteristic, so un-Andy, that Kate laughed.

"Ah, politics," Kate said.

"Don't discount it so quickly. It's a huge factor out here."

"Yeah, well, it's your factor, Sergeant Wyles. Unless it's coughing and having trouble breathing, it's got nothing to do with me," Kate said, leaning back in her chair and stretching.

Andy turned to see someone approaching the desk. She gave Kate a quick look, which Kate didn't have time to interpret. "Wanna bet?" Andy said under her breath. She stood straighter and pulled her face back to professional neutrality.

The man who stopped at the desk in front of Kate was young with bright, determined eyes and a closely cropped beard. He wore a clean button-up shirt and stylish jeans, and had a much-abused messenger bag slung over one shoulder.

"Sergeant Wyles, good to see you again." His voice held neither friendliness nor contempt. When Andy simply dipped her head in acknowledgement, he turned to Kate.

"Are you Dr. Kate Morrison?"

"Yes," Kate said. She suspected she knew who this was but played along anyway. "How can I help you?"

"Are you, Dr. Morrison, currently consulting with the RCMP on several suspected case of influenza in the Hidden Valley area?"

"Again, how can I help you?"

The man waited, his expression expectant, as if his silence would induce Kate to speak again. Kate said nothing. This man clearly didn't know she'd been schooled by Sgt. Andy Wyles in the art of silence.

"I'm Paul Sealy with the *Squamish Herald*, and I'm looking into the story of a viral strain of influenza."

Kate caught herself just as she was about to correct the journalist. Andy would never give away information, even just to correct a medically erroneous statement. The name confirmed for Kate that she should keep her mouth shut.

"Any statements will come through the hospital PR team, as I'm sure you are already aware."

"And Public Health is involved also? I understand you are liaising with Dr. Salinger. We've interviewed him before," Paul said.

"Public Health also has a public relations team, and any media inquiries need to go through them," Kate said again, more firmly this time.

Paul's smile slipped just a little. He seemed truly disappointed this hadn't worked.

"You're pushing this a little, don't you think?" Andy asked mildly.

Now he looked defiant. "I'm doing my job, Sergeant Wyles. Unless you think you've found a link between my contempt of a system that props up the already adequately resourced with a few cases of the flu, there's no reason for me to stop asking questions."

"Your boss seemed a little concerned with the way you asking more questions looked to everyone else, that's all," Andy said, her voice seemingly unconcerned but her eyes direct.

"I can deal with my boss, thanks."

"I believe there's nothing else to say, then," Andy said passively.

The reporter looked back and forth between them, then nodded his farewell and quickly left.

Andy leaned back against the desk, her eyebrows raised at Kate. "You were saying, Dr. Morrison?"

"Shut up, Sergeant Wyles."

The phone rang loudly in the dark hotel room, pulling both Kate and Andy from a dead sleep. Kate sat up in bed and turned on the light as Andy reached for her cell phone on the bedside table, next to her gun. But it was the hotel phone, ringing shrilly next to Kate. She picked up the receiver, wakefulness winning the battle against sleepiness with every heartbeat.

"Hello?" She checked the clock—4:51 a.m.

"Dr. Morrison, it's Dr. Doyle. I'm sorry to wake you."

"Don't worry about it. What is it?" Kate's heart lurched at the thought of her two patients, the x-rays she had memorized lighting up her brain. She started getting out of bed, mentally at the hospital, ready to deal with this emergency.

"It's Keith Grange. We lost him twenty minutes ago."

Kate's heart sank, the image of his chest x-ray results instantly replaced by a pair of scared brown eyes, a pale face, the shaky squeeze of his hand. She sat back down on the bed and closed her eyes, took a breath, then opened them again.

"His lungs?" Kate asked.

"Yes, same as Roberta Sedlak. They just couldn't keep ahead of the infection or the fluid, even knowing this time what to watch for. It happened so fast."

"I'm sure they did everything they could," Kate said robotically. She barely felt as Andy laid a warm hand against her back. It was a light touch, non-intrusive, meant to comfort. "Did Constable Ferris ever find his family?"

"Yes, they were on vacation in Banff. Apparently they're in transit."

Kate rubbed at her eyes while she processed two streams of information and questions. "Autopsy?"

"I'd like to check in with the family first, if we can. I know we can go ahead without their permission, but let's give it a day."

Kate appreciated this modicum of compassion from the stiff, almost cold woman. "Are you at the hospital right now?"

"No, I just got the call at home. Why?"

Kate ignored the defensive note in her tone. "I wanted to know how Serena Cardiff was doing."

"I already checked. No change in her status."

Kate gave a small prayer of thanks.

"Okay, thanks for the call, Dr. Doyle. I guess we'll see you in a few hours."

Kate hung up the phone, staring blankly at the bedside table until she felt Andy's fingers move slightly against her back. A gentle reminder that she was there, if Kate needed her.

"Keith Grange died," Kate said to Andy. "Similar presentation to Roberta Sedlak." The rest she figured Andy had heard or pieced together. Andy said nothing, just continued to run her fingers over Kate's arm. Kate finally twisted her head around to look up at Andy.

"We need those results back."

"Hopefully, we'll find out in a couple of hours."

Kate shook her head. "But what it is. This doesn't make sense."

She let her head fall back against Andy and stared up at the ceiling. None of this made sense. Influenza, viral loads, infections, contagion, pulmonary edema, pneumonia. Acute onset. The words repeated and rebounded in Kate's head until she felt she'd go crazy with it.

"What do you need?" Andy asked gently.

"I need you to take me to the hospital."

Kate held Sharon Grange's hands and let the woman sob. They were sitting in Dr. Doyle's office, Kate with Sharon and Doug Grange on one side of the table, Dr. Doyle fidgeting uncomfortably on the other. Kate reached out for the box of tissues on Dr. Doyle's desk and handed a few to Sharon Grange, who took them without looking up. As Kate studied Doug Grange's face, reading the signs of shock and disbelief and sadness, she wondered how many times she'd watched this scene play out. No ER physician liked this part of the job. It was dark and terrible and tugged relentlessly at the soul.

Some doctors felt a measure of peace with the words and actions of comfort they gave to the families during such an emotional time, but Kate had been on the other side and knew there was very little to remember or absorb beyond the understanding that your loved one was gone. Nothing could cover the sensation of being ripped open. So Kate didn't try. She held a hand, offered tissue, and stayed silent.

Doug Grange was the first to speak, clearing his throat loudly in the silence twice before he could force enough air past his vocal cords to produce sound.

"What now?" He directed his question at Dr. Doyle. She clearly seemed like the woman in charge, a woman who had answers, someone who could direct the course of their grief.

"We'd like to do an autopsy," Dr. Doyle said in her kind but matter-of-fact voice. Kate cursed her silently.

"We'd like to understand why Keith succumbed so quickly to his illness," Kate explained gently. "All we know right now is that a virus attacked his lungs, causing an infection that we couldn't control." Kate squeezed Keith's mother's hand before asking her next question. "I know this is a hard time to answer questions, but had Keith had a lung biopsy, by any chance?"

Sharon nodded, lifting her puffy red eyes to Kate's. "When he was sixteen. A bad bout of pneumonia that just seemed to hang on. Doctors thought it was something else. Sicadosis, I think."

"Sarcoidosis," Kate said quietly.

"Yes, that. But he was fine. He's been so healthy—" Her voice cut off as she choked on the words.

"A post-mortem examination might give us some answers," Kate said gently.

Sharon Grange reached out to her husband, and they locked eyes. Kate looked away, the nakedness of their pain too much to witness.

"Okay," said Doug Grange, gripping his wife's hand. "But soon. I'd like to take our boy home."

"We'll arrange transport for later this afternoon," Dr. Doyle assured them.

Once they were passed into the care of an understanding nurse, Kate sat across from Dr. Doyle, feeling drained. It was barely past ten, but Kate had already spent hours searching uselessly through files, staring at x-rays and blood panels.

As Kate stood to leave, the phone on Dr. Doyle's desk rang. Just as she reached the door, however, Dr. Doyle called out for her to wait. Kate looked out through the window into the hallways where she could see Andy writing in her notepad, cell phone pressed between her ear and shoulder.

Dr. Doyle hung up the phone. "Dr. Kellar is waiting for you in the morgue."

"Now?" Kate asked.

"She'd like to begin immediately."

Kate blinked.

"Dr. Salinger will be in this afternoon with the lab results, so you and Dr. Kellar can update the team then."

Kate said nothing more, just stepped into the hallway. She gave a one word reply to the questioning glance from Andy. "Morgue."

Kate could swear she saw Andy flinch.

"Now?" Andy asked, unknowingly echoing Kate's disbelief from a few moments before.

"Now," Kate said and started walking towards the stairwell. She wished she had time for another coffee, though she was already on her third.

"I can't go with you."

Kate stopped and turned.

"Ferris and I have a conference call with Finns and Superintendent Heath in an hour. I could try to stop by after…"

Kate waved the offer away with her hand, feeling a tension headache starting behind her left eye. "It's fine. Don't worry about it." She kept walking towards the stairs.

"Kate."

Kate stopped, her hand on the railing, already exhausted at just the thought of four plus hours in the morgue with Mona Kellar. "It's fine, Andy. Maybe she'll be better without you there."

Andy snorted. "Not likely."

Kate gave a small smile, all she had at that moment. "I can handle it."

Andy took a step closer and traced a circle across Kate's arm with her finger. It was the first time Andy had ever touched her scar on purpose, and Kate felt a shiver run up her spine.

"I know," Andy said. "I just wish you didn't have to."

"I know," Kate repeated softly. "I should go, she's waiting. See you at the meeting?"

Andy nodded, her grey eyes worried. Kate focused on the stairs in front of her, on the task at hand, not wanting the worry or stress to show on her face. When she faced the dead man's doctor on her own in just a few minutes, she wanted to be a completely blank slate.

By the time Kate made it down to the morgue, showed her ID, and hastily pulled on her gown and booties, Keith Grange's body was already out on the table and Dr. Kellar was vibrating with anger. Olivia stood very still, barely looking up when Kate entered the room.

"In future, Dr. Morrison, if we ever have the pleasure of working together again, I expect you to come immediately when called." Kate tried to ignore the insinuation in the sly grin that followed. "I imagine Ms. Wyles's rules are similar to my own."

Kate looked down at her gloved hands, adjusting them over the fitted sleeves of the gown. "My apologies for being late, Dr. Kellar."

Dr. Kellar switched the overhead microphone on with such force that it swung crazily over their heads for a few minutes before finally settling. Kate felt every muscle in her back, shoulder, and neck tense, waiting for the next insult, the next personal attack.

Hour one went by with no other abuse being hurled across the table, Dr. Kellar taking photos and giving a detailed description of the body. Hour two, as Kate leaned in over Keith Grange's cold, pale body to look into the chest cavity at his infected lungs, Dr. Kellar merely glared and hovered possessively. Hour three, Kate's stomach started to growl with hunger and the acid of too much coffee. Dr. Kellar continued her examination, the oral report given in a trance-like monotone which made the whole setting seem vaguely unreal. Hour four, as Dr. Kellar began her final analysis of the dead, taking what was undoubtedly painstaking measures to return each piece of the body with delicate precision, Kate could only begin to dream she would leave this autopsy unscathed.

Dr. Kellar turned off the microphone, stepped back from the table, and began the process of de-gloving and de-gowning. She indicated with a sharp gesture that Olivia should take over, which the young nurse did silently. Kate stood in the exact position she'd maintained for the past four and a half hours, gloved hands by her sides, staring at Keith Grange's reassembled body.

"Dr. Morrison, I'd like a word before we present our findings to the rest of the team."

How can such a simple request leave me so cold? Kate wondered as she met Olivia's sympathetic glance before beginning to remove her own gown and gloves.

Kate followed Dr. Kellar out of the morgue, down two short hallways, then finally into a nondescript, plain office area. Dr. Kellar closed the door, and Kate felt suddenly very trapped. Trapped by the closed door, by Kellar's intense stare, by Finns's voice in her head telling her she had to be here. Trapped.

Dr. Kellar opened two folders, pulled out pictures, and arranged them on the table. Despite her rising anxiety, Kate was curious and she began pulling the pictures together, automatically drawing comparisons, finding more similarities than differences.

"Tell me what you see, Dr. Morrison."

Kate didn't look up, the purr in Dr. Kellar's voice warning enough that she needed to be cautious.

"I see two sets of lungs, both of which show signs of pulmonary edema and infection." She pointed to Roberta Sedlak's picture first. "I can see where the infection started on this one for sure, but I would guess Keith Grange's point of infection was here, the site of his lung biopsy from three years ago."

Dr. Kellar didn't acknowledge what Kate had said, just folded her hands and stared at Kate across the table. Kate continued to study the pictures until Dr. Kellar swept them away and shoved them back into the folder, forcing Kate to look up at her.

"What do you know about pulmonary edema?" Dr. Kellar said.

Kate didn't have time to wonder how this woman changed moods so quickly, so mercurially. "At its most basic level, it's simply fluid accumulated in the lungs."

"I am not your college-flunky, brain-bashed lover, Dr. Morrison. I expect a complete medical answer when I ask a question."

Kate took her hands off the table and clasped them in her lap, not wanting to betray the fact that she was shaking with anger.

"Pulmonary edema is usually a result of cardiogenic factors, clearly not an issue in this case since the heart does not seem to be affected." Kate waited, knowing somehow that Dr. Kellar would love that Kate had to wait for confirmation before continuing. She did confirm, with a nod, her wild orange hair falling across her forehead. Kate continued. "Next most likely cause is some kind of airway obstruction, aspiration, inhalation of toxic fumes, certain types of medication or, what I believe is the case here, severe infection."

Dr. Kellar drummed her thick fingers on the table, saying nothing for a moment, probing Kate with her bright, too-interested eyes. Kate couldn't help squirming under the gaze, unable to stand up to it as she normally would, afraid she would prompt an attack.

"You're too smart for her, clearly. Though I can understand how she would be a safe foray into the lesbian experience. I wonder at your compatibility, however. You are curious, information-seeking, whereas I imagine Ms. Wyles is wild and somewhat aggressive in bed—"

Kate cut her off, unable to keep the sharp anger out of her voice. "Are we done with the autopsy results?"

"In the meeting this afternoon," Dr. Kellar said, smiling, "and any future meetings which involve non-medical staff, I expect you to give the layman's explanation for my results."

Kate merely nodded, then stood and walked to the door. Dr. Kellar caught Kate's wrist with her hand, her fingers warm and moist against Kate's skin.

"She should have been mine, Dr. Morrison. At least once."

Anger flashed in Kate's eyes, at Kellar's presumption, at the way her words and her tone laid possession to what belonged to Kate. With a control Kate didn't know she had, she pulled her hand out of Mona Kellar's grasp.

"In future I expect you won't touch me again, and that you will keep all conversation about medical findings."

And Kate walked out of the room, desperately seeking a calm that was getting harder and harder to find.

Chapter Eight

Kate stood at the nurse's station and scanned the information in Serena's medical chart from the night shift. Serena had just been cleared by Public Health. She did not have the virus that had already taken two lives. Three other Hidden Valley residents—Tessa James, Chase Noonan, and Mary Johnston—were infected, and Public Health was following up. Kate had just been in the meeting where it was confirmed, but the relief she should have felt was noticeably absent.

Maybe it was the morning spent in the morgue, the tension of Dr. Kellar's presence, the unease of not having told Andy about the implied threat in the forensic pathologist's words earlier. Or maybe it was the statement by Constable Ferris that they would be tying up loose ends. As of tomorrow, they would no longer be a presence on the team. Or maybe it was the look of concern on Dr. Salinger's face as he described what little they knew of this still-unidentified viral strain. It seemed to have components from several different viruses, as if it had adapted multiple codes and strands and enzymes to be ready for anything. Without conscious thought, Kate rechecked Serena's oxygen levels, even knowing it wasn't possible to identify the potential virus in the numbers, to see if it was hiding behind a serious case of pneumonia.

Kate gave herself a brief mental shake and closed the chart. Her role was clear. When Serena's parents arrived in the next half hour—after Natalie Cardiff's daily massage, Lucy had said, rolling her eyes—she was to give the good news to the family, then sign off on her care. She would have no part in the hospital's outbreak protocol, and she would not be assisting Public Health in finding the source of the infection or educating the public or discussing implications with the media.

Kate walked down the hallway to Serena's room. As if reading her unsettled mind, three texts from Andy came through on her phone in rapid succession. The first one simply said, "Montana," the second, "the porch swing," and the third, "the lake." Each brought a vivid memory, a sequence of images Kate could lose herself in, even just for a minute.

The Cardiffs had not yet arrived when Kate walked into Serena's room. A different young man, not Nathan, sat beside a sleeping Serena, holding her hand. He looked to be the same age, with what was obviously a muscled, athletic body under his fitted shirt. He had dark hair, almost the same shade as Serena's. Kate wondered for a moment if this was a relative, but as she stepped closer and could see more clearly the look he was giving Serena, she changed her mind. Definitely not a relative.

The man looked up at Kate as she approached the bed. He didn't drop Serena's hand. In fact, Kate noticed he gripped it tighter.

"Hello," Kate said quietly, not wanting to wake Serena. "I'm Dr. Morrison."

"Chris Ozarc," he said, watching Kate carefully as he gave his name. Kate recognized the name, of course. This must be the reclusive billionaire's son, the one who was taking a year off from college in the States.

Kate smiled. "Nice to meet you, Chris."

Chris seemed to relax a little. Whatever reaction he had been expecting from Kate had not materialized. He turned back to Serena.

"How is she?"

Kate heard Dr. Salinger's voice in her head, clearing Serena of the virus. Swallowing her inexplicable doubt, Kate answered, "She's going to be fine."

The relief on Chris's face was evident. "Do you know when she's going to be released?"

"No, I don't. And I can't release medical information to non-family members," she told him gently.

Chris didn't acknowledge this at first, just continued staring at Serena's pale face, holding her hand tightly in his own.

Kate heard footsteps in the hallway and looked up to see the rest of the Cardiffs entering the room. Michael was in an immaculate tuxedo, his frame somehow heightened by the black suit, making him look absolutely huge. Natalie swept into the room, seemingly unconscious of how beautiful she looked in a long red sequined dress, her hair pinned back in perfect twists. She was pale, though. Kate could see her hand lightly shaking. Julia followed, a tall shadow in jeans and a hoodie, curling herself into the blue chair by the door. Kate caught her eye, gave a quick smile, and was rewarded with a small wave.

"What are you doing here, son?"

Kate looked back to the bed, where an awkward scene was unfolding around a still-sleeping Serena. Cardiff stared at Chris, looking tense but not angry. Mostly Cardiff looked conflicted, Kate decided.

"I heard Serena was in the hospital. I just wanted to see if she was okay," Chris said. Cardiff stared down at the bed, where Chris was holding his eldest daughter's hand. Chris followed his gaze, put both his hands in his lap, though he didn't make any move to rise from his position by the bed.

Natalie looked up at her husband. "I don't think he should be here, Michael," she said very quietly.

Chris stood, though he hadn't been directly addressed.

"I just wanted to see if she was okay," Chris said again. Without another word, he left the room.

Natalie instantly took his position by her daughter's bed, smoothing back Serena's hair from her pale forehead.

"That was rude, Natalie," Cardiff said to his wife, though without much conviction behind it. Kate kept her eyes down on Serena's chart, listening.

"I don't think Serena would want him here," Natalie said.

Cardiff only sighed in response and turned to Kate. "Dr. Morrison, I hear there's an update."

Of course he's heard, thought Kate. *No secrets in Hidden Valley.*

"Yes, good news. I can confirm that Serena has bilateral pneumonia, probably one of the worst cases I've seen, but she's a fighter and should recover with no complications."

Natalie smiled, the first real smile Kate had seen on the woman since meeting her four days ago. It brought life into her face, animated her eyes, and brought colour to her cheeks.

"And what about the rumours of a viral strain of influenza?" Cardiff asked Kate.

Kate made a mental note to talk to Dr. Salinger about educating the public on viruses and influenzas.

"A statement will be released in a few hours to address that," Kate told him.

Cardiff checked his watch. "A preview, Dr. Morrison. As you can see, we're heading out for a fundraising dinner, and I'd like that information before I go."

Kate wanted to laugh at the way he addressed her like she was a secretary or a campaign volunteer.

"I don't have the statement, Mr. Cardiff. The PR team is working with Public Health on it right now."

Cardiff's impatience was evident. "I'm disappointed in you, Dr. Morrison."

"Why?" Kate asked, trying to keep her amusement in check. Cardiff didn't seem like someone who would enjoy being laughed at.

"I got the sense that you weren't someone who always played by the book. You know when it's beneficial to bend the rules."

Kate shrugged. He wasn't too far off the mark, but she still wasn't going to give him the information he wanted. Kate couldn't quite figure out why he wanted the information, anyway. She had just told him his daughter was going to be fine. Maybe he just didn't want to let this idea of a threat go.

"I also rather thought that you would appreciate that rules have recently been bent in your favour," Cardiff continued.

Kate knew instantly that he was referring to the RCMP protocol, to being allowed to work with Andy on this case. She was searching for a way to respond when she heard Andy's voice from the door.

"There's a limo blocking the ambulance bay. I'm going to assume that's yours?" Andy asked, giving no indication that she'd heard the conversation that had just taken place.

He didn't acknowledge Andy, but he did address his wife.

"We should go." He pulled his sleeves smartly down to his wrists, then looked up at his younger daughter, still curled silently in the chair. "You okay, Jules? You sure you want to stay here for the night?" Julia simply nodded. "Okay, we'll see you in the morning, then."

He strode out the door, not even waiting for his wife. Natalie bent swiftly to kiss Serena, then crossed the room to do the same for her youngest daughter. She stopped in the doorway, looked back at Kate, then left without saying a word.

In the silence that followed, Andy's eyes locked on Kate, telling her she'd heard every word of the conversation. "Dr. Doyle would like to talk to you," Andy said.

"Okay, thanks. Could you tell her I'll be there in a minute?"

Andy left to deliver the message and Kate wrote a note in the chart.

"My sister's going to be okay?"

Kate smiled at the quiet girl. "She's going to be fine. You really want to spend a night here?"

"Better than staying at home by myself. I brought my phone and some homework," she said, kicking at her backpack on the floor.

"What about supper?"

"I'll steal some of Serena's. She hasn't been eating much, anyway."

Kate made a face. "Hospital food? Really?"

"I don't mind," Julia said shyly.

Kate thought for a minute. "I had some ravioli from the deli at the grocery store downtown the other day. Do you like that?"

"The squash one is my favourite," Julia said in her feather-light voice.

"Well, if you don't mind some company, then we'll bring some by in a few hours?"

Julia nodded, ducking her head.

Kate took the chart with her as she walked down the hall to the nurse's station. "Hey, Lucy, you on tonight?" Kate asked.

"Yep, just started. What can I do for you?"

"Not much. Serena seems stable. If she wakes up, see how she does off the O2 for a bit. Her sister's in with her right now."

Lucy made a note in the chart Kate handed her. "Was that Chris Ozarc I saw leaving the room?" Lucy asked.

"Apparently. Why?"

Lucy dropped her voice and leaned conspiratorially in towards Kate. "Chris Ozarc and Serena Cardiff are big gossip around here. They're like Hidden Valley royalty. They dated for three years, and then Chris left for the States last fall. When he came home at Christmas, Serena left him. Apparently it was all tearful and heartbreaking. Michael

Cardiff took it especially hard," Lucy said, clearly amused. "It turns out Serena had fallen for the stable boy, Nathan. Needless to say, the Cardiffs are not happy about Serena's choice. The whole thing is very romantic."

Kate rolled her eyes. "Since when are high school breakups such big news?"

Lucy crossed her arms. "We live in a small town with competing millionaires and one billionaire recluse. This is as exciting as things get. Well, until you and Sergeant Wyles came along." She gave Kate a sly sideways grin. "Why didn't you say something?"

Kate laughed, a little embarrassed. She packed up her things, started backing down the hallway.

"I thought I'd try to keep at least one secret in Hidden Valley. I'll come by and check on Serena in a few hours," she said, disappearing down the stairs.

"We've requested a forty-eight-hour extension on your stay," Dr. Doyle said, almost as soon as Kate was seated in her office. She was tidying her desk almost obsessively, moving files and adjusting items. "It's been approved by your supervisor and by the hospital board."

This was news. Kate wasn't sure what to say.

"Who requested me? And for what?"

Kate caught Dr. Doyle's irritated sigh, as if she wished Kate would accept the news without comment. "The team, the hospital, the board, Dr. Kellar, Public Health, the ER." Dr. Doyle's voice rose as the list spewed out. "Apparently, no one thinks we're able to get through this without you."

Kate said nothing. She simply waited. She wondered if Andy knew anything about this. It felt like days since they'd talked.

"I'm sorry," Dr. Doyle finally said. "We're a small team in a small community and we've never dealt with anything like this. I'm fielding more calls than I can handle, the ER is underprepared for an influx if there is one, the public statement is going out tonight, and we're no closer to figuring out how to treat this virus."

It was the simplest, most truthful statement Kate had ever heard Dr. Doyle utter. "I'd like to help," Kate said simply.

Dr. Doyle's shoulders slumped, in defeat or relief, Kate wasn't entirely sure. It didn't matter, really. She was here to do a job, and she could not help the thrill of excitement as her future, if only for two days, was reconnected to Hidden Valley.

Kate considered the virus and the mystifying components that resulted, in at least some of the patients, in critical levels of pulmonary edema. The three other patients exhibited none of the same extreme symptoms as Roberta Sedlak and Keith Grange. But if that changed, the hospital needed to be ready.

"I want to look at what we're doing wrong," she said without thinking. Dr. Doyle looked up sharply, and Kate reconsidered her words. "In patients with compromised lungs, this virus waits and then attacks so quickly. I'd like to come up with a new protocol for treating it in the ER," she tried to explain.

Dr. Doyle looked at her carefully. "We can take a look at the protocol already in place, but the autopsy reports should help in that regard."

Kate had already thought of that. It would be helpful to have the pathologist who had seen the effects of the virus and its ineffective treatment firsthand. Dr. Mona Kellar was the last person Kate wanted to consult with, however.

"When is Dr. Kellar available to meet?" Kate said reluctantly.

"She said she could be here in the morning, if you think we need her."

Kate took a moment and looked out the window of Dr. Doyle's office. She could see the large windows by the entrance as they reflected back the dark of night, the shiny floors of the main corridor, and the cleanly modern and inoffensive paintings lining the walls. How did she end up here? Where was her chaotic, hectic, patched-together city ER? Where was her quirky, comfortable staff? Gone. Left behind. Willingly traded in for a gleaming, woefully underprepared hospital and a hastily thrown-together team.

"Dr. Morrison, should I have Dr. Kellar come back tomorrow morning?"

Kate rubbed at her eyes. She was here now, the other questions would have to wait.

"Yes, please," she said. "And Dr. Salinger, too," Kate said quickly. "Please. If he's available." *Or anybody*, Kate thought. *Anyone that can act as a buffer to that troll of a woman.*

"I'll let you know when you're meeting in the morning," Dr. Doyle said. Her tone was dismissive and Kate stood to leave. "And… thank you," she added.

Kate walked out of Dr. Doyle's office down the hallway to the deserted front desk. She stared unseeing out at the night beyond the windows. The hospital was quiet, as if by some unspoken agreement the town had decided to take it down a notch because the sun had set. Kate saw Andy's reflection in the glass as she walked down the long hallway from the ER and studied it as she approached: her long legs, the belt around her hips with one thumb hooked into a loop, her blond hair held back in a low ponytail, the ever-present soft body armour vest over her short-sleeved shirt. Kate always loved to watch the way Andy moved. She was purposeful, calm, and strong. Finally, Andy stood across from her in the silent hall.

"How are you still standing? You're dead on your feet," Andy said bluntly.

"It's a skill I have."

Neither said anything for a moment. Kate still felt Andy's eyes searching her, as if she could pull out everything Kate wasn't saying. Sometimes Kate wondered if she could.

"So, two days," Andy said, finally.

"Two days."

"You're okay with that?"

"Yes," Kate said firmly. "You'll be here, too?"

"Just for the forty-eight hours. Finns made it clear the investigation is over. Two days to tie up loose ends that are already tied." Andy took a small step closer to Kate, and a little of the light left her eyes. "How was the autopsy?"

"Pretty similar to the last one," Kate said, hedging. Andy's eyes narrowed. Kate sighed. "Later, okay?"

"Okay," Andy said, a little more quietly, as if she was suddenly aware of the intensity of her interrogation. "Are you ready to head out?"

"I need to pick up some files from the ER. And I kind of made plans for dinner. I told Julia Cardiff we'd bring her something to eat."

"Sure," Andy said immediately. "Why don't you give me an order? I'll go pick up food."

Kate looked at her gratefully. "I feel like we're underutilizing your services, Sergeant Wyles."

Andy smiled a slow, private smile that Kate got lost in for a moment before she remembered where they were. She felt herself pull back.

When she and Andy walked into Serena's room, Kate saw Julia wasn't going to need their company. She was sitting on the foot of her sister's bed and Serena was awake, looking alert. Nathan was pulling containers of food out of a plastic bag.

"Looks like a party in here," Kate said on her way in.

Julia looked up and gave a shy, happy smile. Serena smiled, and Kate noticed that she didn't have her nasal cannula in. "How are you feeling?" Kate asked the pale girl.

"Pretty good, actually. Hungry." Her voice was stronger, and the effort to speak from just two days ago was gone.

"Excellent, that's what I like to hear."

"Do you want any, Dr. Morrison? I brought a lot of food," Nathan said, indicating a container.

"No, but thanks."

"Okay. Move over, Junior, make some room for the food."

Kate watched the three of them for a moment. Julia was shy and pink-faced, Serena looked worn but happy, and Nathan was sweet and attentive. She considered what Lucy had said earlier about the Cardiffs not approving of Serena's non-pedigreed choice. She wondered how that was possible. Nathan seemed like a great guy. Kate flipped the chart closed.

"Lucy's going to look after you tonight, Serena. I'll check on you in the morning, but if you keep improving overnight, we can start talking about discharge."

Kate and Andy left the hospital together, first stopping at the ER to pick up the files that Dr. Doyle had left for her. *Homework*, Kate thought. She wanted to be as prepared as possible for the meeting with Dr. Kellar in the morning. She hoped solid prep work would minimize ridicule and keep the meeting short.

Andy's voice intruded into her thoughts the moment she slammed the door shut on the Yukon. "How was the autopsy?"

Kate shrugged, not really wanting to relive it or to have to watch Andy react to what Kellar had said and done. "I'm still in one piece."

There must have been something in her voice, however. She wasn't very good at hiding things from Andy, so there really was no use in equivocating when Andy wanted information.

"Tell me."

Kate sighed and gave her the details. She watched as Andy gripped the steering wheel tightly when she described how Kellar had grabbed her.

"You're not to be alone with her. Ever," Andy told Kate in a tone that left no room for negotiation.

"I'm meeting with Mona Kellar tomorrow morning," Kate said, knowing that wasn't going to go over well.

"At whose request?" Andy demanded.

"Mine, actually. We need to come up with a protocol for treating any future patients with the virus who have respiratory distress. I need to know we've got a plan in place because what we're doing isn't enough. And I need Mona Kellar to help me with that. This is why I'm here, Andy."

Andy said nothing, turning the Yukon down the narrow streets of downtown Hidden Valley until they stopped outside the grocery store. Kate looked out the side window, noticing they only had five minutes until it closed.

Andy followed her in the store, silent and grim. Kate picked up a few things at random: fizzy water, rice cakes, a bar of raspberry chocolate, and then she asked the kid behind the deli counter for the last of the ravioli. Kate took their basket to the front and smiled at the woman behind the cash register, trying to make up for the rigidly angry expression on Andy's face.

"Are you the doctor they've got working at Valley General on those flu cases?"

"Yes," Kate responded simply as she handed over her debit card, hoping that would be the end of it. Knowing it wouldn't be.

"I heard that two people died from it, is that true?" the cashier said.

Kate had seen the press release that had gone out jointly from Hidden Valley General and Public Health, confirming the two deaths. "Yes, two people died from complications from a virus."

"But then how can they be saying that there is very little threat to the public? My little grandson has got a cough and a fever. How do we know it's not the virus?"

"Your grandson probably just has a bug, but if he's having trouble breathing at any point, just bring him down to the ER, and I'll look at him myself."

The woman froze in the act of handing Kate her receipt, eyes round and wide.

"How old is your grandson?"

"Four. Just started kindergarten," she said proudly.

"Well, there you go. Probably picked up something from a classmate, then."

Andy picked up the bag from the counter as Kate thanked the woman on the way out.

Kate climbed back into the car, sifting through the contents of the bag until she found the chocolate bar. She unwrapped it and broke off a piece, handing it to a still-silent Andy.

"Are you attempting to soften me up?" Andy asked, taking the chocolate.

"Yes. Is it working?"

Andy chewed the chocolate slowly as she headed towards the highway. "No. I still won't allow you to be alone with Mona Kellar. Not with what she pulled this morning."

Kate shook her head. "I need to be able to work with her, Andy. This is too important."

"Your safety is important, Kate, and that woman is not safe. Don't forget I know exactly what she's capable of."

"Can we just acknowledge for one minute Mona Kellar is not trying to get at me? Everything she is doing is aimed at you. I'm just the proxy."

Andy's voice was hard when she spoke. "That only makes it worse. I can't stand the thought she's pulling this shit with you just to get at me."

"Well, it's working, isn't it?" Kate said bluntly. "Another pleasant evening in Hidden Valley talking about Mona Kellar." Andy said nothing, and Kate kept going. "And I bet you've already mentally rearranged your entire morning because you think you're going to sit in on that meeting tomorrow."

Andy looked over, surprise in her eyes. "Am I that easy to read?"

"No, love, you're just predictably overprotective when it comes to me."

"Maybe," Andy said. "But you're still not meeting with Mona Kellar alone tomorrow."

Kate sighed. "Fine, but it won't be you in there with me."

"If no one else can be there, then yes, it will be me," Andy insisted stubbornly.

"You're so bossy," Kate grumbled under her breath, realizing there was really no point in arguing.

Andy smiled. "I knew you'd see it my way."

"Just take me back to the hotel, woman. I'm hungry."

Andy laughed and reached over to massage the back of Kate's neck like she did when Kate finished a long, hard shift at work.

"Now who's bossy?"

Chapter Nine

By the next morning, most of Hidden Valley was looking for the same answers and reassurance as the cashier at the grocery store. Kate, suspecting as much, had Andy take her to the hospital early. The ER was already jammed, a tense and frazzled Dr. Doyle buzzing ineffectively in larger and larger circles around the small space, getting in the way of the three doctors shouting orders at overburdened nurses.

"Shit," Kate said quietly as she and Andy stood back and surveyed the chaos. Parents and nannies wrangled toddlers and hyperactive kids, men and women in business suits yelled at each other and their cell phones, and the triage nurse looked like she was going to break down and cry at any moment.

"I'm going to go find Ferris and see if Dr. Salinger is around. Public Health needs to get on this," Andy said.

"Chicken," Kate mumbled, already making a plan to apply order to this familiar chaos.

Andy grinned and touched Kate lightly, secretly on her back. Even distracted, Kate shivered, still not immune to Andy's touch.

"Go work your magic, Dr. Morrison. Call me if you need backup."

"Don't think I won't take you up on that," Kate said, but she was already heading into the very centre of the storm. She descended on Dr. Doyle first, giving her three jobs: call in extra staff to the ER, call local family practice offices and Whistler Health and tell them to expect overflow, and meet with the PR team to come up with a pamphlet to release to the public by the afternoon.

As Dr. Doyle left with her list of jobs clenched in her manicured hand, Kate moved into action. She met with each doctor and nurse, making it clear anyone with flu symptoms combined with difficulty breathing should be flagged. She then pulled two nurses off the floor and out into triage, taking the already overloaded triage nurse with her. She passed them each a stack of charts, instructing them to only input the most basic personal information and to prioritize patients based on a new coding system. Patients with a C for critical would get seen right away, patients with FS on their charts would have a minimum of a three-hour wait to be seen, and the code AB would be used only for patients who exhibited flu-like symptoms.

"I don't understand, what does AB stand for?" asked one of the nurses, writing the new codes on her hand.

"Nothing," Kate told her. "But we are not mentioning the word virus out there. People are already panicked enough. If asked, you tell people they are to treat symptoms as they would the flu and to come in if they are experiencing difficulty breathing." She looked around at the three nurses. "Are we good?"

Kate and the three nurses walked back into the waiting room and started talking to patients, filling in charts and giving most of them the news that it was going to be a long wait. Kate felt the shift of tension in the air before long, from generalized and dispersed to angry and focused on Kate and the nurses. As Kate wrote FS on the top of a chart and got the next one ready, she pulled out her phone and texted Andy that she needed her in the ER.

Kate moved to the next patient. A boy, about nine, coughing and wiping his nose on the back of his sleeve, never looking up from his smartphone, fingers bashing at the screen. A dark-haired woman in worn shoes and a sweater smiled at Kate tentatively.

"His mother is worried," she said, with a heavy accent Kate couldn't place. "She wants him to be seen right now. His doctor is away." She then fished around in her purse, pulled out a cell phone. "I am to call when there is a doctor here."

Kate smiled back at the woman. "Let's check him out first, okay? What's your name?"

"Trenton Clifton III," the boy said, still not looking up.

Kate rolled her eyes internally.

"Tell me about being sick, Trenton Clifton III."

"I've been home from school for three days, and when I cough it's gross, and when I sneeze it's gross."

"Have you been particularly tired?"

"Nope."

Kate turned to the woman. "Has he been sleeping a lot or hard to wake?"

The woman shook her head.

"Has he complained about chest pain or trouble breathing?"

Another shake of her head.

Kate pulled the stethoscope from around her neck and asked the boy to lean forwards. She had to close her eyes and concentrate, away from the noise of the waiting room. Still, she heard nothing.

"I think he's just got a cold," Kate told the woman. "If you or mom wants him to see a doctor, it's going to be at least three hours."

The woman held out her phone, looking worried. "You tell mom this. Please."

Kate sighed and looked over to see Andy and Constable Ferris coming in through the double doors. She waved them over.

"Fine. Call her." She didn't really have time for this.

As the woman dialed, Kate quickly explained what was happening to Andy and Ferris. She told Ferris to be friendly and calm and repeat only the information from the press release yesterday. She told Andy just to walk around. Kate figured her imposing, uniformed presence would be enough to subdue the masses.

The call with the mother was brief and bitter. Apparently, Mrs. Clifton was sure her kid could be seen because his father was on the hospital board. Kate made it clear her son was not sick enough to jump the line and only critical patients were being sent through right now.

That scene replayed itself in varying forms over the following two hours. People cajoled, attempted to influence, and subtly threatened when they were not seen right away. Kate gave everyone the exact same information, not even decreasing the projected wait time as people left. By the end of the two hours, Kate found only two people who qualified for the suspected virus. Neither of them had any fluid in their lungs, nor did they have any pulmonary risk factors. As Kate sorted through the pile of triaged charts, she found the same. She surveyed the ER. It was still packed, people still paced restlessly and shot Kate angry glances, but at least it was calm. At least there was some semblance of order.

Dr. Doyle herself came to collect Kate when it was time for the meeting. Kate sent the two nurses back to the floor before following Dr. Doyle out of the ER.

"I'm getting a lot of calls and complaints, Dr. Morrison," Dr. Doyle said as they weaved their way around patients. "People in Hidden Valley are not used to being turned away."

"We're not turning anyone away, Dr. Doyle. If they want to wait to be seen, then they are welcome to wait."

They passed Andy on the way out. Kate watched as she detached herself from a conversation and resolutely followed them out the double doors.

"Well, it amounts to the same thing," Dr. Doyle said.

"Expect more calls, Dr. Doyle," Kate said, trying to temper the spark of anger that flared in her stomach. "Expect more people to be angry. This hospital can't test every hypochondriac in all of Hidden Valley *and* manage to catch people who are legitimately ill with a potentially fatal virus. My focus is on that last group. You asked me to stay and help. That's what I'm doing."

Dr. Doyle was about to open her mouth, no doubt to give another criticism of the way Kate had managed to get control of Valley General ER, but they were interrupted by a nurse behind them calling Kate's name. She held out a chart, her face grave. Kate immediately followed her back into the ER and listened to the details of their newest potential case.

"Harris Trenholm, forty-three years old, flu-like symptoms including extreme fatigue started four days ago, began having chest pain and difficulty breathing just after midnight." She pulled back the curtain, and Kate saw the man in a rumpled business suit, his legs hanging over the side of the bed, holding onto the O2 mask like his life depended on it. As she watched him try to breathe, Kate wondered if it did.

"Mr. Trenholm, I'm Dr. Morrison. We're going to see what we can do to make it easier for you to breathe." She turned to the nurse. "Medical history?"

The nurse turned the page silently and pointed. Kate's heart sank. Motor vehicle accident eighteen months ago, blunt chest trauma, broken ribs, surgery, diminished lung capacity. Kate saw Keith Grange's lungs in the autopsy. The tiniest sliver of an old biopsy had let in the infection that took over his body and eventually ended his life. She then pictured what Harris Trenholm's lungs must look like with their multiple access points for the virus to settle, infect, and take over. Kate stared at the chart, at the man sitting on the bed, rapidly scanning the information she had, thinking about the charts she'd surrounded herself with last night, trying to come up with a plan for this exact scenario.

She scanned down the chart to the meds section. He was on prednisone for his lungs. *Interesting*, she thought, *let's see what it does.* "Okay, rebreather mask with high-flow oxygen. Cardiac monitor, pulse ox, and a blood panel. And Mr. Trenholm just jumped the list for chest x-ray." Kate pulled out her stethoscope and reached down the collar of his unbuttoned shirt to listen to his lungs. Definitely fluid.

"Mr. Trenholm, we're going to see how you do down here, but if you don't improve I'm going to want to admit you to a bed upstairs so we can keep an eye on you. Is there someone we can call for you?"

The man shook his head, pulling in shallow breaths.

"You're in good hands. I'll be back to check on you, okay?"

Kate turned away and lowered her voice before she spoke to the nurse. "I want a crash cart and surgical tray near Mr. Trenholm at all times. Any changes to his breathing, page me right away, even if it seems insignificant."

Kate checked her watch on her way back out. She was now half an hour late for the meeting. With half her brain still back with the patient, Kate couldn't find it in her to care all that much. Andy was waiting for her by the double doors, but Dr. Doyle was nowhere to be seen.

"Do you know if Dr. Salinger is going to sit in on our meeting?" Kate said.

"Yes."

"Good. Then may I ask why I'm getting an escort?"

"That's why."

Kate looked up to see Andy gesturing with a jerk of her head down the hallway. Dr. Mona Kellar hulked outside the office door, files clutched under her arm. When she saw Kate and Andy walking together down the hall, her eyes narrowed into angry slits and her mouth turned up into a smirk.

"Not one minute alone with her, got it?" Andy's voice was low and tense.

"Yes."

As they came closer, Andy's voice returned to its normal volume, though Kate could still hear the stress in her tone. "I think Dr. Doyle's going to want to piggyback on your meeting here, try to get everyone together in an hour. Does that give you enough time?"

"Sure, we'll make it work."

They were at the door. Kate ignored Dr. Kellar and looked up at Andy. "See you in an hour."

Andy looked into the room, confirmed that Dr. Salinger was there, then nodded curtly and left.

Kate didn't care in that moment what Dr. Kellar thought, what new insult or perverted reference she was going to pull out of a simple good-bye. As she walked into the room and took her seat, Kate tried to focus on why they were here, thinking about the forty-three-year-old man sitting in the emergency room right now, fighting to breathe.

"I thought I made it clear I don't like to be kept waiting, Dr. Morrison," Dr. Kellar said, following Kate into the room and taking a seat.

"I'm not sure what has led you to believe I give two shits about your timetable, Dr. Kellar, but rest assured it's at the bottom of my priority list right now." Kate said it with a calmness she didn't feel. Kate took a breath and ordered her thoughts.

"We have three new suspected cases, one of which is exhibiting early symptoms of pulmonary edema similar to Roberta Sedlak and Keith Grange. We're going to have to come up with a protocol quickly if we're going to stay ahead of this."

Dr. Salinger jumped in. "We're in the process of setting up a temporary lab here at Valley General. I think there are enough suspected cases to warrant the expense involved. Also, if I may get to the purpose of the meeting, I've pulled some literature on similar-acting viruses and their various treatments. It's the best I could do considering we aren't any farther ahead in identifying what we're dealing with."

"Any word from the NML?"

"My understanding is the earliest we would hear from them is tomorrow."

Kate scanned the literature Dr. Salinger had passed her, skipping over the genomes, pathogenesis and virology information, and homing in on the treatment. What she saw wasn't all that reassuring: oxygen therapy, diuretics, steroids, and time. They'd already tried the first two, to little effect. And the fourth option so far hadn't been available to them.

"Dr. Kellar, looking specifically at the treatment given to both patients, could you please tell us what you saw?"

Dr. Kellar took an awkwardly long time to answer. "First a fuck you, now a please. I can't keep up with your moods, Dr. Morrison."

Kate waited, letting the pause lengthen, keeping her eyes on Dr. Kellar, not even attempting to hide the contempt she felt for the woman. Finally Kate decided she'd had enough. She and Dr. Salinger would have to figure this out on their own.

"Too little, too late," Dr. Kellar said, just as Kate turned away. At first Kate thought the forensic pathologist was making another off topic comment, but then realized she was discussing the ER treatment.

"What do you mean?"

"Exactly what I said. Too little oxygen, and the diuretics barely had any effect on the fluid in the lungs. They don't work fast enough, so either find a way to double it without killing off their kidneys or don't bother."

Kate blinked at her, then flipped through the literature Dr. Salinger had pulled, simultaneously reading and recalling information from the medical charts. Keith Grange at least had been maxed out on diuretics.

"What about the oxygen therapy?" Dr. Salinger said.

"Same story. Too little, too late."

"But it wasn't," Kate said, thinking hard, staring down blankly at the sheaf of papers in her hand.

"The two bodies in the morgue beg to differ, Dr. Morrison," Dr. Kellar said.

"No, I mean the oxygen was working fine, at least keeping them stable. But at some point, their lungs reached some kind of critical mass point, and the oxygen wasn't enough anymore."

"And the fluid filled their lungs like a tidal wave," finished Dr. Salinger. Kate looked at him, feeling helpless. This wasn't in the literature. It didn't make sense.

"That's a very poetic image, Dr. Salinger, but it doesn't exactly get us any farther ahead," Dr. Kellar said acidly.

"What about steroids?" Kate threw out. "The newest unconfirmed case has diminished lung capacity from a car accident eighteen months ago, and he's on low-dose steroids. I expected to find his lungs crackling when I listened. I heard fluid, but nothing to cause any alarm."

"Chest film?" Dr. Kellar said shortly.

"I'll check."

Moving to the computer in the corner of the room, Kate pulled up Harris Trenholm's file, found the chest films, and angled the monitor so the other doctors could see.

"Doesn't look like much, does it?" Dr. Salinger said. Kate had to agree. Very few infiltrates, not enough fluid to be too alarmed.

"If he's positive for the virus, then you've got your protocol, I think, Dr. Morrison," Dr. Kellar said in a voice that could almost pass for neutral.

Kate kept her eyes on the films, memorizing them, mentally filing them away with the others. Dr. Kellar was right. There was possibly the smallest glimmer of hope.

There was a sudden knock on the door and Dr. Doyle entered with Andy and Constable Ferris. "Sorry to interrupt, but Dr. Levesque from the NML has just phoned. She has asked for a teleconference to give an update."

Kate felt her stomach drop nervously. Across the room, Andy folded her long frame into a seat, resting her arms lightly on the chair. Kate knew her well enough to read the signs of stress in the grip of her right hand, the tense line of her jaw, the intense stillness of her body. When their eyes met, Kate saw very little. Andy's guard was firmly up. Feeling Dr. Kellar's gaze drilling into her from the opposite side of the room, it wasn't hard to figure out why.

Dr. Doyle was punching numbers into a contoured grey box in the centre of the table, once again the put-together, efficient hospital administrator. Kate considered her hasty, angry words to Dr. Doyle earlier. She added it to the list of things to worry about later. "Dr. Levesque, can you hear me?"

"Yes? Hello?" The voice at the other end was clear with a French-Canadian accent.

"Dr. Levesque, I'll let you know who's around the table. Dr. Clifford Salinger, Public Health; Dr. Mona Kellar, forensic pathologist;

Dr. Kate Morrison, physician liaison with the RCMP; Constable Art Ferris and Sgt. Andy Wyles, also with the RCMP."

"Quite a group. Thank you all for your time."

"We're all quite eager to hear what you have to say, Dr. Levesque."

"Then let me get started. We have the initial findings for what is now classified as HV1A-CS, to include the originator, Dr. Clifford Salinger. Let's refer to it simply as HV1A. This virus is extremely unique. You can imagine that as an epidemiologist, this I do not say lightly."

Kate felt her body tighten, a long line of tension starting in her lower back and spread up her spine, to her shoulders and up through her neck.

"We run every potentially new virus through a database, either to confirm it is one we haven't seen before or to help us identify which classification or virus family it belongs to. HV1A hit one exact match and one partial match. This is not a natural occurrence."

Kate automatically sought Andy's eyes and held them, almost unconsciously, as she listened to Dr. Levesque's next words.

"There can be no other explanation for it. This virus is man-made."

The level of tension in the room increased exponentially as each person absorbed the impact of the information.

"Dr. Levesque, it's Dr. Morrison. Could you tell us what the matches were?"

"Yes. Hantavirus was the exact match, and an unidentified Influenza A was the partial match."

Another silence.

"I'm going to guess by your silence that you all understand the potential severity of the hantavirus. There does seem to be good news, though. Initial reports show that the HV1A virus is not nearly as potent or deadly as the hantavirus. For reasons unknown, the creator of this virus specifically chose the most non-lethal components."

"We have two bodies in the morgue that would beg to differ, Dr. Levesque," Dr. Kellar cut in, reusing what she obviously considered to be a good line.

"But it is not two hundred, which it easily could be with the hantavirus."

Kate thought she heard the woman on the other end of the line sigh.

"This distance is a problem, *non*? It would be much easier to show you. Dr. Doyle, would it be possible to send a member of your medical team down here? Even just a day would allow us to exchange information much more effectively."

Kate saw Dr. Doyle looking around the room, apparently settling on Dr. Salinger. He immediately shook his head and held up his hand in a gesture of refusal.

"I can't leave the office unmanned at a time like this, not even for a day," he told Dr. Doyle.

"Dr. Morrison?" she said.

Kate didn't even need to think. "Yes, I'll go."

"Dr. Levesque, we will arrange for Dr. Morrison to come out to Winnipeg, hopefully by the end of the day."

Kate didn't listen to the uneasy thrum of panic that resonated in her body, and she didn't listen to the end of the meeting as Dr. Doyle signed off. Kate was too busy watching Andy. Her whole posture had changed. She leaned forwards, resting her forearms on the edge of the table, her palms pressed down on the smooth surface. When their eyes met, Kate nodded slightly and Andy flicked her eyes away to address the group.

"As of this moment, the HV1A-CS virus is no longer solely a medical and public health concern. We will also now be investigating this as an act of bioterrorism." Kate felt a thrill of fear at the words as a weight of added urgency settled on her. "For all intents and purposes, the individuals around the table will now be considered the Public Health Emergency Management, or PHEM, team. Dr. Salinger, I'd like you to be in close contact with the Provincial Health Officer. Whatever resources and supports they can offer us from a distance, we'll take. As of right now, though, I want no one else descending on Hidden Valley. I think it will induce the community to panic and make it next to impossible to investigate the source of the outbreak. Constable Ferris and I will work alongside the PHEM team in relation to the investigation."

Andy paused and leaned forwards very slightly, and Kate could feel every eye on her. She didn't raise her voice, but her tone carried the weight of absolute authority.

"The word *hantavirus* does not leave this room. Dr. Doyle, that includes hospital staff as well as board members. This remains an unknown virus with flu-like symptoms. I believe you are working on another press release, so we'll need that immediately. Dr. Morrison..." Andy paused, only slightly. "I guess you have a flight to catch. For the rest of us, let's reconvene here first thing tomorrow."

"What about me, Sergeant Wyles? You haven't handed me my assignment yet."

It was impossible not to hear the condescension in Mona Kellar's tone and equally impossible not to feel the tension in the room as Andy addressed her directly for the first time in almost a week.

"This team would appreciate your continued input and support. Personally, I hope we're not going to need your services again."

Kate could see by the reddening of Mona Kellar's cheeks and the way her eyes went flat that the double meaning wasn't lost. But Andy had already turned away, talking quietly and quickly to Constable Ferris.

Kate left the room, blinking as she entered the bright light of the hallway. It was mid-morning already and bright sunlight flooded through the oversized windows, stretching far down the hallways. Kate felt briefly disoriented as she walked back towards the ER. Everything looked the same as an hour ago, but somehow everything felt darker. Her thoughts free-flowed with information, everything she knew or had read about hantavirus, about influenza A, fluid accumulating in the lungs, the use of oxygen therapy, steroids, and points of infection. Words like *outbreak* and *bioterrorism* hit like pointed daggers behind her eyes. As she pushed open the double doors of the ER, Kate felt not only the weight of urgency, but the weight of responsibility.

Kate forced herself into the present, realizing that the ER, though busy, seemed perfectly under control. She checked in with the sandy-haired doctor, Dr. MacKay, who confirmed three more suspected cases of the virus, though none had been flagged as high risk. Harris Trenholm had been admitted and was stable, but the high flow oxygen was barely keeping him that way. Leaning up against the nurse's station, Kate flipped through charts, surveyed the ER around her, and had to admit she was impressed. Given no warning and very little direction, this tiny ER had managed to control a panicked community dealing with a viral outbreak.

Kate grabbed the phone book behind the nurse's station, picked up the phone, and dialed the local RCMP office. As expected, Judy answered. After giving her overwhelming and genuine thanks for their morning coffee, Kate outlined what she needed: coffee, donuts, éclairs, cookies, and pastries. Basically anything overloaded with sugar and fat. She wanted a pile of it delivered to the ER as soon as possible.

Kate made her way up to the second floor to check on Harris Trenholm. She couldn't find it in her to be surprised when she saw Michael Cardiff in Harris Trenholm's room in another immaculate business suit, talking on the phone while staring out the window. Kate picked up the chart, noting that Mr. Trenholm was breathing at least a little easier.

"How are you doing, Mr. Trenholm?"

"Harris." He had a nice smile, even through his rebreather mask. "I'm all right."

"Which is what everyone says, even when they're not." Kate smiled when he gave a light chuckle, taking it as a good sign that it didn't trigger a bronchial spasm.

Cardiff's voice intruded on their conversation, briefly loud, direct, then back down to a more subdued monotone. Kate raised her eyebrows at Harris, indicating Cardiff with a questioning jerk of her head.

Harris pointed at himself and breathed out, "Campaign manager."

"Ah," Kate said. "Well, not for the next few days, you're not."

Harris pulled down his mask. "Have to. Campaign period starts… two days."

Kate adjusted the mask back onto his face. "And how useful do you think you're going to be when you can't get a complete sentence out?" she asked him gently.

Cardiff strode over to the bed, his phone still clenched in his oversized hands.

"Are you his doctor?" he asked Kate rudely.

"Yes."

"Good. Anything this man needs he gets, whatever treatment or drug therapy or whatever. He gets it."

"Mr. Trenholm will get whatever he needs, Mr. Cardiff, because he's sick and has to have treatment. Not because he's your campaign manager," Kate said evenly.

"Right," said Cardiff, staring down Kate while smiling his politician's smile. "That's exactly what I meant, of course. So, do you know if it's the virus? How can we get the results fast-tracked?"

Kate closed the chart and put it down on the bedside table. "Mr. Cardiff, I have some tests that I need to run with Mr. Trenholm. I'm going to have to ask you to wait outside. Maybe you could check on Serena. I believe she's being discharged this morning."

Cardiff looked from Kate to Harris and back again.

"Right. I'll see you in a few, Harris."

Harris spoke once the door was closed. "Do I have it?"

"We won't know until later today or early tomorrow, but we're treating you as if you do. The damage to your lungs from the car accident puts you at greater risk for developing infection, so you are going to have to be monitored in the hospital for the next few days."

Harris made a face behind his mask.

"I know. I'm sure you're sick of hospitals, but I wouldn't keep you here if it wasn't important."

"I need to work…that's important."

"I'm sure Michael Cardiff can find someone to cover for a few days."

Harris shook his head, pointed at himself. "No, for me…Michael winning this election…important for my career…" he breathed out, sucking on his oxygen.

Kate didn't say anything, letting him get his breath back.

"I know he hired me…for sympathy vote…" He stopped again, took a few long, deep breaths.

"What do you mean?" Kate asked.

"My accident…drunk driver, tourist from Whistler…town rallied around the cause…big news in Hidden Valley…" Harris stopped and rolled his eyes and Kate had to laugh. "Doesn't matter though…still could make my career."

Kate considered the man intently. "Forty-eight hours of nothing. No calls, no paperwork, no sneaking in your laptop. Forty-eight hours of resting, then we'll see how you're doing."

"Boring," Harris breathed out, the smile on his face making soft crinkles around his eyes.

"Buy a book," Kate said bluntly, but she returned the smile. It was hard not to like this guy. "And it's up to you what medical information you want to share with your employer. He'll get nothing from me that you don't explicitly give permission for, got it?"

Harris nodded. "Thanks."

"Rest, sleep, be bored, whatever. I'll see you soon."

Cardiff cornered Kate the second she was out of the room.

"If he has the virus, I need that information contained. It must not get out into the general public."

Kate took a step back, holding up one hand between them to define her personal space.

"Mr. Trenholm is my patient, and all doctor-patient confidentiality rules apply." Cardiff looked satisfied, like Kate had just fallen in line like he'd expected her to. "Which means," Kate stressed, "that I cannot discuss his diagnosis or medical treatment with you, Mr. Cardiff."

Cardiff gripped his phone tighter.

"How is Serena doing?" Kate asked, trying to direct the conversation to more neutral ground.

"Fine, they just need your signature for discharge," he said, still trying to pin her down with a glare.

"I can do that right now," Kate said. She attempted to side step around him, but he blocked her way, moving much more agilely than Kate would have expected. She felt a tendril of alarm unwind in her stomach.

"I understand you're going to a lab out in Winnipeg. I can arrange for a private helicopter transport," he said smoothly, once again overstepping Kate's personal space.

Before she had time to formulate an answer, Kate heard the tread of Andy's boots approaching. Half a second later, Andy stepped in beside Kate, her arms stiff by her side, her grey eyes flashing, giving a clear message for Cardiff to back off, which he did, almost immediately.

"That won't be necessary, Mr. Cardiff. The RCMP has it covered."

Andy's voice contained no inflection, but every muscle in her body was held rigid. She leaned in ever so slightly, the aggressiveness of her stance more like a generalized challenge. Kate knew it would take a bigger man than Cardiff to take her up on that.

He held up his hands in a gesture of placation. It was an empty gesture, Kate was sure. Somewhere not too deep down, this giant of a man was pissed.

"Just trying to help, Sergeant Wyles. Richard James was able to help out with transporting Dr. Salinger to Vancouver, I wanted to extend the same courtesy to Dr. Morrison."

Andy said nothing, and her body did not relax as she turned to Kate.

"Dr. Doyle is waiting for you downstairs and Judy has made all the arrangements for your flight."

Kate swallowed once, trying to keep control of her voice. "I'll just sign Serena's discharge papers before I go."

Andy took a small step to the side to allow Kate to pass behind her. Kate knew she hadn't actually been in any real danger, but she also knew Andy would count any threat against her as real. Michael Cardiff had just made an enemy of Sgt. Andy Wyles. Kate picked up the paperwork, scanned it, and scrawled her name at the bottom, suddenly feeling the need to get away from Hidden Valley.

Andy fell in step beside Kate as they descended in silence to the first floor of the hospital. Michael Cardiff was nowhere to be seen.

"Judy's booked you on a flight to Winnipeg," Andy said as they walked. "You've got a chopper into Vancouver, then connecting through Calgary, but you have to leave soon. You're due to fly back tomorrow night. That's a day to travel and a day to get as much information as you can on the virus." Andy stopped abruptly and grasped Kate's arm. "You're sure you want to do this?" Andy's grey eyes were worried, though Kate wasn't sure what she was reacting to. At this point she had her pick: Mona Kellar, Michael Cardiff, or the animosity with Dr. Doyle. Not to mention a cross-country flight, six new suspected cases, an elusive bioterrorist threat, and the spectre of the hantavirus that hovered over Hidden Valley.

"Positive," Kate said, pushing every one of those previous thoughts aside.

Andy searched Kate's face. "When's the last time you were in Winnipeg?" Andy asked quietly.

Kate's heart dropped as the fact she'd been carefully avoiding for the last few hours slammed into her body.

"Sarah," was all Kate could get out. The last time Kate had taken an urgent trip to Winnipeg had been after a late-night, panicked phone call saying that Kate's younger sister Sarah was in trouble. Lost Sarah, junkie on the street Sarah. Baby sister Sarah. "It was a long time ago," Kate said, finding her voice. "I can do this. I need to do this."

Andy looked at her carefully, and then she reached out and took

Kate's hand, turning it palm up, tracing the barely visible scars with a light touch. They stood together silently until they both felt time catch up to them, and Andy released Kate's hand and led her out the doors of Valley General Hospital.

CHAPTER TEN

The next morning was sunny. A bright blue sky reflected off the hundreds of windows on the Canadian Science Centre for Human and Animal Health, which contained the relatively new National Microbiology lab. Kate walked across the street, the only thing in her stomach a complimentary hotel coffee and a feeling of unease. Kate entered through the front doors of the building and handed over the ID Judy had given her. Kate waited as the man behind the desk processed her information.

She felt a moment of acute panic, like she needed to explain how she was really an ER physician, that this was only the second time she'd consulted with the RCMP. That it was temporary. That her girlfriend had been worried about Kate taking on this assignment. That she didn't want to admit she was struggling. That there was a small possibility Andy had been right from the very beginning.

The man behind the desk handed Kate back her ID, saying Dr. Levesque would be down momentarily. Kate took the few minutes to pull herself together, looking around the lobby at the colourful public service posters on vaccinations, safe food handling practices, outbreak preparedness, and hand washing. By the time she heard her name being called, Kate felt in control of herself again.

Dr. Louise Levesque was a tiny wisp of a woman, with long grey hair pulled back to reveal a broad forehead, bright blue eyes, and a genuine smile of delight.

"Dr. Morrison, it is very nice to meet you. How are you?" she said in her thick French-Canadian accent.

"Fine, thank you," Kate replied, willing herself to make it true.

After signing Kate in and handing her a visitor's badge, Dr. Levesque walked very quickly down several hallways, leaving the brightly lit visitors entrance behind and moving into what Kate suspected was the centre of the building.

"It is very rude of me not to give you the whole tour, the Canadian Science Centre for Human and Animal Health is a fascinating place. But we have such a small amount of time before you are to return to BC, we must make the most of it, yes?"

"Yes. I want to know everything you know about this virus."

The woman smiled again. "Curiosity is a most useful tool."

Dr. Levesque used her passkey to unlock a set of heavy frosted glass doors, the words *Viral Disease Division* stencilled in a thick, dark font. "We have brought the HV1A-CS virus to the Viral Disease Division. There was an argument early on about whether or not it should be here or in the Influenza and Respiratory Division, but viral disease won out. They usually do these days," she added, with a smile.

A long, segmented desk bisected the conference room they entered. A man and two women, all in in lab coats, sat talking. They all looked up as Kate and Dr. Levesque walked in. Kate noted one of the faces looked friendly, one serious, and one disgruntled. Dr. Levesque introduced them to Kate, who only remembered that the serious woman's name was Rayna and the grumpy guy reminded her strongly of Jack. He had curly hair, was unkempt, and constantly fiddled with his laptop.

"Dr. Morrison," Dr. Levesque began, "we'd like to go over our initial results in terms of viral pathogenesis, our hypothesis for viral replication, life cycle, and so on. I realize that as a physician you are more used to looking at patients on a macro level, meaning the onset and progression of symptoms, the broader implications of medical history and drug interactions on illness. So, while I imagine you are eager to put what we have in context of your patients, I would like to encourage you to think micro for the next few hours, try to forget the effects this virus has on your patient and instead think cellular, the effects that one small virus has on a host cell."

Kate looked doubtfully at Dr. Levesque, unsure if she would be able to clear her mind of the chest x-rays, the autopsy results, the picture of Harris Trenholm gasping into his O2 mask. "I'll try," Kate said.

"Excellent," Dr. Levesque said happily. "I truly think once we can begin to understand this virus on a cellular level, it will make the symptoms, the progression, and hopefully the treatment make more sense."

"Okay, let's get started," Kate said, leaning forwards in her chair, attempting to push thoughts of Hidden Valley out of her head.

"Who's up for a game of Go Fish?" Grumpy Jack asked, tapping at the mouse pad on his laptop and looking around.

"I'm in," the not-serious woman with dirty-blond hair said, squinting her eyes in mock challenge at Grumpy Jack.

Kate saw Dr. Levesque shaking her head. "We could at least attempt to make a positive professional impression upon Dr. Morrison," she murmured. "The NML does have a worldwide reputation to maintain."

"Come on, Dr. Lou, we'll still get all the information across but in half the time and in a much more entertaining format." He sat back and folded his hands innocently across his stomach. "Unless you believe our west-coast neighbour here can't hack the content?"

Dr. Levesque looked at Kate with apologetic eyes. "Dr. Morrison, do you have any idea why the most brilliant minds are also the most uncooperative?"

Kate grinned in response, feeling a bit of the pressure relieved in the midst of the banter. These were people she understood.

"Okay, I'll play the hantavirus hand and Nicole, you play the influenza A hand," Grumpy Jack said, without waiting for the go-ahead from his supervisor. Kate saw Dr. Levesque throw up her hands in surrender and take her seat.

"Do you have a single strand?" Grumpy Jack challenged the blond woman, Nicole.

"Yes."

"Point one for me. Do you have RNA?"

"Yes."

"How about a Class 5 on Balty's Classification System?"

"Yep."

"And do you have a negative sense?"

"Absolutely."

"Okay, four points for me," Grumpy Jack calculated. "So far so good, Dr. Morrison?"

"Both the hantavirus and influenza A come from the same group of viruses which contain ribonucleic acid, or RNA, as their genetic material. So far they are more similar than different," Kate summed up. "I take it this means the HV1A virus is also a Class 5, single-stranded, RNA-based virus."

"Single-stranded, RNA, and negative sense we can confirm. Class 5 at this point is only assumed since we don't actually know what we're dealing with," Nicole replied. "Let's make it interesting," she said, with a smile to Grumpy Jack, who scowled across the table. "Do you have eight genes?"

"Go Fish!" Grumpy Jack said haughtily. "I have fourteen. Do you have—"

"Hang on," Rayna interrupted. "Let's make sure we've got the significance of some of this information first." Kate thought she recognized a note of doubt, of condescension. Rayna clearly did doubt Kate's ability to hack the content. "Dr. Morrison, do you need a recap?"

"How many genes does HV1A have?" Kate responded with a question.

"Isolated nine so far."

Kate trolled through the information in her head, not allowing the questioning look from across the table to intrude on her thoughts. "Tell me why you think the number of genes might be significant," she finally asked, not caring if she betrayed her ignorance.

"Viruses reproduce rapidly in part because they have so few genes to replicate once they invade the host cells."

"So the more complex the gene structure, the longer it could take to replicate," Kate said.

"And the more chances of a virus replication fail, let's not forget that," Grumpy Jack said.

"What do you mean?"

"RNA viruses are like kids with ADHD. They often go for speed instead of accuracy. But that means they adapt, mutate, and form new strains."

Again Kate paused and forced herself to remain micro, making pictures of what she was hearing. "Okay, I get all that. But HV1A isn't a naturally mutated strand."

"That's right, Dr. Morrison," Dr. Levesque interjected. "But we think that the creator of this virus would have used the RNA polymerase enzyme adaptation to his or her benefit."

"And don't forget the reassortment factor," Nicole cut in.

"You mean when two influenzas infect the same cell," Kate said.

"Right, the genes can mix and produce new strains. Reassortment."

"But you don't think hantavirus and influenza A could have reassorted," Kate asked.

Nicole shook her head. "I'd give it a ninety-nine percent improbability rate."

"In the lab, we've been able to manually reassort influenzas, but never a virus outside the influenza family." Grumpy Jack jumped in, sounding irritated, as if the discovery that someone else had done it annoyed him no end. He looked over at his boss. "Whoever it is, we should probably hire them."

"As soon as they get out of prison for murder," Kate murmured.

All four pairs of eyes pinned Kate to her seat, and a distinct aura of shock and tension settled on the room. "Sorry," she said immediately. "I forgot to keep it micro."

"No, don't apologize. Sometimes it is good for us to have a reminder of the implications of the viruses we deal with on a daily basis," Dr. Levesque said, looking pointedly at Grumpy Jack.

"I have a question, and I'm afraid it's not very micro," Kate said suddenly, constantly sorting and prioritizing information. "Can you in any way predict the HV1A's...behaviour, for lack of a better word, based on what you know of the hantavirus and influenza A?"

"Short answer? Yes," Grumpy Jack said.

"Long answer, no," Rayna said, giving Grumpy Jack a look that dared him to contradict her. But Jack just smiled and gestured for her to keep talking. "It could take months for us to be able to give an accurate description of the life cycle, from how it binds itself to the surface of a host cell, how it replicates itself, and how those replicated cells are released into the body."

"Rayna's right," Nicole said, almost grudgingly. "There are things we still don't know about the hantavirus, and that's been on our radar for over fifty years."

"Like what?"

"We know it's zoonotic, that it's transmitted by infected rodents.

Humans breathe in the aerosolized virus as it circulates in the air from infected rodent droppings and saliva. We know it incubates for two to four weeks from point of infection to showing symptoms. We don't fully understand how it replicates or how it causes the capillaries in the lungs to leak fluid."

Kate had stopped listening. Now, instead of struggling to make a picture of cellular protease bindings and genetic replication, she suddenly saw a barrage of images. She was not used to thinking on such a small scale. Her macro view of the world was invading the cellular level, and she couldn't help it.

Dr. Levesque came to her rescue. "Dr. Morrison?"

Kate looked up, the flood of images still hijacking half her brain. "Can I see it?" Kate asked. "The HV1A virus. Can you show it to me and tell me what you see? Either hantavirus, influenza, or new. Is that possible?"

Grumpy Jack leaned forwards in his chair and pushed a few buttons on a tablet in the middle of the table. Window coverings dropped down with quiet mechanical efficiency. At the same time, a screen came down from the corner, and Grumpy Jack tapped on his laptop. After moving around a few files, a subdued, purple-stained microscopic image came up on the screen.

"HV1A-CS. A misnomer, but we're going with it for now. Once we isolate the hemagglutinin and neuraminidase involved—"

"Perhaps," Dr. Levesque interrupted, "we can stick to what Dr. Morrison has asked of us." Her tone held little in the way of humour. "John, if you could isolate the hantavirus components. Nicole, the influenza."

They did. In detail. Nearly an hour of detail. Finally, though, with Rayna grudgingly adding in the components of the virus they thought were unique to the HV1A-CS strain, Kate began to understand. She began to make the connections between what she was seeing on the slides in front of her, the information given by the epidemiologists around the table, and of course, the pictures already scanned into memory. She still saw the chest x-rays, heard the sound of the rebreather masks, felt the chill of a body during autopsy.

"Let's take a break," Dr. Levesque finally cut in. "When we return, perhaps you can share with us the symptomology of your patients."

As everyone around her stood, Kate pulled out her cell phone, thinking about Andy for the first time in hours. A No Signal message met her when she turned on her phone, and Kate sighed.

"Why don't you come down for a coffee, and I'll hook you up with a landline," Nicole said kindly.

Kate gave her a small smile. "Thanks, that would be great."

Grumpy Jack—John, Kate reminded herself—accompanied them down in the elevator. The cafeteria was huge and white and thankfully quiet on this Sunday morning. John treated them both, forcing Kate to conclude that maybe he wasn't so grumpy after all.

Just before Kate bit into her cranberry and oat muffin, she remembered where she was and what the labs housed here: microscopic pathogens, invading organisms, rapid cellular replication. She felt John and Nicole's eyes on her, and they grinned knowingly.

"Seriously," John said. "Can you think of a safer place to eat?"

Kate looked at her muffin, then back up at John, smiling guiltily.

"You're not the first, don't worry," Nicole said, taking a huge bite of her bagel and cream cheese. Kate took her cue and popped a bit of muffin into her mouth.

"You eat at work, don't you?" John asked, stirring a fourth packet of sugar into his coffee.

"Sure, when I get a chance."

"See, now that's gross. Do you really go from having your hands all bloody and gory to, I don't know, eating an apple?"

"Uh-huh," Kate said, enjoying her muffin now, feeling the heat and kick of the coffee in her body. "Though it's more likely to be a Pop-Tart than an apple."

"Aren't you supposed to be promoting a healthy diet with your patients?" Nicole said dubiously.

Kate threw the last bite of muffin in her mouth. "I'm very comfortable in my hypocrisy."

Nicole laughed and even John cracked a smile.

Kate wiped crumbs from the muffin off her hands and picked up the large paper cup of coffee, her thoughts wandering back upstairs to the conference room, to the report she was about to give. Questions piled up like a collision in her head.

"So how did you end up here?" John's voice intruded on Kate's thoughts.

"Sorry?"

"I'm just curious. How did you go from toaster pastries in the trauma room to sitting in the NML cafeteria discussing potentially the biggest bio-viral threat in Canadian history?"

Kate felt a hook behind her navel, a disorientation so severe that she was suddenly dizzy. She felt filters over her eyes, a sort of slide show of stills, stacked up and blurry. First the dingy green of the trauma room at Van East, the blinding sun through the wall of windows at Hidden Valley General, driving through the Rockies in the Yukon with Andy, Sunday dinner with her mom and Tyler, joking with Craig at the back of a packed meeting room, the mildew-stained walls of the slum house just ten minutes north of where she was sitting right now. *How did I end up here?*

"Dr. Morrison, are you all right?" Nicole's voice interrupted her thought spiral.

"Yes." Kate managed a small smile. "I'm fine. A little jet lag," she lied easily, her shoulders shifting automatically into a more casual position, her eyes relaxing into a look of fatigue, not stress. Kate ignored the unease that came with the lie, refusing to acknowledge how familiar this was.

"Let's head back upstairs and I'll find you a phone."

A few minutes later, Kate had a small cubicle to herself. She took a long, slow breath before dialing Andy. As the phone rang in her ear, Kate swallowed the last of her unease and double-checked her watch. It was just before seven thirty in the morning in B.C.

"Sergeant Wyles."

"Hi, it's me."

"Kate."

Kate wasn't sure how Andy managed to suffuse that much love, relief, and happiness in such a short word. "Hey, where are you?"

"Still at the hotel. I'm just getting ready to meet Ferris at his office. How are things going down there?"

"So far, so good," Kate told her, feeling her balance beginning to return. "I've got some idea what we're dealing with now, at least as much as the NML has been able to figure out in a short period of time. We're about to go back and discuss what this means for the patients. There are still so many questions."

"I know," Andy said shortly. Kate could hear the tension in her voice. "We've got more than a few down here."

"What's going on?" Kate asked, feeling very far away.

"Ferris and I are attempting to investigate without raising any alarm even though we don't have a clue what we're looking for and all we get is interference from people like Michael Cardiff. It's like finding a small, dangerous needle in a very expensive haystack."

Kate knew how much those kinds of restrictions drove Andy crazy. "What can I do?"

"Do you think your team down there will answer some questions for us? Give us some idea what to look for?"

"I can always ask. You're going to have to be pretty specific. These are lab people, about as far removed from the field as you can get."

"Noted," Andy said briskly. Kate could envision her scrawling in her notepad. "Can you call Ferris's office in an hour?"

"Sure. I guess I should call Dr. Doyle for the patient updates," Kate said unenthusiastically.

"Probably. And be nice, she's getting a lot of pressure from Cardiff and the rest of the hospital board. I think she's holding up pretty well, considering."

"Advice from Andy Wyles to be nice, now there's a change," Kate teased, feeling only the smallest trace of the unease still in her body. Maybe it really was jet lag and lack of sleep.

"Cute," Andy said, sounding half amused, half distracted.

"I'll let you go," Kate said, taking the cue. "Talk to you in an hour."

"Sounds good. Kate?"

"Yes?"

"I love you."

The damp mountain air, Andy's arms around my waist, the rocking of the porch swing.

"I love you, too."

When Kate called the hospital, Dr. Doyle was distracted and brusque. Of the six suspected new cases that had come through the ER, three were confirmed to have the virus, no signs of respiratory distress, no red-flagged histories. Eight new suspected cases, results pending. Harris Trenholm was not improving but was insisting his forty-eight hours was almost up, twenty-four hours early. Kate thanked Dr. Doyle, assured her she would deal with Harris when she got back, and even managed to insert a compliment about how she was holding up.

Kate found her way back to the conference room, her red and white visitor's badge swinging awkwardly around her neck. Everyone was already seated when she entered.

"Dr. Levesque, I was just speaking with Sergeant Wyles, who is heading up the investigation in Hidden Valley, and she has some questions. Would it be possible to have a conference call with her and Constable Ferris in an hour?"

Dr. Levesque looked around the table for confirmation from the others.

"Yes, of course. I only wish we had more information to share."

"I think at this point they could use whatever we've got."

At Dr. Levesque's request, Kate handed over the memory key with all the medical information she had from Hidden Valley General and from Dr. Salinger at Public Health. Kate started from the beginning in September with the first case of suspected influenza. She then focused on Roberta Sedlak, her medical history, the autopsy findings. As the chest x-rays came up on the screen, Kate focused on the details and facts, presenting the case in the most relevant medical detail, forcing any thoughts of the potential new cases to the side. Kate tapped the keypad on John's laptop, and a fresh set of facts, confirmed cases, and autopsy reports raced across the screen in dramatic, macro detail.

The room was quiet as Kate pushed the laptop back towards John, who immediately cycled a few slides back to the graph that had been provided by Public Health on infection rates.

"Newest unofficial information puts those numbers higher. Three confirmed and eight suspected cases," Kate said. "We should have the serological tests back later today."

John opened a new document and created his own graph, inputting the newest information.

"What do you need from us, Dr. Morrison?" Dr. Levesque said.

The list was extensive in Kate's head. A cause, an effective treatment, an antiviral drug. She reined in her thoughts and tried to remain within the realm of possibility.

"Do you see the virus?" Kate finally asked, shifting forwards in her chair. "In the information I just shared with you, do you see the virus? Is it presenting as you would expect? Is it…behaving like you think it would, based on what you know at the cellular level?" Silence again, Kate twisted the ring on her finger, fidgeting with enforced patience. "I know you probably hate these kinds of questions," Kate said sympathetically. "And I'll warn you now that Sergeant Wyles is about to ask a lot more of them."

"Yes and no," Rayna volunteered. "The majority of the patients exhibit influenza-like symptoms, yet the pathogenesis and resulting pulmonary edema in critical patients is more like hantavirus. But it is also acting like the HV1A-CS virus, of which we know almost nothing. So…no."

Rayna spoke without taking her eyes off the screen. Kate heard murmured affirmations from around the table. This information didn't get her any farther ahead, other than to confirm that the small purple-stained slide was exactly what was currently wreaking havoc in Hidden Valley, British Columbia. And for some of the patients, this virus could prove to be fatal. Kate tried not to let her disappointment show. What had she really expected? At least she could see it, at least she was beginning to understand.

"Okay," Kate said finally, looking up at the group. "I think my next questions are going to be similar to Sergeant Wyles's. So instead of making you repeat it, maybe we can call her now."

Kate scrawled the number for the RCMP office in Hidden Valley on a piece of paper and passed it over to Dr. Levesque, who punched the numbers into the tablet on the table.

"Sergeant Wyles? Are we connected?" Dr. Levesque asked, taking her seat again.

"Yes, thanks for your call."

As Dr. Levesque made the requisite introductions on their end and Andy did the same in Hidden Valley, Kate was acutely aware of time. She had less than eight hours before she had to catch her flight back to B.C., and she was just now beginning to feel the pressure.

"Our main focus right now is to try to discover who is behind this. We've spent the last twenty-four hours attempting to uncover any connection to laboratories, virology, immunology, microbiology." Andy repeated the list in short bursts that maybe only Kate could read as frustration. "Nothing. We expanded the list to be more general: pharmacology, genetics, medicine. Again, nothing of interest."

Kate heard Ferris jump in. "Hidden Valley has more of your financial and high-tech types, not so much with your academics."

"Right. So we are looking at two possibilities. One, that the

HV1A-CS virus was made in or around Hidden Valley. Two, that the HV1A-CS virus was imported into Hidden Valley."

"I'd go with the latter," John jumped in. "Whoever created this virus would need some extensive, sophisticated equipment, not to mention access to the live viruses. My guess? Imported from a university lab."

"Why do you say university lab?" Andy asked immediately.

"If you're looking at probability, it's the most likely source. Other than public or private labs, like the NML or the CDC, hantavirus is researched most often at universities."

"I'll need a list," Andy said. "All the universities in North America who are using the live virus to do research."

"Names of the heads of research also?" John asked, typing and talking at the same time.

"Can you do that?"

"It's a shockingly small community," John said drily.

"Then yes. Next question," Andy barely paused before moving on. "Assuming the virus was imported into Hidden Valley, what are we looking for?"

Andy's question was met with silence.

"Think about the kind of containers you would need to transport and store a live virus," Kate prompted. "The size, shape, materials."

"We could generate a list, include pictures, if that would help," Dr. Levesque replied.

"Yes. Next question," Andy said, moving on.

"Wait," Kate cut in, thinking about Andy's request and her own clarification. "High tech and low tech. You need to think about what a lab would use, but also what household items could be used for the same purpose. Think about what you could buy at Walmart that could accomplish the same task."

Four sets of eyes looked at her with incredulity.

"What?" Kate asked, looking around the room.

"Just the thought of someone transporting the hantavirus in, I don't know, a four-dollar Styrofoam container from Walmart kind of gives me the willies," Nicole finally replied.

"Dr. Morrison is right. We can't make assumptions about who is behind this. So a list, high tech and low tech," Andy demanded. "Next, any idea how this virus is being spread?"

"That's our main focus right now, Sergeant Wyles. I'm afraid we have no answer for you," Dr. Levesque answered, almost apologetically.

"I understand. Given what you know, though," Andy pushed. "How can we begin to look?"

"Focus on the hantavirus," Rayna said. "It's spread by rodents. The virus becomes aerosolized so it can be found in the rodents themselves, but also the dust and dirt in their surroundings. Start there."

"Samples, then," Andy said.

"I'm a little confused why you haven't collected samples already," Rayna said with evident contempt.

"Two reasons," Andy said curtly. "Once Dr. Levesque confirmed this was a man-made virus, we weren't convinced we should be looking at how it spreads naturally. More importantly, it will be difficult to collect samples, particularly on private land, without raising alarm. Once the public finds out we are focusing on rodents, we are one Google search away from mass panic."

Rayna had the good grace to redden slightly and Kate was surprised when she spoke again. "Aerosolized means not only that it's in the air but also that it has settled on surfaces. There must be a way to collect samples or swabs that don't raise suspicions."

In her head, Kate pictured Andy and Constable Ferris on one of the Ozarc ranches, kicking up dust as they collected samples.

"That's exactly what we're hoping to do," Andy said. "So thank you all for your time."

"You'll need protective equipment," Kate blurted out, interrupting as Andy tried to sign off. "When you collect the samples, you'll need a way to protect yourselves from the virus."

"Dr. Morrison is right," added John, still tapping away at his laptop. "Though biohazard suits would hamper that whole subtlety approach you're going for, you'll need level three masks and gloves at the very least."

"The Public Health Officer is sending someone up in a couple of hours. He's going to give us a basic safety rundown and a tutorial on collecting samples."

"If it was me out there, I'd want all the protection I could get," John said, making a face. "Take whatever advice that guy gives you."

"Noted," Andy said. "Thanks again for your time."

Dr. Levesque disconnected, the slight whine of the speakers

disappeared, and Andy's voice was gone. Kate quashed the unnecessary concern at the thought of Andy and Ferris being exposed to the virus. Still, she ran through the list of Andy's admitted injuries. Nothing to suggest compromised lungs, nothing that should cause her any alarm. Still…

"Okay, tell me she's six feet tall with a brush cut."

"What?" Kate asked, not sure she'd understood what John had just said. Dr. Levesque was back on the phone, not paying attention. Rayna and Nicole, however, were listening in.

"Agent Wyles or whatever. With that voice, I reckon she's got to be six feet tall with a flat-top. Am I right?"

Kate stared at him. She knew Andy couldn't care less what John or the entire NML or, hell, even what all of Hidden Valley called her. But Kate took it personally.

"She's a sergeant," Kate corrected, her voice hard. "And she's my girlfriend."

John's eyes widened slightly, then his whole face flushed a deep red. He shifted in his seat, his hands fidgeting with his laptop, squaring it to the edges of the table.

"I didn't mean…" he started to say, but Dr. Levesque interrupted, putting down the phone.

"Dr. Morrison, good news. I've got Dr. Peter Hill from the University of Edinburgh on the way down. He's visiting on a lecture tour and just so happens to have some field experience with hantavirus in South America. He's agreed to come down and talk with you, though he's only got an hour."

Kate pushed aside the awkward exchange with John, her worry about Andy, and her sudden and intense exhaustion. "That's great, I've still got a lot of questions about treatment." She looked down at her list, crossed off the questions that Andy had covered and basically avoided eye contact as Dr. Levesque broke up the rest of the team.

Dr. Hill turned out to be short, pompous, and not particularly helpful. The last time he'd seen the hantavirus was over twenty years before in New Mexico, and in the first ten minutes of their meeting, he'd managed to repeat three times that the original hantavirus was genetically distinct from the *Sin Nombre* species Dr. Levesque's team was researching. Kate asked her treatment questions, focusing on the extent of the pulmonary edema he'd seen in his patients, the efficacy of various treatment options, and his input around how the influenza might affect the hantavirus symptoms.

"Oxygen therapy, Dr. Morrison. I can't stress that enough. It's the only thing that worked in the fifty percent of patients who survived," he kept saying, checking his watch.

When Kate asked about steroids, Dr. Hill just shook his head, saying he didn't want to speculate on a treatment he'd never seen as they hadn't had access to that in the field. He did say he would have Dr. Levesque look up the three papers he'd co-authored. Maybe she'd find something of interest in them. Kate, frustrated, managed to thank him for his time as he stood and headed to the door.

"Oxygen therapy, Dr. Morrison!" he called back over his shoulder, as if imparting great wisdom, instead of describing a treatment she had not only tried, but that had already twice proved insufficient.

Kate sighed, rubbed at her eyes, and checked her watch. Just after two in the afternoon, and her flight left at seven-thirty. The disorientation surfaced again, much milder this time, as she remembered where she was. Downtown Winnipeg, a city she avoided thinking about. And she still didn't know enough. Not nearly enough. She felt like she was returning to Hidden Valley empty-handed. This more than anything caused frustration to burn in her stomach.

The frosted glass door of the conference room opened and John walked in, balancing his open laptop on his forearm. He came right over and plunked himself down next to her.

"I'm sorry for what I said earlier. I've got a big mouth, and I'm kind of a jerk, though you probably figured that out already."

Kate gave him a small smile, but didn't say anything.

"Anyway, I'm sorry. I didn't know…" He trailed off.

Kate let him squirm, feeling her own discomfort. *What didn't he know*, Kate wondered, *that I'm a lesbian? And how am I supposed to respond to that? You and me both?*

"Don't worry about it. Apology accepted," Kate said, noting his look of relief as she let him off the hook. She wondered if this was what coming out of the closet meant, a repetition of this uncomfortable scene, constantly managing other people's curiosity and awkwardness, the continuous self-doubt about whether or not she should correct someone's assumptions about her life. And the layers of shame if she decided to just let it go.

"How's the list coming along?" she asked John, breaking the silence, wanting very much to move past this on to more relevant topics.

"I want to run this by you, make sure it fits everything Sergeant Wyles was looking for."

Kate quickly scanned the list of universities and heads of research, not really interested, focusing instead on the pictures and descriptions of containers that could possibly be used to transport and store a live virus. As requested, there were high-tech cylinders and glass vials as well as small foam-packed boxes, dry ice, and small nitrogen tanks.

"How would you do it?" Kate said, looking at the pictures of the containers.

"What do you mean?"

"If you were trying to intentionally spread a virus, how would you do it?"

John thought about this, tapping his fingers on the table in front of him like he was scrolling through his laptop. "Most direct route? Food or water. Most widespread route? Common surfaces or sprinkle it into dust in high-traffic area so it gets kicked up, spread around, and inhaled. That's why the hantavirus has traditionally been so well spread. No one ever suspects the dust because they can't see it when they breathe it in."

"So, you would use different methods of transmission if you were trying to infect one person versus, let's say, a community."

"Right." He suddenly looked uncomfortable. "Not that I've thought about it. You did ask."

Kate had to laugh at him. "Hypothetical, John. It's all hypothetical."

John grinned.

The door to the conference room opened suddenly, and Dr. Levesque walked in, her face serious. Rayna shadowed her, coming over to where Kate sat, pulling the keyboard towards her without asking permission.

"We've tested the most recent samples sent to us by Dr. Salinger. It looks like the HV1A virus is adapting," Dr. Levesque said, her tone grave.

"What?" Kate said, not really caring that she sounded utterly unintelligent. But this piece of information threw her, her overfull brain not able to shift that quickly.

"Four of the most recent cases of HV1A are showing a mutation or adaptation of the original virus," Rayna said, pulling up the purple-stained HV1A slide from earlier and a new one. Kate automatically started categorizing the similarities and differences.

"The protein casing is different," Kate said suddenly, into the silence.

Rayna confirmed with a sharp nod. "We were just concluding that the virus is most likely spread through contaminated dust particles, like hantavirus and not person to person, like influenza, when Dr. Salinger sent over these images. We haven't had enough time to really look at it, but the last four patients are apparently exhibiting a mutated form. One that is spread person to person. Nicole is running the test right now, seeing if it reacts to the protease in the throat and lungs, same as influenza A."

Kate stared at the two nearly identical slides, the phrase *person to person* looping through her head in a continuous, awful chant. She forced herself to say the next words, to ask the next question, to hear out loud the results.

"So the same effects, the same symptoms, the same risk of acute onset pulmonary edema in compromised patients. Just a faster transmission rate." She turned away from the slides to look at Rayna. "Is that what you're telling me?"

Rayna's face was grim.

"I'm afraid that's exactly what I'm saying, Dr. Morrison."

CHAPTER ELEVEN

Kate woke alone in the motel room in Hidden Valley, disoriented and still tired. She watched the bedside clock click over to eight thirty and a peppy, static-driven talk show host announced the wet, cold weather for the day. Kate vaguely remembered Andy setting the alarm on her way out the door to meet Ferris, hours earlier. Kate flicked the switch, got up and showered, feeling the sluggishness in her body, wondering how she'd managed to find her way out of the airport late last night, let alone rent a car and drive to Hidden Valley. Despite her exhaustion, Kate had been anxious to get back here. As she soaped and rinsed, Kate felt a kind of desperation, like something had to break. Soon. Maybe it would be treatment protocol or maybe it would be a solid lead for Andy and Ferris. Considering the bleak look on Andy's face last night, she wasn't feeling any farther ahead either.

As Kate drove the darkened highway to the hospital, it felt like the kind of day when the sun doesn't really rise, and it remains dark and shadowy all day before sinking back into night in imperceptible degrees. The rain didn't help, making her hunch her shoulders and duck her head to keep it all out. In contrast, the windows of Hidden Valley General were bright, warm, and welcoming, as if the hospital had been built specifically to shelter people from days like this.

The first person Kate saw when she pulled her rental car into the parking lot at Valley General was Chris Ozarc, standing outside in the rain looking up at the hospital. In her headlights, Kate caught a glimpse of his sombre face. His expensive grey jacket was completely soaked, as if he'd been there a while. Kate pulled the hood up on her jacket and ducked out in the rain, avoiding puddles as she went.

"Chris?"

Chris turned around at the sound of Kate's voice, and she could see a deep weariness in his eyes. It looked strange, out of place, though Kate knew a privileged life could not protect him from pain. Chris acknowledged Kate with a slight nod of his head, then turned away again, coughing loudly.

"Sick?" Kate said.

Chris shrugged, a spasm of some emotion crossing his face.

"Are you coming in to get checked out?"

"Thinking about it."

They stood silently side by side in the pouring rain, looking up at the inviting lights of the hospital. Kate couldn't tell from here how busy the ER was, though she knew from Dr. Doyle a constant, steady flow of patients had been coming in over the last few days. *And about to get worse*, Kate thought.

Kate tucked her hands in her pockets as cold rain seeped around her wrists. "It could be a long wait, but at least you'll be dry."

Another shrug from Chris.

"There's nobody here you need to worry about," Kate said gently.

Chris turned to her then, his eyes suspicious. Kate kept her expression open, understanding. Whatever judgement Chris had been expecting to see, he didn't find it, and his shoulders slumped.

"Come on in, we'll get you registered in triage and find you a corner that isn't full of screaming three-year-olds."

They walked into the hospital together silently, Chris keeping his head down. Still, his already bloodless face paled even more when he saw the number of people in the ER waiting room. To Kate, it didn't look too bad. It was noisy and chaotic, with almost every chair full, but controlled and efficient. Kate had to wonder if all Chris saw was a room full of people who knew everything about him, who gossiped mercilessly at his expense. Chris stopped and surveyed the waiting room, then backed up slowly.

"Chris—" Kate started.

"I can't," Chris said, barely a whisper, turning to go.

"Wait," Kate said impulsively. She grabbed a piece of paper from the desk and scrawled out her cell phone number.

"If you start to feel worse, give me a call. We'll figure something out. And if you have any trouble breathing, you *have* to come back. Got it?"

Chris stared at the piece of paper, and then back up to Kate. She could see him struggling with something. She waited silently, unmoving.

"Dr. Morrison, the meeting's about to start," Dr. Doyle's annoyed voice came from behind them.

Kate looked back over her shoulder, trying to keep her own annoyance out of her tone. "Yes, thanks. I'll be right there."

When Kate turned back, Chris was already gone, the glass doors of the front entrance closing slowly behind him. Kate sighed, wondering if she'd done enough. A moment later, the doors opened again and a man walked in. Not Chris. Jack.

"Hi, Katie!" Jack's wild, curly hair was plastered against his head, but nothing seemed to dampen his enthusiasm.

"Hey, Jack," Kate said, giving him a quick hug. "Andy said she was calling you in."

"Yep," he said happily. "Just had to finish up a project for Finns, but now I'm here and you guys have got my full attention."

"Good, we're going to need it," Kate said fervently. She was so incredibly happy Jack was here. Something about Jack's youthful smile, his kind brown eyes, and his boundless energy and enthusiasm was absolutely infectious. "Follow me, our team meeting is about to start."

The meeting room was packed. Their small team had grown since the threat of epidemic had heightened after the NML's discovery late yesterday. Dr. Salinger and Ferris were deep in conversation at one end of the table, and another officer Kate had never seen before, young and keen looking, was listening attentively. Dr. Doyle was talking with Dr. MacKay, who looked supremely relaxed. Kate couldn't help thinking that he looked more like the lead singer in a boy band than a doctor. Andy was at the front of the room, carrying on a simultaneous conversation with someone on her cell phone and with a man with light brown skin and salt-and-pepper hair, dressed plainly in khakis and a button up shirt. Mona Kellar sat on her own in the corner, the same hungry, contemptuous look plastered to her face that had been there for the last week.

Andy looked up and caught Kate's eye. She acknowledged Jack with a brief smile, then spoke to the group.

"Quick introductions before we get started," Andy said as Kate and Jack took their seats. "Constable Slater is on loan to us from the Whistler detachment. My partner, Jack Sharpe, will be helping with information gathering. And this"—she indicated the man she'd just been talking to—"is Dr. Ahmed Din, an investigator with the federal branch of Public Health's Emergency Management Team, sent to us by the Provincial Health Officer.

"Given the most recent information that the HV1A virus is now able to transmit person to person, we've gone up one threat level. I'll let Dr. Salinger and Dr. Din explain what that means for health management and community containment. Investigating this as a biological threat, any subtle, under-the-radar approaches we were going to attempt are now too conservative. The RCMP has two objectives. This first is to apprehend the person or persons responsible for making and releasing this virus into Hidden Valley, and the second is to assist with handling the public, as the panic levels will undoubtedly be increasing in the next few days."

Andy paused and looked around the table, meeting each member's gaze, including Mona Kellar's. Andy was too focused, too perfectly controlled to allow any kind of distraction to pull her from her goal.

"Dr. Salinger? You're up."

"The goal of Public Health at this point is also twofold. First, we must track the spread of the HV1A virus, both in its original form and now in its mutated form." Dr. Salinger swallowed, and Kate could only imagine how he'd taken the news the virus was now being spread person to person. "Second, to educate the public. This includes not only the general public, but also communicating with Squamish-Whistler Health and local physician's offices. I believe quite strongly that education and understanding can go a long way in preventing the kind of wide-scale panic that Sergeant Wyles was alluding to. Something we disagree on." Dr. Salinger said it with a small smile.

"We don't disagree with you, Cliff." Ferris jumped in, apparently speaking as the only local representative of the RCMP. "We just think it's important to have both education and a police presence."

"He's right," Dr. Din said from the other end of the room. All eyes swiveled back to the far end of the room. Dr. Din looked to Andy for permission to speak, and she gave it with a curt nod of her head. "Constable Ferris is right. Studies of pandemic viral outbreaks show that the best community outcomes are acquired through a combination of the most up-to-date and transparent information as well as a strong authority presence. What I am trying to say is that you should let the public see that you are working together."

Dr. Salinger and Constable Ferris looked at each other across the table.

"We can do that, no problem."

Dr. Salinger simply nodded, strain still evident on his lined face. Andy looked back and forth between Dr. Salinger and Ferris.

"The public needs to see this whole team work together, especially those of you who are residents here. Disagreements are a natural part of the process and can even help us problem solve, but they happen in here and only in here." She tapped the table with one hand, emphasizing her point. She looked around the room. "Constable Ferris, Dr. Salinger, Dr. Doyle, Dr. MacKay, as the most visible and well-known members of this team, a great deal of that will fall to you."

"You should include Dr. Morrison on that list," Dr. Doyle added. "She has proven herself enough at this hospital and in this community that I think people will look to her for guidance."

Kate tried not to let her surprise show. She hadn't been expecting praise from Valley General's chief of staff this morning. Andy looked at Dr. Doyle, then at Kate. Kate raised her eyebrows ever so slightly to convey her own shock.

"And Dr. Morrison," Andy conceded. "Dr. Doyle, if you could give the hospital updates. It will be the first and most visible response to our increased threat level."

"As of this morning, Valley General Hospital is instituting our viral threat and containment policy." She stood and pulled a cardboard box onto the table, pulling out large white face masks, surgical gowns, and gloves. Kate's face itched just looking at the masks. "All front-line staff will be required to wear protective gear at all times, no exceptions. We are also in the process of isolating one ward for acute patients. I'll update you as I know more. Dr. Morrison and Dr. MacKay, I will be looking to the two of you to run the ER and the containment ward."

Kate looked across the table at Dr. MacKay, who shrugged playfully and smiled. Kate didn't know much about this doctor, but she got the sense he was a bit of a cowboy.

"Lastly," Dr. Doyle said, "all staff is required to report any fever or related flu symptoms to their immediate supervisor. No one is to come to work sick and risk spreading this virus. I will be in contact with Squamish-Whistler Health to work out a plan for maintaining sufficient staff."

"Priority one is the hospital, and that's where we are focusing our efforts right now," Andy was saying as Dr. Doyle took her seat. "Jack is here to work on a website as a joint initiative between Public Health and the hospital. When it's up, you'll all be able to direct inquiries from the public and the media there. Are there any questions?"

Silence.

"Let's meet tomorrow, early. Eight a.m." No one disagreed. Andy was not an easy person to disagree with.

As everyone else rose to put their piece of the plan into action, Kate stayed in her seat, making grooves on the empty Styrofoam cup with her thumbnail.

"I guess we should get to know each other a little better."

Kate looked up to see Dr. Eric MacKay smiling pleasantly. He seemed almost cockily unconcerned about the weight and severity of what they'd just heard.

Kate returned the smile cautiously. "I guess we should." She extended her hand across the table. "Kate."

"Eric," he said, shaking Kate's hand. "You're causing quite a stir here at Valley General. The redheaded doctor who is everywhere at once. Shaking things up."

"Not my intention, I assure you."

"Between the two of us, we should be able to whip this hospital into shape, don't you think?" he asked.

Definitely cocky, Kate decided. But not unreasonable. "I intend to lead by example, Dr. MacKay," Kate said drily. "We'll only bring out the whips as a last resort."

Kate looked over as Dr. Ahmed Din pulled out the chair beside her and took a seat. Up close, his face was much younger than his salt-and-pepper hair would suggest. His brown eyes were kind and apologetic.

"Pardon my intrusion, but am I to understand you two will

be disseminating the information to the hospital staff in terms of precautionary protocols?"

"Yes."

"A word of advice then, if I may." He posed it as a question, treading carefully. "You must find a balance between calmness and adherence. They must understand from the very beginning that there will be absolute and complete compliance with all regulations, but without causing them to panic."

"A healthy dose of fear, then," Eric said, grinning at the man.

"No, not fear," Dr. Din said, not returning the smile. "Fear is exactly what we are trying to avoid."

The grin slid off Eric's face. Kate was glad to see him knocked down, just a little. She was also glad it didn't have to be her who did it, though she was sure Andy would have gotten around to it eventually.

"I was in Toronto," Eric blurted into the silence. "When SARS hit, I was working at a hospital in Toronto."

Dr. Din seemed to brighten at this. "That is good. Tell the staff that. Let them know you have been through this before. It will build their confidence in you as a leader."

"Let's split it up," Kate said to Eric. "You run the ER. I'll be there to back you up, but let's give the staff one person to focus on. I'll take the new acute ward." She scrawled her cell phone number on a paper in front of her, thinking briefly of doing this same thing for Chris Ozarc only an hour ago. Eric took a moment and inputted the number into his phone, quickly texting back his own. "We'll be in close contact. Anything comes up, we'll keep the other in the loop."

Eric nodded, his face serious for the first time. He stood to go. "I'm going to check in with Dr. Doyle. I think the first time the staff hears about the new safety protocols, it should come from her."

"Good idea. I'm going to go check on a few patients." Kate's thoughts instantly went to Harris Trenholm, wondering if he had checked himself out of the hospital yet or if his condition had deteriorated enough to keep him admitted.

"Dr. Morrison?" Kate had almost forgotten about Dr. Din.

"Yes?" Kate was curious about this man and his background. He seemed intensely focused, less so on *what* information was being shared than *how* it was being distributed.

"I am being forward, and I apologize if I make you uncomfortable, but there is something I want to say." He shifted in his seat, his fingers fluttering over the sleeve of his shirt. "I think I have heard and seen enough in the short twenty-four hours I've been here to know that Hidden Valley is precariously balanced right now. This is a community of intelligent and aware individuals but also suspicious and self-centred, I think." He paused, and Kate had to admit he'd pretty much nailed Hidden Valley. "I think you will be key in maintaining the balance. You are a trusted outsider with a transparent agenda. I have been through enough similar scenarios to recognize a key player when I see one."

Kate took a moment to consider Dr. Din's pronouncement. She'd spent less than an hour in a meeting with this man where she'd said very little. Kate decided he must be basing his conclusions on what he was hearing from others. She didn't like the thought of other people talking about her. Empathy for Chris Ozarc welled up in her chest.

"I'll do whatever it takes," she said finally. "But I'm going to need a lot of help."

Dr. Din patted her hand gently. "That's what we're here for."

Ten minutes later, with only a too brief, too public check-in with Andy, Kate went upstairs to what was quickly becoming a closed ward. Orderlies were moving patients through the hall, charts wedged at the foot of beds, and gowned patients inched slowly along the wall railing, supported by nurses and IV stands. Kate checked in at the nurse's station and found Lucy typing quickly into the computer, flipping hard-copy files as she went. She looked up as Kate said her name.

"Hey, you're back! Sorry for the chaos. Dr. Doyle wants the viral containment ward…sorry, Ward B up by the end of today."

"Ward B?" Kate repeated, impressed by how the nurse could carry on a conversation and continue to input data into the system.

"Yes, Dr. Doyle says we need to manage community fears, and that includes the consistent use of medically neutral language." Lucy stopped typing and looked up at Kate. "Any idea what that means?"

Kate looked into the nurse's face, reading stress and annoyance. She didn't blame her, especially as she could imagine how Dr. Doyle would have delivered the message. She briefly thought about her recent discussion with Dr. Din. *Precariously balanced.*

"It means Hidden Valley is about to get a pretty big shock, and the public is going to look to how this hospital deals with the crisis.

So we do our jobs and we do them calmly and we do them without throwing enough medical jargon around to scare the shit out of the people listening."

Lucy looked at her thoughtfully, then nodded. "I'm glad Dr. Doyle put me on your team," she said. The nurse leaned back and sorted through a stack of charts before handing Kate Harris Trenholm's chart.

"You like this team because we've only got one patient," Kate said.

Lucy laughed. "That and I hear you had half a bakery delivered to the ER. I'm looking forward to the perks."

Kate paused in the act of opening the chart, staring at the nurse. Lucy met her glance, then spoke quietly. "I know it's going to be a long haul, Dr. Morrison. But we've got some good people working on this. I'm hopeful."

Kate didn't say anything more as she left to see her patient.

Harris Trenholm's condition had changed very little, and Kate decided this was more than she could have hoped for, given how much time she'd spent in the morgue recently. He was sitting up in the hospital bed, propped up by four oversized pillows, the half table meant to deliver food overflowing with files and a laptop. He looked up as Kate walked in. She shook her head.

"Forty-eight hours…you said…" Harris said through his re-breather mask. Definitely no improvement to lung capacity, Kate decided. She looked at his O2 saturation levels for the last twenty-four hours. Not great, but steady.

"How's the campaign going?"

Harris's eyes brightened. "Exactly as planned."

"Except the part where you're stuck in here."

Harris held up his BlackBerry and pointed at his laptop. "Wonders of modern technology."

This short sentence caused a bronchial spasm, but Harris just closed his eyes and sucked the high-flow oxygen through his mask until it passed. Kate held up her stethoscope, and he nodded and leaned forwards. She heard the rales, the bubbling and crackling of the fluid. It was present but controlled. Against her medical training, Kate willed them to stay that way and not reach the crisis point that had swamped Roberta Sedlak's and Keith Grange's lungs with fluid. She'd started thinking of it as the hantavirus tidal wave.

"Discharged soon?" Harris asked as Kate removed her stethoscope, allowing him to lie back.

Kate gave him a sceptical look. "What do you think?"

"I think you're going to be…on my ass about not…working too much."

Kate laughed. "Smart man. I need to see at least forty-eight hours of oxygen sats in the normal range, and I need to know that the fluid in your lungs is decreasing."

"And that I'm…not contagious," Harris breathed out through his mask.

Kate watched him intently, Harris's eyes never leaving hers. She let it go, deciding not to get into the details of what she knew about the virus.

Harris's BlackBerry vibrated insistently on the table in front of him. "Pardon me, Dr. Morrison…just going to…step into my office."

Kate smiled and flipped his chart closed. "I'll let myself out."

As she walked back to the nurse's station, she could see a crowd had gathered. Eric and an orderly were pulling masks and face shields and gowns out of huge cardboard boxes.

"Your team's gear, Dr. Morrison. The ER has already started the fashion trend downstairs. Face masks and shields are very in this season."

The nurses laughed, though they also rolled their eyes, fingering the thick, itchy fabric of the face mask. Kate pulled out her own gear from the box, putting it on without saying a word.

"We've got a buddy system going on downstairs," Eric was saying, still passing out masks. "Medical professionals are notoriously bad at taking care of themselves but highly effective at managing other people's illness. So, a buddy system. At the start of each shift, you are assigned a buddy. You check for an elevated temp, feelings of fatigue, sniffles. If your buddy passes, they get a smiley face on their gown." Eric pulled a Sharpie out of his pocket, drew a happy face on Kate's shoulder. More laughs from the nurses, more eye rolling. Kate looked down at the upside-down smile, then back to Eric. Kate's confidence in the doctor kicked up another notch.

The hospital quickly became a sea of light blue gowns and full face masks, conversations muted and swallowed by the fabric stretched from ear to ear. Kate admitted only to herself that it was annoying, that it took more time than she felt they had to offer, to slow down her speech, enunciate her words enough for patients and nurses to understand her. She could also feel a shift in the patients, in the people walking through the ER. It wasn't panic, at least not yet. They were quiet, more subdued.

By late that afternoon, Kate was fending off the four hundredth question about where private citizens could obtain the face masks. Kate's explanation that the hospital-grade masks were only for front-line staff was insufficient for the frustrated, overbearing woman in front of her. Kate sighed and leaned up against the admit desk as the woman walked away, making sharp gesticulating motions in the air as she talked on her cell phone. That hadn't gone well at all. She wondered if Dr. Doyle and Dr. Din had been wrong. Right now she didn't seem to be holding on to any public confidence at all.

"Dr. Morrison, could I get a consult?"

Kate looked up to see Eric just down the hall, holding up a chart. She pushed herself away from the desk, feeling an ache in her back.

"Jim Beckett, age seventy-two, severe emphysema, exhibiting flu symptoms, difficulty breathing, and chest pains."

"Ward B candidate?" Kate said, trying to remember her own medically neutral language.

"Tests haven't come back yet. Looks like the lab's backed up."

"I take it we've been sending down more tests than normal today?"

Eric shrugged. "I don't think so. I just know it's taking about four to six hours to get results back."

Kate filed this away, along with the question of how they were going to address the community's need to understand contagion and universal precautions. It was a growing list of things she had to do before her head hit the pillow tonight.

"What do you want to do with him?" Kate said.

"He needs to be admitted regardless. I don't want him exposed to the virus if he doesn't have it, but I'm not sure we should admit him to acute care and risk spreading it if he does."

Kate weighed the risks in her head. He should stay in emerg until the tests confirmed his viral status, but Eric was right. The ER was too busy to keep such a high-risk patient while they waited for test results. "Let's admit him to Ward B. There are enough isolation rooms right now and only one patient. If he needs to be moved after the tests come back, we'll deal with it then."

"Perfect, thanks," Eric said, scrawling in the chart, calling a nurse over and giving the orders. "He'll be yours in an hour."

"Sure," Kate said, distracted, tapping the pen she was holding against her cheek.

"What's up, Red?" Eric asked, pulling her back.

Kate raised her eyebrows. "Kate, Morrison, Doctor…any combination of those three will work for me," Kate told him pointedly.

"My apologies, nicknames are a bad habit with me. What's got you going in circles, Kate?" he tried again, unabashed.

"Labs. I'm curious why they're taking so long. Is there any way to pull numbers off the system?"

"Sure, no problem." Eric moved to the computer, banged at the keys with gloved hands, cursing as he had to correct himself. "Three days ago was our peak at forty-seven submissions. Yesterday we sent down thirty-nine, and today we're already at thirty-six, with another six hours to go until midnight," he said, checking his watch.

"So why the backlog?" Kate asked, knowing he didn't have an answer. Eric shrugged again.

Kate considered going through Dr. Doyle, but she didn't. She told herself it was because Dr. Doyle already had a long enough list of things to deal with. If she was being honest, though, the real reason was she just couldn't handle her passive-aggressive attitude this late in the day.

"Let me see what I can find out," Kate said to Eric, pushing herself away from the desk. "Call me if you need anything."

"Will do, Dr. Kate Morrison," Eric said and laughed.

Kate shook her head on the way out the door. She knew full well she could have been stuck with someone much worse than Eric MacKay. She descended quickly down to the lower level of the hospital, listening to the echo of her own footsteps on the stairs. She scratched again at her mask, wishing she could pull it off and take a real breath. She followed the signs for the lab, pulling out her hospital ID when asked. As she tucked the plastic tag back into her pocket, sliding it in beside her temporary RCMP ID, Kate had to wonder what this pocketful of temporary identification meant about her life.

After asking a few people, Kate found a small, glassed-in area where a man in contaminant protective gear stood against a counter, putting small glass vials into an industrial-sized centrifuge. Kate watched as he closed and latched the lid and pushed a series of buttons.

The whirring of the machine could be heard through the partition. She tapped at the window, and the startled man turned around. Kate guessed he was in his late twenties with dark hair and three piercings in his eyebrow just visible under his white cap.

"No one's supposed to be down here," he said through the glass, by way of greeting.

Kate pulled out her ID and held it up. He grudgingly opened the door.

"I've heard about you. You're the one running the show upstairs."

"One of many, right now," Kate said, unsure how'd she'd gotten this reputation. "How are things in the lab?"

"Backed up," he grunted at her, "which is why I'm guessing you're down here." Definitely defensive.

"Is it just you?" Kate asked.

"Just me." Kate looked at him for a moment, holding back her next question, waiting to see what he would offer into the silence. "Dr. Doyle said she was looking into either more staff, which is useless because there isn't enough room, or not running all the tests in-house which is just as useless because once you add in transportation delays, you might as well just wait for me to do it and not deal with the hassle."

Kate nodded but didn't speak.

"And since she's doubled the number of samples today, there's just no way—"

"Doubled the samples? What do you mean?" Kate interrupted.

"Dr. Doyle herself sent down twenty-eight samples this afternoon. She didn't so much *say* they were priority, but it was pretty clear. And that's on top of all the ER samples you guys keep sending down." He gestured back through the door at his tiny space. "So there are all the reasons for the backup. Take your pick."

Kate took a breath. "What's your name?" she finally asked.

"Ryan. Everyone calls me Trick, though."

Kate had a feeling Eric and Trick would get along just fine. "Trick, how long have you been on shift?"

He seemed surprised by this question. "I got here at seven this morning."

"Almost twelve hours, then."

Trick shrugged. "I've got to catch up somewhere. I figured it might as well be tonight."

Kate gave him a long, disbelieving look.

"Are you going to lecture me now on the occupational hazards of working tired? 'Cause I've got them memorized," he nearly growled.

Kate laughed and again he seemed surprised, his defensive posture relaxing a little.

"No, no lecture. But if you're still here when I leave in a few hours, I'm sending in the cops to haul you out."

"Right," Trick scoffed at her, but she could see the amusement in his eyes.

"Fine, don't believe me. You'll see."

"Is there anything else?" Trick asked, obviously wanting to get back to work.

"No," Kate said. "Thanks for your time, Trick. It was very nice to meet you."

"Sure. See you and the rest of your army in a few hours, then?" he grinned through his mask.

Kate laughed at him as she pushed open the glass doors on her way out. Walking back through the basement maze, Kate cycled through the information Trick had just given her, wondering how she would confirm her suspicions. The sound of a heavy boot tread on the stairs ahead of her startled Kate. Her first thought was that it was Andy, then she changed her mind. Andy always walked so lightly, even in her heavy boots. As she turned the corner, halfway up the stairs, Mona Kellar came into view, an oversized jacket over her T-shirt and jeans.

"Dr. Morrison, to what do we owe the honour of your presence below ground?" Mona Kellar asked. Her grating purr made Kate shudder.

"Dr. Kellar." Kate acknowledged her presence with a quick glance and tried to keep going. The stairwell, however, was too narrow, and Mona Kellar only had to take a small, almost casual step to the side to block Kate's way. Kate considered shouldering past the woman, but the thought of having to touch her, to slide her body next to Mona Kellar's made her hesitate. The hesitation cost her. Dr. Mona Kellar now commandeered the stairwell.

"Where's your guard dog?" Mona Kellar glared down at Kate, who was standing two stairs below, gripping the railing, her knuckles white with strain.

"Don't..." Kate said sharply, then bit her bottom lip, keeping the rest inside.

"Don't what, Dr. Morrison? Don't talk about Ms. Wyles? Don't ask the questions all of Hidden Valley wants answered? You two have become quite the celebrities in this town."

Kate looked back down the stairs, wondering which would take more bravery, to withstand the interrogation or to swallow her pride and retreat. Mona Kellar took one step down, holding Kate's eyes, then another until they were on the same step. Kate looked up the stairwell this time, sensing escape. Then Dr. Kellar leaned in, brushing up against Kate until she cringed.

"A word of advice before you scurry away, Dr. Morrison," Mona Kellar whispered harshly in her ear. "Just because she fucks you doesn't mean she loves you. Just because you can make her come doesn't make you a lesbian."

Kate moved without thinking, pushing Mona Kellar aside with her shoulder and racing up the stairs, her heart hammering in her chest. She made it to the main floor in seconds, leaning against the wall to catch her breath. The lobby was thankfully quiet by now and Kate took a moment, breathing carefully, letting the adrenaline run through and out of her body, her brain, her muscles. She trembled slightly, feeling a sick twisting in her stomach as Mona Kellar's words repeated and rebounded in her head. Kate was angry, embarrassed, ashamed, and she clenched the muscles in her abdomen, squeezing those feelings until they became smaller and smaller, until they barely registered.

Kate heard Andy, the unmistakable tread of her boots down the long hallway. Kate quickly swallowed whatever traces of fear or anger were left, not wanting to deal with a confrontation right now between Andy and Mona Kellar. Because there would be if Andy knew what had just happened in the stairwell. Hidden Valley could not afford to have Andy or Kate distracted by one twisted, sick mind.

"I've been looking for you," Andy said from down the hallway. Even from where she stood, Kate could see Andy was preoccupied, focused somewhere else. Kate gave her a careful smile, trying to not show how desperately happy she was to see her.

"I was just checking in with the lab tech downstairs," Kate told her, letting go of the railing and meeting Andy halfway.

Andy's eyes flicked to the stairwell, then back to Kate. Kate could see her register a question, a suspicion, some intuition flickered behind her grey eyes. Kate jumped in before she could fully form that thought.

"How did things go today?" Kate knew Andy and Ferris had been questioning residents, trying to find the source of the outbreak.

It worked. Andy's eyes darkened. "Not well." She didn't elaborate, but Kate assumed Andy wanted privacy before unloading the frustrations of her day. "How long until you're done here?" Andy said.

"An hour or two, but you can go whenever you want. I've got the rental car," Kate reminded her.

"I'll wait."

Kate didn't argue and Andy's eyes flickered again, as if Kate's lack of fight waved a red flag.

"Give me an hour, then," Kate said. She touched the sleeve of Andy's shirt, running her thumb very lightly over the contoured muscle of her arm. "Let me get this patient settled, and then we'll go."

Andy smiled and let her go. With Andy's eyes on her back, Kate started to feel the weight of all the things she wasn't thinking about, all the things she had pushed aside and pushed away. She hurried up the last few stairs, hoping to outrun it all.

CHAPTER TWELVE

Kate sat in the passenger seat of the Yukon, pulling her sleeves down over her hands to keep them warm. A cold front had settled over the mountains while they slept, reminding them of the winter to come. Kate stifled a yawn, taking a sip of her Judy blend coffee and catching Andy's eye. They smiled at each other but didn't say anything. Having stayed up late last night talking, they didn't feel the need to fill the morning air with random chatter.

Last night had been hard for Kate. She knew it was wrong to keep things from Andy. Not just the latest incident with Mona Kellar, but the growing sense of unease, the questions she had about herself, the all-too-familiar feeling of being lost. But right now, in the face of the growing bioterrorism threat in Hidden Valley, answering or even acknowledging those questions seemed indulgent. So Kate had kept Andy talking. Curled up in her pyjamas and Andy's sweatshirt on the bed, she'd watched Andy pace the room, the frustration of inaction evident in each step she took across the small space.

While Kate had been managing patients the day before, Jack, working through the data he'd been given over the last two days, had given Andy and Constable Ferris the most highly probable infection site as the James Ranch. It linked Tessa James, of course, as well as Chase Noonan and Keith Grange, who had both worked there. Mary Johnston had taken her granddaughter there for riding lessons. But it did not include Roberta Sedlak, who they were having a hard time definitively linking to any of the other patients.

The James Ranch was the best guess, so Andy, Constable Ferris, and Dr. Salinger had gathered their protective gear and headed out.

But Richard James had refused to even allow them on the property, threatening them through the intercom attached to the front gate. Apparently he assumed this was all a set-up by Michael Cardiff to discredit him in the community. Constable Ferris had attempted to be persuasive, holding back a severely pissed-off Andy. Richard James told them to come back with a warrant before he'd let them on his property.

Andy wasn't ready to give up that easily. She and Ferris knew that without a more firmly established link between *all* the initial incidences of the HV1A virus, getting a warrant would be difficult. Going to Superintendent Heath was a possibility, but Andy knew that would be more trouble than it was worth. It would only confirm Richard James's paranoia. So Andy wanted to bring in Kate, thinking her neutral medical stance and her visibility in the community would bring him around.

"Why were you down in the lab yesterday?" Andy said as they drove to the James Ranch. "I never got around to asking you last night."

"Dr. Doyle submitted twenty-eight samples to the lab yesterday on top of what the ER was sending down. I don't know for sure, but I'm guessing most of Valley General's hospital board and their families jumped the queue for getting tested."

"Christ. And here I was thinking Dr. Doyle was starting to stand up to them, when really she was just being underhanded."

Kate took a sip of her coffee. It was nice to have Andy on her side, to share in the frustration.

"Some team leader," Andy grumbled, turning onto a neatly paved side road as the sun began to peek its way through the clouds. "What do you want to do?"

"Confront her," Kate said decisively. "Privately, of course. Make sure she knows how backed up the lab is getting without doubling the samples for no reason other than to make her life easier."

Andy nodded approvingly. "Let me know if I can help."

Kate smiled. "How about another vacation at the end of this? I bet you could find us another cabin in the mountains somewhere," she said, teasing.

Instead of returning the smile, Andy gave her a long, searching look, and Kate's hand trembled lightly. What had she just given away? "I take it you're not anxious to return to Van East?" Andy said, pulling down the visor to block the sun that had erupted from behind the clouds.

Kate blinked, utterly unprepared for this conversation. She sipped her coffee, wondering what her chances were at avoiding this. *Pretty slim*, she thought, as Andy pulled onto the shoulder of the road, a tall black fence separating the road from neat green paddocks.

"I was making a joke, Andy," Kate said sharply, wondering if Andy would back off if she got annoyed.

"I know. But that doesn't answer my question," Andy said, not backing off even a little. Kate hadn't really expected her to. "I know you're struggling, Kate. I know Winnipeg was hard." Andy's voice was soft and Kate swallowed convulsively. Winnipeg had been hard, but not in the way Andy thought. The last time she'd landed in that city, it had been about finding her lost sister. This time, it was not her sister who was lost. "Kate…" Andy waited until Kate looked up. "I know you're avoiding something."

Kate had to look away again, away from those grey eyes that saw to the very centre of her, past any hastily shut doors, past every sad attempt at distraction. Andy could see, she always had. *What does she see that I can't?* Another convulsive swallow. The question was close, too close.

"You don't have to talk to me, you know." Andy was still trying, her voice carrying that sweet, understanding softness that had always tugged at Kate's heart. "Just know that you can. And that you don't have to waste any more energy trying to hide from me."

From me, Andy. I'm hiding from me.

Those were the words Kate knew she should say out loud. She didn't. Instead, she took three slow breaths, counting the spires of the long black fence framed in the side window until those words in her head disappeared. As if the thought had never existed in the first place. Finally she looked at Andy, who waited patiently, quietly, like they had all the time in the world to work this out.

"Thanks," was all Kate said into the silence.

Andy looked at her for a long time and Kate, her defenses terrifyingly low, let her. She didn't know what Andy saw, but whatever it was, it was enough.

"Are you ready for this?" Andy said, indicating the large, black gate in front of them.

More than ready. Anxious to get at something she had some hope of solving.

"Yes. Maybe you should let me do most of the talking?" Kate asked, giving a tentative smile. Andy returned it, put the truck in gear, and eased forwards into the driveway. She then lowered the window, pushed a button on the intercom, and waited until a subdued voice at the other end answered.

"James residence."

"This is Sergeant Wyles with the RCMP. Could you let Mr. James know that Dr. Morrison is with me and would like to speak with him."

"One moment."

The speaker clicked off, and Kate and Andy waited in silence. A moment later Richard James spoke through the intercom. He was angry.

"Sergeant Wyles, I thought I made myself clear yesterday—"

Kate leaned across Andy, raising her voice to be heard through the speaker.

"Mr. James? This is Dr. Kate Morrison, I'm one of the doctors working with the team at Hidden Valley General regarding the community virus. The one linked to your daughter's recent illness."

A brief pause. "Dr. Morrison, are you here to discuss my daughter? Is something wrong?"

Kate could hear the anxiety in his voice, remembered Dr. Doyle describing how overprotective he was of his only child.

"Tessa's fine, Mr. James," Kate reassured him. She was unwilling to play on a worried father's fears to get them in the door.

"Then I fail to see—"

"It's the rest of Hidden Valley I'm worried about," Kate interrupted.

"I don't understand."

"If you would please meet with us, Mr. James. Give us twenty minutes of your time."

Another pause. "All right."

The intercom buzzed, and the huge black gates swung slowly, mechanically on their oversized hinges. Andy followed the long, winding driveway, edged in an assortment of evergreens, the house coming into view as she took the last turn. Even on this cold, grey day, the house set back against the trees was absolutely stunning. Kate's first thought was of the bow of a ship, its most prominent peak coming out from the house at an angle, giving the impression of movement, of moving forwards. The house was a perfect assortment of wood and glass, the expanse of the roof betraying its monstrous size.

"Nice," Andy noted neutrally. "A little on the small side maybe."

Kate smiled. "Any advice before we go in?"

"This is your show, Dr. Morrison. I'm just along for the ride."

"All right, then. Just try not to glower too much, okay?"

Andy scowled playfully, then pushed the driver's side door open. As Kate got out too, her heart suddenly lurched in her chest and she froze. *I love her. God, I love her.* Kate knew she had to get this under control. She couldn't let Andy keep worrying about her, not on top of everything else. Another thought occurred to her, and Kate felt sick at its implications. What if Andy grew tired of always carrying the weight of Kate's worries? What if…

"Kate?"

Andy was at the passenger side door, looking in at Kate, concern in her grey eyes.

Kate looked down at her hand, still clenched around the door handle. She pulled at it, felt the metal give way, and a gust of cold air swept in through the open door.

"Are you all right?" Andy said. "You're so pale."

"I'm fine…I'm good," Kate said as she got out of the truck. She couldn't meet Andy's eyes. "You have Dr. Din on standby for collecting samples, right?"

"Yes, he's with Ferris at the RCMP office," Andy said, frowning. "That is, if Richard James allows it."

"Let's see what we can do," Kate said.

As they approached the massive front door, it opened. A man in a long-sleeved pink polo shirt and neatly pressed khaki pants held the door open and smiled politely. "Sergeant Wyles and Dr. Morrison, Mr. James said he will receive you in his study."

Kate and Andy followed the man down the hall. The house was magazine perfect, the wood and glass and stone of the exterior brought inside to reflect warmth and opulence and a distinct tone of grand comfort. Kate barely noticed the details, only that the house made her feel small. She had never been in such a grand house, had never been *received* anywhere, and was feeling more than a little intimidated at the thought of trying to persuade the owner of this house to do anything he didn't want to. Kate felt her lack of confidence acutely, a hard, immovable line down her chest.

As the man led them through an open door, Kate felt Andy touch her wrist, then trace her thumb in a quick, light pattern across Kate's palm. It reminded Kate of the first day they'd met, the first time Andy had touched her and the amazing, confusing, instantaneous connection between them. Kate remembered also *why* Andy had touched her. Against Andy's explicit orders, Kate had slammed her fist into a patient's chest, restarting his heart. She remembered being so sure of her actions, so confident it was the right thing to do. Now Kate caught Andy's eye, silently thanking her for her absolute confidence.

Richard James sat behind an expansive wooden desk in front of a large window that threw him into dark relief. He was an average-sized man, generically good looking, almost nicely forgettable. As Kate and Andy were shown into the room, Richard stood immediately, came around the desk to shake their hands, and then invited them to sit in one of the chairs set casually around a small coffee table. Kate was surprised and more than a little relieved by the gesture. She wasn't exactly sure how the conversation would go with Richard behind his giant desk. As she sat in the chair, surveying the man in front of her, Kate thought this was the exact opposite gesture to what Michael Cardiff would have made.

"Sergeant Wyles, I see you found another way in," Richard said as a greeting. Kate noticed he didn't seem angry, just very, very cautious.

"Dr. Morrison can be persuasive," Andy said, matching his tone.

"Well then, Dr. Morrison, perhaps you'd like to tell me why you're here. What does my house have to do with the virus circulating through Hidden Valley?"

He was direct. Kate appreciated directness.

"The Public Health Emergency Management team, of which Sergeant Wyles and I are both members, is trying to track down the source of the original viral outbreak. Given the data that has been collected, four of the original five cases can be traced to your property."

This was obviously news to the man. He sat up in his chair. "Who? Tessa, obviously, but who are the others?"

Kate shook her head. "That's information I can't share with you, Mr. James. I am bound to keep their confidentiality just as stringently as I keep Tessa's." It was a not-too-subtle reminder, if he needed it, of her absolute neutrality.

"Yes, of course. I shouldn't even have asked," he said. "I'm just shocked to hear it, that's all." He took a moment to digest the news. "But isn't this thing like any other flu bug? Doesn't it just, I don't know, sweep into a community and then out again?" He waved his hand vaguely in the air to show how easily it could descend and retreat. Kate wished with everything in her soul it could possibly be that easy.

"No, it's not like any other seasonal influenza. It's more like salmonella. There's a point of contamination that can be tracked and then isolated. We're hoping to do the same for the virus."

It was a lie. The HV1A virus was nothing like salmonella, but the PHEM team *was* trying to isolate the point of infection. Kate knew she had left out the most unique and alarming feature of HV1A virus, but it needed to remain with as few people as possible.

"And you think you might find it here? In my home?" Richard asked, a perfect wrinkle of worry across his forehead.

"On your property, yes." Again, Kate wanted to try to give the most accurate information without revealing too much.

Richard leaned forwards in his chair again, running his hand over his mouth. "What do you need from me?" he finally asked.

"We'd like to bring in a team to take samples," Kate said, without elaborating.

"What does that look like?"

"They'll come in biohazard suits and collect dirt and dust, mainly, and take swabs from common surfaces," Andy added, better than Kate at evasive responses.

"In the house," he clarified.

Andy kept her eyes on Richard, her expression unreadable. "And the outlying buildings."

Richard held the look, obviously thinking about the virus in his home and on his property. And how it had gotten there.

"How many staff do you have, Mr. James?" Andy jumped in.

Kate mentally shook her head. Why had she even bothered using these diversionary tactics on Andy? Andy had them perfected.

"In the house? Six regular staff. If you want to include the whole property, closer to twenty."

Kate made a mental picture of that number of staff, working and interacting on this massive farm. She thought about Chase Noonan and Keith Grange, working on more than one farm. It didn't make sense. Out of a possible thirty people potentially exposed to a virulent bug, only three were sick? She considered her conversation with John at the NML, how different it could look if the target was a few people as opposed to an entire community.

Kate tuned back into the conversation.

"You have my permission, of course you do," Richard was saying. "But why didn't you share this with me yesterday?"

"It wasn't information I really wanted to share over an intercom, Mr. James," Andy said.

"You must think I'm a fool, acting the way I did yesterday. I will admit that Michael Cardiff's bid for MP has me more than a little paranoid."

Kate felt Andy shift, very slightly, almost casually in her chair. Kate noticed because Andy didn't fidget, certainly not in front of someone she was questioning. Going with her gut, Kate pressed him on the subject.

"May I ask why?"

"A long history. You'd have to be a resident of Hidden Valley to truly understand how interconnected everything is out here." He looked back and forth between them. "It's not a very interesting story, I assure you. Michael and I disagree on a great number of things, and at the end of the day, I just don't trust him to do right by me, my family, or this community." He paused, like he was considering saying more. Then he turned to Andy. "Will you be getting started on the samples today? I'd like this done before my wife and daughter get home this afternoon."

"Right now, if possible," Andy said, pulling out her phone. Kate assumed she was texting Ferris and Dr. Din the go-ahead.

"I'll have my property manager show you around." He stood up and picked up the phone on his desk, speaking into it quickly before setting it down again. "His name is Tony, he'll meet you out front." Richard reached forwards to shake their hands again. "Let me know what else I can do to help."

Ferris pulled up outside the massive James house less than fifteen minutes later. Dr. Din began pulling on biohazard gear, a puffy, thin white suit with a built-in face shield and a rubber mask which looked shockingly uncomfortable. Dr. Din didn't seem to care as he moved efficiently, preparing his tool kit full of swabs and bottles and clear evidence bags. Ferris also began the process of putting on the suit. A second pair of eyes, Kate assumed, as well as a measure of protection.

After seeing Dr. Din and Ferris off with a clearly suspicious Tony, Kate and Andy got back in the Yukon and began their trip back to town. Just down the road from the James Ranch, they pulled up to a flashing red light strung across the road, announcing to nobody else that it was a four-way stop. Andy leaned over suddenly and kissed Kate on the cheek.

"What was that for?" Kate asked, laughing, grateful Andy knew how to pull her out of her own head, as usual.

"I like working with you. It's very helpful to have you there reading my mind when I'm questioning someone."

"Well, it's probably good you didn't decide to make out with me at the James residence."

Andy leaned in again and kissed Kate on the lips this time, lingering just long enough for Kate's heart to begin racing in her chest before she pulled away again.

"Too many cameras," Andy said, eyes shining.

"I didn't see any cameras."

"That's why you're the doctor and I'm the cop." Andy put the car in gear again, surging through the empty intersection.

They were quiet as Andy wound their way back towards Valley General. A few fat drops of rain splattered against the windshield before the sun made a brief, bright appearance.

"How long until the samples are back?" Kate asked.

"Two to three days minimum, I've been told."

"And until then?" Kate asked, curious where the investigation led next.

"We're still looking into how the virus was transported. We're hoping it will give us some physical evidence to follow. We wanted an RCMP officer with Dr. Din, to be on the lookout for anything that looks like it could have been used to transport the virus into Hidden Valley. We've still got very little to go on, no clear targets or motives or patterns in who was infected."

"And now that it spreads person to person, there's no way to even guess if anyone was exposed intentionally or accidentally," Kate added, following Andy's thought process.

"Exactly, which means a full ER for you and virtually meaningless data for us."

Kate skipped from an image of the packed ER to the graph she'd shown the team at NML to the boxes of files she'd mined on her first day in Hidden Valley. She thought about the first cases, the tenuous links they'd found between the original four cases. She wanted to trace it backwards, understand the *when* and *where* of their exposure to the HV1A virus.

"We need to know how long." Kate blurted the half-formed thought into the silence.

"What do you mean?"

"How long from exposure to the onset of symptoms. It would give you a timeline, a rough estimate of when the original four were exposed to the virus. From there…"

"It could tell us where they were," Andy finished the sentence for her.

"Maybe. Hopefully." Kate cautioned.

"Do they have that information? The NML, can they figure that out?"

"When we get back to the hospital, I'll call Dr. Levesque."

"Good, let me know what you find out," Andy said. The hint of the playfulness in her tone was gone.

As they pulled into the Valley General parking lot and walked quietly beside each other, Kate's thoughts were already in the building, two floors up with her patients, when she heard Andy mutter under her breath beside her.

"Here we go."

Kate looked up at Andy's stony expression, then saw the figure who had detached itself from the shadow of the front entrance. She couldn't place him for a moment, then she realized it was Paul Sealy from the *Squamish Herald*.

"Sergeant Wyles, could you comment on the team of scientists who are currently investigating the James Ranch in connection with the viral outbreak?"

Andy kept walking until she was right in front of the reporter. "Did you get your invitation to the press conference this afternoon?"

"Yes, uh, thanks for that," Paul replied, somewhat awkwardly. Kate kept her face neutral, though she wanted to smile.

"Then we'll see you this afternoon," Andy said politely but dismissively as she continued walking into the building.

"The team led by Dr. Ahmed Din, currently on the James farm. Could you comment on what's happening right now?" he tried again.

Andy stopped and pinned down the man with an unflinching glare. "Let me guess, you followed the van but couldn't get onto the property."

Paul didn't answer, just lifted his chin somewhat defiantly. He was very young, Kate realized, having been fooled by the beard.

"We'll see you this afternoon," Andy said again, this time firmly, and kept walking into the hospital. As Kate hurried to keep up, she saw out of the corner of her eye as Paul scribbled something furiously into his notebook.

"Always making friends, aren't you?" Kate said under her breath.

"You know me," Andy muttered.

Kate stopped at the main desk to pick up her compulsory mask and gown when she heard Andy for the second time.

"And again…"

A second later and Michael Cardiff was on top of them. "We need to talk," Cardiff said, his voice an angry hiss.

"Okay," Andy responded calmly.

"Not here," he said, leaning in slightly. Kate felt the inherent threat in the gesture, even when it wasn't directed at her.

"I can speak with you here or in four hours at the RCMP office downtown. Which would you prefer?" Andy said. Either Cardiff hadn't learned bullying Andy would get him nowhere, or it had never failed him before and he had no backup plan. Kate imagined it was the latter.

Cardiff looked around at the number of people moving around them. They had caught more than one person's attention, Kate noticed. Cardiff and Andy were difficult people to overlook.

"I imagine this is not information you want out in the general public, Sergeant Wyles. Please be assured that I keep your best interest at heart also when I ask for a private meeting." His voice had lost the hiss, replaced by the slick politician.

Andy's eyes grew hard but her tone never changed. "You're right. Follow me."

With a quick glance at Kate, Andy turned and walked towards the office that had become PHEM headquarters. Kate picked up her mask and gown and followed, sure in that moment Andy wanted her there. A witness perhaps, or another set of eyes. Or to read her mind the way she'd done with Richard James just an hour earlier.

Andy took a seat quickly, her back rigid, her eyes not betraying a hint of the contempt she held for the man. Once everyone was seated, Andy spread her hands on the desk, gesturing for him to get started.

"I'm hearing rumours that the virus that's spreading in Hidden Valley was released intentionally," Cardiff said, eyeing Andy very closely as he said it. Kate quickly covered her own shock, not nearly as practiced as Andy in the art of neutrality.

"Part of the RCMP's role in a public health crisis is to manage circulating rumours," Andy said, almost immediately. "I'd like to know where you heard this."

"Doesn't matter," Cardiff said with brisk wave of his hand, still trying to read Andy's reaction. She wasn't giving him anything.

"I'll let you know if it matters, Mr. Cardiff," Andy said sharply. "Where did you hear this rumour?"

Cardiff stared at her for a long time, passively attempting to engage Andy in a pissing contest. Andy kept eye contact, pulled out her notepad and a pen, and the sound of them smacking on the table in front of her was loud in the silence.

"A business associate I know whose brother-in-law is on the hospital board said he heard something," Cardiff finally offered up, watching intently as Andy scribbled in her notebook.

"Is that it?" Andy asked, looking up again.

"Yes." He seemed taken aback at the casualness of her question.

"I will follow up on it," Andy said, flipping shut her notebook, making as if to rise out of her seat.

"I'd like a confirmation or a denial, Sergeant Wyles," Cardiff said, the anger back in his tone.

"I can't, Mr. Cardiff, as I'm sure you already know. The Public Health Emergency Management team has strict protocols which we are following rigidly in the face of this crisis. Circulating rumours, such as the one you are presenting us with right now, is one way to induce panic in a community already in a heightened state. Rest assured I keep Hidden Valley's residents', who I understand you hope to make your constituents, best interests at heart when I refuse to elaborate."

Kate felt like cheering.

Cardiff clenched his hand into a fist, then almost immediately relaxed it. "I suppose I should thank you for your time," he finally said, the insult evident in his tone.

Andy said nothing.

He turned suddenly to Kate, leaning back in his chair, aiming for a casualness that fooled nobody. "I don't suppose you'll tell me anything either, will you, Dr. Morrison?"

"I'm bound by the same protocols that Sergeant Wyles just spoke about, Mr. Cardiff," Kate said quietly.

"Closing ranks, I see," the man said, smirking almost suggestively.

What is it with these people? Kate thought as the anger rose, unbidden, in her chest.

"Are you questioning our motives, Mr. Cardiff?" Kate asked.

Cardiff didn't say anything, leaning back in his chair with a look on his face Kate was sure he wouldn't have used on Andy. As it was, Kate could see Andy's shoulders tense, her jaw lock, the protective instinct triggered. Kate had a brief moment to be thankful she hadn't told Andy about the incident with Mona Kellar in the stairwell before she focused back on Cardiff.

Kate tried to end it. "The situation in Hidden Valley is far too critical for you or any other resident to not be a hundred percent confident in the team leading them through this crisis. Any concerns you have should go to my supervisor, Staff Sergeant James Finns." Kate paused. "Or I suppose it could go directly to your father-in-law," she finished quietly.

It was her own version of a threat, one she knew he would not hesitate to slap back on her or Andy if things were not going well. But right now he had nothing to go on, no complaint other than the fact that he did not like being left out of the loop.

Cardiff stood. "I'll thank you both for your time. You have given me a great deal to think about." He left the room, closing the door firmly behind him.

Kate and Andy looked at each other from opposite ends of the long table.

"This is going to get messy, isn't it?" Kate asked.

"Yes. And quickly," Andy answered, her eyes still on Kate, though also somehow faraway. Distracted.

Kate's phone buzzed in her pocket, she pulled it out and read the text. Lucy, Ward B. Kate stood. "I have to go. I'll call the NML when I get a chance, okay?"

"Yes, text me if I don't answer my phone," Andy said. "I think I need to talk to Finns, figure out the best way to handle the press conference this afternoon."

"I'll be up on Ward B or in the ER if you need me."

"Okay."

Kate closed the door quietly behind her and pulled the mask over her face as she ascended the stairs. She wondered how many times she'd been up and down these stairs in the week that they'd been here. They felt familiar already, the time it took to climb them giving her just enough space to clear her head and prepare for the next meeting or crisis or problem.

"Dr. Morrison, I didn't know you were in the hospital," Lucy called from down the hall.

"Just got here. What's up?" Kate asked, wondering what had the nurse so stressed.

"Jim Beckett's been stable since he checked in. Then about an hour ago, his O2 sats started falling, and he admitted to continued difficulty breathing as well as chest pain." Lucy handed her the chart as they walked down the hall towards the older man's room.

"Last films?"

"You saw them this morning," Lucy answered. Kate hadn't remembered any change from when he was admitted. She had been cautiously optimistic, but that was gone now. "Send him down for a repeat, ASAP," she said, quickening her pace.

Lucy started to turn, then stopped. "Wait, you haven't been checked in, Dr. Morrison. Any elevated temperature, cough, or difficulty breathing?"

"No."

Lucy pulled out a marker, happy-faced Kate's shoulder, and then she immediately headed back to the nurse's station to fill the orders for the patient.

As she walked, Kate scanned the chart quickly, reading the

information she already knew. Rebreather mask at one hundred percent oxygen, diuretics and steroids on board. She knew the next step was a ventilator. Kate hadn't spent too much time with her second Ward B patient, but she had a feeling that the ventilator was going to be a tough sell.

Jim Beckett reclined in an uncomfortable-looking half-sitting position, sucking at the air coming through his mask. Kate took in his pale face, the scared look in his watery blue eyes, and without saying anything, she pulled his mask away. His lips were dusky, a sure sign not enough oxygen was getting in.

"Mr. Beckett, the oxygen therapy isn't working. We need to put in a tube to help you breathe," Kate said directly, knowing she didn't have time for another chest x-ray.

Jim Beckett shook his head. "Don't want it," he gasped out.

She'd been up against patients like this before. "What do I need to do to convince you?" she said, hoping to bypass the usual routes.

The man smiled a blue-lipped smile. "Direct…I like that," he said, his voice barely audible. "Save your breath…no ventilator…unless you can guarantee…that I'll get off it."

Kate frowned. "I think you know I can't. I *can* guarantee that if your oxygen saturation levels don't go up soon, then you are going to begin to feel dizzy and the chest pains are going to get worse. Your heart is working too hard to deliver too little oxygen to your body."

"I know how it works, Doctor…still don't want it…"

Kate sighed and threw the chart onto the foot of the bed. She found a stool and pulled it up to the railing of the hospital bed and sat down.

"Let's play a game," Kate said to the man, surprising him.

"Better not be…a smoking lecture…" he grumbled.

"Nope. I'm guessing I'm about five decades too late for that."

Another blue-lipped smile. "Six."

"There you go, then. So, I'm going to try to guess the three words most often used to describe you. And I only get ten words total."

Kate saw the blue eyes light up. "Seven," he countered.

"Fine, no problem," Kate said, shifting in her seat, thinking. "Stubborn," she guessed.

"Too easy," he said.

"Doesn't matter, one down, two to go," Kate told him. "Smart," she tried again.

Jim Beckett looked surprised. "I'll give it to you…though it's usually…followed by *ass*."

Kate had to laugh. She wondered, though, as she caught a glimpse of his monitor, if she had any hope of changing this man's mind about the ventilator. Kate didn't want him to know she was frustrated at being unable to talk him into the treatment. As she took the rest of her guesses, mainly variations on stubborn, Kate tried very hard not to picture the tidal wave of fluid and infection that had recently haunted her dreams.

"I give up," she told him. "What's the last one?"

"My wife…when she was alive…always called me sweet," Jim said, the softness in his voice having little to do with his lung capacity.

Kate put her hand out to the man, feeling his racing pulse on the inside of his arm.

"All right then, Mr. Stubborn, Smart, and Sweet, what's it going to be?"

He shook his head and Kate's heart sank. "No ventilator."

"Do you understand that by refusing the ventilator, you are limiting the measures we can take to save your life in the event that you stop breathing or your heart begins to fail?" Kate asked, her hand still touching the man's warm arm.

"I understand…I'll sign to that effect."

Kate sat with him for a moment longer, not saying anything. "Okay," she said finally and stood up. Jim reached out for her hand and gave it a squeeze.

"Thanks," he said.

"For what?"

"No lecture."

Kate walked quietly out of the room as he lay back, each forced breath barely strong enough to make it to the next one.

Back at the nurse's station, Kate asked Lucy about his family. He had two kids living in the States, both of whom had been in phone contact already. Kate then checked on Harris Trenholm and was surprised to find him sleeping, his laptop open, his BlackBerry with its blinking message light on the half table. She checked his vitals—unchanged—and then left again quietly.

An hour later, Kate was winding up her phone call with Dr. Levesque at the NML when the code blue was called for Jim Beckett's room. She slammed down the phone, instinct pushing her forward, itching to wrap her hands around the flexible tracheal tube. But as Kate entered the room again, Lucy calling out his rapidly dropping vitals, she remembered the man's refusal.

Kate went right up to the rails of the bed, looked Jim straight in the eye. "Mr. Beckett, your heart isn't getting enough oxygenated blood. Unless it does, soon, your body is going to shut down. Do you want a ventilator?"

A shake of the man's head.

"In the event that you stop breathing or your heart stops beating, do you want us to take heroic measures to save your life?"

They were words Kate hated to say, an admission of her failure, or at the very least a directive of passivity and impotence. Two things Kate hated. She took a deep breath and watched Jim's face carefully. This wasn't about her.

"No…no measures…"

Kate turned to Lucy. "Could you witness, please, Lucy," Kate said quietly.

Lucy picked up the chart, printed in her neat block lettering and passed it over to Kate. She signed, then closed the chart, giving it back to Lucy to take away. They weren't going to need it. Kate held his hand. With the drugs in his system to try and make him more comfortable, it wasn't long until Jim was unable to speak. They sat in silence for longer than Kate could account for.

Jim Beckett's eyes were closed when he died. His last words had been his own directive to let him pass peacefully. As Kate turned off the monitors, pronouncing his time of death, she couldn't decide if this was a cause for joy or sadness.

Lucy took over with calm efficiency, handing Kate the chart and the forms she needed to fill out and sending her back to the nurse's station. Kate sat at the desk and phoned Jim Beckett's two children, managing the daughter's instant, unchecked grief. The son's shock came in the form of continuous questioning, but Kate knew he'd never remember the answers.

Finished with the forms, finished with the phone calls, including one to Dr. Doyle, Kate called up the files on the computer. She clicked through x-rays, autopsy results, oxygen levels, viral loads, white cell counts, steroid dosages, and a hundred other factors for the forty-three people who had now tested positive for the virus. The clicking of the mouse became a steady rhythm as facts and files raced across the screen and raced through her head. Kate knew she should phone Andy, should update her on what she'd learned from Dr. Levesque, but instead she continued her obsessive searching.

The phone ringing on the desk behind her jarred Kate out of her half-conscious daze. Lucy picked it up, then looked over at Kate and spoke quietly before putting the receiver back down again.

"Dr. Morrison, Sergeant Wyles is in the ER."

Kate looked at the nurse, confused. "Does she want to see me?"

"No, I mean she's being treated in the ER. That was Dr. MacKay, Sergeant Wyles is in the ER, something about a face lac…"

CHAPTER THIRTEEN

Kate ran down the hall, halfway down the stairs before she thought clearly. A laceration. Lucy had mentioned a face lac. Not a gunshot, not a bullet, not her heart, not her lungs, not her vital organs. Still, the panic continued until Kate rounded the corner of the curtained-off area and saw Andy sitting on the edge of the gurney, holding gauze to her right temple.

"It's just a cut," Andy said instantly, reading Kate's panic. Kate said nothing, letting her heart rate return to normal as she looked at Andy, injured but whole, sitting in front of her. Blood had dripped onto her collar and Kate noticed that it had already lost the shocking brightness of fresh blood. She stored this fact for a moment as she approached Andy sitting on the bed.

"What happened?" Kate asked, taking the gauze from Andy and lifting it gently. A three-inch laceration cut diagonally from just above her brow line towards her right temple. The edges were slightly jagged and uneven, something sharp enough to break skin, but not sharp enough to do it cleanly.

"Someone was trying to break into my truck in the parking lot," Andy said quietly. Kate stopped inspecting the wound for a moment to look at her. *A suspect?* "Who?" Kate asked, also keeping her voice low.

Andy shook her head, frustrated, but Kate held her chin and stopped her from moving.

"I don't know. It was too dark to see anything. I chased whoever it was into the trees behind the hospital, up into the mountain. I got close but a branch snapped back and caught me here…" She pointed to her temple. "And I lost them."

"When was this?" Kate asked as she snapped on clean gloves. She touched the edges of the laceration lightly, half thinking about the best way to close the wound, half picturing Andy running full-out through a pitch-black forest after a suspect.

Andy shrugged. "A couple of hours ago, two maybe."

Kate shook her head but made no comment.

"Ferris and Slater are out there now, but I don't think they'll find anything. Too dark." Kate noticed the way Andy flexed her hand, clenched it around her leg. She hated sitting still right now.

Dr. Eric MacKay pulled back the curtain around the bed. "I thought you'd want to take a look," he said to Kate.

"Thanks. Do you guys have plastics on call?" She ignored Andy's glare.

"It's Hidden Valley, Dr. Morrison. Of course we have plastics on call," Eric said drily. "Might be another hour before he can get here, though."

Kate looked at the wound again, Andy's grey eyes now silently shooting daggers at her. "Could you call him?"

"Sure thing. Let me know if you need anything else."

Andy waited until he was out of earshot before launching her protest. "Plastics? Seriously?"

"It's a large, uneven laceration on a highly visible part of your face. So yes, plastics."

"I don't care what it looks like, Kate."

"You'll notice I didn't ask for your opinion," Kate said, still manipulating the jagged edges of torn flesh.

"Can't you just stitch it up and get me out of here?"

"If you don't mind, I'd prefer not to be responsible for more than one horrible scar on your body," Kate said evenly.

Andy went perfectly still, then she lifted her hand and rested it against Kate's arm. Kate looked her in the eye.

"You think you're the only one who irrationally blames themselves for the other's scar?" Kate asked.

Again, Andy said nothing, staring silently into Kate's eyes.

"I see it all the time," Kate continued softly. "I can hear myself refusing to go with Angler out of the hotel room. I can see that man kicking you in the side, punishing you for my refusal. And every time

I see that awful scar above your hip, I think about how long it took you to get it looked at because you were taking care of me."

Andy ran her thumb along Kate's arm, from her wrist up to her forearm. "You don't have to carry that, Kate."

Kate yanked at the sleeve of her gown, pulling it up over her elbow until they could both see the pink scar. "And you don't have to carry this. But I know that you do."

Andy looked at Kate, then reached up and touched the scar with her thumb, running it up and over the pink line, lightly at first and then with more pressure. As if she was trying to smooth it away with her touch.

Andy dropped her hand. "Fine. Plastics. How long do I have to sit here?"

"A couple of hours, probably," Kate responded, pulling down her sleeve again. "Why don't you give me an update? I haven't heard anything all day."

"Sure. I need to check in with Ferris, and then I'll give you an update. Not here, though."

"You call Ferris, I'll find a room."

A few minutes later, they were in the small suture room with the door closed. Andy had a sterile blue cloth wrapped around her shoulders and neck as Kate used a syringe to irrigate the wound, wanting it clean and ready when the doctor arrived. Andy didn't wince once, even as Kate probed deeply with the syringe, spraying saline down into the wound.

"How did Ferris and Dr. Din make out this morning at the James Ranch?"

"Apparently, it was pretty straightforward. Nothing to cause Dr. Din any alarm, and Ferris didn't find anything that could resemble any kind of virus containment device," Andy said, sitting perfectly still. "The samples are off to Vancouver, but results will take a few days. Not surprisingly, there were a lot of questions about the collection of samples at the press conference."

Kate stopped. The press conference earlier in the afternoon had completely slipped her mind. She had been sitting in Jim Beckett's room, holding his hand.

"Shit, I totally forgot," Kate said.

"Don't worry about it. You didn't need to be there. I don't think you would have liked it much anyway," Andy added with a small smile.

"Why?"

"You tend to get irritated when people verbally attack me."

Kate shrugged, put down the syringe and pulled the magnified light over. "Close your eyes for a minute." Andy complied and Kate satisfied herself no debris remained in the wound. She flicked the light off again and put a sterile bandage over the laceration, taping it in place. "The media gave you a hard time?"

"The media and then Dr. Doyle. She and I met just after the press conference."

"What? What's her issue this time?" Kate could feel her temper flicker in her stomach.

"To be fair, I had just accused her of putting the community in jeopardy and slowing down the testing process by allowing an information leak."

Kate stopped cleaning up the gauze and saline. "How did she react?"

"Well, she didn't deny it and proceeded to give me several shockingly lame excuses for her behaviour. When that didn't work, she threatened to have me thrown out of the hospital."

Kate looked at Andy, stunned. "And you…"

"As the lead of the PHEM team, I threatened to have her removed as chief of staff at Valley General, to be reinstated once the health crisis has passed, unless she could ensure that all information would be secure," Andy said succinctly.

Kate blinked. "I bet that went over well. What did she do?"

"I didn't exactly leave her a choice," Andy said. "So she's promised to run all decisions through the team, but I'll keep an eye on her in case she decides to hide something."

"You're not an easy person to lie to," Kate said as she checked her watch, thinking the plastics consult should be here anytime. She missed the look Andy was giving her.

"And yet you do it all the time," Andy said softly. Kate looked up, searching Andy's face, a trace of panic in her chest. "I won't ask you anymore how you're doing because I don't think I can take it if you lie to me one more time."

The panic multiplied, Kate flinching with its impact. "I lost another patient," Kate blurted out. "About an hour ago. That's where I was during the press conference."

Andy touched Kate's hand, a light touch. "I'm sorry," she said. They both knew that wasn't the extent of it. Not even close.

They were interrupted by a knock at the door, Eric coming in followed by a man with grey hair and a full beard. His eyes were kind as he smiled.

"Dr. Morrison, this is Dr. Fullworth. And this is Sergeant Wyles, our patient."

Eric indicated to Kate that he needed to talk to her as Dr. Fullworth began washing his hands in the sink. Kate could feel Andy's eyes on her back as she left the room.

"I hear we lost Mr. Beckett," Eric said when they were just outside the suture room door. "He refused treatment?"

Kate did nothing but nod. Eric could read the chart if he wanted all the details.

"I've got two more Ward B candidates for you," Eric continued, taking Kate's cue. "Brothers. Age thirty-one and thirty-four, rising stars in the Hidden Valley financial community, so very high profile," Eric added.

"Great," Kate mumbled, taking the charts that Eric held out for her.

"Both had severe asthma as kids, both hospitalized more than once with collapsed lungs. Grew out of the worst of it in their mid-twenties."

"Meds?" Kate asked, scanning the charts.

"This is where it gets interesting. One takes a daily low-dose prednisone because his asthma is still exercise-induced."

Kate looked up at Eric. "Both presenting with fluid build-up?"

"Yes, I just sent them down for x-ray and the samples are already downstairs in the lab."

"Good. Perfect," Kate said, her thoughts on three different floors: the ER, Ward B, the lab. "I want to push the steroids, high dose, right away. There's a reason Harris Trenholm is still with us and Jim Beckett isn't. And let's meet tomorrow morning after the PHEM meeting. You, me, Dr. Salinger, and Dr. Kellar, let's run a differential and see what we come up with."

"Will there be an autopsy on Mr. Beckett?" Eric said.

"I think that's pretty much a guarantee." Kate handed him back the charts.

Eric left to transfer the patients upstairs, and Kate walked back into the suture room. Andy was lying on her side on the gurney, a sterile drape over her face and Dr. Fullworth bending over the opening, inspecting the skin.

"Just waiting for the freezing to take effect, and then I'll get started. A little tricky with these edges, but I should be able to close it up with minimal scarring."

Kate wheeled over a stool and sat in front of Andy.

"Dr. Morrison, am I to understand that you are a lifer over at Van East ER?" Dr. Fullworth asked, his eyes twinkling.

Kate looked up, surprised at how familiarly he spoke about her hospital. "I don't know if I qualify for lifer status, but that's my day job." It seemed like a strange way to describe the job that, until recently, had been her entire life.

"Oh, well, anything over five years qualifies as lifer in my books. I know the population you serve, Dr. Morrison."

Kate looked at the man carefully, trying to figure out how a plastic surgeon from Hidden Valley had any connection to the grime and crime of downtown Vancouver.

"Are you Dr. Sean Fullworth, by any chance?" Kate said. "As in founder of the Fullworth Clinic?" Kate referred to the eastside drop-in clinic that provided day-to-day medical services for Vancouver's poorest and sickest residents.

"The very same. Though I regret on a daily basis I allowed them to use my name. Too high profile," Dr. Fullworth said. He picked up a small needle and touched the tip carefully to different spots around Andy's cut. "Sergeant Wyles, can you feel that at all?"

"No."

"Good, I'll get started, then." He picked up the suture materials and very precisely began to pull the jagged edges of skin together. Kate knew she'd been right to call him in. Her own attempt would have definitely left Andy worse off. "Are you wondering why a plastic surgeon opened up a clinic to service the homeless and destitute, by any chance?"

"Yes."

"I was a trauma surgeon years ago. Decades ago, really. My wife grew tired of the hours, though, tired of being a single parent to three very rambunctious kids in a city she hated. So I pursued a more family-friendly specialty, and we moved to Hidden Valley. But I couldn't stand leaving it behind. I hated being surrounded by the *haves* just as much as my wife despised having to live in the city so I could work with the *have nots*. So we joined forces and opened a clinic."

Kate continued to watch him work, trying to imagine the shift from being a trauma surgeon in downtown Vancouver to a plastic surgeon in Hidden Valley. How did those two things even exist in the same space? Didn't those two identities compete and battle on a daily basis? And how could he possibly allow someone else, even his wife, to dictate the direction of his life?

"It seems impossible to you, doesn't it?" Dr. Fullworth asked kindly, looking up at Kate. "That level of compromise seems unimaginable."

"I guess it does."

"When you two have been married for thirty years, we'll talk then. The world looks very different from this end, let me tell you," he said, laughter in his eyes.

Kate didn't bother being surprised by his knowledge of her relationship with Andy. It was all over Hidden Valley by now. "So, compromise is the secret to your success?" Kate said, focusing on his careful stitches, Andy's wound now almost closed. Andy remained perfectly still under the sterile drape, just the gentle rise and fall of her shoulders as she breathed evenly.

"It works for us. I try to bridge the gap here in Hidden Valley between the two polarities of this region. I feel strongly about community, a coming together of people from a variety of backgrounds. My wife and I host an annual fall fair every Labour Day weekend. But it's a public event, no flashy show ring or prize money. There's riding and roping and a plowing match and a bale-throwing contest."

"Hidden Valley meets Calgary Stampede?"

Dr. Fullworth laughed. "Yes, I suppose you could say that. It's a good community event."

Kate saw Andy move. Her hand, which had been curled in a loose fist, opened as she spread her fingers against the white sheet. It was a small gesture, but a very deliberate one. Kate immediately thought back over the conversation, wondering what Andy was reacting to. *The clinic, marriage, compromise, community, a coming together of people...*

"Dr. Fullworth, how many people attend your fall fair?" Kate asked as she abruptly shifted gears, prompted by Andy's typically astute mind.

"We had our highest attendance this year with over a thousand." He looked up at Kate. "Are you looking for an invite for next year?"

"No, nothing like that," Kate said, distracted. "Was Tessa James at this year's fair?"

"Yes. She and the eldest Cardiff girl organized the craft table for the little ones."

"How about Chase Noonan and Keith Grange?" Kate continued, meeting Dr. Fullworth's eyes as he looked up from his last stitch.

"Chase Noonan I can confirm, I'm afraid I don't know Keith Grange," he said slowly.

"Mary Johnston?"

"I believe she was there with her grandkids."

"Roberta Sedlak...do you know Roberta Sedlak?" Kate asked, her stomach flipping.

"Yes, of course. But I don't recall seeing her that day. Is this about the virus, Dr. Morrison?"

"Yes."

"Do you think my farm might have been the point of origin?" he asked directly, his voice calm but with an undercurrent of strain.

"Possibly."

Instead of asking another question as Kate anticipated, Dr. Fullworth inspected his stitches. Then he took a pre-medicated swab from the metal tray, smeared an antibacterial cream across the wound, and covered it with a bandage, taping it carefully in place. He then pulled the sterile covering off Andy's head and shoulders. As she sat up, she locked her grey eyes on Kate for a moment before looking to Dr. Fullworth.

"What do you need from me?" Dr. Fullworth asked.

"Full access to your property in the morning. I'd like to get some samples and send them in first thing tomorrow," Andy said.

"Of course," said Dr. Fullworth. "Is my family in any sort of danger?"

"No, not as far as we know," Kate said.

Dr. Fullworth looked down at his hands. "Still, this might be a good time to take my wife to visit her relatives in Montreal, don't you think?" He tried for a smile, coming just short of being convincing. He then sighed. "I'd hate to think we had anything to do with the spread of this thing."

"We don't know anything yet," Andy said. "We'll have results in a few days, but if you go away, just leave us a number where you can be reached."

Dr. Fullworth pulled a card and a pen out of his inside pocket, scratched some numbers in the back with sharp strokes. He handed it to Andy. "My personal cell phone, I'm never without it."

"Thank you, Dr. Fullworth. For your cooperation and for stitching me up," Andy said to him.

"You are most welcome." He stopped and looked between them. "Best of luck to you both. I truly hope you can put this community back together again."

He left them then, Kate sitting so still on the stool that her legs were vaguely numb, Andy on the gurney, the spatter of blood on her white shirt now brown. Andy shifted, pulled her cell phone out of her pocket, and dialed.

"Hey, where are you?" Andy said into the phone, her voice clipped. "Good. We'll be right there." She stabbed the Disconnect button and stood quickly.

"Where are we going?"

"Meeting room, to see Jack," Andy said, holding the door for Kate.

They made their way down the quiet hallway and into the half-lit boardroom where Jack sat surrounded by two laptops, a portable printer, and the remains of what looked like lunch and dinner. Kate had almost forgotten how absorbed he could get when he was working. Kate checked her watch—almost ten p.m. She couldn't remember the last time she ate. She could barely remember the beginning of the day.

"The fair wasn't overlooked, Wylie," Jack was saying. "It just didn't have enough data to support it as a site of interest."

"How could it not? Most of Hidden Valley was there," Andy said, frustrated at his answer. Kate knew she only let her frustration show around her and Jack. If it was anyone else, she would have hid it entirely.

Jack hit a few keys on his laptop, then pointed at the screen to back up his answer.

"Tessa James, Mary Johnston, and Chase Noonan were at the Fullworth fall fair. Keith Grange has yet to be linked and Roberta Sedlak was definitively not there."

"According to who? Where is this definitive information from?" Andy barked out, pulling out a chair and sitting down.

Jack hit a few more keys. "Ferris questioned her husband over the phone about a week ago."

"Do we know where she was?"

"We don't have that information," Jack said, apologetically.

"Well, we need it," Andy said to no one. She was sitting rigidly in her chair, eyes trained on nothing. "Who is our best contact for finding out where Keith Grange was that day?"

Jack scrolled quickly. "Ferris questioned his two roommates, one of whom was at the fair and one working at another location."

Kate could see her formulating a plan, mapping out the best strategy to take this on.

"Okay, I'll put Ferris and Dr. Din on obtaining samples from the Fullworth farm first thing in the morning. Slater and I will find out definitively where both Keith Grange and Roberta Sedlak were that day," Andy said, the authority in her voice absolute. She zeroed in on Kate, sitting across the table. "Maybe you should be there, too. You get information out of people faster than I can. Can you clear your morning?"

"I'll do rounds on my patients early. If everyone is stable and Dr. MacKay is managing things in the ER, then I'll come with you and Constable Slater."

"Good. Did you ever hear back from Dr. Levesque?"

"Yes. They've got one team working on the original presentation of the virus and another on the mutated, airborne presentation. The team looking at the original virus is very close to finding out how it spreads and how long until onset of symptoms, possibly even tomorrow. That information is still a few days away for the new strain."

"Excellent. If we can confirm either the point of origin or the onset of symptoms…"

"We can backtrack," Kate finished for her.

Andy flicked her eyes back to Jack on his two laptops. "Jack, can you pull up all the data from last week? I want to look at it again."

Leaving them to talk data, Kate went upstairs to meet her two new charges, Jackson and Trent Ross. They were nearly identical, both medium build with neatly parted, glossy black hair. They were both polite and attentive as Kate explained the treatment course and the concerns about their history of asthma. Even with this cautionary news, they both flashed perfect white smiles through their oxygen masks.

When the night shift came on at eleven, Lucy dragged Kate back downstairs, depositing her at the door of the meeting room where Andy and Jack were both silently and independently working on their laptops. Andy looked up first, checked her watch, then powered down her laptop without saying anything. She jerked her chin at Jack, who did the same.

"I guess the Three Musketeers needed to sleep sometimes, didn't they?" Jack asked no one in particular.

"Kate, give Jack your keys. I'll drive you home."

Kate gave her a tired smile, handing Jack the keys to the rental car. "Don't I wish," she said.

The drive was quiet, each lost in her own thoughts. As soon as they got to the room, Andy immediately pulled out her laptop again and set it up on the desk. Kate sighed but didn't say anything. She was too tired, and she wouldn't win the argument anyway. As Kate brushed her teeth, barely looking at herself in the mirror, she saw Andy through the half open door taking off her bloody shirt and carefully pulling on her basketball hoodie. Kate thought about their earlier conversation, how they both carried scars, how they worried more about the other's than their own. Finally, Kate pulled back the covers and crawled into bed, Andy giving her a sweet, slightly distracted kiss. Kate closed her eyes and tried to put her thoughts on pause, focusing on her breathing instead of her brain. It worked as she was pulled quickly and deeply into sleep.

Angler stood leaning against a wall, an invisible spotlight above his head illuminating his grossly puffy face and his thin blond hair,

everything around him darkened in shadow. He stared at her, his smirking eyes locked on Kate, telling her unequivocally that he knew something she didn't. He began to laugh, a simple heave of his chest at first, and then it built until he was roaring, his pink mouth opened wide, his eyes now streaming with the tears of laughter. He pointed at her, ridiculing her because she still didn't know. But then she did. All of sudden she knew why he was laughing. Andy was dead. Angler had killed her. Andy was dead.

Kate woke with the scream of her dream choked in her throat. Every thought was centred on the constricting panic in her chest that wouldn't allow her to breathe in or out. She sat up, clutching her abdomen, having no idea where she was. Andy was at her side in a heartbeat, gently touching Kate's face. But Kate couldn't see her, could just feel the fear as it locked her down.

"Kate, it's a nightmare. It's just a nightmare. You're fine, no one is going to hurt you, you're fine," Andy repeated the words, smoothing Kate's hair back from her face.

"No…" Kate said, the first glimmer of reality intruding on the dark nightmare. It barely helped, only made her shake, made her question what was real. "He's alive. He was there…"

"Angler's dead, Kate. You saw him die," Andy said firmly, knowing instantly who Kate was talking about. "He can't hurt you. No one is going to hurt you."

"Not me," Kate said fiercely, remembering why Angler was laughing. "It was you…he's alive, he killed you." Kate was just awake enough to know she wasn't making sense, but afraid enough that she couldn't be sure.

Andy held Kate's face between her hands, pressure along her jaw, fingers on her cheekbones. Kate focused on Andy's serious grey eyes, on the words coming out of her mouth. "I'm right here. I'll always be right here. Tell me what you saw the night Angler died."

Kate recalled the details. Even through the haze of a drug overdose, she remembered. "Two bullets. One shattered his left orbital floor and went into his brain. The other bisected his aortic valve and he bled out instantly."

"Which means…" Andy prompted, still not letting her go.

"He couldn't have survived that," Kate said, feeling her own heart rate slow as she said it. She took a breath, the oxygen easing the tight panic in her chest. "He couldn't have survived either one of those shots."

"Right, which means he's gone. You and I are here, and Angler is gone. It was a nightmare, love. We're fine." Andy kissed her forehead, and Kate started to cry. The awful fear still clung to her, an unwanted shadow.

"I'm sorry, Andy." Kate leaned into her.

"You don't have to apologize for a nightmare, Kate."

Kate looked up to meet Andy's worried gaze. She felt vulnerable. She felt a massive weight, huge, unnameable, threatening to crush her. It contained every fear and every thought she had ever pushed away. Somehow in the pushing, each thought had gained incredible mass.

"I'm sorry for lying to you," Kate whispered. She had to say it quietly. Any louder, and the weight would come crashing down.

Andy touched her face gently and the familiar feel of her fingertips calmed Kate almost instantly. Kate touched the bandage above Andy's eye, convincing herself this was the extent of her injuries. She was here. She was very much alive.

"I'll come to bed," Andy said.

Kate stayed sitting up, watched Andy move around the room. She looked at the clock. Just before two in the morning. This made her tired, so deeply tired. Then Andy finally crawled into bed, pulled Kate down into her arms, and eventually they both slept.

Kate stood at the nurse's station, trying not to think about how dry and itchy her eyes were from lack of sleep. She was staring at Harris Trenholm's sats for the last few days. Her gut told her there was a downward trend, though the printout showed continuous results in the normal range. The computer program at least showed no red flags, but Kate worried. Harris seemed much too tired these days. As the election ramped up, he seemed to be fading. Kate shook her head. *Fading* was not exactly a medical term, but her instinct had been right too many times to ignore it.

Double-checking that the nurse on call had her cell phone number, Kate made her way downstairs. The PHEM meeting wasn't starting for another half hour, but thinking of the red-flagged computer system made Kate think of Jack. He was sitting at the far end of the table, his sweet, boyish face scrunched in concentration.

"Good morning, Katie!" Jack said, his exuberance infectious. "Have you tried Judy's coffee? So good. I told her she could make millions with this blend. Seriously."

"Morning, Jack."

Kate and Andy had missed out on their morning coffee, gone from the hotel long before the sun was up. She thought with a pang of those two large Styrofoam cups sitting at the front desk of the Sea to Sky Inn as she reached for the carafe of hospital coffee in the middle of the table.

"I've got a question for you," Kate said.

Jack happily pounded at a button on his computer and turned all his attention on her. "Shoot," he said.

"I haven't thought this all the way through, so bear with me," Kate said, sipping her coffee, trying to organize her thoughts. "My gut is telling me Harris Trenholm is about to get much worse, but his tests are all falling within the low-normal range. I want to see if there's a trend the system isn't picking up on, something that it's not anticipating. Something outside each individual patient's test results. Does that make any sense?"

"So there's a system in place already for tracking patterns, but you think it doesn't have all the factors," Jack summarized in his own computer tech way.

"Exactly."

"What data did you want to use?" Jack was already clicking through screens on his laptop.

"Autopsy results, specifically those dealing with oxygen saturation levels, fluid levels and lung capacity. There should be three sets by this afternoon. I know it's not much…"

"Three is a pattern, Katie. Maybe we'll find something." Jack tucked his head down and got to work, the sound of keys and clicking filling the silence.

Kate smoothed her fingers over the flat, black wood of the tabletop. She was trying to figure out what she had seen or understood that she couldn't yet put into rational thought. There was something…

Kate just hoped she could figure it out before Harris Trenholm took the downward turn she anticipated. The one she had little confidence that she could turn around.

A moment later, Andy walked in, her tall uniformed frame filling the doorway. Kate's heart gave her a nudge as Andy smiled at her. Even with the bandage above her right eye, she was still so incredibly beautiful.

"How are your Ward B patients?" Andy asked, sitting down at the head of the table, pulling out her case notes.

"Stable for now," Kate said, hoping it would remain true. "I was planning on running a differential after this, get the medical team together and see what we come up with."

"Kellar's scheduled the autopsy for right after this," Andy said, giving Kate the bad news.

"This afternoon, then, if we could schedule it for this afternoon," Kate said. She supposed there was no point in meeting unless Kellar could be there. And they could use the results regardless.

"I'm hoping to have something for you by then, too, Katie," Jack said helpfully.

Constables Ferris and Slater came in next and sat down. Kate looked at the young constable as he adjusted his holster after he'd sat down. Slater wore his uniform with the puffed-up pride of the still new. The holstered belt around his hips had not yet become an unconscious extension of his body, as it had with Ferris and Andy. Kate then looked closer at Ferris. His usual, affable smile was absent this morning. She had to assume she wasn't the only one losing sleep over the HV1A virus.

Lost in her scrutiny of the two cops, Kate hadn't noticed Mona Kellar come into the room. She dropped her bulk noisily into a chair near the door, drawing Kate's attention. Mona Kellar was looking at Kate with her bright, interested eyes, and she seemed almost happy. Kate didn't want to know what was behind that, but then Mona Kellar turned that same eager, anticipatory look down the table to Andy.

Kate's heart lurched, though Andy returned the gaze in her professional, guarded way. Mona Kellar looked back and forth between them, and her eyes grew brighter. She shifted about excitedly. Immediately Kate understood. Cornering Kate on the stairwell had never been about hurting her, it was meant to provoke Andy. But by not telling Andy what had happened, Kate suddenly realized that she had played right into Mona Kellar's hand.

As more people filled the room, Kate could not tear her eyes away from Mona Kellar, dreading what she would say or do next. Kellar raised her hand in an accusatory gesture.

"You didn't tell her," Kellar hissed, her eyes too probing, too eager.

Kate couldn't help looking at Andy at the end of the table, and the look she got told her quite clearly that yes, Andy had heard and no, Andy was not happy.

"All right everybody, let's start with updates," Andy said, taking a moment to pull the rest of the team to order. "As most of you know by now, someone attempted to break into one of the RCMP vehicles last night. He or she was unsuccessful in their attempt, and they took off before I was able to apprehend them for questioning. Constable Slater, could you update the team on the evidence and the consequent actions we are taking."

Even distracted, Kate could see this was a big moment for Constable Slater. He sat up straighter in his chair and cleared his throat.

"We found a few partial boot prints in the mud, which we're taking to the lab to have analyzed. There were no fingerprints left on Sergeant Wyles's car or on the surrounding areas. After meeting with Dr. Doyle first thing this morning, we are increasing the number of hospital security on each shift, and we are putting one RCMP officer on site as well."

Andy stared down the table at him and Kate could see her thinking. "Let's make it two," she said suddenly. "I'll talk to Staff Sergeant Finns, but I think we should make it two more constables to come up and supplement the hospital security."

Kate's instinct twigged, her suspicions raised. She had a feeling where this sudden need for increased security came from.

Andy updated the team on the samples collected yesterday and the samples being collected today. Kate saw Ferris nod as Andy indicated he would be going back out again. He really didn't look very good. Next, the Public Health update. The numbers were climbing so rapidly, they were assuming all flu cases were now a result of the HV1A strain.

Testing would only be done on patients who had any of the listed risk factors, and those would be flagged for Kate and Eric.

As Dr. Salinger finished his update, Andy took over the meeting again. "Dr. Kellar will be performing the autopsy on Jim Beckett this morning—"

"And Dr. Morrison will be there to assist," Mona Kellar interrupted.

Andy met Mona Kellar's challenging glare. "Not possible this morning," Andy said neutrally. She then looked down the table. "Dr. MacKay, would it be possible for you to take a turn assisting Dr. Kellar?"

"Sure, no problem, though I'll need someone to cover the ER," Eric said in his laid-back way.

"Dr. Doyle?" Andy asked, turning her eyes to the chief of staff. Apparently Andy had this all worked out.

"Yes, I could make myself available," Dr. Doyle said somewhat stiffly.

"Good. Lastly, Dr. Morrison would like to assemble the medical team later this afternoon, once the autopsy results are in. Four o'clock." She didn't pose it as a question. "Same time tomorrow. Any issues that come up over the day, bring them to me."

As the meeting broke up and people filed out of their seats, Kate looked down the table to Ferris and Slater, who were talking in low voices. Kate watched as Ferris stood. He seemed to be moving slowly. Her heart sank as she watched him cough once, quietly.

Kate met him at the door before he could leave. "Constable Ferris, do you have a minute?"

"Sure, Dr. Morrison, what is it?"

Kate waved him into the hallway. "How long have you been sick?" she asked him quietly.

Constable Ferris looked guilty. "I didn't sleep well last night and woke up feeling like crap. A pot of Judy's coffee, and I'll be just fine."

Kate surveyed him with a critical eye. "You have a cough, fatigue, and I'm going to guess by the way you're talking that you're starting to get congested. Any fever?"

Constable Ferris shrugged miserably. "I don't own a thermometer."

Kate told him to wait and headed back into the meeting room. Andy was off the phone, writing in her case notes.

"We have a problem," Kate said, and Andy looked up immediately. "Ferris is sick." Kate opened the box of masks and pulled some out. "I'm going to take him down to the ER, check him out and take a blood sample, but if he's got a fever, we're going to have to assume he's got the virus. I'm going to have to send him home."

Kate watched Andy cycle through the implications of this news. She didn't swear, didn't visibly react like Kate would have.

"I'll call Finns back. We're going to need a more senior officer up here to replace Ferris," Andy said.

"What about this morning? Are you going to go with Dr. Din to the Fullworth farm to collect samples?"

Studying Andy's face, Kate knew what her answer would be before she opened her mouth.

"No. Constable Slater has been briefed on the NML information. He's been studying the files since before he got here, so he knows as well as Ferris what to look for." Andy paused. "Let's give them an escort, though. We'll drive down to the farm with them before meeting with Keith Grange's roommates."

"Okay, give me half an hour to sort out Ferris."

"Send Constable Slater in. I'll give him the news he's flying solo," Andy said and Kate quickly left the room. Soon enough, she would be stuck in a car with Andy where she could be grilled about the details of her latest run-in with Mona Kellar.

Ferris had a fever. He slumped miserably on the hospital bed while Kate went through the long checklist of risk factors. Ferris had none of them, nothing to indicate this virus would develop into anything more than a week-long enforced vacation. As Kate drew his blood, she made it clear that Andy and now Staff Sergeant Finns were aware of his condition so he would not be allowed to actively participate in any PHEM-related business until he was better.

Once Kate had sent the constable home, she and Andy caught up to Constable Slater and Dr. Din in the parking lot as they loaded supplies into the back of the van. Dr. Din gave a thumbs up, and both vehicles pulled out, ignoring the media vans parked along the road leading into the hospital.

Kate waited for Andy's onslaught of questions, for her anger and hurt and accusations. She knew she deserved all of it. It had been supremely stupid to keep the incident with Kellar from Andy, not only a wasted effort, but a damaging one.

Andy was silent. Not grim, not angry. Just silent. She didn't look at Kate, didn't prompt her to begin. Nothing. She just followed the van in front of them, occasionally checking her rearview mirror to see if they were being followed.

Kate couldn't stand the silence. She just wanted to get it over with.

"The night I went down to the lab to check with the lab tech, Mona Kellar cornered me on the stairwell. She was surprised to see me, but she knew I was alone. Then she called you my guard dog and offered me advice, something to the effect of you only being with me for the sex, and that I would never really qualify as a lesbian."

Now Andy was angry. Kate could see it in the tense line of her jaw, in the way she gripped the steering wheel, in the hard stillness of her body.

"Why wouldn't you tell me that?" Andy asked, controlling the anger in her voice so Kate could barely detect it there. Kate also guessed she was controlling the hurt and the worry.

"Because I didn't want you to go after her, I didn't want it to start something or to have it affect you or the team." Kate tried to explain, knowing the excuses were feeble. "With everything else going on, it seemed kind of insignificant."

"I bet it didn't feel insignificant. When she said those things, are you really going to tell me it didn't bother you?" Andy said.

"Of course it did."

"Then why wouldn't you tell me that?" Andy repeated.

"I guess I just didn't want to add anything else to your list of things to worry about."

"I don't need you to protect me like that, Kate," Andy said, and the rebuke in her tone was evident.

Kate thought immediately of their morning meeting. "While we're on the topic of protection, do you want to tell me why you decided to double the security team?" Kate said, her own irritation rising.

"I think it's called for."

"So it's not about me."

Andy didn't answer.

"I don't need a babysitter, Andy," Kate said, her voice now sharp.

She couldn't explain why she was suddenly annoyed at Andy. She knew Andy had every reason to be upset with her, and this just seemed like more evidence of how Kate was failing on multiple levels. "I need to be able to work without an armed guard attached to my hip." She knew from Seattle what that felt like.

Andy continued her silence.

"Andy…" Kate said in a warning tone.

"What do you want me to say, Kate?" Andy said tiredly, like she didn't have the energy for this.

"I want you to say that you trust me enough to deal with this," she said stubbornly.

"Well, I don't," Andy said bitterly. "You have the worst self-preservation skills of anyone I've ever met. I don't understand how you can make rapid, complex decisions about the treatment and care of others, but when it comes to yourself…" Andy shook her head angrily, unable to even finish the sentence.

Kate felt the fight ebb out of her completely. Part of her reeled from the shock of the criticism. She stared blankly out the windshield, amazed at how Andy had perfectly, if painfully, summed up her greatest weakness. She didn't feel angry or even really hurt. She just felt completely empty.

"I'm sorry," Andy said. "I shouldn't have said that."

"But it's true."

Andy didn't contradict her. The van in front of them pulled up outside a large, unadorned fence surrounding the Fullworth farm. They both watched in silence as Dr. Din and Constable Slater were buzzed through, Slater waving an all clear to Andy as the gates closed behind them.

"We'll head to Keith Grange's apartment first," Andy said, glancing at Kate as if checking they were okay to move past this. They had to be, Kate decided. There were too many other things to think about.

Andy pulled into the small working-class neighbourhood, the houses only shabby in comparison to their opulent neighbours. Andy indicated a three-story building as she killed the engine. "Top floor," she said. "Our objective is to place Keith's whereabouts the day of the Fullworth fall fair."

The Yukon doors slammed in the silence as they got out and

walked up to the building. Andy tried the main door to the triplex and shook her head as she found it open.

"Clearly we're not in Vancouver," she muttered and headed inside.

They walked to the top floor and Andy gave two sharp knocks on the boot-scuffed wooden door. A moment later a young guy, nineteen or twenty, with tousled hair and wearing only plaid pyjama pants, answered the door. His bloodshot eyes got instantly round as he saw Andy on the landing outside his apartment.

"Riley Hanson?"

A tousled-hair nod.

"Sergeant Wyles and Dr. Morrison with the RCMP," Andy said, holding up her badge. "We have some questions for you about Keith Grange."

Kate saw a genuine wave of sadness cross Riley's face, like he'd forgotten just for a moment, and the reminder was a sharp jab. Kate thought he was about to open the door wider, then he looked almost furtively behind him, unsure.

"You've got thirty seconds to get rid of whatever it is you don't want me to see, and then you will invite us in and answer our questions," Andy said, pinning him down with her grey eyes. Riley hesitated. "Twenty-seven seconds," Andy warned, and Riley disappeared from view.

Kate looked at Andy silently, her eyebrows raised. She couldn't help smiling.

"What?" Andy mouthed.

"You're cute when you're tough," Kate whispered.

Andy rolled her eyes, but Kate could see the corner of her mouth turn up in the smallest of smiles. "Focus, Dr. Morrison."

Riley returned, slightly breathless, a sweatshirt pulled on over his bare chest. He opened the door wider, gesturing for them to come in. The apartment was fairly small, a tiny kitchen opening onto what looked like a dining room/living room/game room combination. A large TV, game controllers, and wires dominated the room.

"You wanted to talk about Keith?" Riley asked, standing by the window, running his hands nervously and ineffectively through his messy brown hair.

"Yes. Are you familiar with the Fullworth fall fair?" Andy said, standing just inside the doorway.

A look of confusion crossed Riley's face. This clearly wasn't where he was expecting the conversation to go.

"Sure. I worked it this year," he answered.

"Did Keith?"

Riley shook his head. "No, he was supposed to have the weekend off. He kept ribbing me about being behind the scenes and missing all the fun." Riley stopped and took a breath, again like his memory had just kicked him into recalling that his friend was gone.

"So he attended the fair," Andy prompted.

"No, he ended up trading weekends with someone. He wanted the following weekend to go camping with some friends who were coming up from Vancouver. He worked at the Cardiffs' that weekend, I think."

"You never saw him at the Fullworth farm, then," Andy said.

Riley shook his head again.

"What about that night? Where was Keith that night?"

"We had a party here that night, sort of a last-minute thing. Keith came in late with one of the girls we hang out with."

"Name?" Andy pulled out her notepad.

"Alicia. She works at one of the coffee shops downtown."

Andy looked at him, waiting.

"Alicia Davidson," Riley said hurriedly. "The coffee shop's called the Green Bean. It's just a few blocks from here," he added helpfully.

Andy flipped her notepad shut and stared silently at Riley. Kate watched Riley shift nervously under her glare. Finally Andy took a card out of her pocket and handed it over.

"If anything else comes to mind, give me a call."

They walked back outside, a quick gust of wind cutting through Kate's jacket. At least it was sunny out today. Andy indicated they should walk the three blocks to the coffee place.

"You didn't need me after all," Kate said, hunching her shoulders up around her ears. "He was very cooperative."

"Of course he was. It was that or get busted for possession of marijuana. Cooperation was clearly the better choice," Andy said, zipping her own jacket up higher. "I'll talk to this Alicia Davidson, but I'll need you to take the lead on talking to Al Sedlak. That might require some more delicacy."

"Are you saying you're not delicate, Sergeant Wyles?" Kate teased.

"You think you're pretty funny today, don't you?"

"Let's call it lack of sleep," Kate said. "And maybe an act of contrition for not having told you about my latest run-in with the troll," she added.

Andy looked at her as they walked the few short blocks back towards the main street of Hidden Valley. "Can I confess something to you? Promise you won't judge," Andy said to Kate.

"Of course," Kate said, curious.

"I want to punch Mona Kellar in the mouth every time I see her. Hard. Broken teeth, split lip, ten stitches, not able to eat for a month kind of hard," Andy said, her voice cold. Then she looked quickly back to Kate, gauging her reaction.

"Not bad," Kate said casually. "Every time I see her I think about forcing her to run a comb through her hair for the first time in a decade, and then tell her she has to perform her next autopsy in six-inch stilettos."

Andy stopped in the middle of the sidewalk, threw back her head, and laughed. Kate loved that sound, loved how in that moment Andy's shoulders relaxed and her eyes glinted mischievously. Kate suddenly, without thinking it through, balanced up on her toes and gave Andy a light, quick kiss on her still-laughing lips. Then she took a step back, almost shy, wishing she could kiss Andy without wondering in the back of her head who might be watching or what they might be thinking.

"I love you, Andy Wyles," Kate said quietly. "I know I'm doing a shitty job of showing it these days, but I love you."

Andy smiled and reached out to run her finger over Kate's cheek, tucking an escaped curl back behind her ear. "I love you too, you know. And I'm glad you're here."

Kate took that moment to look into Andy's grey eyes, not caring that they were standing in the middle of the sidewalk. She could almost hear the rain hitting the roof of their cabin in Montana, almost feel the damp wood of the porch swing and Andy's arm wrapped protectively around her. Perfect.

The Green Bean coffee bar had a classic green awning over the front entrance, the letters slashed across it in a slanting, almost impossible to read font. The windows were steamed, but Kate could see large, glinting machines and even from outside could hear the sharp motorized hum of a milk frothing machine. There were three people behind the counter, all extremely serious looking. Coffee baristas. This was definitely not Kate's kind of coffee place.

Just as Andy was about to open the door, Kate's phone rang in her pocket. She checked the caller ID.

"It's the hospital, I better take it," Kate said, looking up at Andy.

"Sure, I'll meet you back out here," Andy said, the bells on the door jangling cheerily as she walked inside.

Kate hunched her shoulders against the cold as she connected the call. It was the Ward B nurse with an update. Harris Trenholm's O2 saturation levels had slipped just below the normal range. They had returned to baseline since then, but she thought Kate would want to know. Kate thanked the nurse and told her to call again if his numbers dropped, adding that she should take him down for an x-ray next time he woke up. She thought about Jack and wondered if his algorithm could possibly predict or confirm her instinct.

Kate disconnected her phone, running her fingers over the blank screen as she processed the new information, trying so hard to figure out what she was missing. She watched Andy distractedly through the window, not really paying attention, barely remembering what they were doing here in the first place. There was something critical, something the NML had covered but Kate hadn't understood. Something…

The bells jangled again, Andy making her exit, just as Kate's phone rang for the second time. The hospital, again. Kate answered it and listened with a sinking heart, asking rapid-fire questions to the person on the other end. She was vaguely aware that as they walked back towards the Yukon, Andy's phone had also rung and she was talking in a clipped tone. Kate hung up first, thinking hard, still tuning out Andy's conversation beside her. They climbed into the Yukon, Andy still talking, reading now from her notes. Finally she hung up, and the air was heavy with news.

"You first," Andy said, starting the engine.

"Harris Trenholm is losing the battle, and I've got a fourth Ward B patient," Kate said, looking up at Andy. "It's Serena Cardiff."

"I thought she was discharged," Andy said, frowning.

"She was. Readmitted by Dr. Doyle about a half hour ago," Kate said, for some reason holding up her phone as evidence. "Serena is showing all the signs of the HV1A virus, and we already know she has two risk factors. I need to get back to the hospital." Kate hated to say it, to draw up her mental image of Serena's chest x-rays, the crack in her ribs from a fall, the imagined bruising of the lung tissue. That, along with her recent bout of pneumonia, put her at higher respiratory risk. "Your turn," she said to Andy.

"Alicia Davidson places Keith Grange at the Fullworth farm the night of the fall fair. She called him for a ride and he stayed to help with the clean-up before they left," Andy said, like she was reading from her notes. Her voice was distracted, though, and Kate could tell she wasn't thinking about Alicia Davidson's information.

"What else?" Kate asked.

"The phone call was from Slater. They think they found the viral containment device at the Fullworth farm. I think we might have our point of origin."

CHAPTER FOURTEEN

Kate looked at Serena Cardiff's pale face through the oxygen mask. So little had changed in the nine days since Kate had stood right here at the foot of Serena's bed, flipping through her medical chart. She felt absolutely no farther ahead, had no better plan for dealing with this virus than they did nine days ago. Kate pushed away the thoughts of helplessness. Instead, she thought about the samples Dr. Doyle had sent down to the lab, the chest x-ray results which should be up any moment, the O2 saturation numbers she had already memorized, and the high-dose steroids that they'd slammed Serena's body with the second she'd been admitted. And still, Serena's pale face, her breathing careful and shallow through the mask, felt like an accusation of inaction.

"No tough-guy act this time, Serena," Kate warned, putting down the chart. "You need to let someone know if there are any changes to how you're feeling. I don't have Nathan or your sister around this time to act as interpreters."

Serena nodded, her eyes slightly wide.

"How are you feeling right now?" Kate asked, testing her.

"Tired."

No wonder, thought Kate. She'd come in with low O2 sats, and they'd only marginally improved on a hundred percent oxygen.

"Dizzy?" Kate checked.

Serena shook her head. "Not anymore." Serena's voice was muted through the mask.

"And if you start to feel dizzy again?" Kate knew she was pushing, but Serena's history of hiding her symptoms scared Kate. Serena had been feeling sick again for two days before she told Nathan. Apparently, Nathan had immediately phoned Mrs. Cardiff, knowing she was the only one who could force Serena to get to the hospital.

Serena reached out to the buzzer clipped to the white sheets of the bed, and she held it up to Kate as an answer.

"Good." Kate nodded approvingly. "Use it. I'm going to go see if your chest films are up, I'll be back."

"Dr. Morrison?" Serena asked, just as Kate turned to go.

"Call me Kate, it takes less time," Kate said to the girl, smiling.

"No visitors?"

Kate shook her head. "I'm afraid not. This is a closed ward, only medical personnel are allowed on this level of the hospital."

Serena nodded, then closed her eyes, and Kate's stomach twisted with worry. She added it to the pile.

Back at the nurse's station, Kate scratched at her face mask and wrote in Serena's chart. She thought about Andy out at the Fullworth farm, directing the team sent up from Vancouver, as they secured the property. Checking her watch, Kate decided she should probably eat before meeting the rest of the medical team down in the PHEM meeting room. She gave her orders to the nurse and headed back down to the main floor of the hospital, nodding politely to the masked RCMP officer standing outside the doors of Ward B.

Kate grabbed a sandwich and headed into the meeting room. Jack was still there or he was back again, either way looking like he hadn't moved in days. Impossibly, he had three laptops open and the hospital computer monitor was on behind him, streaming seemingly senseless reams of data.

"How are you doing, Jack?" Kate said, dropping into a seat near him.

"You know me, Katie. Never happier than when I'm multitasking."

"Good. Have you heard from Andy?"

"She called about a half hour ago for some information from Constable Ferris's notes." Jack leaned in, looking excited. "Looks like they pulled a print off the viral containment device."

"Already?" Kate asked, surprised. Things finally seemed to be moving on the criminal investigation end of this health crisis. Unfortunately, it put Kate and her patients no farther ahead.

"Wylie also told me to find somewhere else to work 'cause you and the medical team are taking over the room," Jack said, peering at her from over one of his laptops.

"Doesn't bother me. You can stay," Kate told him distractedly.

"Good, I'm just mining the medical files from the NML for information around the pattern, like you asked me to," Jack was saying excitedly, and Kate forced herself to tune back in. "There wasn't enough data in the charts, so I thought about what other information you had in your head that could be considered a variable. So I created a search based on the same parameters you gave me." Jack tapped a few buttons on one of the laptops. "Should be done soon," he finished.

"So you basically created an algorithm to run a pattern search on my brain?"

"Yes!" he said happily.

"Huh. Okay." Kate didn't really want to think about all the information in her head and how little of it was useful.

"Hopefully it will give you what you need," Jack said as he picked up his sandwich and took a bite.

Eric MacKay entered the room without his usual smile and swagger. He immediately reached for the coffee, pouring himself a cup and taking three long gulps of the hot, dark liquid before leaning his head back against the chair and closing his eyes.

"That was the longest fucking morning of my life," he groaned, keeping his eyes closed. "And there have been a lot of long days recently, but this one wins, hands down."

"Dr. Kellar?" Kate asked, sympathetically.

"Yes." Eric shuddered. "I know she's the brilliant eccentric and all that, but does she have to be so nasty?" he asked, opening his eyes and looking at Kate.

"Did she give you a hard time?"

"A hard time?" Eric repeated, sitting up. "It felt like medical school. I couldn't do anything right, always handed her the wrong thing, and I swear I got every answer wrong. And it's creepy down there. And cold." He sat up, taking another long gulp of coffee.

"If it makes it any better, it's not about you," Kate told him.

"Whatever it is, if I wasn't motivated to keep the residents of Hidden Valley from the morgue before, I'm doubly motivated now. No way do I want to be on morgue duty with that woman again," he said and shuddered one more time.

Kate couldn't help feeling guiltily glad that it wasn't her just surfacing from the morgue after five hours with Mona Kellar. As her phone rang on the desk in front of her, Kate silently thanked Andy for keeping her above ground today. She checked the caller ID. It was the NML.

Kate was expecting to hear Dr. Levesque's warm, accented voice on the other end of the line, but it was Rayna. She sounded awkward at first, like a kid learning to use the phone for the first time. But as she updated Kate, giving her the details of their most recent discovery of the HV1A virus, she became more animated. She answered Kate's questions precisely, and just before they hung up at the end of their short conversation, Kate thanked her profusely.

"Seven to ten days," Kate said to the room, which now included Jack, Eric, and Dr. Salinger. "From exposure to onset of symptoms, it's seven to ten days."

"Original virus or mutated strain?" Dr. Salinger said, taking a seat.

"Original. Mutated strain they are estimating four to six." He looked surprised, echoing Kate's reaction when she'd heard the news.

"Interesting," Dr. Salinger continued, his eyes bright. "So it's longer than the influenza A virus but considerably shorter than hantavirus."

Mona Kellar opened the door, looked around the room with her mean eyes, and chose a seat across from Dr. Salinger.

"What's interesting?" she barked. She did seem to be in a worse mood than usual.

"The NML in Winnipeg just called. Original strain of the virus, exposure to onset of symptoms they are estimating at seven to ten days. Four to six for the mutated strain." Kate tried to include every detail, to avoid the angry, commanding voice. But Dr. Kellar seemed almost uninterested in this detail. Maybe if it didn't affect her autopsy results, she didn't really care. "Dr. Kellar, are there any more details to report from your most recent autopsy?" Kate asked, aiming for a tone that walked the careful line between meekness and hostility.

"Not much," Mona Kellar grunted. "Except Jim Beckett wins for most fluid pulled off a patient's lungs. The combination of emphysema and HV1A is not for the faint-hearted." She smiled cruelly, aiming it at Eric, who picked up his mug to avoid eye contact.

"Mr. Beckett was given high-dose steroids in the ER. Did you see any effect at all?" Kate asked. She knew the answer already; there was a reason she aimed the question at the forensic pathologist, the dead man's doctor.

"No," Mona Kellar said shortly. "No effect. Looks like you're back at square one."

"But that might have been the emphysema," Dr. Salinger cut in. "I'm not sure we should throw out the initial high-dose steroid protocol based on this one patient. If he presents atypically—"

"They all present atypically, Dr. Salinger," Mona Kellar sneered. "In case you hadn't noticed, we haven't had one patient who presented the same."

"I recognize that," Dr. Salinger said evenly. "I'm just saying we need more data to either support or negate our current protocol."

"I agree," Kate added in. "But let's lay out the protocol, see if we can add to it or adjust. Let me pull up Harris Trenholm's most recent results. He's been on the newest protocol the longest."

As Kate was pulling up the files she wanted to see, the intercom in the room made her jump.

"Dr. Morrison, code blue to Ward B. Dr. Morrison, code blue to Ward B."

Kate was completely unaware of the faces around her as she opened the door to the meeting room and took the stairs two at a time. It wasn't until she was at the top of the stairs, fumbling with her ID to show the RCMP officer stationed there, that she realized Eric was right behind her.

Kate took the corner into Harris Trenholm's room quickly, the picture of him sitting up in his hospital bed, laptop open not making any sense.

"Dr. Morrison, down here!" Eric called from down the hall.

Kate followed his voice one room over to the double room of Jackson and Trent Ross. The nurse was calling out vitals, saying they'd all been in the normal range twenty minutes ago. Kate pulled out her stethoscope, listening to the sharp crackle of fluid, and watched as the man strained for each wet breath.

"There's no point in tubing him without getting some of this fluid off," she said to Eric, who was reading the EKG printout. Kate read the printout upside down, judged that his heart was holding up. For now.

"Drain first, then tube?" Eric asked, pulling over a cart, adjusting the light.

Kate looked at the man's face, scared, half-there eyes too far gone already to even plead. "Same time," she said shortly, then looked up at the nurse.

"Laryngoscope and six millimetre tube," Kate said. She pulled the scope through her hands, adjusting it until it sat just right in her palm. Then she spoke to the man as he sucked oxygen hungrily through his mask. "Mr. Ross, we need to put a tube down your throat to help you get oxygen. I need you to relax, don't fight it. Dr. MacKay is going to put in a drain, and it's going to hurt. Do you understand?"

No response from the patient. Kate could see his eyes swimming in and out of focus. She hated to think what was about to be done to this man. Even half-conscious, it would be at best torturous. But if she wanted him to live through the next ten minutes, it was going to mean a measure of pain.

Kate nodded at Eric and they both began their procedures. Jackson Ross didn't fight, barely flinched as the tube slid down past his tongue, only a slight gag reflex as Kate pressed the tube past his cords. She was in, pulling the lead from the tube and attaching the ventilator handed to her by the nurse. The ventilator only offered a small increase in oxygen absorption rates. His lungs couldn't process anything with that much fluid. So much depended on getting that fluid cleared up or cleared out. Kate watched Eric slide the flexible tubing through the small incision, his movements efficient and confident, with absolutely no hesitation.

"Get x-ray up here," Kate said to the nurse as she watched Eric stitch the tube in place. As he finished, they both pulled out their stethoscopes and listened as the ventilator forced air into fluid-dense lungs.

"What's the output?" Kate asked.

Eric checked the bag hanging over the side of the bed.

"Five mils already," he told her, looking up. She shook her head, unsure if this would be enough. They both watched the monitor, waiting for his O2 saturation levels to reach acceptable levels.

By the time the x-ray tech arrived and took the pictures, the number on the monitor had slowly started to rise. Jackson Ross was far from stable, but he was holding his own for now. For the first time, they'd been able to bring someone back, to keep the tidal wave of fluid at bay. Kate wished she could feel confident that this would be enough.

Kate spoke briefly with Trent Ross, explaining what had happened, trying to reassure him they were doing everything possible for his brother. Leaving the room with Jackson Ross hooked up to a ventilator and Trent Ross coughing into his oxygen mask made the worry in Kate's stomach turn to anger.

"Let's bring everyone up here," she said to Eric. He complied silently while Kate went behind the nurse's station, grabbing clipboards, paper and markers. The anger in her belly pushed her into overdrive, rapidly sorting through information, feeling like she was running the pattern algorithm faster than Jack's computer.

Salinger and Kellar came upstairs, their face masks not quite hiding his curiosity and her annoyance. Kate didn't care about either. She needed their perspectives, she needed them to see what she couldn't. A moment later Jack followed, his face mask making his curly hair stick out comically, one of his laptops tucked under his arm. That was good. She could use him right now. Writing names in big block letters with the marker, Kate attached them to clipboards and handed one to each person, pulling in a nurse and a security guard so everyone was representing one patient. Each of the four Ward B patients had a clipboard, as did the three deceased patients.

Everyone looked at her silently, no one quite knowing what to do or say. Kate was thinking about the Go Fish game in Winnipeg, how it had helped her sort through some of the facts and categorize the information. She hoped this would do the same for the medical team.

"Jackson Ross experienced acute onset pulmonary edema about twenty minutes ago even though he's being closely monitored, and even though he had received initial high-dose steroids upon being admitted. Dr. MacKay was able to insert a drain and Mr. Ross is currently on a ventilator. This combination is giving him enough oxygen to keep his heart going for now, but we need to know why this is happening."

"Why what is happening, Dr. Morrison?" Kellar said in her impatient, superior voice. "Why you can't predict it, or why you haven't figured out how to treat it?" The question was asked with all the insulting implications intended.

But Kate took a moment with the question. Kellar was right. Kate was asking too many questions. She had to pick one and follow it through.

"How to predict it, let's focus on that," Kate said finally. "Everyone got a chart and a marker? Good. Bear with me on this. Okay, if your patient has the original strain of the virus, over here, mutated strain, over there," Kate directed.

There was a brief shuffle of confusion, the poor security guard being yanked by Dr. Kellar into a group. Roberta Sedlak and Keith Grange were in one group, the current Ward B patients and Jim Beckett were in the other.

"Write it down. Next." Kate barely allowed them to scratch the information underneath the patient's name. "Compromised lungs from injury or illness older than a year over here, under a year over there."

This was more complicated. They threw questions at Kate. Did Roberta Sedlak's tumour count as a new illness? What about Harris Trenholm's ongoing injury? People were talking loudly, directing each other into groups, shaking their heads in disagreement.

"Wait, enough. Sorry, that question wasn't specific enough," Kate said, thinking.

"Try severity of injury, Dr. Morrison," Dr. Salinger called out.

"Yes," Kate said, looking up. "Severity of injury upon being admitted, specifically. Likert scale, one to five being the least severe injuries over here, six to ten being the most severe over here."

More confusion, more questions, though this resolved itself much faster. In the end, only Jim Beckett and Harris Trenholm qualified for severe pre-existing injury or illness affecting their pulmonary system at time of admittance.

"Interesting," Dr. Salinger said, looking at the two groups. They both ignored Mona Kellar rolling her eyes.

"Write it down," Kate commanded. "Next, initial high-dose steroids given."

A quick shuffle. Only Roberta Sedlak and Keith Grange were not given high-dose steroids. Without waiting for Kate's command, people scratched on their clipboards.

"Of the group given the high-dose steroid protocol," Kate said, turning to the one group, "divide yourselves into those who were already taking steroids for a pre-existing condition before they were exposed to the HV1A virus."

A third group split off: Harris Trenholm and Trent Ross.

"Okay," Kate said, eyeing the three groups.

"Wait," Eric called out. "Serena Cardiff should qualify for that group," he said, indicating the most recent divide. "She was given steroids proactively a week ago, before we knew if she had the virus. So she would qualify for taking steroids before she was exposed."

"You're right, yes."

As the nurse holding Serena Cardiff's name moved into the third group, Kate handed her own chart to Eric to hold and stood in front of everyone. Three groups. Roberta Sedlak and Keith Grange were in the first group, both already lost to the virus. The second group held Harris Trenholm, Trent Ross, and Serena Cardiff. The last, Jackson Ross and Jim Beckett. This didn't look good. This last group held one deceased, one currently on a ventilator. Something tugged at Kate, something wasn't quite right.

"It's the timing of the steroids, not the dosage," Dr. Kellar said, throwing her clipboard onto the desk behind her. "That's why I'm seeing no effect in the autopsy, Dr. Morrison. Only those lucky enough to already be on the steroids prior to exposure are surviving," she finished bluntly.

A wave of unease moved the group as the implications of those words settled. Dr. Kellar was right, of course. The evidence was in front of them. Kate looked at the charts with Jackson Ross's name on one and then at Serena Cardiff's name. Had the steroids been in Serena's system long enough before exposure to have a therapeutic effect?

"Dr. Morrison?" Dr. Salinger was trying to get her attention. "Should we stick to the protocol?"

Kate tuned back in, to the group in front of her still holding the charts, to the buzz of hospital activity around her. The feeling that they were getting somewhere had vanished with the news that the only thing that could help their patients was utterly out of their control. But they were all watching Kate, looking for direction. Kate fought the urge to let a scream rip from her throat, admitting defeat.

"Yes, we stick to the protocol."

Mona Kellar skulked away, muttering angrily under her breath, and the rest of the group broke up quietly. Kate leaned up against the nurse's station, absently pulling the papers from each of the charts, looking at the marker scrawls.

"You okay, Katie?" Jack asked, standing beside her.

"We're not doing enough, Jack. I don't know how to treat this thing," she told him, wanting to sag under the weight of the admission.

"You're doing everything you can," he said to her kindly.

"And it's not enough." She looked down the hall to the Rosses' room, then she sighed and pushed herself away from the desk. "I'm going to go sit with my patient. Call me if anything comes up, okay?"

Jack patted her arm gently, his brown eyes shining sympathetically from behind the mask. Kate was glad he was here. Jack possessed a steadiness. Something about the singular way he looked at the world made her feel calm.

Kate moved between her Ward B patients, trying to anticipate their needs and their test results. She mentally filed each piece of information, medical or personal, vital or irrelevant, adding to the growing list of things she was trying to keep in her head. Sometime after the shift change, Andy came upstairs to get her, saying she and Jack had food waiting in the meeting room downstairs. Kate compulsively checked on each of her patients one more time, comparing their most recent vitals to the last four hours, knowing she would stay if Jackson Ross even hinted towards instability. But everyone was holding steady, Ward B settling in for another long night. As she closed her last chart, Andy tugged at her hand and Kate let herself be pulled off the ward and down the stairs.

Jack was already unpacking Styrofoam containers from the bag, passing out cutlery, racing a bottle of water down the table which Andy caught deftly as it careened off the edge.

"So, did you hear that you're brilliant?" Jack asked Kate, popping the lid off one of the containers. Kate shook her head, folding herself into a seat. She felt tired and nowhere near brilliant. "My algorithm came up with two variables. The first one you figured out faster than my computer, which is the one that covers patients who were on steroids before exposure to the virus. The other is whether or not they had the flu in the last six months."

Kate put down her fork. She'd been chewing her food without really tasting it anyway. "Tell me about that last one."

"I ran a scan of all the patients who had tested positive for the virus and found an overlooked pattern. Your Ward B patients not only had some kind of respiratory risk factor, but none of them had the flu last year."

Kate tried to compartmentalize all the possibilities. She looked from Jack to Andy, both of them staring at Kate, neither of them understanding the implications.

"It's local," Kate finally blurted out.

"What do you mean?" Andy asked.

"It's a local strain of influenza, or at least part of one. That's why some people are sicker than others. That's why the fluid build-up is so bad. The Ward B patients have double risk factors: compromised respiratory systems and no form of immunity." Kate was talking to herself, not even sure that Andy and Jack were keeping up with her. It made sense. It didn't help her treat her patients, but it made sense.

"Is this good news or bad?" Jack said, taking a bite of his chicken sandwich. Very little could keep Jack from his food.

"Neither, but it gives us more information. And possibly a way to predict who is going to get sick. If we can test for immunity to the right flu strain, we can guess the trajectory of their illness. You should send the findings to Dr. Salinger." Kate picked up her fork again. At least it was something.

"And it confirms that whoever made the HV1A virus is a local," Andy added, her eyes on Kate.

"It confirms that the strain of influenza A used to create the HV1A-CS virus was the same strain that probably went through Hidden Valley last flu season," Kate said. She paused. "So yes, most likely a local."

Kate watched as Andy pulled out her notebook and wrote it down. She could see how tired Andy was. The dark circles under her eyes were getting more pronounced. They were similar that way: the more urgent and focused they needed to be, the less they slept. Kate absently stabbed at a cucumber with her plastic fork, dipping it in ranch dressing before taking a bite.

"Tell me what they found at the Fullworth farm," Kate said to Andy.

Andy looked at her partner down at the other end of the table.

"I'll do one better, I'll show you," Jack said, wiping his fingers on his shirt and opening his laptop. A white square appeared on the screen beside Kate and she shifted in her chair so she could see better. Jack clicked on the mouse a few times and an image appeared. It looked to Kate like a telephoto lens, the black casing cracked and dirty. It was partially hidden in a pile of hay or straw. Kate studied it and then turned to Andy, waiting for an explanation.

"Slater and Dr. Din discovered this in one of the outbuildings on the Fullworth farm. It seemed out of place, and when he picked it up"—Andy indicated Jack should go to the next image—"this is what he found."

Kate looked at the newest image. The telephoto lens casing was just that, a shell. Inside was a smooth metal cylinder with a small screw-on top. It looked almost like a flask.

"You can just see traces of residue, most likely dry ice, which John at the NML had told us to look out for."

Kate kept looking at the picture, thinking of the HV1A virus living in that small, innocuous container. She pictured it being opened, the virus spreading and adapting. She couldn't imagine who had let this go. "You found a print?"

"Yes. And an hour ago we got a match."

Kate looked back to Andy, tearing her eyes away from the image on the screen. She waited.

"It's Roberta Sedlak," Andy said. "Her prints are in the system because she had to get periodic vulnerable sector checks to work in the school system."

Kate's eyes narrowed. She thought about the sixty-four-year-old retired teacher, someone who had lived most of her life in Hidden Valley. "You don't think she had anything to do with spreading the virus, do you?" Kate asked.

"I'm not ruling anything out," Andy said automatically. She then paused, changed her tone, like she'd just remembered who she was talking to. "I'm thinking that Roberta Sedlak had contact with whoever had this container in their possession. We need to know where she was the day of the fair."

"I take it we're heading to see Al Sedlak tomorrow, then," Kate said.

"He's expecting us in the morning."

Kate absently picked up some more food, looking at the image still projected on the screen. "Did you get anything else from this? Can you track any of the components down, where it was made, that kind of thing?" Kate said. She caught Andy's tired smile.

"Thinking like a cop now, are you?"

"Yeah, well, you're rubbing off on me." Kate tried to return the smile while pressing her palm into her left eye, trying to stop the pounding. Andy's smile disappeared, replaced by a look of concern. Kate headed her off. "So, can you get anything else?"

"I've got someone on it," Andy said, keeping her eyes on Kate's face but answering the question. "Now that we know where and what, Slater and I are going to try to narrow down who had access to that area of the barn and who had access to this kind of equipment. If we can find out—"

"And if they wear a men's size eleven MEC hiking boot," Jack added, looking up from his laptop. "Results just came in from the boot print you picked up. The suspect who tried to break into your truck."

"Make sure that gets to Slater," Andy said automatically, then checked her watch. "Now, if you don't mind."

Jack put his head down and typed away.

"Ready to head out?" Andy asked Kate quietly.

Kate wanted nothing more than to leave with Andy, to crawl into bed and feel warm fingers against her skin, to kiss Andy gently and longingly until nothing else could compete with the feel of her lips. But something tugged at Kate, the patients in Ward B, the image of Jackson Ross hooked up to the ventilator, his latest O2 sat levels, the EKG showing how hard his heart was working. Kate sighed and looked into Andy's grey eyes.

"I think I'm going to stay here tonight," Kate said, and then she waited for the argument.

Andy opened her mouth to protest but closed it again. Kate watched her struggle, to fight her instincts to run interference. After their conversation in the car this morning, Kate realized how often Andy jumped in to try to protect her. *Because apparently I never do it myself*, Kate thought as she waited for Andy to say something.

"I guess crashing together in the on-call room isn't an option."

"We're already pretty high on the gossip list."

"Yes, we are," Andy said quietly.

"Just for tonight," Kate reasoned, though Andy hadn't asked for an explanation. "Just until I know Jackson Ross is stable."

"Do what you need to do, Kate," Andy said softly. "You can call me anytime, and I'll be here first thing in the morning with your coffee."

Kate stood and walked around to Andy's side of the table. Andy pushed her chair back and Kate sat in her lap, putting her arms around Andy's neck. Andy wrapped her arms around Kate's waist, and they sat like that for a long time, not saying anything. Kate listened to the sound of Andy's heartbeat, wondering when she'd gotten used to cuddling up to soft body armour. Eventually Kate stood and kissed Andy lightly on the lips.

"I'll see you in the morning," she said.

"Sweet dreams, Katie," Jack said as she passed him on the way out the door.

Kate impulsively leaned down and gave him a kiss on the cheek, making him blush. "Thanks for your help today," she said.

"You're welcome," he said, sweetly flustered.

Kate hooked her mask back over her ears as she left the boardroom and made her way slowly back up the stairs to Ward B.

CHAPTER FIFTEEN

It was impossible not to breathe in time with a ventilator, though there was nothing calming about its predictable rhythm. Unlike falling asleep with someone, when your breathing unconsciously fell in synch with the person beside you, listening to the ventilator was slightly alarming. The machine was too forceful, each controlled breath slightly delayed but also too sudden. Other than the fact that it was keeping Jackson Ross alive, there was nothing peaceful about it.

Kate sat between Jackson and Trent Ross for a long time, dawn filling the room with a faintly orange glow. She'd slept in the small, cold on-call room, uneasily, lightly, but she had slept. Part of her had stayed on alert, waiting for the nurse to come in and wake her up, listening for the code blue over the intercom. Kate knew she couldn't lose another patient. She needed to keep every Ward B patient alive, to carry them through the effects of this virus and see them out the other side. When she'd woken alone just before five, the weight on her shoulders had felt enormous.

Jackson Ross's monitor beeped, and Kate silenced it. He was ready for more meds. She checked his drainage output, noting the slow trickle of fluid. It had remained slow since the initial flood after Eric had inserted the drain, but it was enough to raise his O2 sats. Kate wondered about taking him off the ventilator. She worried, she questioned, she debated. No clear answer, so she sat back down, the sharp puff of air from the ventilator forcing her to draw in her own, shallow breath.

"How's he doing?"

Trent Ross struggled to sit up in his own hospital bed. She immediately went to him and put a hand on his shoulder to have him lie back down again. She pressed the button to raise the head of the bed. His dark hair was no longer neatly parted, and his perfect smile came slower, no longer lighting up his pale face.

"Holding steady," Kate said to him. "He had a good night." She took her stethoscope from around her neck and held it up. Trent nodded resignedly and Kate listened to his chest, making a picture of the free-flowing fluid in his lungs. Satisfied, Kate let him lie back again.

"My asthma was always worse than his," Trent said, adjusting the pillow awkwardly behind his head, looking over at his younger brother. "For the longest time I thought he played his up, just so he could get as much attention as me. It took me a while to figure out he didn't want me to be alone while he ran around with his friends."

"Doesn't sound like your usual bratty brother type," Kate said quietly.

"He was that, too. We spent a lot of time together as kids, obviously. My dad taught us about stocks and trading before I was ten, trying to keep us entertained. Guess that worked in our favour." He shrugged and let out a loud, drawn-out cough. Kate watched him struggle through it, his shoulders shaking, his head hanging low. She realized he was trying to stay quiet, concerned about waking up his brother. A sharp edge of sadness wedged itself in Kate's chest. The cough passed, and Trent Ross looked up at Kate. "Is he going to stay on the ventilator?"

"I haven't decided. Let's see how he does this morning. Why don't you try to sleep? Breakfast is still another hour away," Kate said, standing.

"It would be nice to talk to him again, if only to complain about the food," he said and leaned back against the overstuffed pillows, closing his eyes.

Kate left the room, followed her own well-worn path to the next room. Harris Trenholm was still asleep. His vitals had drifted down again, dancing the line of instability. She let him be, knowing he'd be awake soon enough, taking calls and trying to work on his laptop. At least, Kate very much hoped that would be the case.

Serena was awake, lying on her side and looking out the window when Kate quietly entered her room.

"Good morning," Kate said quietly.

Serena blinked her acknowledgement, but didn't say anything.

"How did you sleep?" Kate asked, checking her vitals.

"Crappy," Serena said, her voice low.

Kate frowned down at the pale girl. "Are you having trouble breathing?"

Serena took a minute to answer. "A little," she finally admitted.

Kate grabbed the mask hanging over the oxygen monitor and handed it to Serena. She put it on without protest, and Kate adjusted the flow. Kate pulled up a stool, not saying anything, the only sound in the room the hissing of the high-flow oxygen.

"Thanks," Serena said eventually. "Kate, am I getting worse?"

Kate very much wanted to know the answer to that question herself. "You're still recovering from pneumonia, so it's complicating your body's ability to fight the new virus," Kate explained. "Take my advice, use the oxygen whenever you need to. Don't make your body work so hard."

Serena nodded and turned to look out the window again.

Kate headed to the nurse's station and told the nurse about Jackson's meds needing to be changed. Then Kate lifted her arms above her head and stretched, pulling in a deep breath before checking the clock on the wall. It was twenty to seven; the rest of the day shift would be coming on any time. Kate suddenly wanted to be outside, to pull down her mask and breathe in real air. She felt like she'd been on this ward for days, not just overnight.

Walking down the stairs and out the doors, Kate wondered if Andy had slept in, or gone for her run, or had stopped to eat breakfast. She knew she had most likely stayed up late working, going over case notes, writing reports, and following up on the details of the entire PHEM team.

As soon as Kate stepped outside, she could tell the cold snap had broken. A light, warm breeze, just at the edge of cool, met her as she walked out the front doors. The sun was making its climb over the mountain behind the hospital, its yellow rays shooting up into the sky. It was going to be a beautiful day, but she wouldn't get to see it. Not with the four sick patients, whatever chaos the ER was going to throw at them, and a meeting with a deceased patient's husband. The thought made Kate sag against the wall beside her, the chill of the stone a shocking contrast to the warmth of the morning sun. Kate closed her eyes and leaned her head back for a moment, breathing in the fresh air. When she opened her eyes again she looked around. It was all familiar, this building and that tree-covered mountain behind her and the slant of the sun as it rose. But it was strange, this familiarity, how quickly she could acclimatize to her surroundings, immerse herself in the people and the environment. Taking off her mask completely and shoving it in her pocket, Kate remembered her conversation with Andy outside RCMP headquarters in Vancouver. Andy had considered Kate's ability to blend in an asset, as if it was a skill Kate had learned and honed. Right now, though, it felt like nothing more than a survival technique, a practice she'd adopted out of necessity.

As another gust of warm wind whipped around the side of the building, Kate closed her eyes again, let the thoughts drift out of her head.

"I didn't know you were into morning meditation."

Andy's voice was sweet, welcome, and made Kate smile before she'd even opened her eyes.

"I'm not into morning anything, you know that," Kate replied, opening her eyes to see Andy walking up to her, handing her one of the two coffees she was holding. Kate caught the scent of Andy's shampoo and watched the morning sunlight glint off her hair.

"I know nothing of the sort," Andy said, leaning in to kiss her.

Andy's kiss was gentle, sweet, but Kate pulled her in suddenly and kissed her back with an intensity that startled them both. She needed this, needed Andy's touch to blot out the crowding awful fear that lurked so close to the surface. Kate felt it again, that weight that seemed to hang just over her head. It shifted slightly, dangerously. She pulled away from Andy with a small gasp.

"Kate? You okay?" Andy's eyes were now cloudy with longing and concern.

"Yeah," Kate breathed out. Her heart wouldn't settle. The shock of cold and warm, desire and fear, the effort to speak and stay silent. "Long night."

Andy stayed silent, her free hand still on Kate's hip. Kate felt the warmth of her touch and willed that feeling to spread through her whole body.

"Guess we should get the day started," Kate said finally.

As they walked together into the hospital, Kate felt for the edges of calm and tried to imagine a time when no weight existed in the world.

❖

Al Sedlak's hand shook slightly as he set down the tray of cream and sugar. They were sitting at the kitchen table, and Kate pressed her hands against the wood, feeling the bumps and divots of a well-used table. It fit perfectly in this two-story red brick home, just off the main street of town. It spoke of craftsmanship and age and family.

"Coffee's coming right up, should just be a moment," the man said, lowering himself into a chair.

Kate studied him as he sat. He was clean-shaven, his grey hair combed, a button-up shirt tucked neatly into belted pants. He looked very together for someone who had so recently lost his wife of forty-six years. Though Al Sedlak wasn't her patient, she still mentally went through her checklist, evaluating how well he was coping with his grief.

"How are you doing, Mr. Sedlak?" Kate leaned forwards a little in her chair.

"I'm managing, that's about all I can say," he said with a small, tired smile.

"I imagine that's a full-time job some days," Kate said in a soft, understanding voice.

Al Sedlak studied her with his blue, watery eyes. "Yes, that it is. But my Roberta told me when she first got sick that I had exactly one week to fall apart and wallow after she passed. And then she expected me to shower every morning, put on clean clothes, and pick up the papers from the end of the driveway."

"Sounds like she was a very practical woman," Kate said with a smile.

"Yes," he responded with a small laugh. "Always practical." His shoulders slumped suddenly, his body listing forwards, leaning his weight on his arms. He ran a shaky hand over his eyes. "Sorry, I'm so sorry," he said, his voice thin.

"No need to apologize," Kate told him gently. "I'm sorry we're bothering you at such a difficult time." She placed a hand on his arm, giving him a moment to recover.

"I understand you are trying to track the virus that's spreading through Hidden Valley," the man finally said, looking up. Kate must have looked surprised because he gave her a smile. "My wife was a newsophile, especially local or provincial news. So I've been keeping up with what's going on." He stopped and looked between Kate and Andy. "I suppose you think that's morbid, don't you?"

"Not at all, Mr. Sedlak," Andy assured him. "I happen to think curiosity is the sign of an active mind."

"You would have gotten along well with Roberta, then," he said, seeming happy to make a connection. "So, go ahead and ask the questions you came to ask." He straightened his shoulders, sitting up a little in his chair.

"We are trying to track the movement of the five original patients who contracted the virus," Kate started, after a slight nod from Andy at the end of the table. "So far, we can place four of the patients at the Fullworth fall fair on Labour Day, but not your wife."

"No, Roberta said she didn't feel like going this year. Usually she loved to go, seeing so many of her former students there. But this year she was tired. Said she wanted to take advantage of the market being quiet to get some shopping done."

"So she went shopping in town?" Kate pressed, knowing Andy needed a confirmation.

"Yes, most likely the organic market, possibly the bakery, though I can't remember if she went that day specifically," he said.

"How did she usually pay for things?" Andy said. "Maybe we could look at receipts or a bank statement."

"Sure, yes. I think I have that. Let me get that and the coffee," Al Sedlak said and pushed himself up from the chair.

Kate looked at Andy as they listened to Mr. Sedlak moving around the next room.

She wasn't there, Kate said in her head, shrugging her shoulders at Andy.

Andy gestured with her fingers, *keep talking, keep asking questions.*

Mr. Sedlak returned with a silver coffee carafe and an overstuffed envelope, one edge ripped neatly with a letter opener. He filled each of their mugs of coffee before sitting down again slowly, pulling the bank statements out of the envelope. Kate shifted in her seat, feeling a little on edge, a little impatient to figure this out.

"Here we go, last month. Roberta was at Market Organics here in town and Best Bakery, that's just on the edge of the highway. Both just after noon, which makes sense." He looked up from the bank statement. "Does that help?"

"Yes," Kate assured him, though there were still so many unanswered questions. "Can you remember if your wife mentioned anything about who she ran into that day?"

Al Sedlak picked up his coffee mug, shaking his head in a seemingly unconscious motion. He took a sip of his coffee, still obviously thinking back to a few weeks ago.

"She was always stopping to talk to people, so it wouldn't have stuck in my mind if she said she ran into someone in particular. Wait, yes. She stopped to give someone a ride, I'm sure that was Labour Day."

"Who, Mr. Sedlak?" Andy asked.

"That I don't remember. She might not have even said. A former student, but there are hundreds of those around here, I'm afraid."

Both Kate and Andy waited silently, watching as the man thought back, both hoping that the name would come to him.

Instead, he shook his head again. "I'm sorry, I really don't remember." He looked sad again, almost defeated. Kate's heart went out to him.

"Don't worry about it, you've given us enough to go on," Kate said, trying to reassure the grieving man. "Thank you for meeting with us today, I know this must be a very difficult time for you."

"Yes, a difficult time," he repeated, almost unconsciously. He took a sip of his coffee, made no move to rise from the table. "How many people has this virus taken?" he asked suddenly, looking up at Kate.

"Three," Kate said quietly.

He shook his head again. "Again, please don't think me morbid, but I think Roberta would have preferred this, to lose the battle so quickly against a small virus instead of the cancer that she'd been fighting for so long."

Kate smiled at the man, saying nothing about what she knew about how the virus had invaded his wife's body so effectively through a tumour in her lungs.

"I miss her every second," he said suddenly, quietly. "Every second. I find myself talking to her, calling to her from upstairs when I can't find something. I wake in the night and think she's just downstairs making herself some tea. I put some of her clothes in with mine when I did the wash last week, just so I would have something of hers to put away. Strange, the things you do in grief, isn't it?" Tears were in his eyes, the sadness pressing down on his vocal cords making his words waver.

Kate put her hand on his arm again, and the three of them sat in silence as the sun from the perfect blue sky day streamed in from the windows.

"Do you have family close by, Mr. Sedlak?" Kate said, not able to ignore her concern.

He smiled and wiped at his eyes. "My daughter is just in Vancouver, and I have a whole community of people looking out for me. But I thank you for checking, Dr. Morrison."

Andy pulled a card and a pen out of her pocket and put them on the table. Kate wrote down her cell phone number before passing the card to Al Sedlak.

"Call, anytime. About anything," she told him.

"Yes, I will."

Back in the Yukon, Kate squinted against the bright light, checking her silent cell phone. She felt pulled in too many directions, thinking of her patients, of the widowed man they'd just left, of whoever had been in that car with Roberta Sedlak on Labour Day weekend. Kate was debating whether or not to call Lucy and check in on her patients when Andy spoke.

"I'll take you back to the hospital. I've got to meet with the new officers back at the RCMP office in half an hour."

"Sure," Kate said absently, now twisting her silver ring around her finger.

"What is it?"

"That's who you're looking for, isn't it?" Kate said. "Whoever Roberta Sedlak offered a ride to, that's who you're looking for."

"Most likely," Andy said, checking her blind spot as she pulled out onto the highway.

Kate wondered how she could sound so calm when they were tantalizingly close to the information they needed. Kate itched to know. It drove her crazy to have those missing pieces just out of reach.

"I need Ferris," Andy said suddenly. "It's not going to be easy trying to question people without a local to help."

"What about Judy?" Kate asked as farms and fields whipped by the windows. "I know she's not an officer, but she has all the information, and she's definitely a local."

Andy looked quickly at Kate, calculating. "Yes, brilliant."

"That's why I'm here," Kate said, her thoughts drifting back to Ward B. She silently repeated the vitals for her four patients, or at least what they'd been almost two hours ago when she'd left. She was relieved when Andy finally pulled up to the front doors of Valley General.

"Wait," Andy said as Kate got out of the car. Andy was staring intensely at a point just over Kate's shoulder. Kate turned to see Michael and Natalie Cardiff just inside the doors of the hospital. Michael Cardiff looked furious. "Maybe I should come in with you," Andy said immediately and turned off the car.

"We need to talk," Cardiff said the second they walked in the door. Natalie was silent, fidgeting with the sleeve of her quilted coat.

Andy said nothing, simply led them to the board room. Jack was there, plugging away at his laptop. Andy gestured at him with a jerk of her head, and Jack immediately picked up his laptop and cleared out, giving Kate a wide-eyed look on his way out the door. Kate closed the door behind him.

"I want you to consider that this virus was intentionally released in Hidden Valley to compromise my election bid," Cardiff said immediately, apparently too keyed up to sit.

Andy surveyed him carefully, and Kate couldn't read surprise or derision on her face.

"What made you come to that conclusion, Mr. Cardiff?" Andy asked, her voice neutral.

"Both my campaign manager and now my daughter have been targeted. I know you were checking the James Ranch for evidence, and I also know that you are well aware of our political rivalry because you have been asking questions about it since you arrived here." His voice rose in anger, and it ricocheted off the walls of the small room. In contrast, Andy's voice remained even, almost subdued.

"So you believe Richard James is responsible for the release of the virus?" she asked pointedly.

Cardiff looked suddenly evasive, knowing it wasn't a question he could answer with any reasonable authority. "I'm saying it should be investigated."

"I can assure you that it is being investigated. The politics of Hidden Valley have been on my agenda from the beginning. Which is why I've been asking questions since I arrived," Andy pointed out.

"But specifically, Sergeant Wyles. I want you to specifically look at me and my family as targets. I want to know exactly how you plan to keep this virus away from me and my family."

Andy looked at the man impassively for a long minute before leaning forwards in her chair. The movement somehow added weight to her next words. "There are currently seventy-one confirmed cases of the virus in Hidden Valley. Are you telling me that you can trace even a third of those cases specifically to you, your family, or your campaign?"

Another trap, another question with no answer. "But my daughter…" he started, his shoulders tight with anger.

"Your daughter and Mr. Trenholm both unfortunately have additional factors that put them at a high risk for complications from this virus," Kate jumped in. "Very different factors, I might add. I don't see how that can be more than a coincidence."

"And I don't see how you have the authority to make that assessment," Cardiff said sharply. "Stick to the medicine, Dr. Morrison. You are one wrong move away from being packed up and sent back to your dingy ER in Vancouver."

Kate kept eye contact with the man, refusing to flinch under his gaze or the weight of his threat. She could feel Andy tense on the other side of the table, reacting to the insult.

"You two aren't any farther ahead since you got here. The virus is spreading, the community is in turmoil, and you are no closer to finding a way to stop it or catch who's responsible. What exactly have you two been doing since you arrived in Hidden Valley? Or is that a *private* matter?" he sneered.

Kate felt the heat of embarrassment rise in her cheeks as the accusations and insinuations reverberated in her head. She automatically looked to Andy, probably the worst thing she could have done in that moment. It made her look guilty and feel weak. Andy, however, kept her eyes on Michael Cardiff, her gaze intense and unwavering.

"Is there anything else you wanted to discuss, Mr. Cardiff? If not, both Dr. Morrison and I need to get back to work." Andy's voice was even, betraying none of the stress Kate could read in her body language.

He turned to look at his wife, who met his gaze, her right hand clenched tightly at her side. She seemed to plead with him with her eyes, but whether it was to cease his fighting or to push harder, Kate couldn't be sure.

"Don't be surprised, Sergeant Wyles, when you are asked some very pointed questions by my father-in-law in the next few hours," he said, his voice hard, his tone doubling the threat of his words.

Finally he turned and headed back out the door, his wife following quickly behind.

"I need to get upstairs," Kate said immediately after they left. Her heart pounded, her spine felt tight with stress, the blood vessels behind her eye throbbed, and as she moved towards the door, she felt a momentary dizziness.

"Kate?" Andy's voice reached her just as she got to the door.

Kate turned, wishing more than anything that Andy wouldn't ask her any questions. She needed desperately to get upstairs and update the patient information that streamed in a constant backdrop in her head. But Andy didn't ask anything, just subjected Kate to her full body scan, like Kate needed to pass some sort of test before she was allowed to leave.

"Call me if you need anything," Andy said, her voice cautious. Kate gave only a brief thought to what Andy had just seen, what signs of stress were evident in her body and her face. She simply nodded, hooked her mask back behind her ears, and headed out into the hallway.

At the top of the stairs, just as Kate was reaching for her ID to be admitted to Ward B, she heard her name being called. Natalie Cardiff was coming up the stairs, her one arm wrapped almost protectively around her body. Again, Kate got the sense that this woman was literally trying to hold herself together.

"I'm sorry—" she started, but Kate held up a hand.

"Please don't," Kate said, her voice sharper than she had intended. "It's fine. And I really need to get in and check on my patients."

Natalie Cardiff fidgeted, hands tightly clenched. "If there's any way I could see my daughter…" Her voice was pleading, like she already knew what Kate would say but couldn't stop herself from asking.

"I'm sorry, this is a closed ward. I can't allow you access." It felt beyond cruel, barring this woman from seeing her daughter. But Kate also knew it was a necessary precaution. "Have you been able to video chat with her? I know it's not the same…" Kate said, her voice softened a little.

"Yes, this morning. It was hard with the mask on, and she couldn't take it off for very long, she had trouble breathing almost as soon as it was off." Tears pooled in her eyes and ran down her cheeks.

Kate sighed as alarm for Serena and compassion for her mother warred for space in Kate's body. She felt it as she took the weight on, made it fit amongst the details and the worry, the sharp-edged fear and the guilt that she wasn't doing enough. But even still, Kate knew she had to take on Natalie Cardiff's pain. It was what she did. It was how she functioned.

"I can't imagine how hard this is for you, Mrs. Cardiff. I know you're dealing with a lot right now, but we need to keep this ward restricted. For everyone's protection," she tried to stress.

"I know, I know," Natalie said quietly, still crying. "I'm sorry," she said, though Kate wasn't exactly sure what she was apologizing for. "I'm trying so hard keep it together, for my kids." She took in a deep, shaky breath, like she was heading off a complete breakdown.

Kate sighed again, looked down at Natalie's clenched hands, a thin edge of metal showing between her fingers and palm. A shock of recognition passed through her then as she saw what Natalie had been holding tight in her fist. Natalie followed the direction of her gaze, then slowly opened her fingers. A perfectly smooth, dull medallion sat in her palm. An AA chip. Kate went back over every detail she knew of Natalie Cardiff, adjusting and resorting information.

"It's not a massage appointment you go to every morning," Kate said.

"No, though I let everyone think that," she said, closing her hand again.

"How long?" Kate asked gently.

"Sixteen years," Natalie said, still looking down.

Kate was silent, thinking about the age gap between Serena and Julia, deciding that maybe the woman standing in front of her wasn't so fragile after all. She also thought about her own number, the one she tracked unconsciously in her head. *Seven years, eight months*. She didn't offer this into the silence. Right now, she could not imagine letting this small piece of her float freely. Everything had to be held so carefully right now.

Natalie suddenly looked up, her eyes pleading.

"I know you're doing everything you can, Dr. Morrison. But I need my daughter to walk out of here. I will not survive, our family will not survive without Serena."

"I promise that I will do everything I can, Mrs. Cardiff." She repeated the promise automatically, forcing the words through tight lips. Then she turned and walked through the double doors of Ward B.

CHAPTER SIXTEEN

Kate sat on the on-call bed staring down at her hands. The faint lines of old scars, the slight roughness of patched skin. She took off her silver ring, Sarah's ring, and put it on the bedside table. Looking carefully at the slight indentation, she saw the familiar groove against her finger. Cross-hatched lines, puckers of skin, the shiny stretch over bones and knuckles. Kate inspected her hands until they crossed the line from familiar to foreign. Until they belonged to someone else entirely.

They'd lost Jackson Ross.

Kate's shoulders sagged as she saw the replay of the scene in her head, watched her hands—fast, useless hands—trying to save him. Another tidal wave of fluid, his lungs filling so rapidly she had no hope of staying ahead of it. She watched the scene again, reliving the moment when she decided to put a drain in his other side, weighing the risks of a double drainage, of yet another hole in his already severely compromised lungs. Eric, on the other side of the bed, handing her the tube, calling out vitals, yelling at the nurse to close the curtain around the bed. Trent Ross crying, choking behind her. A moment, so brief, when they thought it had worked. Then crashing, heart rate wild, his system screaming for oxygen. Eric telling her they were done, repeating the words until Kate removed her hands from Jackson Ross's still chest. Trent Ross screaming, thrashing on the bed behind them, and Kate didn't have it in her to feel his pain, too. Eric having to subdue him as he tried to get out of bed, pulling at his IV, at his mask.

Her hands. Useful hands, competent hands. Kate tried to remind herself of this. But the sentiments echoed hollowly and unconvincingly in her head.

Kate looked up as someone knocked on the door to the on-call room and opened it without waiting for a response. Lucy. Kate was thankful she hadn't cried.

"Dr. Doyle is looking for you," Lucy said, her eyes kind and tired.

Kate forced herself to remember she wasn't the only person losing here. "Thanks, I'll be right out," she said.

She took enough slow, steadying breaths to feel like she could face another person. Then she deliberately pulled the sleeves of her gown right down to her wrists and walked out.

Dr. Doyle was standing at the nurse's station, two charts in hand, her mask looking out of place over her perfectly made-up face. "Dr. Morrison, I've got two new patients, both borderline, both in good condition. But they also present with risk factors and neither has been on steroids. Dr. MacKay thought it best to admit them."

"Have they had their initial dose here?" Kate asked automatically.

"Yes, in emerg, before they were sent up," Dr. Doyle replied, handing over the charts.

"Good," Kate said, though it wasn't really. It hadn't been enough for Jackson Ross. Why did she think it would be enough for these patients?

"I'm sorry about Jackson Ross," Dr. Doyle said suddenly, awkwardly.

"So am I," Kate said, not looking up from the charts.

"What's the status of the rest of the patients?"

"Harris Trenholm and Serena Cardiff are holding steady. Trent Ross is sleeping off a dose of sedative that Dr. MacKay administered a few hours ago and his sats are in the normal range, only supplemental oxygen needed occasionally."

She had a sudden, bizarre thought that Dr. Doyle would ask her who would be the next to go. That she would want a prediction about the inevitability of Kate losing another patient. Kate shook her head, forced herself to read the charts in front of her. Twenty-nine-year-old woman, lung infection last year; forty-seven-year-old man, car accident over a decade ago. Low risk factors, but still risk factors.

Kate closed the charts, handed them to Lucy, and met Dr. Doyle's eyes for the first time. "Anything else?" she asked, knowing the question sounded rude.

"Autopsy scheduled for the day after tomorrow. I'll let you and Dr. MacKay fight that one out," Dr. Doyle said, completely unsympathetic.

Kate acknowledged her with a quick nod of her head, wanting Dr. Doyle gone off the ward as quickly as possible.

"I have to go inform PR of the Ross death. We'll have to prepare another media alert. Perhaps you should check in with Dr. MacKay tomorrow, since the ER is sure to be busy with the news of another death."

"I'll make sure the ER is covered tomorrow," Kate said.

"Good, do that," Dr. Doyle said, almost sharply. She turned to go then stopped, looked back at Kate. "I've got two doctors coming on tonight to cover Ward B, and they should be here in an hour. Go get some sleep, Dr. Morrison."

She had no room to feel grateful, no thought Dr. Doyle was being kind. It was simply another accusation, a questioning of her competence as a doctor. As Dr. Doyle turned away, Kate sagged heavily against the nurse's station, covering her now pounding head with her hands. She stood like that, listening to Dr. Doyle's high heels on the floor, clacking their way down the hall and through the double doors.

"Dr. Morrison, is there anything I can get for you?" Lucy's voice, tentative and kind, intruded on Kate's self-depreciating thoughts.

"A new protocol to treat acute onset pulmonary edema would be great." Kate tried for a joking tone, but she must have missed. Lucy looked at her with wide, worried eyes. "No," Kate sighed, "there's nothing you can get for me, Lucy."

Kate admitted the two new patients, adding their data to the loop in her head. They both seemed so healthy, so vibrant in comparison to her other Ward B charges. Kate remembered both Jackson and Trent Ross seeming so carefree just two days ago. The thought stopped her, forced the air from her lungs, and it was a moment before she could breathe again.

She was cycling through chest x-rays, trying to crack the viral code when she heard Jack down the hall.

"Hi, Katie," he said in his gentle, warm voice.

Kate looked up from the monitor, met his kind brown eyes, and felt the sudden urge to cry, to let her guard down for one second and just cry. But she swallowed it, too aware of the precariously balanced weight.

"Hey Jack, what are you still doing here?" Kate checked her watch—nine o'clock. Where had the day gone?

"Wylie sent me to get you. She's back at the hotel. Conference call with Finns and Heath," he said.

Andy. Kate felt the warmth and the worry mix in her chest. She'd barely allowed herself to think about Andy in the last few hours. Now she very desperately wanted to see her.

She didn't even fight. "Give me twenty minutes, I'll meet you out front."

Half an hour later, the Ward B patients transferred over to two doctors for the night, Kate made her way outside. She briefly remembered the morning, standing in the sun, feeling the warmth on her face. It seemed like so long ago, as she climbed into the rental car and Jack drove out onto dark, empty streets. They didn't talk, Jack fiddling with the radio and muttering about the lack of quality stereos in newer vehicles.

Kate used her pass key in the lock of the hotel room, pushing the door open to see Andy sitting rigidly at the desk, her shoulders tight, her voice perfectly controlled as she spoke into the phone. Kate's heart ached at the sight of the stress in Andy's body. Andy half turned and looked at Kate before she spoke again, turning back to her case notes spread on the desk. Kate silently took off her shoes and coat and walked across the room. At the very least, she could be there for Andy, to offer her silent support as Andy had done for her so many times over the last few weeks. Kate put her hands lightly on Andy's shoulders, just a gentle pressure to let her know she was there. She felt Andy's body tense, and was sure Andy had barely resisted moving away from her touch. Kate let her hands fall, a sick, useless feeling in her stomach. Andy reached up and tried to catch her hands, but Kate let them slip out from underneath and walked away again.

Walking into the bathroom, she quietly closed the door behind her. She started the bath, welcoming the loud creak of the pipes, the splash of the hot water against the cold tub, drowning out the silence. She took off her clothes, leaving them in a pile behind the door, and sat in the tub before there was much more than a few inches of water.

When it was almost full, she turned off the tap with her foot, hearing Andy's muted voice through the water. There were no distinct words, just the familiar tones of her voice.

With just her head above the water, Kate looked down at her body, examining it as she had done earlier with her hands. She inspected the folds of her body, the curve of her waist, the shape of her legs, the lack of colour in her pale white skin. Kate wished she could see her face, to go through the same scrutiny, to refamiliarize herself with her own reflection. She wished she could empty the contents of her brain, of her memory. Wished she could inspect and sort, identify and examine. Maybe then she could find something familiar, to connect all these pieces of herself into some semblance of a whole being.

Kate heard Andy's tread on the floor, light thumps as she crossed the room. A moment later, the door to the bathroom opened. Andy came in, her shirt untucked, her beltless pants low on her waist. She sat on the edge of the bath and leaned back against the tile wall. Kate was still, watching Andy's cautious face.

"I'm sorry," Andy said, and her voice sounded so loud in the silence.

Kate nodded but didn't speak. What did Andy have to be sorry for? She wasn't the one fucking up at every point, reading every situation wrong.

"It's not going well," Andy continued, when Kate didn't speak.

"I know that," Kate said sharply, stung by the judgement and criticism Andy had not intended.

"That's not what I meant."

Kate sat up, leaning back against the cold tile. Her blood pounded through her body in slow, sluggish waves, her body dealing with the overwhelming heat of the bath. They didn't say anything for a long while, each sizing up the other, testing the air.

"I know it's been a long day," Andy finally said, and Kate had to stop the flood of images that threatened. She focused on Andy's voice, focused on keeping it together. "I'm glad you came back here tonight."

"The on-call room was too cold," Kate said, aiming for conversational, wondering if she could make the climb to normalcy. Wondering if that was even something to aim for.

Andy smiled. "Well, I got all the pillows last night, so I didn't miss you too much."

Kate flicked some water at her in response, leaving splotches on Andy's pants and shirt.

"Watch it," Andy said in a mock, warning tone, "or you'll get some company."

Kate kept her eyes on Andy, waited a beat, then flicked water at her again.

Andy slid fully clothed into the bath, lifting one leg over Kate's head until she was positioned between Kate's knees, her legs wrapped around Kate, eyes shining.

"I did warn you," Andy said, reaching around Kate, her fingers cold against Kate's warm, wet skin.

Kate had to laugh, the sensation feeling only slightly strange, only slightly out of place. She wondered how one person could so easily make everything slip away, as if she could eclipse, merely with her presence, anything difficult.

Kate hesitated, uncertain if she could give voice to her worry. Or if she should reach out, as she knew Andy hoped she would, and begin to unbutton Andy's soaked shirt.

A heartbeat, two, three…

Kate trailed her fingers down the collar of Andy's shirt. And when she met Andy's eyes, smiling, relieved, she had only one thought before she took her up on her offer of oblivion. *Andy was right.*

❖

Kate spent the next day moving between floors, checking in on her Ward B patients and triaging patients in the ER. She knew it was a waste of time to sit by Harris Trenholm's bedside and watch him fight for breath. His sats were no longer fluctuating, they were firmly in the grey area between critical and low-end normal. They had a tube tray ready, the ventilator on standby. Kate wanted to pray they would remain untouched but couldn't find the energy for hope. She hadn't slept well last night. Not with Andy's arms around her, not after the distraction of their lovemaking, not even with the intense tiredness of her body and soul.

She saw patients in the ER, listened to their lungs, catalogued their complaints, scrawled out scripts, ran down the risk factors, assured, feigned patience, forced a smile, remained calm behind her mask. Always remaining calm. Back upstairs, wanting to see the monitors for herself, compare chest x-rays and saturation levels. Her thoughts moved rapidly, always thinking, always searching for the elusive key, something to ward off the fluid, to stop the build-up, to keep the oxygen flowing through their body. And down again to the ER, pick up a chart, ask the questions, stay alert for red flags, question history, listen to their lungs. And again. And again.

"Katie, want to stop for lunch?" Jack met her on yet another trip up to Ward B, wondering what she would find when she got there.

"No, not now, Jack," Kate said, distracted.

"Okay, but can I show you something?" He seemed nervous, fidgeting and rocking.

Curiosity won over impatience. "Sure, what is it?"

Jack motioned for her to follow him into the office.

"Maybe it's nothing, but maybe it's something, I don't know, not enough data yet, but I thought you should see it," he babbled, clearly nervous. He hit a few keys on the laptop and turned it so Kate could see. It seemed to be the patterns algorithm she had asked him to work on a few days ago. The columns of information meant nothing to her, so she looked at him and waited for an explanation.

"I keep inputting data, mining the patient files for whatever fits into your parameters, just wanting to see what it comes up with," Jack said, still fidgeting. Kate was surprised. She hadn't realized he was still working on it. "So after I put in Jackson Ross's information, the program flagged something. Now, it needs more data to confirm, I'm not even sure I should bring it to your attention since it's still so raw—"

"Spill it, Jack," Kate commanded in her best Andy Wyles voice. She needed to know what had been flagged. Right now she could use anything.

"Okay, last we checked, the data suggested that the acute onset edema occurred only in patients who had not had any proactive steroids. But the newest data suggests that the steroids only delay the onset. It doesn't and can't prevent it entirely. The bigger the dose and the longer the exposure are factors, but this data suggests an inevitable downward course to potentially fatal pulmonary edema," Jack finished, his hands flicking at the keys with apprehension.

Kate's body felt cold and she shivered. It made sense, it added up. Even if it wasn't definitive at this point, Kate's instinct told her that Jack was exactly on track.

"How long?" Kate finally asked. "Can it predict how long? For Harris Trenholm, can the program track his exposure to steroids, what his O2 sats are now and how long until the pulmonary edema catches up to him?" She was afraid to ask. She had to know.

"Maybe, but it would be ballpark at best," Jack cautioned.

"Do it. Send it to my phone," Kate commanded. She moved automatically towards the door before she stopped and turned. "Thanks, Jack."

"Sure, Katie. And stop for lunch sometime soon, okay?" Kate smiled but shrugged it off, needing to get back upstairs.

As soon as she reached Ward B, Lucy handed Kate a chart. "Mr. Trenholm's sats are down, and here's his latest EKG results."

Lucy handed Kate the printout, and Kate's heart fell. Harris Trenholm's heart showed signs of stress, the arrhythmic dips and peaks an indication of the strain on his body.

"Shit," Kate said, scanning the entire printout, hoping to see some good news. Nothing.

"Maybe it's a blip," Lucy said, trying to be helpful. Trying to be hopeful. "He's taken worse turns and come back from it."

"No," Kate said sharply, not capable of hearing hope. Not with what Jack had just shared with her. "We need to treat him like he's dying, not like we're just hoping that he'll live." It was a cruel thing to say, especially to Lucy, whose optimism had been helping keep Kate afloat these last few weeks. But Kate didn't offer an apology. She walked into Harris Trenholm's room and sat heavily in a chair.

When her phone chimed that she had a text half an hour later, Kate could do nothing but stare at the screen: *24-48 hours from initial sustained drop below normal range O2 sats.*

A day or two. Maybe more, maybe less. The numbers trickled through her head, streamed and screamed, pounded behind her eye. She was worse than useless, not even able to think let alone put thought into action.

A sickly cheerful voice intruded into Kate's rapidly deteriorating thoughts. "Word on the street is that you're losing it, Dr. Morrison."

Kate looked up to see Mona Kellar sauntering into the room, a look of near glee on her thick face.

"Go harass someone else, Dr. Kellar, I'm not in the mood for your shit," Kate said coldly. She had to admit, though, that she was almost glad Kellar was there, someone she could attack without the smallest trace of guilt.

"Don't flatter yourself that I came here to spend time with you," Kellar said, taking a seat on the other side of Harris Trenholm's bed. "The morgue is filling up fast, and I'm afraid to say you and I are the best Hidden Valley's got at the moment."

Kate surveyed the woman across the bed, thinking about how much trouble she had caused in the past ten days, how much anger and humiliation and more than a little stress. But she had also driven samples to Public Health, made herself available for every meeting, and treated each victim of the virus with a simple kind of respect.

"What do you want?" Kate asked cautiously.

"You need me," Kellar said, her voice so close to suggestive that Kate almost screamed at her to get out. "You need a mind smart enough and fast enough to keep up with yours. No more collaborative medical teams, no more pussyfooting around ideas and conservative treatments. Quit wallowing in self-pity and find a way to treat your patients, Dr. Morrison."

Kate looked away from her, down at Harris Trenholm. She didn't need his chart to know how low his sats were, didn't need an x-ray to confirm his lungs were slowly, stealthily filling up with fluid, even as she and Dr. Kellar discussed the morgue over him. Kate looked back up, meeting those bright, shrewd eyes over her mask. She nodded once in acknowledgement, not trusting her voice.

"Start at the beginning, everything you know. Go," Kellar barked in her drill sergeant's voice.

So Kate started at the beginning. Every detail from every chart of every patient in the past two weeks. Every discovery by Public Health, by the National Microbiology Lab, and even by Jack just a few hours ago. Kellar grilled her with questions, forcing her to connect those pieces of information, not allowing for any breaks in the information chain. Kate began to get frustrated, feeling they were coming back to the same conclusion.

"Then make a conclusive statement, Dr. Morrison." Dr. Kellar's voice was heavy with condescension.

Kate barely controlled the anger in her voice as she answered. "We need to stop the acute onset pulmonary edema," Kate said through clenched teeth.

"Do you?"

Kate stopped the instant retort that sprang so easily to her lips. She paused, eyes on Dr. Kellar, thinking.

"Why are the patients dying?" Kellar asked, leaning forwards in her seat.

"Fluid build-up in their lungs prevents oxygen from being absorbed which causes multi-system failure," Kate said automatically. She watched this exact scenario with Jackson Ross play out in morbid detail in her head.

"So lack of oxygen is the issue," Kellar prompted.

"Yes…" Kate said absently, watching the rise and fall of Harris Trenholm's chest, the re-breather mask fogging over with each strained, wet breath. She knew he needed to be on a ventilator soon, needed to force the oxygen down into his lungs. She wished they could find another way to supply the oxygen his body so desperately needed. She imagined, wildly, an O2 bath, immersing him in the simple molecule, letting it absorb through his skin like a life-sustaining bath…

Kate's body jolted, both her feet hitting the floor, her heart pounding with a sudden rush of adrenaline.

"What is it?" Dr. Kellar asked immediately.

Kate opened her mouth to speak, but she was having trouble forming words. "Not taking it far enough…oxygen therapy…" She stumbled over the words, over the thought in her head, picturing the useless researcher in Winnipeg yelling those same words over his shoulders.

"We've been over that," Kellar said derisively, leaning back in her chair, disappointed.

"No!" Kate shouted at her, angry that she couldn't spit it out. "Oxygen therapy, use a hyperbaric chamber to flood their bodies with oxygen. If we can manage the fluid while keeping their O2 levels up, we can get them through the critical period, let the virus run its course. We can stay ahead of it," Kate finished, looking desperately now for approval from Dr. Mona Kellar.

Dr. Kellar said nothing for a moment, her eyes calculating. Kate fidgeted, the adrenaline in her body making small tremors run through her chest and arms.

"Yes," Dr. Kellar said finally, simply. "Yes."

"Where?" Kate asked, her relief only temporary.

"One in Whistler, two in Saskatchewan," Dr. Kellar said immediately, standing also. "Dr. Doyle needs to get on this, now. I'll find her, you prioritize the patients. Use that algorithm predictor, find out who's the next most critical."

Kate agreed, already calculating vitals and oxygen levels in her head, staring unseeing at Harris Trenholm.

Dr. Kellar had almost left the room when she stopped and turned back. "Good work, Dr. Morrison," she said, grudgingly.

"Thanks for your help," Kate added, striving for genuine appreciation, even now struggling with it, knowing who Dr. Kellar was and what she was capable of.

True to form, Mona Kellar gave a sly wink. "Maybe now you'll put in a good word for me with Ms. Wyles. See if she and I can't come to an understanding." The emphasis on the last word made Kate's skin crawl. It must have shown on her face because Dr. Kellar laughed as she walked out of the room.

Kate pushed it out of her head, not letting it intrude. Her body felt utterly re-energized as she inputted Harris Trenholm's most recent vitals in the chart and walked quickly to the nurse's station. They had a plan. Not a definitive plan. No guarantees. But a plan. And Kate's gut told her they were on the right track. If they could keep their patients steady through the peak of fluid, the virus would run its course and they could walk away from this. Just as Natalie Cardiff had asked of her not so long ago.

Kate moved quickly, inputting the data into the system, brushing off any offers of help from Lucy, wanting to do it herself. Wanting Jack to be able to use this data to help her prioritize the patients. Kate checked in on Serena just before she went downstairs. The young woman was asleep. She'd been on O2 all day, her breathing laboured. Even with a plan, Kate felt the sick worry thud in her chest. She thought she knew who would be next highest on the priority list.

She took the stairs quickly, almost running down the hall, skidding into the meeting room. Jack looked up as she came in, breathless.

"You okay?" he asked, alarmed.

"Hyperbaric chamber. We're going to try a hyperbaric chamber with the critical patients. But there aren't very many available, so we need your algorithm to predict timing, which is the next most critical patient. Can you do it?"

"Sure, I can," Jack said, "I just need the most recent data."

"I inputted it myself and I told the nurses the updated vitals have to go directly into the system every half hour so you can have it immediately," Kate finished, almost breathless. Everything seemed too slow. She wanted to be three steps ahead already, could almost feel the lift-off of the helicopter transport, taking Harris Trenholm to what she desperately hoped was a cure.

"Have you talked to Andy today?" Kate asked Jack.

"Yeah, she was talking her way around Hidden Valley this morning, trying to figure out who Roberta Sedlak offered a ride to," Jack said, talking and typing at the same time.

Kate decided not to interrupt Andy, though she wanted to share the news. There would be time. Kate stood quickly, deciding to go see Eric after all.

"Call me if you need anything, okay?" Kate said to Jack, already half out the door.

It had been so long since Kate felt this light, this normal. But no, that was an illusion. The weight still shadowed her, hovering just overhead. Kate forced it away, focusing on the good news, on the excited expression on Eric's face as she walked him through the new plan. Though they were both supposed to be going off shift in less than an hour, Kate would stay, manage the remaining Ward B patients and continue to update the priority list. Eric would take Harris Trenholm on the transport to the first available hyperbaric chamber. He promised to stay in constant communication.

As Kate left the ER again, feeling almost light with the promise of action like a drug in her system, her phone rang. She checked the screen—somewhere from in the hospital. She answered, hoping it wasn't Lucy with bad news, hoping each patient could make it through to the next treatment stage.

"Dr. Morrison? It's Trick…from the lab?"

It took Kate a moment to place the voice and the name. "How can I help you, Trick?"

"I found something a little odd, I thought maybe you'd want to know."

"Okay, shoot," Kate said quickly, leaning up against a pillar, focusing on Trick's voice. She watched absently as people moved around the main lobby, masks and gown obscuring faces and expressions.

"Well, you know how you sent down more blood samples, wanting to test the Ward B patients for immunity to last year's influenza?"

That already seemed like a lifetime ago, like old news. But Kate forced herself to listen. "Yes."

"Well, when I ran Serena Cardiff's sample and compared it to her other blood work, I noticed something different. Serena Cardiff has the original strain of the virus, not the mutated strain as first assumed."

"Are you sure?"

"Double-checked and then sent my findings to John Crann at the NML to confirm. It's the original strain."

Kate's thoughts slowed, pulled back, shifted gears. She watched one hospital staff member walk up the stairs, his gown tied hastily, his feet hitting the stairs with athletic precision. Kate watched him pull out ID and get admitted to the ward, all the while calculating, counting, and trying to make sense of this newest information.

"Dr. Morrison?"

"Yes, thanks. It's good that you called," Kate said automatically into the phone. She hung up without waiting for a reply and walked quickly back to the meeting room.

"Call up Serena Cardiff's chart," she said the moment she walked in the room. Jack complied immediately without question. He hit a few buttons and looked up for his next instructions.

"When was she admitted for pneumonia?" Kate asked.

"October third."

"Discharged?"

"October ninth."

Kate's head hurt. "Today's date?"

"October fifteenth."

It didn't make sense. It didn't add up. They'd assumed Serena had contracted the airborne virus after she left the hospital. Her immunity was already low, her body ripe for this virus to find its way into her lungs and take up residence. If she had the original strain and had started to show symptoms only four days ago… Kate's brain did the math.

"She contracted it here," Kate said, her voice a monotone.

"What's that?"

"Serena Cardiff contracted the virus here," Kate said, doing the math again in her head, counting back from her onset of symptoms. Seven to ten days before that put her right here at Valley General. *How is that even possible?* Kate wanted to pound her brain into making it make sense.

"What does that mean?" Jack asked, his eyes round.

"I don't know, but I think I need to call Andy," Kate said just as her phone chimed in her pocket. "Unknown number," Kate mumbled as she read the screen, her thoughts in too many places.

Jack picked up his own phone. "I'll call Wylie, you get that."

Kate looked at the screen on her phone as it signaled she had a message. She opened the text.

I need your help.

She quickly texted back. *Who is this?*

Jack called her name and held out his phone. "Wylie wants to talk to you," he said. Kate detected a note of urgency in his voice.

"Andy?" Kate asked, pinning Jack's phone between her ear and her shoulder, watching the screen of her own phone in her hand.

"I think we know who we're looking for," Andy said, her voice intense and focused. "We retraced Roberta Sedlak's route, adding in the Fullworth farm as a waypoint and came across a backpack. It's a camera bag, which fits, given what was found there."

Kate listened, trying to follow as another message came through on her phone. She hit the button automatically.

Chris Ozarc, I need your help, please.

"Kate, are you listening?" Andy said in Kate's ear, annoyed by her obvious distraction.

"Chris Ozarc," Kate mumbled into the phone, reading the name on her screen.

"How did you know?" Andy demanded.

"Because he was here a week ago. He gave the virus to Serena," Kate said as she worked it out in her head. "And he just sent me a text, asking for my help." Kate was struggling to track all of the details. A sudden image intruded into the barrage of information flooding her thoughts. She'd seen him, Chris Ozarc. Just now she'd watched him climb the stairs: the dark hair, the athletic body, the hastily tied gown. He'd been admitted to Ward B.

Andy was talking in her ear, asking her questions, but Kate didn't hear it.

"He's here," Kate blurted out.

"What?" Andy asked, stopping mid-sentence.

"Chris Ozarc. Andy, he's in the hospital."

CHAPTER SEVENTEEN

Confusion. Mass confusion. Andy yelling in her ear, Jack picking up the landline and dialing, the sound of the Yukon's engine racing in the background. Kate gripped her cell phone tightly and stared at the message on the screen.

"Kate!" Andy's voice commanded on the other end of the phone.

"What?" Kate asked, trying to focus.

"When did you see Chris Ozarc in the building?" Andy asked. Kate could hear someone talking in tense, commanding tones in the background. Constable Slater probably, Kate thought.

"Five, maybe ten minutes ago," Kate answered, checking her watch.

"And you're sure it was him?"

"I didn't see his face, but I'm sure it was him."

"Slater's on the phone confirming. We should have an answer soon. We've got security starting a lockdown. Slater and I and the two other officers should be there in about five minutes…"

Kate had stopped listening at *lockdown*. "Andy, I've got to get patients out," she said urgently. "Harris Trenholm, at the very least. Dr. Doyle was arranging helicopter transport—"

"Ward B is going into lockdown," Andy said firmly. "We won't be able to get anyone out until this situation…"

Kate was already moving, Jack's cell phone pressed to her ear, her own cell still clenched in her fist.

"We'll see how quickly we can apprehend Chris Ozarc. Any idea what he wants?" Andy asked, and Kate could hear that she was on the highway.

Kate moved quietly out of the room and down the hall, trying to even out her breathing, so Andy wouldn't know she was walking. "No, he just said he needed my help."

"And how does he have your cell number?"

"I gave it to him last week when he came by the hospital. I thought he wanted to get looked at in the ER. He looked so lost, I gave him my cell phone number and told him to call me about anything," Kate said, taking the stairs slowly.

"Of course you did," Andy said, under her breath. "We're almost there, two minutes out."

"Okay," Kate said. She pulled out her ID for the security guard as his two-way radio beeped and squawked loudly on his shoulder. Kate knew she only had seconds.

"Kate, where are you?" Andy asked suddenly.

Kate didn't answer.

"Kate Morrison, answer me! Where are you?" Andy demanded.

Still she didn't answer, showing her ID, getting the nod from the guard even as he picked up the receiver and pressed the buttons. Kate was through the doors and down the hall as he got his orders to lock down the ward.

"I'm on Ward B," Kate said as calmly as she could into the phone.

Andy swore violently. Kate felt a moment of guilt. She knew she'd just made everything harder for Andy. But she couldn't sit downstairs with Jack in the meeting room. She needed to be with her patients, needed to get Harris Trenholm out of here, soon. Twenty-four hours. The clock was ticking down.

"What do you need me to do, Andy?" Kate asked, approaching the nurse's station. Lucy was on the phone, and her face was bloodless, her eyes wide with fear.

"Where is Chris Ozarc now?"

Kate made a questioning gesture with her hand to Lucy. She pointed with a shaking finger to Serena's room, and Kate moved down the hall and peeked through the blinds.

"He's in Serena's room," Kate said quietly into the phone. "He's sitting by her bed, holding her hand. That's all I can see,"

"Get back to the nurse's station, immediately. We're here," Andy said, and Kate could hear her moving.

"Andy, I'm putting the phone in my pocket, so just listen, okay?"

Kate didn't wait for an answer, dropping Jack's open phone into the pocket of her gown. She still held her cell phone in her other hand as she walked into Serena Cardiff's room.

"Hello, Chris," Kate said quietly. Serena was asleep, and even from the doorway, Kate could hear her laboured breathing. *Twenty-four to forty-eight hours*, thought Kate. Dr. Doyle had better find two available hyperbaric chambers.

Chris Ozarc's mask and gown lay discarded on the floor. He sat exactly as he had last time Kate had seen him in Serena's room, holding her hand. This time though, there was no look of pain. His face seemed blank, completely devoid of emotion.

"Dr. Morrison, tell me Serena's okay," Chris said, his voice an alarming monotone.

"She's not," Kate said. "But I've never seen anyone fight as hard as Serena," she added. Kate calmly picked up Serena's chart and flipped it open. Lowered O2 sats for the past four hours. Kate checked the monitors and inputted the newest vitals, all the while feeling the intensity of Chris's gaze on her. She adjusted the O2 monitor on Serena's finger and checked the flow of the oxygen through the mask. The familiar, routine movements calmed her. She could see Chris's posture relax a little out of her peripheral vision.

"You said you needed my help," Kate said quietly, looking over the bed at Chris.

He stared down at Serena. "I don't know what to do," he finally said, in the same, deadened tone. "I don't know what I'm doing."

"You came here to see Serena," Kate said, posing it as a statement, trying to keep any accusation out of her voice.

Chris met Kate's eyes again, and she felt a flash of fear. That wasn't the only reason he was here. He had some desperate, half-formed plan. He looked away again, back to Serena, and Kate could now see the pain in his eyes. This was good. This was something she could connect with.

"Chris, we have a plan to help Serena and the other critical patients. We need to get them out of the hospital, though." Kate watched as he gripped Serena's hand convulsively, and her heart sank.

Kate let the silence stretch, forcing herself to not check her watch, not to feel the countdown of the minutes. If only she could get Harris Trenholm out of here. She heard the muted squawk of a radio in the hallway, and Chris looked up at Kate, then out the open door.

"Who else is here?" he demanded. His body was tense again, and the hand farthest from Kate hung awkwardly down by his side.

"Last I checked there was a nurse on the floor and a security guard at the doors," Kate said evasively. Chris's eyes narrowed dangerously. Kate sighed and sat down in the chair and looked directly at Chris. "The RCMP were on their way when I came in. I assume they're here by now," Kate told him evenly.

"I'm making them nervous."

"Yes."

"Am I making you nervous?" he asked Kate in the same monotone, but his eyes were pleading.

Kate considered this. "What makes me the most nervous is that you're trying to hide," she said gently. "If I'm going to help, I need to know what's going on in your head."

Chris glared at her from across the hospital bed, but Kate looked back at him impassively. After a moment, his shoulders sagged. He slumped forwards in the chair, resting his head against the bed.

"Why are you helping me?" His voice sounded muffled.

"Because you asked me to," Kate said. "I'm a doctor, Chris, it's kind of what I do." Another minute, another sound from the open door, and Kate wished she'd thought to close it on the way in. "Chris, there are four other patients on this ward and one of them is in critical condition. I need to go and arrange transport for them."

Chris looked up in a panic, one hand gripping Serena tightly, the other reflexively touching his jacket pocket. Kate didn't need to be a cop to figure out whatever Chis had hidden wasn't good. Her hope this would be resolved easily and peacefully dissolved in a heartbeat.

"Are you here to hurt Serena?" Kate asked quietly.

"No!" Chris shouted, sitting up. "No, no, no, no…" His body twisted in panic, every muscle tight, like he was fighting off the accusation. Kate felt alarm at his reaction, how unstable he was, how unnervingly quickly he moved between numbness and fear. At the very least, though, Kate was convinced that he wouldn't hurt Serena.

"It's okay. Chris, listen to me. I trust you, I need your help," Kate held her hands up, a gesture of peace and calm. Eventually he listened, his breathing returning to normal, and he looked to her for direction. Good. That was good. "I'm going to go move the other patients," she said. "I will be back. While I'm gone, I need you to watch this number." She pointed to the O2 monitor. "When I come back, I want to know if the number has gone below eighty-five."

"Eighty-five," he repeated, staring at the monitor.

"Eighty-five," Kate said calmly and she stood up. Chris looked up at her movement, uncertainty etched in every nuance of his body language.

"You'll be back." It was a statement, not a question.

"I am going to arrange to have the other patients moved and then yes, I will be back," Kate said. "You'll hear us moving in the hallway, and you'll probably hear the police radios, but it will just be me who walks back into this room. Promise." God, Andy was going to be pissed.

"Okay," Chris said, staring back down at Serena.

Kate moved towards the doors, watching for signs of movement in the hallway. Nothing. But as soon as she stepped out of the room, a familiar hand gripped her upper arm and pulled her down the hallway. Andy said nothing, her face an angry, stone mask, marching Kate quickly and quietly to the nurse's station. Constable Slater was there, along with two other officers Kate didn't recognize, a security guard, and Lucy. They all looked at Kate, wide-eyed and cautious. Kate didn't have the time or energy to wonder what they thought of her in that minute.

"He's not here to hurt Serena," Kate said immediately, addressing the group but looking at Andy. "He's got something in his pocket. I'm guessing a weapon but I don't know. If he's got a plan, it's not very detailed. Right now I think he just wants to sit with Serena and know that she's okay."

Andy looked at her with calculating eyes. Kate could see the sharp edge of her anger as Andy forced herself to breathe evenly. "Do you think moving your patient will set him off?" Andy asked, her voice direct, devoid of emotion, though her grey eyes pinned Kate to the spot.

"I think it will be fine, as long as no one mentions anything about moving Serena at this point. Is there a transport available?"

"Yes," Lucy jumped in, her voice a nervous whisper. "Dr. Doyle said Whistler is sending an air ambulance." She checked her watch. "Should be arriving in twenty minutes." She looked back to Kate, waiting for direction.

"We need to get him out now," Kate said.

Andy finally looked away from Kate and gave a curt note to Slater. "Let's go."

Kate followed them to Harris Trenholm's room, waiting for Andy's objection. It never materialized. Kate updated his chart, wedged it against the bed, unhooked the IV bags from their poles, and attached them to the bed frame. Andy and the officers watched and waited for direction as Kate moved around the bed with urgent efficiency. Kate triggered the wheel lock mechanism on one side of the bed and indicated the officer on the other side should do the same. They wheeled Harris Trenholm out of the room and down the hallway, the complete silence strange and ominous. Kate focused on Harris's dusky face. *Please let this work*, she thought. *Please let this be enough.*

Out in the hall, Kate waved for Lucy to take her spot with the patient.

"The others," Kate said once the elevator doors had closed. No time for relief. "They're not critical, but we need them out. Do we have somewhere to take them?"

"We can't move them," Andy said, cutting in. "We would have to send multiple staff past the room multiple times. It's too risky. If the patients aren't critical, they should stay."

Kate shook her head, ignoring Andy's irritation. "I've already told Chris what was going to be happening. If I'm in the room with him, I think he'll stay calm. I don't think he'll even notice."

"You are not going back in that room," Andy said, her voice deadly.

"Yes, I am," Kate said, aiming for calm, for certainty.

Andy said nothing, staring down at Kate. Kate couldn't help but fidget, knowing others were watching, but she kept her chin up and refused to look away. The silence stretched.

"Serena needs to be treated," Kate tried again, when it was clear Andy couldn't or wouldn't speak. "She's the next most critical patient and someone has to be in there with her in case she crashes. I think Chris trusts me, he just needs someone to help him end this. You heard him, Andy." Kate took a breath. "I think he's here to hurt himself, not anyone else."

Andy still said nothing, and Kate could see her working through the details, coming up with a plan. She watched Andy wrestle, her grey eyes boring into Kate's. In that moment, Kate knew she had won. Kate was the best chance they had of ending this quietly.

She heard muted shouting down the hallway, by the locked doors leading out of Ward B. Kate could see indistinct shadows against the frosted glass and could hear someone pulling frantically at the doors. "What's going on?"

Andy looked up briefly, gestured sharply at one of the new officers, indicating he should deal with it. Then she looked back to Kate.

"Michael Cardiff," she said shortly, her body rigid with stress.

"He knows already?"

Andy nodded once, quickly. Kate watched the officer slip through the doors of Ward B, caught a very brief glance of a furious, terrified Cardiff, trying to get through the doors to his daughter. For the first time Kate actually felt empathy for the man. She knew what that kind of desperation felt like.

"Have you called anyone for Chris? Maybe his dad could talk him out of this."

"I've got Ferris on it," Andy said. "But I wouldn't count on it. Ferris said Chris was basically raised by a series of household staff. His father might not be the best option."

Kate thought about the man, possibly armed, sitting in the room three doors down. She thought she would be afraid of the person who had released a fatal virus into the community. But she wasn't, not really. She mostly just wanted to talk to him until that haunted, dead look left his eyes.

"When I go back in," Kate started, meeting Andy's gaze, "what's my best approach with Chris?"

"You aren't trained for this," Andy said through gritted teeth.

"Really?" Kate said, her own anger rising to the surface. "You think I'm not trained to deal with an unstable patient with mental illness? You know the clientele I work with on a daily basis, Andy. I can handle this."

Andy glowered at Kate, her fear showing as anger. Kate wished she could offer some kind of reassurance. But there was absolutely nothing she could do to make this easier on Andy other than end it, soon.

"Take off your gown," Andy said suddenly, tersely.

Kate didn't understand at first, then she watched as Andy undid the Velcro straps of her own soft body armour vest. Kate untied her gown and stood still while Andy placed the vest over her head, her movements almost rough. She spoke as she secured the straps around Kate's ribs.

"You have time, so use it. If he can't handle the possibility of Serena being taken from him, then you'll have to make him give himself up. Don't push him there, lead him there." Andy pulled the last strap tightly across Kate's body. "Any hint that he's threatening you or Serena, and we will take him down. If we forcibly enter the room, you will immediately hit the floor. That will be your only reaction, leave the rest to us," Andy finished fiercely.

"Okay," Kate said quietly. She put her gown back on. The bulky vest was still warm from Andy's body.

Andy glared at her, and then she suddenly took Kate's face in her hands, forcing Kate to look at her. "However important you think Chris Ozarc and Serena Cardiff are to their families, you need to know you are that important to me. To me and your mom and Tyler, you are that important, Kate Morrison. You will remember there are three of you in that room, and three of you need to come out again."

Kate's heart hurt as it thumped wildly in her chest, beating strangely against the tightness of the armour vest. She wanted to twist away from Andy's gaze, away from her words, the ones that struck the uncomfortable chord in her body.

"Yes," was all Kate could manage to say, as if she was simply accepting orders from a commanding officer.

A moment passed, two, with Andy's hands still clenched around Kate's face. Then suddenly Andy released her and Kate walked immediately back to the room, not stopping for a final look at Andy or anyone else.

Chris was in the exact spot Kate had left him. He looked up when Kate walked in, then his shoulders relaxed when he saw it was Kate.

"How is she doing?" Kate asked. She wasn't quite able to keep the shakiness out of her voice. She clenched her hands in her pocket, released them, clenched them again, trying to get her body under control.

"I watched the monitor. It didn't go below eighty-five," Chris said. "Shouldn't she be waking up?"

Kate sent a random prayer of thanks that Serena wasn't awake. "Her body is trying to heal itself, that's why she's sleeping so much."

"But she'll be okay. You said you found a way to treat the critical patients," Chris pushed, desperately seeking reassurance. There was so little of that to give right now. To anyone.

"We think so. But we can't do it at Valley General. Serena will have to be airlifted out of here at some point," Kate said carefully, thinking of what Andy had said.

Chris didn't react. He just looked back at Serena and pushed a lock of hair off her forehead.

Kate charted Serena's vitals, listened to her lungs, and adjusted the flow of oxygen, Chris closely monitoring each movement. Then she hooked her stethoscope back around her neck and sat in the chair opposite Chris. She sat comfortably, giving no indication they were in any hurry. She waited, letting the silence stretch, while Chris worked through whatever end he'd come here to seek out.

"Is it four?" Chris said suddenly.

"Is what four?"

"The…the death count. From the virus. Is it four?" Chris stuttered, his body tensed as if for impact.

"Yes." Kate tried to keep any emotion out of her voice as she confirmed it. Tried not to feel the impact of each of those deaths.

Chris sagged under the weight of it. Kate knew almost exactly how he felt.

"Will you tell me about it?" Kate asked after a moment of watching Chris wrestle and shift restlessly in his seat. "It might help to say it out loud."

Chris didn't answer, and Kate wasn't sure he'd heard. She heard a sound out in the hallway, a muted whisper, the steady squeaking of wheels over the floor. If Chris noticed, he gave no indication. Kate pushed away thoughts of Andy and focused on the two people here in the room with her.

"You won't understand," Chris said, the dead tone back in his voice.

"What won't I understand?"

"You said it yourself, you're a doctor, you help people. How could you understand?"

Kate thought about the best way to answer. "You're right," she said. Chris flinched. "I spend all my time trying to make sure other people are well. But I'm still human, and I do know what's it like to feel out of control. I know what it feels like to not recognize yourself. To wonder exactly what it is you're capable of. I know what it's like to feel lost."

Kate watched as Chris slowly turned towards her, his eyes evaluating and judging, as if he was testing her story. Then he leaned back in the chair, his head bowed. It was exactly what he needed to hear, the understanding and the lack of judgement. Kate knew in that moment she should have been saying the same thing to herself and to Andy. The weight above her shifted.

"Nathan Tomms," Chris said, enunciating the name carefully, as it was the key to everything. "I wanted to hurt Nathan Tomms. I wanted him to feel sick and disgusting. I wanted him to feel so awful he couldn't speak or focus on anything other than being sick. I wanted there to be nothing that anyone could do for him, I wanted him to get no relief. Because that's exactly how I felt when Serena left me for him."

He paused and looked down at Serena before continuing.

"I knew a guy at Princeton in the virology lab. He got drunk one night and was telling me about some crazy shit he was doing, making up viruses, mashing them together. He's not a bad guy, kind of geeky. I don't think he once thought about the implications. I paid him ten grand to give me one of the viruses. He said he'd use my immunity to last year's flu so I wouldn't get sick. He gave me a case to carry it and told me the best way to make sure someone picked it up. I think he was curious, more than anything. To see if it would work."

Kate watched Chris carefully as curiosity, empathy, and disgust competed for dominance. She thought about her conversation with Lucy, the seemingly sweet and sad love story of Hidden Valley's royalty. It ended badly, apparently. Very, very badly.

"I decided to go to the Fullworth farm on Labour Day. No one would pay attention to me there, at least no more attention than they usually did," Chris added, bitterly. "I found out where Nathan was working in one of the barns, took out my camera from my bag, made it look like I was just changing lenses. But I got spooked, kind of freaked out and I left it in a stall. I don't know, it must have spread like crazy.

That's not what I intended, I swear." He looked to Kate, searching her face for any hint of judgement or persecution. Kate tried to keep her face free of both, tried to quell the questions in her head. This wasn't the time for curiosity.

Chris jumped as a monitor beeped. "What is it?" he demanded, his hand reflexively tightening around Serena's, jerking her arm. Kate was surprised, then alarmed, that she didn't wake up.

"I don't know Chris, give me a minute."

Kate read the monitors. Her O2 sats were drifting down in the now familiar descent from low-normal to critical. Kate thought about Jack, about his algorithm. She wondered how much time that initial dose of steroids a week ago had bought her now.

"I need to make a call," Kate said evenly.

"Who?"

"His name is Jack Sharpe, he's a computer tech with the RCMP. He generated a computer program that might be able to tell me how long until Serena's condition turns critical. We need to know, Chris."

Chris looked back and forth between Serena and Kate. She tried not to twitch with impatience. Andy said that they had time, that Kate should use that. Perhaps it wasn't an advantage that she had after all. The monitor continued to beep, but Kate made no move to silence it. Chris was tense again, his muscles jumping spasmodically.

"Okay, make the call."

Kate pulled out the cell phone, realizing she still had Jack's. *Shit.*

"I'm going to connect through Sergeant Wyles—" Kate started to say, dialing.

"No!" Chris shouted, reaching across the bed and hitting the phone out of her hands. Kate's arm stung, but she tried not to react, straining to hear whether or not Andy would take this action as a threat. She held still, waiting for her breathing to calm.

"What's the problem?"

"You're telling them to take her away, aren't you?"

"I'm not trying to pull anything over on you, Chris. I've been totally honest with you so far, and I don't intend to change that. I need to call Sergeant Wyles so she can connect me to Jack since that"—she pointed to the phone that had skidded across the floor—"is his cell phone. Okay?"

He nodded.

Kate pulled out her own cell phone, took a breath, and called Andy, very aware that Chris was going to listen and interpret everything she said.

"I need to talk to Jack," Kate said, as soon as Andy had picked up.

"I'll call on the landline," Andy said immediately. "What's going on, Kate?"

"The patient is stable for now," Kate answered carefully, knowing Andy would understand. "Give Jack the following stats, tell him to assume that Serena Cardiff has entered the first sustained dip below normal O2 sats and tell him to text me the results of his algorithm." Kate read the latest vitals off the monitor.

"Okay. Are you all right, Kate?"

"I'm fine," Kate said, then immediately wished she hadn't. It was a blatant lie, and they both knew it. Nothing about this was fine, nothing about Kate was fine. She took a breath, feeling suddenly and completely overwhelmed. She felt the same tug of disorientation that she'd had in Winnipeg, a slip of reality. Then she focused again on the monitors, on Serena lying on the bed, on Chris watching her so intently.

"We're fine," Kate said, needing to be just convincing enough that Andy wouldn't storm the room. "I need Jack's answer as soon as possible. Please," she added. Then she hung up, knowing if she stayed on the line with Andy any longer, she would lose it entirely.

"He's going to text me shortly," Kate said to Chris. "It's a ballpark of how long until Serena needs more treatment than I can provide for her in this room or this hospital." Kate judged Chris's response to this reminder. He seemed steady. "What are we doing here, Chris?"

"What do you mean?"

"Why did you come to the hospital?"

"To see Serena," he started, then stopped himself, his face contorting in pain, reacting to whatever he hadn't said.

"To see Serena…" Kate prompted, waiting. He didn't speak. "To see Serena for the last time?" she offered into the silence.

Chris flinched, but he kept his gaze on Kate, the uncertainty of what he should do holding him still.

"You can trust me, Chris. Tell me what's in your pocket." Her voice was calm, even though her heart pounded. He continued to stare at Kate like she was someone who had all the answers.

"I didn't know the virus would kill all those people. I couldn't have known, right?"

Kate said nothing, keeping her face free of judgement, refusing in that moment to hear Jim Beckett's raspy, smiling voice through his mask or see Roberta Sedlak's cold body in the autopsy room.

As if he could read her mind, Chris suddenly blinked and looked down.

"Mrs. Sedlak..." he said, his voice raw. "She saw me on my way to the Fullworth farm, offered me a ride. I couldn't say no. I wanted to tell her, I almost did. As I was getting out of the car my bag split and the camera lens fell out, cracking the casing. She picked it up before I could stop her." Chris hung his head low. "I couldn't have known," he said, almost to himself.

"Tell me how Serena got this virus," Kate said. Her instinct told her he needed it all out, the whole story. A complete confession.

"I knew he was coming to visit her. I knew I'd missed my target the first time. But I thought she had my immunity, we were both sick last year. It wasn't meant for her."

Kate could see he was shaking now with nerves, adrenaline, regret, fear. She would have to move carefully, slowly. *Lead him there*, Andy had said. Kate needed to find a way to do that. Her phone chimed loudly, and Chris jerked up from his hunched over position.

"Eighteen to twenty-four hours. Hyperbaric chamber in SK, three-hour flight."

Kate's heart sank. It was even less time than Harris Trenholm. Eighteen hours, fifteen if you took off the flight time. Less if the ballpark was generous. Kate breathed slowly, reading the text again and again.

"What does it say?"

"It says we don't have a lot of time to decide what we do here. Serena needs to be out of here in the next few hours."

"What will happen?" he whispered.

"Her lungs are already beginning to fill with fluid. At some point in the next few hours, I will not be able to stop the fluid from completely filling her lungs, making her body incapable of getting the oxygen it needs. When that happens, she will die no matter what I do. We need to get her to a specialized facility, Chris. Soon."

Nothing. No sound, no movement. Kate wanted to hold her breath, but she kept it steady, slow. Minutes ticked by, measured by Serena's laboured breaths and the steady beep of the monitors. Kate needed to try again.

"You came to say good-bye, Chris. I think you should say it now."

Chris didn't look up at her, but he did pull his hand from his pocket. He lay a small gun on the bed, dark against the white sheets. A thrill of fear shot through Kate, though she'd expected as much. She wondered if Andy could see but she refused to turn and check, refused to move even one muscle. Chris took Serena's hand in both of his, lowered his head, and kissed her fingers. He said something quietly under his breath, gentle murmurings. When he looked up at Kate again, the deadness had returned to his eyes.

"I can't live with what I did and I can't live without her."

Kate slowly leaned forwards, her movements careful, keeping her eyes on Chris the whole time. She leaned her arms on her knees and clasped her hands together.

"It's amazing what you can learn to live with, Chris. I think you should try."

"You don't know—" Chris started to say in the same dead tone.

Kate cut him off, her voice just sharp enough to get his attention. "Yes, I do. I let my sister live on the streets, I let her suffer, and I let her die. I live with that every second of every day. So don't tell me I don't know. Don't tell me you think you're the only one who has ever lived through regret and a broken heart."

It was a risk, a gamble. As she watched Chris waver, neither of them looking at the gun on the bed between them, Kate had time to remember Andy's words. *The worst self-preservation skills of anyone I've ever met*. True, in this instant. Absolutely true. Kate could not deny the pull; every muscle in her being screamed to keep Serena and Chris safe. But herself? She was irrelevant, her own safety barely registered.

"What should I do?" Chris barely choked out the words.

"When you're ready, go stand by the window and close your eyes. Think about how warm Serena's hands feel. Because she can recover from this. And so can you, Chris."

A knife edge, sharp, painfully thin. So hard to balance, so unsure which way they would fall. Kate did hold her breath now, waiting. It was out of her hands.

Chris looked at his hands covering Serena's for a long moment, closed his eyes, and turned his face towards the ceiling. Then he opened them again, and without looking at Kate, he stood and walked to the window, his hands loose at his sides.

Kate turned in her chair and raised her voice just enough so the sound would carry. "Andy."

Andy came in with her gun drawn, held low. She looked from Kate, to Chris standing at the window, to Serena on the bed, to the gun. Andy locked on Chris and strode across the room, Constable Slater shadowing her steps. Kate watched the scene unfold before her, feeling a bizarre break from reality in that moment. She wanted to tell Andy to be careful, to not hurt Chris. But Andy was holstering her weapon, pulling out handcuffs, approaching Chris with careful, tense movements.

"Chris Ozarc, you are under arrest for manslaughter. It is my duty to inform you that you have the right to retain and instruct counsel without delay. Do you understand?"

Andy's voice seemed loud though her voice was careful, neutral. No accusations, no rough movements as she pulled his wrists behind his back and bound them with cuffs. She turned him with a hand on the shoulder, always staying just to the side. *So careful, so controlled*, Kate thought, watching her move.

"Do you understand?" Andy repeated. "Do you want to call a lawyer? You are not obliged to answer, but anything you do say may be given in evidence."

Chris nodded but kept his eyes down and closed.

Andy gestured to Constable Slater, who took control of Chris Ozarc. Then she raised her voice and called in the other officers. The room was suddenly full, too many bodies, too loud. Kate stayed hunched in the chair, watching Serena now, trying to tune out the action, not able to watch as they marched Chris out of the room. Kate felt a distant sense of relief, then sadness. Then, most terrifying, emptiness.

"Kate."

Kate centred her attention on Andy's voice, reading her evident relief edged with distraction, stress, needing to be somewhere else. Kate could hear every small nuance, every change in tone and pitch. She knew that voice so well. Kate watched as one of the officers lifted the gun on the bed with a blue-gloved hand, checked the chamber, and dropped it into an evidence bag. This seemed to be some kind of signal for Kate and she stood up, her legs shaky.

"Is Serena's transport waiting?" Kate said, pushing past the sick feeling as the adrenaline leaked out of her body. She picked up Serena's chart and inputted the latest stats.

"Yes, the air ambulance and Dr. MacKay are on standby," Andy said carefully.

Kate watched Andy move around the bed with those same careful, tense movements. As if the person in front of her was unpredictable. Kate still couldn't meet her eyes.

"I'll take her," Kate said, as she removed the IV bag from the stand.

"No, Kate," Andy said, and her voice was very soft, very gentle. It would have been easy if she had resisted angrily. Kate could have fought back against that. But this understanding, this gentleness…it was too much.

Kate slammed her foot down on the release brake of the bed, walking around to do the same on the other side. She didn't have enough strength left to move the bed by herself, her upper body shaking by now. Still she tried. She didn't know what else to do.

Andy walked to the door and called for assistance. Two people Kate didn't recognize came in and pulled Serena's bed easily out from under her grasp. She watched Serena get wheeled away, wanting to fight to stay with her patient but knowing she didn't have it in her.

And suddenly the room was empty. No more patients or suspects. No more gun. No more cops. Just Kate and Andy.

Andy walked towards her and Kate met her eyes. They were very beautiful. Even this worried, even with the lines of stress making light folds in the delicate skin, her clear eyes were absolutely beautiful. Andy raised a hand and touched her, fingers drawing a soft line across her cheekbone. Kate felt the weight shift with that touch, with the memory of Andy touching her like that for the first time, with the feeling of peace that threatened with that touch. Kate wrestled with it, fought the desperate urge to lose herself in that touch.

"Are you all right?"

Such a loaded question. There was only one answer that would be acceptable.

"No," Kate said and watched as Andy pulled every possible meaning from that simple answer.

Andy's radio squawked on her belt, and she reached back and

pulled it out. Kate barely understood the message, something about squad cars and suspect transport. She wasn't listening, didn't want to listen, too intent on the inevitable crashing about to occur. She almost had a sense of relief in that thought. She knew without a doubt she could no longer hold it together.

"Kate, I'm the arresting officer, so I have to take Chris Ozarc down to Whistler. I'll be a couple of hours at least, but I'll be back as soon as I can. I'm going to get Jack to stay with you at the hotel, and he's going to run you through a statement and some paperwork. Can you handle that?"

Paperwork, yes. Everything else, no. She met Andy's worried eyes and nodded. Andy pulled Kate closer and wrapped her arms around Kate's exhausted, shaking body. Kate leaned her forehead against Andy's chest, letting herself feel protected, committing to memory exactly how this felt. Because soon there would be no protection. Soon it would just be her and the contents of that precariously balanced weight. Kate closed her eyes, fighting the waves of fear and sadness. Not yet. She couldn't let it go yet.

Andy's radio squawked again and Kate pulled back. As Andy spoke into the radio, Kate slowly took off her gown and pulled at the tough Velcro straps around the soft body armour vest. Andy helped her lift it over her head, let it dangle from one hand.

"I'll be back as soon as I can," Andy repeated as Jack walked in, his laptop bag slung over his shoulder. Andy looked up and pinned him with hard eyes. "Take her back to the hotel. We need her statement and her signature. After that…" Both Andy and Jack looked at Kate. She wondered what they saw. It couldn't be good, but Kate didn't have the will to hide it anymore. "Just take care of her, please," Andy pleaded with her partner.

Kate walked through the hospital in deadened silence. She saw familiar faces, shocked faces, wary expressions, a look of awe, of thanks, and relief. Lucy, Dr. Doyle, Michael Cardiff, the ER staff, Paul Sealy from the newspaper. Kate couldn't sort through which expression belonged to which face. It didn't matter. None of it settled on her, none of it seemed relevant. She kept her feet moving, down the stairs, across the lobby, and out into the night air. She took a deep breath, and it felt so good, she took another. And that felt so good, she cried. Just a few tears escaped and she breathed through it, fighting the constriction of her throat. Kate sat in the rental car beside a silent, concerned Jack. She closed her eyes instead of watching the now familiar route between Valley General and the Sea to Sky Inn. It didn't matter anymore. Almost none of it mattered.

"My patients…" Kate croaked out, like it had been days since she'd last spoken, not just a few minutes.

"Harris Trenholm showed improvement one hour post dive. Serena Cardiff should be landing in Saskatoon in a couple of hours. The rest are in isolation in the ER, everyone stable," Jack reported. "They're all being taken care of, Katie. You can relax."

Kate closed her eyes again as she thought about that word. *Relax*. It didn't fit, didn't make sense. That wasn't her goal. So she let it drift out into the night air. She let herself drift as Jack pulled off the highway, pulled up outside the hotel door. Kate walked into the empty, cold hotel room, her things scattered across the room, Andy's neatly folded or tucked away. Kate sat on the edge of the bed, pulled off her shoes, and let them drop heavily to the floor. Jack watched her carefully, and then he brought the desk chair near the bed and opened his laptop.

"Ready?" he asked.

Kate started to speak. This was easy. She chronicled every step of the last several hours. She referenced times, medical charts, interactions, movements, and decisions in precise details. She excised each piece, slowly and painstakingly putting Hidden Valley behind her. There was no pride in what she'd accomplished, only a satisfying closing up, one last stitch in a soon-to-be-healed wound. But it was Hidden Valley's wound. Her own was huge, raw. The crashing of that ever-present weight would cause bodily damage. And there would be fallout. Innocent bystanders. Andy. Kate squeezed her eyes shut. *Andy.* How could she even consider it? How could she even imagine walking away from her, let alone do it?

Kate stood suddenly, ignoring the pins and needles in her legs from sitting still for so long. It was hard to breathe suddenly. Her body felt jumpy and on edge. She pictured leaving Andy again, and the pain hit her so hard in her chest that Kate wrapped one arm protectively around her body. Breathe, focus, breathe.

"Katie?" Jack's voice was alarmed.

"I need to pack," Kate said suddenly. She pulled her bag out from the corner and threw it on the bed. Then she walked into the bathroom, sorting through their shared collection of toiletries, pulling out her own, not letting herself think. Back into the main room and Jack was on the phone, speaking furtively into the phone, presumably to Andy. Kate wanted to tell him not to bother. She was fully aware of her alarming behaviour, the dead expression on her face. She was so close to losing control, she almost wanted to hurtle herself towards it. Get it over with.

Jack was off the phone, watching her warily. "Please just wait until Wylie gets back, okay? Please," Jack begged.

Kate stopped what she was doing and looked up into his earnest, panicked brown eyes. Of course she would wait. What did he think she was capable of? What did Andy think she was capable of? Kate felt a piercing in her chest, an understanding that brought no comfort. They knew better than she did what she was capable of. Kate no longer had a clue. But she would wait for Andy. That was the point of this. To tell Andy that she'd been right.

"I'll wait," she said to Jack, aiming for a neutral tone to reassure him she was not yet completely broken. Only fractured. "But will you do something for me?" Knowing he would do anything for her.

"Sure I will, Katie. What is it?"

"Will you drive me home tonight? When I need you to, will you take me back to Vancouver?"

Heartbreak in his eyes as the understanding sank in. Kate averted her gaze and looked down at the uniform brown of the carpet. She couldn't take that, not now. She couldn't explain to him how necessary this was.

"I can do that," he said softly.

Kate nodded her thanks. She finished her packing, pulled on her shoes again and sat on the bed. She listened to her heart in her chest, tested the strength of her resolve, compared it to the massive proportions of the weight above her. It wasn't hard to convince herself that this was vital. Necessary. That didn't make it any easier.

But what would she say? How could she form her disordered, chaotic thoughts into words? She repeated the same words over and over in her head. *I love you, I love you, I love you...I'm lost, I'm lost, I'm lost.*

Kate sought the ring that was always on her right hand, but her finger was bare. She'd left her sister's ring in the on-call room at the hospital. Kate felt the last vestiges of control splinter and fall away. She put her head in her hands and cried. Jack came to sit beside her on the bed, but she was so far from being comforted. She had so far to go and nothing to go on. Even as she pulled herself together one tiny piece at a time, enough to stop the wracking sobs in her body, Kate felt only empty.

Minutes stretched and tumbled into hours, the blood in Kate's body pooling in her core, leaving her fingers and feet frozen. Then the sound of the key in the lock. Kate zeroed in on the door, every sense suddenly heightened, drawn to Andy walking in through the door. In that moment she wished Andy could understand everything without Kate having to witness the impact of her own words as they sank in.

Andy flicked her eyes to Jack, who walked quickly to the door; a brief look at Kate and then he was gone. Andy moved away from the door, her shoulders rigid with strain. It was a deliberate action, telling Kate she would not hold her here. That she wouldn't fight this, whatever it was. Kate hadn't expected her to do that, but the understanding still caused sadness to blossom in her chest. The silence stretched, Andy waiting for Kate to speak. Kate waiting to find the words.

"I need some time," she said finally, her voice thin. Wavering.

Andy said nothing to this, just a curt nod of her head. Kate took a breath. It wasn't enough.

"I need some time…to figure things out." It would be no comfort to Andy that she'd been right. No comfort at all.

Andy nodded again, pain flickering in her grey eyes. There was a question though, too.

How long?

The question hovered silently in the room between them. Kate wanted to know, too. How long? How long had she been lost? A month? Four? A year? Since she took the Chief Resident job which she could now admit that she hated? Since her sister died? Before? Was there a mathematical equation, a computer-generated algorithm she could use to predict how long? She wanted to believe it could be that easy. She knew it wouldn't be. Not with all the shit that she'd spent years shrugging off. The accumulation was too great. And now, with Andy standing before her, so close to heartbreak, the stakes were too high for Kate to do anything but face it head-on. And no choice but to do it on her own.

Kate stood shakily, willing her body to make it down to the car before she lost it completely.

"I love you, Kate."

The smell of pine trees in the rain, Andy's voice in my ear, arms holding me so tightly.

Kate locked her eyes on Andy, infusing everything she had left in her next words.

"I love you, too, Andy."

They both knew that wasn't the problem. And they both knew it wasn't enough. Kate wrenched her eyes away first, then her body, feeling the emptiness, the loss almost immediately. She forced herself to walk to the door, pull at the handle, and step outside. And as Kate closed the door behind her, she forced herself to hold two images in her head. One was of Andy watching her go, pain and hurt in her eyes. And the one in her memory, that perfect moment on the porch in Montana. She held them there fiercely, promising herself that she would get back there. That she would do whatever she had to. That she would never be responsible for that look in Andy's eyes again.

About the Author

Jessica Webb spends her professional days working with educators to find the why behind the challenging behaviors of the students they support. Limitless curiosity about the motivations and intentions of human behavior is also a huge part of what drives her to write stories and understand the complexities of her characters and their actions.

When she's not working or writing, Jessica is spending time with her wife and daughter, usually planning where they will travel next. Jessica can be found most often on her favorite spot on the couch with a book and a cup of tea.

Jessica can be contacted at jessicalwebb.author@gmail.com.

Books Available From Bold Strokes Books

Arrested Hearts by Holly Stratimore. A reckless cop with a secret death wish and a health nut who is afraid to die might be a perfect combination for love. (978-1-62639-809-2)

Capturing Jessica by Jane Hardee. Hyperrealist sculptor Michael tries desperately to conceal the love she holds for best friend, Jess, unaware Jess's feelings for her are changing. (978-1-62639-836-8)

Counting to Zero by AJ Quinn. NSA agent Emma Thorpe and computer hacker Paxton James must learn to trust each other as they work to stop a threat clock that's rapidly counting down to zero. (978-1-62639-783-5)

Courageous Love by KC Richardson. Two women fight a devastating disease, and their own demons, while trying to fall in love. (978-1-62639-797-2)

One More Reason to Leave Orlando by Missouri Vaun. Nash Wiley thought a threesome sounded exotic and exciting, but as it turns out the reality of sleeping with two women at the same time is just really complicated. (978-1-62639-703-3)

Pathogen by Jessica L. Webb. Can Dr. Kate Morrison navigate a deadly virus and the threat of bioterrorism, as well as her new relationship with Sergeant Andy Wyles and her own troubled past? (978-1-62639-833-7)

Rainbow Gap by Lee Lynch. Jaudon Vickers and Berry Garland, polar opposites, dream and love in this tale of lesbian lives set in Central Florida against the tapestry of societal change and the Vietnam War. (978-1-62639-799-6)

Steel and Promise by Alexa Black. Lady Nivrai's cruel desires and modified body make most of the galaxy fear her, but courtesan Cailyn Derys soon discovers the real monsters are the ones without the claws. (978-1-62639-805-4)

Swelter by D. Jackson Leigh. Teal Giovanni's mistake shines an unwanted spotlight on a small Texas ranch where August Reese is secluded until she can testify against a powerful drug kingpin. (978-1-62639-795-8)

Without Justice by Carsen Taite. Cade Kelly and Emily Sinclair must battle each other in the pursuit of justice, but can they fight their undeniable attraction outside the walls of the courtroom? (978-1-62639-560-2)

21 Questions by Mason Dixon. To find love, start by asking the right questions. (978-1-62639-724-8)

A Palette for Love by Charlotte Greene. When newly minted Ph.D. Chloé Devereaux returns to New Orleans, she doesn't expect her new job and her powerful employer—Amelia Winters—to be so appealing. (978-1-62639-758-3)

By the Dark of Her Eyes by Cameron MacElvee. When Brenna Taylor inherits a decrepit property haunted by tormented ghosts, Alejandra Santana must not only restore Brenna's house and property but also save her soul. (978-1-62639-834-4)

Cash Braddock by Ashley Bartlett. Cash Braddock just wants to hang with her cat, fall in love, and deal drugs. What's the problem with that? (978-1-62639-706-4)

Death by Cocktail Straw by Missouri Vaun. She just wanted to meet girls, but an outing at the local lesbian bar goes comically off the rails, landing Nash Wiley and her best pal in the ER. (978-1-62639-702-6)

Lone Ranger by VK Powell. Reporter Emma Ferguson stirs up a thirty-year-old mystery that threatens Park Ranger Carter West's family and jeopardizes any hope for a relationship between the two women. (978-1-62639-767-5)

Love on Call by Radclyffe. Ex-Army medic Glenn Archer and recent LA transplant Mariana Mateo fight their mutual desire in the face of past losses as they work together in the Rivers Community Hospital ER. (978-1-62639-843-6)

Never Enough by Robyn Nyx. Can two women put aside their pasts to find love before it's too late? (978-1-62639-629-6)

Two Souls by Kathleen Knowles. Can love blossom in the wake of tragedy? (978-1-62639-641-8)

Camp Rewind by Meghan O'Brien. A summer camp for grown-ups becomes the site of an unlikely romance between a shy, introverted divorcee and one of the Internet's most infamous cultural critics—who attends undercover. (978-1-62639-793-4)

Cross Purposes by Gina L. Dartt. In pursuit of a lost Acadian treasure, three women must work out not only the clues, but also the complicated tangle of emotion and attraction developing between them. (978-1-62639-713-2)

Imperfect Truth by C.A. Popovich. Can an imperfect truth stand in the way of love? (978-1-62639-787-3)

Life in Death by M. Ullrich. Sometimes the devastating end is your only chance for a new beginning. (978-1-62639-773-6)

Love on Liberty by MJ Williamz. Hearts collide when politics clash. (978-1-62639-639-5)

Serious Potential by Maggie Cummings. Pro golfer Tracy Allen plans to forget her ex during a visit to Bay West, a lesbian condo community in NYC, but when she meets Dr. Jennifer Betsy, she gets more than she bargained for. (978-1-62639-633-3)

Taste by Kris Bryant. Accomplished chef Taryn has walked away from her promising career in the city's top restaurant to devote her life to her six-year-old daughter and is content until Ki Blake comes along. (978-1-62639-718-7)

The Second Wave by Jean Copeland. Can star-crossed lovers have a second chance after decades apart, or does the love of a lifetime only happen once? (978-1-62639-830-6)

Valley of Fire by Missouri Vaun. Taken captive in a desert outpost after their small aircraft is hijacked, Ava and her captivating passenger discover things about each other and themselves that will change them both forever. (978-1-62639-496-4)

Coils by Barbara Ann Wright. A modern young woman follows her aunt into the Greek Underworld and makes a pact with Medusa to win her freedom by killing a hero of legend. (978-1-62639-598-5)